PRAISE FOR

The Card Game

"*The Card Game* literally shouts: 'freedom, adventure, fun, travel, friends! And let's never pay for any of it!' Take this road trip, this head trip, with these three girls, and you'll give Bonnie Lee all the credit in the world."

—David L. Robbins, *New York Times* bestselling author of *War of the Rats* and *Isaac's Beacon*

Also, by Bonnie Lee

*Taxpertise, The Complete Book of Dirty Little Secrets
and Tax Deductions for Small Business that the
IRS Doesn't Want You to Know*

Taxpertise for the Creative Mind

Taxpertise The Heist, 50 Shades of Green

The Card Game

By

Bonnie Lee

Published by Little Star

Richmond, VA

Contact the author at *bonnieleeauthor.com*

ISBN 979-8-9861299-2-1

Book and cover design by Wendy Daniel

Cover illustration by Wendy Daniel uses Adobe Stock images.

Printed in the United States of America

For

Granny Bee whose spirit, wit, and wisdom inspired me

Prologue

December 1975

Turning the corner, Edith spots the dim outline of a bus through the fog. She takes two quick steps but there's no way she will catch it before it roars from the curb.

Grumbling in the doorway of a vacant storefront, she plops down her purse and shopping bag. She buttons her camel coat up to her chin. The chill and her arthritic hands make the task difficult.

She starts at the sound of breaking glass. Three teenage boys round the corner then block her from the sidewalk. Edith yanks up her purse and shopping bag. They trap her in the doorway, laughing.

"What do you want?"

"What's in the bag?" The tallest one wears tight black leather pants over boots with silver spurs. His black hair is streaked with purple and spikes from his head. Silver studs embed a leather eye patch. This darkness against his pale skin makes him ghoulish. Identical twins in blue coats flank him, waiting.

"What do you want?"

The ghoul presses his face close, tobacco stains his breath. His one unveiled eye is a road map of veins. He sways, rights himself, then grabs her by the lapels.

She whispers, "Please don't hurt me."

He pulls her closer; she cringes against an expected blow.

A large sweaty hand across her mouth, he shoves her against the door.

The twins' laughter makes Edith's skin crawl. The doorknob jabs into her back. The tall one's eye has a dilated pupil, it is unnaturally wide and wild looking. Plainly he is drugged up.

One twin rips away her shopping bag to peer in at the wrapped gifts.

The tall one-eyed boy asks, "She got any booze in there?" He takes his hands off her lapels, his breath from her face. He sways again as he looks down at the blue twin and the bag.

Edith cannot see beyond the three to the sidewalk. Somebody might be there, might save her. Should she scream? Make a break for it? Others had done that and paid for it with their lives. She focuses, gulps at the cold air, tries to control her rising panic. Her heart thunders in her ears.

The packages hit the pavement; the twin has upended the bag.

"No. Those are for my friends."

The ghoul slaps her. "Shut up!" He asks the blue twin, "Anything good?"

The twin shreds candy cane wrappings off the packages. The shards of a black ceramic cat, a broken bottle of Tabu and an aluminum fondue set litter the sidewalk.

"Shit! That's all she's got is shit."

Again the tall one grabs Edit by the lapels. "Nothing to spike your eggnog? You're starting to piss me off, old lady. You got any money?" He jerks the purse from her hands. She inches closer to the blue twin who kneels over her packages. He smashes the Tabu bottle against a wall.

"Two bucks. No credit cards! Fucking old people." He pockets the dollars and hurls the purse at her feet. He steps back and nods to the standing twin, the silent lookout. This blue boy snaps open a switchblade.

In desperation, Edith pushes the drugged and unsteady one-eyed boy into the twin with the knife. She pushes off the door, dashes past the three. She runs to the street.

They shout after her.

Edith does not look back. In front of her, people scatter. She runs crying, "Help!" She doesn't hear the warning, "Look out!"

Another bus arrives. Invisible arms toss her into the air. Higher, wingless, weightless, above the busy street.

x

Chapter 1

Outside, a gray mist rolled through the Tenderloin.

Sarah turned from the window, enough grayness.

In the hall, a stained glass pane lit a path for no one. Under a bent Christmas tree lay boxes of ornaments and rolls of wrapping paper. Edith hadn't decorated, and never would.

After forty two years as best friends, Edith's death felt too abrupt, unfair.

When Sarah's husband died, she'd been ready. The doctors gave him six months. Her grief was natural and expected, with time to play it out, to say goodbye, speak her heart and put words to all the gestures and meaningful looks of their forty-three years. All the things she'd taken for granted.

Her husband was lucid to the end. In his final dying moments, Sarah thanked him for being her provider and fulfilling his vows to love, honor, and cherish. He'd given her a son, and a lifetime of love, companionship, and friendship.

She'd held the weak bony threads of fingers that had gripped hers with strength for so many years. Of all the loving moments in their life together, this stood out.

He smiled to express what he could, thanking her as well. He motioned her close to whisper his last words: "Don't forget to roll out the trash cans tomorrow."

His eyes grew distant, peering at something beyond her. His head rolled back into the pillows, a low hiss slipped from his lips. She envisioned him leaving through his open mouth. She watched his unseen spirit rise through the ceiling of their Corte Madera home. Through a screen of tears she waved goodbye, feeling a bit foolish. She was thankful that he had been released from agony and missed him instantly.

Tenderly she kissed him, dropping tears on his unblinking eyes. Sarah smoothed his thin white hair. The afternoon streamed through the windows, spotlighting his stillness with rainbows from the prism hung on the drapery rod. She would remember his death as filled with love and tenderness, a natural and well-done ending to a good life.

She settled deeply into Edith's armchair, to seek some remnant of her murdered friend's warmth there.

Edith was gone, abrupt, a consequence of dark forces. No time to say goodbye or I love you, not even a moment of remember when. Sarah's throat caught with regret, sadness, fear, and anger.

Jeanette asked, "Do you want more coffee?"

She stood close, to pick a coffee mug off the end table.

"That's not my mug."

Sarah and her good friend Jeanette fell silent. This was Edith's last cup of coffee. Jeanette ran her finger over the lipstick mark on the rim, a remnant of Edith. She peered down into the mug. Jeanette all but tiptoed into the kitchen to pour the cold remains down the sink.

Minnie quietly slid up beside her. "I can't hardly take this. How are you doing in here?"

Jeanette rinsed the coffee mug. "I'm almost done. Just a few more things left to pack up. I'm worried about Sarah. She doesn't look so well."

"I know. Poor thing. Look, I'm almost done in the bedroom." In the other room, Sarah blew her nose.

Minnie said, "I can't wait to get out of here. And get her out of here too."

"I know what you mean. It's a shame. Especially with the trip to Spain coming up."

Jeanette sighed. A five-bedroom villa in Malaga was waiting for the three of them. Forty years ago a friend of Jeanette's had bought the villa. Jeanette was only twenty then, a model for *Vogue*. A photo shoot found her exploring the area with her friend Jeff. They came upon a dilapidated structure with a *"Por Vender"* sign out front. It had good bones and a ton of potential. In an attempt to win her heart, Jeff bought the house, and promised to leave it to her one day when he died. He kept his promise. The letter announcing his bequest arrived two days ago.

Jeanette had been formulating a plan before springing the marvelous news on her three best friends. The villa was leased out to others until the end of May. After that, the three of them would get themselves to Spain, leave this low-income housing project, the poverty of their lives, and spend their final years together basking in the sun, paying no rent.

Jeanette picked up a sponge to wipe up toast crumbs off the counter. Flipping the sponge into the sink, she said, "I'm going to finish packing up her desk. Then I'll be done."

In Edith's bedroom, Jeanette stood on the spot where Edith's prize possession and sole family heirloom once stood, a two hundred year old walnut armoire with exquisite floral inlay. The outline of the armoire remained in the faded wallpaper. The fog had begun to disperse, and mute sunshine bled into the room through the old mangled Venetian blinds to spotlight the empty space. Edith had sold the desk three weeks ago, probably for grocery money.

On a mahogany secretary in the corner, a pile of unsent Christmas cards rested on the folded-down door. Should Jeanette mail them, discard them, or open them and add a note about Edith's passing? She shoved them into a shoebox and set it aside. Beneath the pile of cards lay a plain stationary tablet. Jeanette read:

December 10, 1975

Dear Pansy,

It's another foggy day in San Francisco. I'm just starting to decorate for Christmas. I love the holiday season.

It's good to hear you are feeling better. I bet you'll soon be up and running like we did when we were kids.

I've saved a little money and finally, after 17 years, I'm coming up to see you. I can't wait to

The way the letter ended, Edith likely got up to answer the phone or the door. What could she not wait to do? Finally do a little traveling? 'I can't wait to' – get out of this miserable dump?

Jeanette swiped away hot tears. She opened desk drawers to rummage through more paperwork, dried-up pens, a box of staples with no stapler in sight. She chucked everything into the trash.

She found an antique wooden box in the bottom drawer. Jeanette ran her hands over the art deco carving of the face of a woman with flowing hair. She lifted the lid and thrilled at what lay inside. Jeanette peered down the hallway. Sarah had joined Minnie in the kitchen. Minnie shoved a box along the floor with her foot while Sarah pulled pots and pans from a cabinet.

Jeanette quickly stuffed over a dozen credit cards into her smock, and patted the pocket.

Chapter 2

Pandora's wasn't crowded. The lunch crowd had pretty much come and gone. A Maître d' seated them at a table overlooking a tropical garden. The large, dimly lit dining room was decked in red against dark walnut wainscoting. On each scarlet tablecloth burned a crimson candle beside a red rose in a small crystal vase. Elegant and sensuous, the room had been created for lovers who looked at each other and not the bill.

"This is too expensive." Sarah scanned the menu. Her clear gray eyes, magnified behind her thick glasses, widened more at the prices.

Jeanette said, "Think of this as a wake for Edith."

A waiter arrived. "Good afternoon, ladies. My name is Rafo. I'll be your server. May I start you with a cocktail?"

Jeanette gifted the waiter with one of her 'Come hither, big boy' smiles. Rafo was tall, elegant, in his fifties, with a full head of black hair, ample lips, and a regal Roman nose. Jeanette loved his Italian accent. When they made eye contact, she guessed he liked the looks of her, too. Jeanette crooned, "Yes, cocktails would be perfect."

Minnie and Sarah gave their drink orders. Jeanette figured if she plied them with enough liquor, they might be more inclined to hear her out. She wasn't worried about Sarah, the follower. Minnie was conservative, with no-nonsense ways and a straight-and-narrow approach to life. She would be the tough one to convince, if at all.

By the time the escargot arrived, they were well on their way. Stingers on empty stomachs was just the formula for obliterating the shock and sadness of the past few days.

Jeanette waited until the moment seemed right.

"I can't remember the last time I had a meal like this. I wish we could live like this all the time."

She slid a snail onto a torn bit of French bread and spooned garlic butter over it. She closed her eyes on the first taste.

Minnie agreed. "Hah! Wouldn't that be nice."

Jeanette said, "This reminds me of the good old days. Alex and I used to eat like this every night."

Though Minnie rolled her eyes, she did not lose her good humor.

"Here we go. Another reminder about your elegant life as a model and actress."

Sarah pitched in, pretending ennui. "Three marriages, all wealthy, doting men. Traveled the world with the rich and famous. Blah and blah."

Unperturbed, Jeanette continued. "You know, Alex was eating at Henri's when the IRS came to arrest him. He died eating escargot." Jeanette punctuated her description as if the IRS, for disturbing Alex's dinner to hand him a public humiliation, should be sued. "The poor man couldn't take it. At first we thought he was choking on his food. One Fed tried to clear his mouth and when he found nothing there, he performed the Heimlich, then pounded on Alex's back." Jeanette sipped her stinger. "His last words were 'Yelp! Yelp!'"

Her friends' drunken smirks suppressed what would have been truly inappropriate laughter.

Jeanette goaded them. She cocked her head and said in a small voice, "Yelp! Yelp!" then slid another escargot into her mouth. Sarah and Minnie giggled. All three women dissolved into laughter. Sarah fell sideways into Jeanette and put an arm around her.

Minnie gasped, "Yelp! Yelp!" She knocked over her Stinger reaching for it. Her drink splashed onto the pile of snail shells.

"Yelp! Yelp!" Sarah cried. "The snails are drowning!"

Jeanette held a slender finger to her lips. "Shhh, the waiter's coming." Minnie and Sarah sat up straight. Jeanette was casual as Rafo placed the salads before them, ground pepper over the greens, and smiled openly at Jeanette.

The friends forked the salads, lost in their own thoughts. Jeanette was rehearsing her approach when the restaurant door opened. The Mayor-elect of San Francisco entered with his entourage of bodyguards and assistants.

Jeanette beamed as they passed her table. "Mr. Mayor," she drawled, extending her hand.

The mayor paused; he smiled mechanically. "Good afternoon." He took the proffered hand and squinted.

Jeanette asked, "Why, you don't remember me, do you?" She twirled a curl of auburn hair with a finger of her free hand. His smile froze while he tried to recall her name.

Killing the suspense, Jeanette said, "It's been five years, dear. The Black and White Ball, 1970? We danced to Moonlight Serenade."

He snapped his fingers. "Jeanette Compton. How is my favorite constituent these days?"

"Well, I'm just fine, sugar. You're looking dapper, Mr. Mayor. Tell me, do you still tango under the stars in Golden Gate Park?"

His grin flirted as though recalling a steamy encounter. "Not since that night. Politics doesn't allow for much leisure time, especially lately." He put his palms on the table and leaned in to whisper, "Tell me, Jeanette, did you vote for this old has-been last month?"

"You always have my vote."

"That's my girl. It's wonderful to see you again." He patted her hand, then nodded to a flabbergasted

Minnie and Sarah. The Mayor of San Francisco strode off, assistants with clipboards and briefcases scurrying after.

Minnie asked, "What was that all about?"

"He's a real sweetheart. But that's ancient history." Jeanette waved a hand dismissively.

Minutes later, champagne cocktails arrived. From a table in the corner, the Mayor raised his glass to exchange an air toast with Jeanette.

Sarah said, "Back to Alex. You never talk much about him."

"Alex was the third of three. He didn't stand out that much."

"Well, what happened? I mean, the tax thing."

Jeanette felt a thread of bitterness enter her voice. "Something about oil depletion allowances and real estate in Hawaii. I don't know. I was never any good at business. His attorneys handled it. They said I should have kept my property separate. Fine time for them to tell me that. The IRS got everything, of course. Except." Jeanette put down her fork; she struck a pose behind one hunched shoulder. "There was one other thing they overlooked. Or really, I should say, I beat them to." A little sloshed, Minnie and Sarah leaned to her.

Sarah said, "Oooh, secrets."

"A hundred thousand dollars. Cash. Hidden in a vault behind a secret panel in the bedroom. I got it all before the sheriff closed down the house. And of course, this." She showed them the emerald ring circled with diamonds that was a fixture on her right hand.

Minnie asked, "And? What happened to the money?"

"My God, that was seven years ago. What do you think?" Jeanette busied herself with the salad fork.

"You spent it." Minnie wagged her own finger. "Jeanette, you've got to invest money like that. Plan for the future."

Jeanette immediately regretted telling the secret. "It wasn't going to last forever."

"It could have, if you'd invested properly. Why didn't you ever tell me this before? I thought we were best friends."

"Because of this right here. I knew you'd lecture me. Get on my case for, how do you always put it? My lack of common sense."

Matter-of-factly, Sarah said, "You must have gone through it in a year. You've been living on our floor for six years now." Sarah returned to slicing her tomato, taking Jeanette's admission in stride.

Minnie said, "A year. That's preposterous! I don't see how anyone could do such a wasteful thing. If you've got that much money in hand..." Minnie stopped when Sarah shot her a warning look.

Sarah refilled their glasses, a comforting gesture. "Have more wine."

"I really shouldn't." Jeanette took a sip. They laughed again.

"Besides," Jeanette said in a merry tone, "if I had invested, I wouldn't be here with you, my dearest childhood friends. Now, how about a toast to Edith."

Minnie and Jeanette raised their glasses.

"Sarah?"

"Oh dear, if I start, I might go on forever." Sarah's rosy jowls and the whites of her eyes blended with the decor. She sighed and simply said, "I love you Edith. I miss you. And none of this was fair."

Jeanette added, "To Edith, our dear departed friend. We miss you."

Minnie said, "To Edith. We love you and we're going to get those punks." The thought of five foot, skinny Minnie going after hoodlums made the tipsy women guffaw. They clinked glasses and chugged.

"Poor Edith," Sarah said softly. "God, I do miss her."

"At least she died with her boots on. If it were me, I'd rather go out with a bang like that, better than inch by inch. Ugh." Minnie shuddered. "Which one of us is next?"

"Stop it," Jeanette lay a warm hand over Minnie's. The waiter approached. "Here comes the scaloppini. Another bottle?"

Sarah said, "By all means." Two weeks of grief and tears, then outrage, had finally relented before wine. "You were right, Jeanette. It was definitely a good idea to get out of the house. We'll have to do this again tomorrow."

Weaving slightly, Minnie said, "And on Thursday we'll declare bankruptcy, right?" Her eyebrows disappeared under her curly gray bangs.

Sarah's laughter turned sodden. "How are we going to pay for this?"

"Sssh!" Jeanette shot her a stern look.

Rafo arrived with the scallopini. He hesitated, serving dishes suspended in midair. "Is there a problem, madam?"

"Everything's fine." Jeanette smiled coyly.

Rafo set the plates before them. "Would you care for anything else?"

"Another bottle, please." Jeanette smoothed a few strands of hair at the nape of her neck.

Sarah added,. "A little more French bread, too."

Rafo inclined his head. "Of course." He lingered to smile at Jeanette, then walked off to the kitchen.

Minnie mimicked the waiter's throaty voice: "Of course. Would you like me to bring you another mink stole, as well? Perhaps a lovely diamond lavaliere?"

Sarah snickered. "Or the skin from a snake? After all, your charm is considerable."

"Ah, he doesn't count. He's at least fifty-five. Now if he was forty."

"Fifty-five and stay alive." Sarah toasted with her empty glass.

Jeanette frowned. "Maybe we should take the wine home and order coffee. Honestly, you two are getting out of hand."

Minnie teased, "I could call Rafo back."

"No. Have some lunch. Fill those empty tummies." Jeanette wiggled her fingers in another hello to the Mayor. He grinned and waved back.

Minnie gazed solemnly at Jeanette. "Listen. All of this wine at thirty bucks a bottle, this fancy lunch. I'll help you pay for it. We can split the check. I'll put it on my Master Charge."

"Don't be silly, Minnie. Wait. Master Charge? I didn't know you had any credit cards."

"Are you kidding? I have a drawer full of them at home. Bank cards, Magnin, Saks. Even oil company cards and I haven't had a car in ten years." Minnie laughed and dropped her salad fork which tumbled off the booth seat to disappear under the table. She looked downward then shrugged. "I was done with my salad anyway."

"Don't change the subject. That's something you never told me about."

"And for good reason. You'd want to borrow them. I'd end up in the poor house. Oh my, why am I telling you now?"

"You're already in the poor house. Use them and maybe you could get out. And Saks? Hmmm. I'd love to owe them a lot of money."

For Sarah, Minnie jabbed her thumb in Jeanette's direction. "See what I mean?" Then to Jeanette, she said, "I only use them on special occasions, like today. I don't owe anyone a cent."

"Magnin, too? How about Neiman Marcus?"

"Needless Markup." Sarah winked.

"And Nordstrom's?"

Minnie grumbled, "That's enough."

Jeanette took a bite of scaloppini, chewing thoughtfully. It was time to broach the subject.

"You know, if we're going to be living in Spain, basically become expatriates, I think we should leave from New York, not San Francisco."

Sarah asked, "What do you mean?"

Minnie leaned forward. "A road trip? See this country one last time. Is that what you're thinking?"

"That's exactly what I'm thinking." Minnie was always one step ahead, knew what was going on in Jeanette's head. To men, Jeanette was a mystery. To Minnie, an open book.

That came with the territory. They'd grown up one farm apart in Missouri and had been inseparable until age eighteen, when Jeanette left for a modeling career in New York and Minnie went to teacher's college in LA. So different in character, yet with the same hopes and dreams to get off the farm. To do something with their lives besides milk cows, marry, make babies and drive pickups.

In high school they met Sarah. She lived in town. Sarah was sweet and shy but had the same desire to live in the big city. She got on the bus to Los Angeles and the teachers' college with Minnie, both flushed with the excitement of new possible lives.

The three kept in touch, but over the years they went in different directions until six years ago; they landed together in the same low-income housing complex on Geary Boulevard where Edith lived. Sarah had become best friends with Edith long ago. She was a comfort after Don's death. Minnie had accepted her new living conditions, but Jeanette had fallen into deprivation kicking, screaming, and still dreaming of a way out.

"Hmmm. A road trip. And we would pay for it – how?" Minnie shook her head, quizzical.

"With these." Jeanette pulled a pink envelope from her purse. She emptied the contents in the center of the table. At least twenty credit cards scattered across the red cloth. The bright logos of bank, oil company, department store cards reflected under the candlelight.

"Where did you…?" Minnie picked up a Master Charge. The name Edith Clarke was printed in raised letters under the account number.

"Are you crazy?"

"I've called all the eight-hundred numbers on the back. They're all good and none have any balances on them."

"No, no, no, no, no." Minnie said with finality as though she'd decided against it weeks ago. She shook her head, slumping into the booth. "Jeanette, are you insane? We could end up in jail."

Sarah asked, "How would they ever find us?"

Jeanette said, "Good question. Seven years ago when I left New York, none of them ever found me again."

Minnie said, "What does that matter? It's wrong. Now, put those away before someone sees."

Jeanette put the cards in the envelope and stuffed them in her purse. She pouted dramatically and sighed.

Now came the hard part. The coaxing and the pleading. Maybe it wouldn't be so bad. Sarah appeared to be in favor of the idea.

"Minnie, didn't I hear you say something about which one of us is next?" Jeanette set her jaw. "What if a plane crashed into the room right now? Could you honestly say you've lived to the fullest?"

Minnie set her own jaw. "Oh, I see. You'd like me to round out my life with a nice little prison sentence?"

Jeanette sucked her teeth. "Nobody's going to jail over this. Even if they caught us and pressed charges, we'd get out of it easily." Jeanette puckered childishly. "But your honor, we were all so grief-stricken and scared. We're so old and sad, we just weren't thinking properly."

Sarah asked, "Will that work?"

"Believe me."

"Maybe you could get away with it." Minnie crossed her arms, sour. "It's wrong, wrong, wrong. Now change the subject."

Jeanette did not comply. She and Minnie bandied about it at length. Sarah listened without much input.

By the time Rafo brought the bill, Minnie had not budged from her stance. She dug through her wallet looking for her Master Charge, but before Minnie could move, Jeanette whisked up the brown billfold and slid inside one of the cards from the pink envelope.

Minnie opened her mouth to protest but Jeanette raised a finger to her lips. "Just watch how easy this is."

Rafo gathered up the check. Minnie watched in earnest as he processed the charge. When Rafo picked up the telephone, Minnie's eyes widened. "What's he doing?"

Jeanette said, "He's calling for an authorization. We ran up a pretty high bill."

Minnie wrung her hands. Jeanette placed a warm palm on her squirming wrists. "Don't worry. It'll be fine, you'll see."

When Rafo returned, he presented Jeanette with the sales draft, which she signed with a flourish. He glanced at the draft and the big tip, then smiled at Jeanette.

"Thank you so much Mrs. Clarke."

"It's not Mrs., and please, call me Edie."

Minnie hissed. "This is another of your harebrained schemes. After all these years, you haven't changed one bit. You have a good heart but it's larcenous. And now, thanks to you, we're headed for trouble. I can feel it in my bones. Sarah, you've got to help me talk some sense into her."

Sarah, the follower, only shrugged. Unsteadily, Minnie rose. "I'm going to the restroom."

When she was gone, Sarah asked, "Are we going to jail?"

Jeanette patted Sarah's arm. "Good Lord, no." Jeanette stood. "I'll see you all later."

"Where are you going?"

"I've got some errands to run."

Chapter 3

With the promise of spring in the air, Minnie trotted down to the lobby to check her mailbox. She emerged from the elevator into the foyer.

"Butch, you're late today."

The mailman doffed his cap and rubbed his brow, then returned to sorting the mail.

"They changed my route. Are you collecting Edith's mail this time?"

"What do you mean, this time? I thought all her mail was being returned to sender."

"No, ma'am. Your friend Jeanette's been picking it up. Said she's taking care of Edith's affairs." Butch didn't look up from shoving stacks of mail into the banks of mailboxes.

Minnie was dumbstruck. She faltered before saying, "Okay. I'll see Jeanette gets it."

"Here you go. You might need a forklift today. And here's your mail."

Edith's stack of correspondence was big as a brick. "This is all hers?"

"Afraid so." Butch closed the mailbox block with a solid click. "It's mostly junk mail and bills. Have a good day."

"Bills?" Frozen, Minnie watched him wheel away his pull cart out the door, letting in a burst of sunshine.

Alone in the elevator, she sorted through the pile. Many letters were credit card bills.

"Oh my God."

Jeanette. She should have known. Minnie tore some open. She gasped at the balances. "Oh, no, no, no."

Minnie rode the elevator to the sixth floor, willing it to go faster. Storming down the hall, she pounded on Jeanette's door, but got no answer. She raced to Sarah's apartment. When Sarah answered, Minnie thrust the statements into her hands.

"Look at this. Good Lord in heaven. Look at this."

"What? What is it? My goodness, Minnie, calm down." Sarah squinted at the fanned-out stack.

"Calm down? Calm down? You won't be so calm when you see this."

"I was napping, dear. Sit down, catch your breath."

"Would you just take a look? Where are your glasses?"

Still groggy, Sarah put a hand to her mouth. "Good question. Now, where was I sleeping?"

Minnie found Sarah's bifocals on the end table next to an avocado Lazy-Boy. "Quick. Take a look."

Together they pored over the statements, clicking their tongues when they saw the charges at Gump's. The itemized purchases corresponded by date and description to the Christmas gifts they'd received from Jeanette. Sorting through the stack, Minnie couldn't believe what she saw: The emblem of Master Charge on one, the return addresses of banks and department stores.

Minnie said, "What in the world has gotten into that woman? She swore she wasn't using Edith's cards. She lied. She told me she'd gotten some money from Jeff's estate."

She ripped open an envelope from Magnin's. "Jeez, she's probably run out of room in her closet. Where is she anyway? Jeanette's going to be in so much trouble."

"Buying a new closet, I don't know." Sarah opened a bill from City Security Bank, then read a long list of Master Charge transactions, "Pandora's, Pandora's, Pandora's. Everyday Pandora's."

"What time is it?"

"Twelve twenty."

"Come on."

Minnie was not surprised to find Jeanette flirting with the same waiter who'd served them a few months ago. At her table, he was pouring white wine into a crystal glass. She and Sarah marched up and sat abruptly. Rafo smiled graciously.

"Ah, nice to see you again. Would you lovely ladies care for some wine?"

Sarah rolled her eyes and plopped her purse on the red tablecloth. "I think not."

Minnie mustered a snobbish tone. "Maybe we will partake." She leaned to Jeanette. "After all, you are buying, aren't you, Edie?"

Clearing her throat, she said, "Two more glasses, please, Rafo."

Rafo, sensing trouble, backed away.

Minnie asked, "On a first-name basis with the help now, are we?"

"Well, a woman's work is never done. How did you find me?"

"This gave us a clue." Minnie tossed the credit card bills onto Jeanette's Caesar salad.

Jeanette removed the statements from her plate and set them aside. She sat up straighter. "Angry because I didn't invite you today?"

"Don't play with us, Jeanette. This is disgraceful. Using Edith's cards. And not just using them, either. You've been out binging."

"Like you would have gone along."

"Gone along? Good grief! How in the world are you going to repay these debts?"

"I am repaying them." Jeanette sipped her wine.

"There's been a few minimum payments made. How did you manage that?"

"Easy. Just get a cash advance on one to make payments on the others. Keeps them alive longer."

Rafo's return to pour more wine silenced Minnie in mid-epithet. With a slight bow he asked, "Will you be ordering lunch as well?"

Before they could answer, Jeanette said, "You haven't lunched yet have you, dears?" To Rafo, she said, "A Ceasar salad for Sarah, here, and Minnie, you must try the Coquille St. Jacques. I believe we'll also need another bottle of Pouilly-Fumé. Thank you, Rafo."

Sensing the tension at the table, Rafo all but fled.

Jeanette asked, "So what are you girls doing about getting ready for the road trip, for Spain?"

Sarah said, "It doesn't look like we're as ready as you are."

Minnie again threw the bills on Jeanette's salad. "Do you know how much you've spent?"

"Stop that." Using her fork, Jeanette flipped the bills aside and took a bite of her salad. "I don't particularly care."

"I don't believe this." Minnie slumped, exasperated.

Calmly, Sarah asked, "Why are you doing this?"

"Because, because." Jeanette considered for a moment, then leaning forward, whispered.

"Because, oh hell, I don't know why. Because they were there. Because it was easy. Because I'm sick and tired of living like a bum. And after I bought Christmas presents for you two, I couldn't stop. I could think of a million things to get with them. I just couldn't stop. And believe me, I never intended to hurt your feelings."

Sarah interjected, "Well, you did."

Minnie sputtered, "I'm surprised at you."

Sarah said, "I'm not."

Jeanette sighed. "We're not getting any younger. What have we got to show for our lives? Look at how we've ended up. I can't stand it! And I don't see how you can either. Both of you had good lives. You had nest eggs. But look what happened." Jeanette reached across Minnie to cover Sarah's hand. Dropping her voice, she said compassionately, "Sarah, your husband got so ill and your entire savings went to pay the medical bills. I remember when you told me that. Now some doctor is living in a fine house on Russian Hill using your money for petty cash. You and Don were supposed to travel, see the world. Now he's gone and you can barely make ends meet. It's not fair. It doesn't have to be that way. And I'm going to make it right for you."

Minnie glared, intending to make Jeanette flinch, but Jeanette didn't flicker an eye. Instead, Jeanette gazed back with a challenging expression.

Sarah said, "Well, I do feel cheated."

Minnie's jaw went slack. "Here we go."

Minnie turned back to Jeanette. "You can't justify it. It's just how things are, that's all."

"And you, Minnie. You spent your life teaching little children. Worst paying job in the world. Yet you shaped the future of this country."

"That's a bit melodramatic, even for you."

"Nonsense. It's the truth."

Sarah looked off, to the few patrons at nearby tables. All were eyeing them and their argument. In a low voice, she said, "Let's calm down. We don't want to create a scene. We've got a problem here. It doesn't make any sense to fight. What we need to do is figure out a solution." To Minnie, she said, "Now I'm inclined to go along with Jeanette on this."

"Sarah!"

"Sshhh. Think about it. You saw those balances. There's no way we can pay it back."

"We? We aren't the ones who ran up those balances! Our klepto-buddy here is the one. Why should it even be our problem?"

"Because we're best friends, that's why."

"Thank you, Sarah." Jeanette reached out to take Sarah's hand again, but pulled it back quickly when Sarah slapped it.

"Stop that. Sometimes I don't think you have a brain in that pretty head of yours."

Jeanette rubbed her stung hand. Sarah continued.

"We have to stick together. You could be in a lot of trouble for this." To Minnie, she said, "Jeanette's right about one thing. I'm bitter. Very bitter. Since Don died, I've felt betrayed. He worked very hard and it all came to nothing. The insurance maxed out but the medical bills kept rolling in. Then the bank foreclosed on my house. Put me right out on the street. I feel like a statistic."

Sarah paused for a sip of wine. "We're in it this far, we might as well go all the way. Since we'll be living in Spain in a few months, I don't see why we couldn't tour the United States for the last time. See the country. That's what Don and I had planned. We were going to buy a Winnebago. If we use all of our credit cards together, we could do it. By the time the bills come in, we'll be long gone."

Jeanette agreed. "My thoughts, exactly."

Minnie's mouth made a small 'O' and stuck. They'd finally done it. They'd struck her speechless.

Jeanette was giddy now that she had an ally. She wiggled in her seat, grinning brightly. "We could trade the airline tickets for a New York departure. That way, I could see Natalie and my little Jeannie before we fly out to Spain."

Minnie asked, "And who'll drive the Winnebago? Maybe you could talk Rafo here into chauffeuring."

Jeanette answered breezily. "Forget the Winnebago. We'll rent a Lincoln touring car and drive. In comfort and style. We'll take our time. See all the sights. Stay in fancy hotels. Eat fancy meals."

Sarah said, "I want to see David. He's in Albuquerque."

"New Orleans!" Jeanette rubbed her hands together. "And Washington D.C. I want to visit my daughter and grandbaby in New York City."

Sarah and Jeanette bounced ideas and destinations back and forth. Minnie sat between them feeling like an observer at a tennis match. "Two against one. Is that how it is?"

"C'mon, Minnie, why the hell not?" Jeanette slammed both palms on the tabletop.

"Because I'm afraid your mind has short circuited. You're off in some fantasyland. I'm not just angry. I'm scared for you. You've lost it. You too, Sarah. This is criminal."

Jeanette fumed. "You think I'm going to live out the rest of my life in the slums, waiting to get picked off like Edith? Why don't we just go join Edith now and get it over with?"

"See, you have lost it."

"Figure of speech. Look, I'm trying to make a point. None of this is a fantasy. The villa in Spain is a reality. The credit cards are real! And they're the key to escaping this cage we're in."

"Why don't we just leave right now? Fly directly to Spain from here, right now? We've got the tickets. We can take our knocks if we have to about Edith's cards."

"Because the place won't be vacated and ready until summer, remember?"

Sarah said, "I've got to see my son first."

Jeanette nodded. "And I'm going to see Natalie and my granddaughter for sure. That means Albuquerque and New York. Minnie, don't you have any desire to see anyone before you go?"

"I don't have anyone except Marc. And he's right here."

"Well, lucky you. Then what about seeing America? Once we get to Spain, we may never make it back. As much as you've carried on about traveling, I'd think you'd be gung ho."

Sarah fidgeted with her silverware. "The geography teacher. And you've never been anywhere."

The bill arrived. Jeanette slid Edith's Master Charge onto the tray.

"By the way, Minnie, did you enjoy your meal?"

Rafo returned the credit card slip for Jeanette's signature. "Thank you so much, ladies. Please visit again.

I trust everything was to your liking." He whispered something to Jeanette. Jeanette blushed and, laughing, said, "Of course."

Rafo kissed her hand, "Edie, it's always a pleasure."

Chapter 4

The phone woke Minnie after midnight. She answered to Sarah sobbing.

"What's wrong? Are you okay?"

"I'm sorry to call so late. No, I'm not okay. I just need to talk to you."

"Have you come to your senses?"

Sarah's blubbering made way for a small laugh. "No, I can't say that's happened. But, well, I'm just afraid of losing you. We've already lost Edith. I don't mean losing you that way. I mean losing your friendship. Our little group. What's left of it." Sarah blew her nose.

Minnie's heart sank. She didn't know what to say.

Sarah went on, sniffling, "It's just that, oh, sometimes you can be so stubborn."

Minnie clicked on a lamp. "Sarah, I thought I knew you. I was shocked when you said all those things today at Pandora's. I can see Jeanette going off the deep end. She's always been out there. But you agreed with her. I just don't know what's going on anymore. Or where anyone's sense of right and wrong has disappeared to."

"But it makes sense, what Jeanette wants to do. I'm scared, Minnie. I don't want to end up like Edith. All those things Jeanette said at lunch, you know she's right."

Minnie curled her finger in the torn satin trim of her blanket. She reminded herself to mend it. "Why don't you come down and have some tea."

"All right. I'll be right there."

Minnie put on her blue fuzzy slippers and a robe, then shuffled to the kitchen to start the teapot. A moment later, Sarah tapped on the door.

They sat at the kitchen table. Sarah's bathrobe, homemade a decade ago from a thermal blanket, was pilled everywhere. It was so old the original pink color was washed out to shades of rosy gray. Sarah apologized again, "I'm sorry to wake you."

"That's okay. I was tossing anyway."

"I know it seems farfetched. It seems like a crazy thing to do. But haven't you ever wanted to do anything crazy?"

"It's breaking the law."

Sarah blew her nose again. "You know, that just doesn't matter to me. We're so old now."

"Call yourself that if you want to. Age is in the mind, dear. I don't feel old. Not yet."

"I'm sixty-two." Sarah paused, lost in thought. "All my life, all I got was old. I've lived by the rules. My family's rules first, then my husband's rules. And now, well, now I want to bust out. Do something. And this seems like the perfect chance. Time goes by so fast. We don't have that much longer. Twenty years give or take, if we're lucky. And what I do have left, I want to enjoy. It's worth the risk. Even if I get in trouble, it will be worth it."

"So you're definitely going to do this? With Jeanette?"

Sarah nodded, then buried her face in her hands. "I want to see my son. David's been so distant since Don died. For twelve years, I've barely heard from him. I want to talk to him, find out what's eating him. This will probably be the last time I see him."

The teapot whistled. Minnie poured hot water into a pair of mugs on the counter.

"You would leave me here alone?"

After a long silence, she turned to the table with the tea to find Sarah crying once more. From the bathroom Minnie brought a box of tissues. She needed one herself.

Sarah said, "I can't stay here anymore. Every time I pass Edith's door, my heart aches. When I met Edith we were both twenty. You'd already transferred to San Francisco State. I'd married Don and we lived in that little house behind the big house in San Gabriel. Remember that place? You visited us there."

Minnie nodded.

"You remember my backyard had the low fence with the gate that opened to Edith's backyard?" Minnie nodded again. Sarah continued: I remember a spring day. The gate was open like it always was, and Edith, young and beautiful Edith, brought me a basket of fresh-picked green beans from her vegetable patch."

Sarah shook her head. "All those years. How did they pass so quickly?"

Minnie wanted to reach for her friend. "They just do."

Sarah continued. "Edith and I were pregnant at the same time, raised our kids together, were neighbors for years and years. Our husbands were best friends. They died two years apart, hers first, then Don. By then we were both in Marin County. We did everything together, saw each other every day. Now, just like that, she's gone. I can't believe it. And I'm furious about it."

Sarah slapped the tabletop. "I can't stay here. I have to get away, start over somewhere else. Too many memories, too much loss."

Sarah sipped the tea to wash away the sad words.

"I can't get her out of my mind and it's eating away at me."

Minnie covered Sarah's hand with her own and sat in quiet empathy to let Sarah recover a bit. Then she said, "Go on."

"You know, when you and Jeanette moved into the building it became the four musketeers. Now there's only three. No more bridge parties. I looked forward to those afternoons."

"I did, too."

"Edith was a night person, like me. Long after you and Jeanette would retire, we'd be up to all hours talking, working on our knitting or sewing projects. Now at night, I'm awake, I'm alone. It's so scary. You know what the worst is?" Sarah shivered and ran her hands up and down her arms. "It's so cold in the apartment now at night. I don't remember it being like that when Edith was here."

Minnie put an arm around Sarah's shoulder and squeezed. "I know how hard this must be for you. But I don't want to be the old fool. I don't want to go to jail. In essence, I agree with you two. I don't want to stay here, especially alone. And traveling would be great. But I'm having a hard time with this credit card business." Minnie tried to figure how to word it properly. Unable to, she blurted it out. "Don't you think using Edith's cards is disrespectful?"

"What?" Sarah seemed genuinely puzzled. "No. No, I don't. In fact, I picture Edith up there cheering us on. Look, Jeanette is your best friend. But she'll go, with or without you. Believe me. Then for you, it will be like me losing Edith. You'll have lost Jeanette. And she'll have lost you. You'll have three empty doors to pass every day."

Sarah sipped her tea, then became cheery. "You worry too much. Come with us. Say you'll do it. You know how Jeanette is. Once she's got something set in her mind..."

Minnie nodded; she knew exactly how Jeanette could be. And no matter what harebrained scheme Jeanette got herself into, she always came out smelling like a rose.

In the silence of sitting together, taking in the cold quiet midnight and sipping chamomile tea, Minnie couldn't resist considering how life would be without her best friends. Opening the mailbox to find a postcard from the Spanish Riviera, or Paris, or London. Alone in her apartment with no one to talk to. Only looking forward to her monthly outings with her nephew, Marc. Yes, it would be too much to bear.

"I have an idea. Why don't I just meet you in Spain. You and Jeanette can have your road trip and if you survive, if you come out unscathed, I can fly out from here." As soon as she said it, she felt like a traitor.

"No, no. You have to come with us."

Traitor or not, she pressed on. "But why? You two are hellbent on pulling this scam. Personally, I don't want to have anything to do with it. I'll just meet you in Spain."

"It just wouldn't be right. You've got to come with us." Sheepishly, Sarah added, "Besides, we need your credit cards, too."

"I should have known. Why don't you just take them!" Minnie rose to storm for her purse. She pulled out her wallet.

"Stop it, Minnie. I didn't mean it like that."

"No, go on, take them. I don't use them anyway. I'll wait until you're safe in Spain then I'll report them stolen. I'll say I was mugged or that I had misplaced them. I'll think of something. Don't worry, I won't incriminate you."

"You get mad so fast. I've never seen anything like it. The whole point is for the three of us to go together, to have a really good time, to escape this awful place, our awful futures. See the country. A road trip."

Minnie stopped tugging out credit cards. She sat again at the kitchen table.

"I'll never talk you two out of it."

"We'll take you kicking and screaming."

Despite herself, Minnie grinned. "I'll sleep on it."

Sarah finished the last of her tea. At the door, she took Minnie in a bear hug. "I love you."

"I love you, too." Minnie felt the return of tears. She stayed in the doorway while Sarah shuffled down the hall looking like a ragamuffin. Turning at her front door, Sarah smiled and waved with waggling fingers.

Minnie made herself memorize the gesture. How deeply would she be sorry if she stayed in San Francisco? How deeply would she regret it if she went with them?

Chapter 5

"Don't speed. Are you going to drive with the top down?"

Her nephew said, "Absolutely."

Minnie dug through her purse for a long pastel blue scarf. "After all that rain, I'm glad to see a little sunshine. Where shall we go?"

"We haven't been to Muir Woods in a while. What do you think, Na Na? We could have lunch in Sausalito afterwards."

"That would be nice. This scarf isn't too long is it? I don't want to end up like Isadora Duncan."

Marc chuckled and started the Alfa with a vroom. "Is that a new scarf? I like the color."

"Jeanette gave it to me. I bet you don't miss that old VW bug, do you?"

"Nope. This is my pride and joy."

Marc took off. He was a good driver; she felt safe. Minnie thrilled at flying around curves, loved the racecar sound and admired the car's sexy, sleek Italian styling. She felt young and reckless.

"You look more and more like your father every day. I sure miss him.

"I do too." Marc tugged on his mustache. He zipped into the far right lane.

"Your dad and I were like two peas in a pod. Running through the corn together, playing with the farm animals. We were inseparable. Sometimes I have to do a double-take. It astounds me how much you look like him. Good looking man, he was."

"Nice gene pool. I'm lucky," Marc accelerated around a pickup truck.

Marc's features were dark and rugged, with sparkling brown eyes and high cheekbones. His hands were large and nicely curved, with prominent veins like his father's. A workingman's hands, but not quite, and not a workingman's tan which would come from a tractor and not a tennis court. Still, her nephew was trim and tan, in khaki pants and a UC Berkeley sweatshirt, the picture of an athlete, and her brother.

On their monthly outings, Minnie most enjoyed the discussions, everything from reincarnation to politics. They'd agree, debate, and disagree. She was glad he, too, left the farm, made it to college at UC Berkeley, not to spend his life plowing fields.

Yet after all that hard work at school, graduating Phi Betta Kappa, he still hadn't gotten into medical school. Though he'd shrugged it off, saying "Well, if Dad had been rich enough to build a library for UC Irvine, maybe

I'd get in." He was disappointed. But youth and energy persevered over disappointment and Marc had found a new love and frontier, computers.

"What are you thinking, Na Na?"

"I'm just so proud of you."

Crossing the Golden Gate Bridge, they left the sunshine. Fog rolled across the span, sprinkling them in the open car. Between patches, the sun shone on Angel Island and Alcatraz. A barge made its way under the bridge heading to sea toward the shrouded Farallon Islands.

On today's jaunt, Minnie intended to ask Marc for some answers about credit cards and Jeanette's predicament. While attending college, he'd started his career as a bill collector in City Security Bank's Master Charge department. She'd have to be discreet, and privately rehearsed what and how she would ask him.

Walking between the redwoods in Muir Woods, Marc took Minnie's hand to help her over a mushroom-encrusted log. Two blue jays soared low across the path, to disappear into the tall branches.

Marc said, "That whole thing with Edith was awful. How's everyone holding up?"

"We're okay. Sarah was hit the hardest. But she's starting to smile again." Marc had created an opening; Minnie went through it. "Now everyone wants to take a little trip. You know that villa in Spain that Jeanette inherited?"

"You're going to Spain?"

"Actually, Jeanette wants to move there and since the place is so big, she'd like Sarah and me to live there, too."

"Whoa! When were you going to tell me about this?"

"Right now."

"So are you going?"

"It's a big decision. Jeanette and Sarah are determined. I'd like to. But, well, there's you and…I just don't know."

"If you really want to, if that's what your heart is telling you to do, then you ought to do it. I'd miss you of course. But they're your best friends. They're practically family. I don't think you should stay just because of me. You've always wanted to live in Europe. You're a geography teacher. Besides, I could come for vacation. A villa on the Spanish Riviera. I could dig that. And I could fly you back here for Christmas. Man, Jeanette's got some highfalutin friends."

"Almost too la-di-da for me. You know me, I'm just your basic farm girl."

"Come on, Na Na. As educated as you are? You could hold your own anywhere, with anyone. I remember when you made me learn all the state capitols. And that big globe you had. Showing me all those itty-bitty, funny-named countries. You were always excited about traveling, but you never got to. This is your big chance. Why are you hesitating?"

"Maybe because it's so permanent."

"Hell, nothing's carved in stone. If you don't like it there, you could come back."

"I suppose you're right."

And face criminal charges.

"Besides, if you didn't go, would Jeanette and Sarah go anyway?"

"They've made it perfectly clear they intend to go."

"You'd get pretty lonely. Do you have any other close friends here?"

Minnie couldn't think of even a short list of acquaintances, much less friends. She'd never been very social. "Not really. I'd miss them terribly. So you really think I ought to do it?"

Marc threw an arm around her. "Sure. When is this supposed to happen?"

"Pretty soon. The villa's leased out until the end of May. So June, I suppose."

"I'll miss you. But it sounds too good to pass up."

"You're right, honey. Besides, you've got better things to do than drive your old Na Na around. Like today, you should be out playing tennis with your buddies."

"I finished a quick set this morning."

"I thought you slept in on Saturdays."

"No way. Sunday, yes. I make a big pot of coffee and pull the Chronicle back into bed with me."

"And your Saturday night date?"

Marc shrugged sheepishly.

"When are you going to settle down, young man? You're twenty-five."

They hiked deeper into the redwood forest. The massive trees darkened the path and wild brush around them. Beside the trail, a slender stream trickled. Marc led Minnie to a bench; here, they breathed the earthy fragrance of the redwoods and listened to birdsong and the peacefulness of the rolling water.

Marc broke the silence. "If you want, I'll take you to the airport."

"Actually, Sarah and Jeanette have been talking about doing a road trip across the country and then leaving from New York. Sarah wants to visit her son and Jeanette wants to see her daughter."

"That sounds great. A road trip."

"True. But I don't know if we can afford it."

"I've got some money put aside. I'd be happy to contribute to the cause."

"Oh, no, Marc. Keep that money. I'm glad you've got something in savings. Good for you. As far as this trip is concerned, I've got my part handled. So does Sarah. It's Jeanette I'm worried about."

"Jeanette. I'll bet she blows through every dime she gets."

"Tell me about it. Did you know she came to San Francisco with a hundred thousand dollars seven years ago? She spent it all in one year. One year! Now she doesn't have two nickels to rub together. But she's got these credit cards. She's thinking she could use them for the road trip. But what if she doesn't pay them back? Would they extradite her from Spain and put her in jail?"

"I'd say no. Jail's only for people who steal credit cards or commit fraud to obtain them.

There's no debtor's prisons in America, Na Na. Lots of people can't pay their bills. They file bankruptcy. It ruins their credit, and some skip town. Others might get their wages garnished. But they don't go to prison."

"They don't? I thought they jailed people who run up their credit cards with no intention of repaying."

"It's pretty hard to prove intent. Of course, no one in their right mind would tell a court of law that they had no intention of paying their bills. They would claim financial reversals. Or say they were expecting a windfall that didn't come in. If they misrepresented themselves on the initial application, that would be fraud. And fraud charges are pressed in only the most extreme cases."

"So what would they do about Jeanette? I mean, if she ran up the cards and went to Spain?"

"They couldn't do much at all. They'd try to track her down, try to collect. But eventually they'd just charge it off." Marc tossed a pebble into the stream. "She'd be long gone. They probably wouldn't even find her. And if she didn't do too much damage, it would be cheaper for them to forget about it. When it becomes international, it gets too costly and time-consuming to go after. Say, how did Jeanette get credit anyway?"

Minnie waved the question away. "I saw a story in the paper last week about a man who ran up thirty thousand and took off to South America. They extradited him and put him in jail."

"I saw that, too. Yeah. You know, a month ago, there was another guy who'd stolen a City Security credit card from one of our customers. Lots of other bank cards were involved as well. He ran up fifty grand and fled to Mexico. They had to charge that one off but only because they couldn't find him. Stolen cards. If they'd caught him, he would have gone down on felony charges. But this guy was clever. Stayed under the floor limits, moved around a lot. It takes a few days for the sales drafts to float in, longer if the charges are made in a foreign country. You think you've got him in Florida, and next thing you know, you're looking at sales drafts from Brazil. They had a hell of a time finding him."

Minnie barely heard, stuck on his earlier statement. "Felony charges?"

"Robbing a bank with a credit card instead of a gun."

"Floor limit. What's that?"

"When a merchant signs up with the bank to accept credit cards he's assigned a limit on the amount he can accept before having to call in for an authorization. That's a floor limit." Minnie recalled Rafo placing the phone call on their first lunch at Pandora's. He was asking about the floor limit of Edith's card, exactly what Jeanette said he was doing. Maybe she knew more about the ins-and-outs of this than Minnie realized.

Marc continued his explanation: "A liquor store, for example, has a floor limit of twenty-five bucks. If a customer charges fifteen dollars of liquor, the merchant can accept the charge without calling it in. But he has to check the warning bulletin to see if the credit card has been reported lost or stolen. If the purchase is twenty-five bucks or more, he must get an authorization from the credit card company. So if the account is delinquent, or over the limit or closed, the authorization is refused. And if it's listed as lost or stolen, he has to call the cops."

"How do they know if the card is lost or stolen?"

"The cardholder reports it."

"That makes sense. So, for example, what's the floor limit on airlines?"

"Three hundred."

"What about restaurants?"

"Fifty, I think, or twenty-five. I can't remember exactly. I think it varies. The more expensive restaurants have higher floor limits."

"And hotels? Do the fancier ones have higher floor limits than, say, a Motel Six?"

"They do." Marc cut himself off to look Minnie square in the face, "What are you up to Aunt Minnie?"

"Up to? Nothing at all."

"No, you've got that tone in your voice. And you're asking an awful lot of questions."

"I just find this very interesting. You're so smart. No wonder the bank made you a hotshot computer manager." She stood and stretched. "Let's go get some lunch. I'm famished."

Marc remained planted on the bench. "No, no, wait a second. Flattery will get you nowhere." He patted the bench. "Tell me what's going on. Jeanette's already in trouble, isn't she?"

Minnie eased back onto the bench. She took a deep breath.

"Okay, here's the thing. When we were cleaning up Edith's place, Jeanette found a bunch of her credit cards. I don't think Edith ever used them. Those are the cards I was referring to. Jeanette has this wild idea that she could finance her part of the trip with them. After all, she doesn't have a single charge plate in her name. And she's not likely to ever get one. Her credit is horrible."

"I knew something was up. It doesn't surprise me that Jeanette would try to pull a stunt like that. That's pretty tricky."

"What should I do? What should I tell her?"

"I'd advise her against it. Even so, Jeanette might make a case for herself with a good lawyer. At her age, maybe an Alzheimer's defense. If not, with her good looks and acting experience, who knows? She could try to charm one of those old judges." Marc eyed Minnie suspiciously. "She's already used those cards, hasn't she?"

"What? No. Good grief, Marc, I just asked you a few simple questions. I'm probably overly worrying. Jeanette talks a lot, but I don't think she'd really do anything that foolish. Now obey your elders. Take me to lunch like you promised."

"Okay." Marc clapped and rose off the bench. "But something smells fishy. When you get home, I want you to get those credit cards away from Jeanette and destroy them. Don't even let her think about it anymore. I can easily picture her going berserk with them."

In Sausalito, they had a fabulous lunch of fresh scallops and Dungeness crab. Patrons arrived and departed at the dock near their table, Minnie and her nephew enjoyed the sun and talked about everything but credit cards. A breeze arrived with dessert and seagulls sailed aloft on the currents of air.

As usual, Minnie quibbled with Marc over who would take the check. Today, he wouldn't hear of her paying even a part of it.

"Okay, bigshot." For years she'd been the one who treated. She made him loans and gifts while he was a struggling student. With no children of her own, she was happy to help Marc.

The loans had long since been repaid and the roles seemed reversed. Now he was self-sufficient and eager to reciprocate. This disconcerted Minnie, and hinted that he no longer needed her. She'd known this for a long time, but today was the first time she'd acknowledged the truth of it, and this left Minnie a bit vacant and sad.

Cars packed the Golden Gate Bridge on their return. Minnie didn't mind. The bumper-to-bumper traffic let her ponder her decision. She'd promised Sarah an answer, soon. They wanted to start the road trip in May.

The early fog had burned off; the Hermes scarf had been shoved into her jacket pocket. Minnie loved the way the late afternoon sun cast a golden glow over San Francisco and on the sailboats gliding across the bay. Was there French bread in Spain? Could it be as good as the French bread at Fisherman's wharf? Other than bread,

Marc, and this amazing view, what else was here for her? With Jeanette and Sarah gone, she could think of nothing else strong enough, attractive enough, to hold her here.

The road trip was an appealing opportunity. Edith would have gone at the drop of a hat. Minnie was supposed to go shopping with her that fateful day. Edith wanted her opinion on which of the two items she had found to give Sarah for Christmas. Feeling too tired, Minnie had begged off. If she'd gone, maybe Edith would be alive today. But Minnie might have been killed, too. She pushed the thought away, and considered Spanish French bread.

More images, of Venice, London, Paris, and Amsterdam, rushed at her like clips from travel logs. Could they really get away with it? And even if Jeanette stopped charging now, isn't it already too late? She's already in big trouble. It just hasn't arrived on her doorstep, yet.

What if they all got caught? Alzheimer's defense, that's what Marc advised. The repercussions might not be so bad if Minnie used her own cards. She wouldn't be in too much trouble. As long as she didn't use Edith's cards.

Suddenly she felt ashamed of the notion that she might let Jeanette take the fall. No. Minnie had to stand by her friend. Her best friend. She and Sarah won't make it if they try this on their own. Jeanette's wild, with not a lick of common sense. She'd trip herself up right off the bat. And Sarah, under Jeanette's spell, was vulnerable, following like a puppy. They needed Minnie along for more than just access to her credit. She was good at math. She had common sense.

And if they did get in trouble, Marc could help. He was clever, he loved Minnie, and he knew the world of credit cards.

Marc smiled as if in agreement with Minnie's thoughts. The convertible sped onwards, whipping the wind across them.

What the hell. Minnie was going to find out what Spanish French bread tasted like.

Chapter 6

Jeanette stepped out of the dressing room onto the dais. She admired her reflection in the full-length, tri-fold mirror. She examined her profile, then twirled like the model she was. The green satin was her best color, matching her eyes and complementing her auburn hair; it floated against her creamy skin. Her hand moved down the front of the dress. The flattering light picked up the sparkle of the emerald on her finger.

Six years of waiting. Not being able to shop, of watching her fine clothes go out of style and become shopworn. So nice to ignore price tags again; just buy it. She pirouetted before the mirror.

Minnie rounded the corner, arms laden with cocktail dresses. "Oh, my, Jeanette. That is stunning!"

"Exactly what I was thinking." Jeanette pivoted to study the back. She noted an elderly woman with a cane, watching from the clearance rack just outside the dressing room area. The woman wore a threadbare coat, a faded navy scarf tied below her chin. She smiled her approval at Jeanette then returned to rummaging through the clearance rack of Saks Fifth Avenue.

A clerk approached her. "Excuse me, can I help you with something?"

"Oh, just looking. Browsing really."

"I see." The clerk rolled her eyes, then moved beside Jeanette. Animated, she exclaimed, "Mrs. Clarke, that dress is you! Would you like me to find some accessories? Shoes perhaps?"

"That would be very kind."

"I'll be back in a moment. I know the perfect shoe, a satin pump with a waterfall of rhinestones on the heel. What size?"

"A five, maybe a five and a half. Bring a six, just in case. You know how sizes vary."

"Better bring a seven," Minnie said. "That's the size she wears."

The clerk departed with a glance at Jeanette's feet.

"Really, Minnie."

"You didn't destroy those cards did you? I agreed to do this only because we decided we would not use Edith's cards."

"Don't be silly. I was in here last week as Mrs. Clarke. I can't very well tell her I'm someone else, now, can I?" Jeanette extended the long full skirt and fanned it, turning in a waltz step. "We'll have to go out dancing. Some really fine club, maybe when we're in New Orleans. This is just the perfect dance dress."

Jeanette turned her attention to the mirror to watch the woman rifle through the clearance rack. The woman pulled out a gold lame gown and fondled the material to check the workmanship. Holding it up to herself, she checked the price tag, then put the dress back on the rack.

Jeanette murmured sadly, "Pathetic."

Minnie looked and nodded. "Reminds me of Edith at Gump's. But at least Edith washed and repaired her clothes."

Minnie put a hand over her mouth. "I am embarrassed and sorry I said that."

"That could have been us in ten years. What have you got there?"

Minnie pulled the top dress off her arm, holding it out for Jeanette to see.

"Wrong color, Minnie. Your skin will look gray in that. You can't wear that shade."

"Oh. What about this one?" She held up the next dress, a deep blue.

"That's a better color. But it's cut wrong. You're too short for it. You'll look like a little square box. Next."

Minnie hung the first two dresses on the mirror's hook. "I wish I were tall like you."

"Don't be silly. You're incredibly cute."

"Nothing looks good on a tiny woman. And men are in awe of tall gals."

"Men are in awe of all gals. I think most men prefer petite women. It makes them feel big, masculine. There are plenty of outfits that look great on tiny, cute women." She indicated a lavender dress on Minnie's arm. "That looks like one of them."

Minnie held up the dress.

"That might work if you accessorize it properly." Jeanette made a closer examination. "It's a nice color. Try it on. I'll have Marie find a strand of pearls to go with it."

Next, Minnie held up a black cocktail dress.

"You're not going to a funeral, dear. Hang on a second." Jeanette disappeared into her dressing room. She emerged with six dresses. "I picked these out for you. Go try them on, dear, and let me see."

When Minnie emerged from the dressing room, she wore an outfit of luminescent pink. In front of the triple-fold mirror, she was transformed. Her breasts protruded, looking larger than they were. The fabric clung to her small waist then opened onto her hips, hugged her to mid-thigh and finally fled into a flirty skirt. Jeanette spun a finger in the air and Minnie made a slow, provocative turn.

"Well?"

Minnie said, "At first I thought it was too youthful."

"And now?"

"Oh. It's not."

"I knew you had a figure under all those turtlenecks and cardigans."

"It is beautiful." Minnie did a Chubby Checker twist to flip the flirty skirt. "But."

"But what?"

"Do you think it's too sexy?" Minnie barely squeaked out the last word.

Jeanette rested her head on Minnie's spaghetti-strapped shoulder and looked with her in the mirror. "Don't you think it's about time for a little of that?"

"At my age?"

"If you wear this, maybe you won't feel so uptight." Jeanette gave Minnie a peck on the cheek. "You might even get yourself a man." She winked in the mirror.

Sarah flung open the door from her dressing room. At the mirror she nudged Minnie out of the way, and held her head high.

Jeanette said, "You look like a million bucks."

"This makes me feel forty again." With a hand on her hip, Sarah turned a circle, to view the sea foam green Armani suit from all sides.

Minnie said, "You look like you've lost fifteen pounds."

Jeanette advanced on Sarah. "The top designers always make you look good. Plus, you stand up straighter in expensive clothes. You're more confident." Jeanette straightened the collar on Sarah's blouse. "What's with that grin? You're jazzed. You got the shopping bug. It's fun to spend money, isn't it?"

"Especially if it's not my own."

Minnie stood shyly to the side, arms crossed. Sarah pretended to jump at the sight of her.

"My goodness, Minnie. You better watch out. You just might get yourself a man with that one."

Minnie thrust out her chin. "I'll buy this if you'll just drop the subject."

Jeanette clapped. "Sold."

The woman who'd been flipping through the clearance rack walked over.

"Sarah?"

Sarah squinted first at the reflection, then turned from the mirror and came down off the platform, arms open to the old woman.

"Mrs. Timmons. How are you? I haven't seen you in years."

"I'm fine. Just fine. A little ache in my hip. I broke it in '73, you know. I was at the zoo. Clumsy of me, really. I was walking toward Monkey Island. Just love those monkeys. There's this one, I call him Hopscotch; he's the littlest one. Jumps around from rock to rock, like playing hopscotch. So I'm looking at Hopscotch, and I didn't notice, but somebody had lost their ice cream off a cone. Well, here I am turning on a dime, and slipped in the mess of it. Went right down, banged my head too. I think I was out for a minute. They made such a big fuss. Everyone gathered around. The resident vet looked me over, he put my sweater in a little ball behind my head. Big crowd. I was so embarrassed. I couldn't move at all, so much pain. They called an ambulance, of course, and took me right into surgery. Doctors didn't think I'd ever walk again. But I showed them." Mrs. Timmons lifted her cane off the floor to demonstrate her ability to stand unaided.

Before anyone could murmur a word, she rushed on. "I was in the hospital for a month. Then they put me in this horrible sanitarium. Physical therapy and all that. Awful food, oh just wretched."

Sarah tried to wedge in some words. "How terrible for you."

Oblivious to Sarah's voice, Mrs. Timmons barreled on. "I was there for six months. Then my daughter moved me in with her. She has this beautiful place in San Rafael. Her husband's an attorney, you know. Let's see, what law firm was that? It's a big one in the financial district. Six Jewish names. Oh, what was that?" She tapped her chin.

Sarah opened her mouth, again to no avail. Mrs. Timmons said, "Doesn't matter. He's been made a full partner, you know. So I stayed there for a year. They have this little granny unit off the garage. Very nice. Wallpapered. They installed bars in the shower, went out of their way to make me feel comfortable. But I just couldn't help but think I was imposing. By the time the year was up, I was so much better. I wanted to get back on my own. You know what I mean? So, last year, I moved back to the city. Live out in the Avenues now. Wish I lived in Noe Valley though. More sunshine there. The fog is just terrible in the Avenues. Usually wake up stiff and sore. But I do my stretching and physical therapy every day. I'm fine. Just fine."

Mrs. Timmons paused. Jeanette and her friends stood stock still, overwhelmed by this slow moving, soft-spoken chatterbox.

Sensing the momentary opening was up for grabs, Mrs. Timmons plunged back in. "Of course, last week, I had the sniffles. I thought it might turn into pneumonia. And me all by myself. My daughter is so busy with the kids, didn't want to bother her. She'd have to drive all the way from Marin. And pay fifty cents toll to cross the Golden Gate. Fifty cents. Bridge maintenance, they say. Personally, I think some higher ups are skimming."

Jeanette touched the woman's shoulder, making her start and interrupting her. "What do you think?" She pointed to Sarah's outfit.

"Oh my, yes, lovely. I was admiring all of you from over there." She gestured toward the sale rack.

The clerk returned with a stack of shoeboxes. She had no smile for Mrs. Timmons. The clerk lay the boxes on the carpet and pulled from one the pump she'd described to Jeanette.

Jeanette said, "These are exquisite."

"I found two other pair that I think you'll also like." She propped shoes on the edges of the boxes.

Mrs. Timmons nodded appreciatively. She said to Sarah, "Looks like you have plans. Some fancy event?"

Jeanette said, "Lots of fancy events." She tried on the pair the clerk recommended, in size seven.

"Those days are past now." The old woman shook her head. "Do it while you're young and able. That's what I say. Because one day you're weeding the garden, and the next you're watching weeds grow. But I fooled them. Now I get out every day. I go into all the shops on Union Square. At night I think about all the pretty things I saw and all the things I wished I had done. All I can do now is covet my neighbor's ass."

That had been one of Edith's favorite expressions.

"Well, I'm off. The coffee shop on the corner has the best meatloaf sandwiches. Bye now." To the clerk, Mrs. Timmons said flatly, "Thanks for trying to help me."

The old woman and her cane hobbled away between the racks of chic garments toward the elevator.

◈

Minnie surprised herself.

She resented the old lady. Mrs. Timmons had interrupted their happy shopping spree, talking on and on about her problems. Six months ago, Minnie would have listened, sympathized, maybe offered a hand. But now she didn't want to hear bad news of any sort, didn't want to discuss old age, broken hips, and poor living conditions. Minnie was leaving all that behind to embark on a new life filled with thrills and larceny and travel. She cringed at the notion of larceny, but it was better than the idea of living alone, growing older, becoming Mrs. Timmons.

Minnie drove the old woman from her thoughts as she went into the dressing room to try on more dresses.

◈

An hour later, the girls followed Jeanette to the sales desk. The clerk hung each garment in heavy plastic bags, then wrote up the sales ticket. Jeanette handed over Edith's Saks card.

When the card hit the counter, Minnie couldn't help herself and recoiled, just enough for Jeanette to notice.

"Minnie, why don't you go look at coats. I'll join you in a minute."

Sarah jumped in. "I'll go with you."

The two left, and the clerk rang up the purchases. "That will be $2,573.08." If this charge went through, it would be their last purchase at Saks. The clerk slid the plastic through the imprinter plate. She picked up the phone.

Jeanette straightened a bobby pin in her French roll and tried not to appear nervous.

The clerk read the account number into the phone. It seemed an eternity before she completed the transaction. Finally, she hung up. "Mrs. Clarke?"

"Yes?"

"Would you sign the sales ticket, please?"

"Of course." Starting to write, Jeanette caught herself completing the J of her first name. Quickly, she turned it into a clumsy E and continued signing 'Edith Clarke.'

The clerk snapped off the top of the invoice, and handed Jeanette the pink copy along with her purchases. "I hope when you come in again, you'll ask for me. Here's my card."

"I will. You've been very helpful."

Outside, Sarah and Minnie waited on a bench across the street.

Minnie said, "You took so long, we started watching for the cops. I'm surprised to see you without handcuffs. Now, give me all those credit cards. I knew I shouldn't have trusted you to do it yourself."

"Stop it, Minnie. The heat's not on yet. Besides, knowing you, you'd be stingy with your own cards. We should keep these for emergencies."

"A Saks Fifth Avenue emergency?" Minnie mimicked Jeanette: "'Oh my God, I need a new tiara to go with my evening gown.' Now give me the damn cards."

"Fine. Here, take it. We're up to the limit there anyway." Jeanette angled her wallet away from Minnie to pull out just the Saks card.

"And the rest."

"I don't have them with me."

Minnie seemed ready to force the issue. Jeanette stopped her. "I'm starving. What time is it?"

Jeanette's new diamond encrusted watch told them it was noon.

Sarah said, "I don't want to stop for lunch. Let's keep shopping."

"No," said Minnie. "Let's get our hair done."

Jeanette hoisted a finger. She had just the place.

They headed to Sacramento Street. A block before the colorful entrance to Chinatown stood Jeanette's favorite salon, housed in a 1930's Art Deco structure. The only recent addition was imported Italian pink marble sheathing the walls and the floor of the entryway.

They spent the next three hours absorbed in the lavish surroundings, pampered and treated like queens.

Attendants brought them icy bubbling water, towels, and robes. The girls got massages, makeovers, hairstyling, manicures, and pedicures.

When they'd finished their luxury and indulgences, all three changed into new clothes from Saks. In the dressing room they admired themselves in the mirrors. For each, the makeup was impeccable, professional. The new hairstyles made them look years younger; the gray was gone from Minnie and Sarah's hair, replaced with softened shades that brought out each woman's best features. The stylists had given them all tips on how to care for their hair and sold them all the right products.

"This is just too marvelous." Sarah touched a strand of her perfect hair.

Leaving the salon, they strutted down Grant Street toward Market. An elderly gentleman in a suit and tie, carrying a cane curved over his arm, walked toward them. His eyes lit up when he saw Sarah. "Excuse me, young lady, could you tell me how to get to Coit Tower?"

Sarah blushed. "Oh, why yes. Go up to California Street, there's a bus that will take you there. You'll have to transfer at Sansome."

The gentleman's blue eyes crinkled. "Thank you, madam." The man was no spring chicken but he was handsome in a cultured fashion. He made no secret of ogling Sarah head to toe before he tipped his hat. "Toodle-ooo."

As he strolled off, Sarah broke into nervous laughter. "My goodness. Was he flirting with me? Did you see that?"

Minnie said, "Oh, yes."

"I never realized what a new hairdo and some decent clothes could do."

Jeanette said, "You look like a different woman. But it's not just dress and hair. This is a new you. The whole package. You're confident and beautiful, and it shows."

Minnie said, "For all of us."

Jeanette hugged her two friends. "For all of us."

Chapter 7

Marc set down his chopsticks to peer out the window. "What the hell?"

There on the street below the restaurant was his Aunt Minnie and her two best friends. They appeared to have undergone complete makeovers. A dapper, elderly man approached them on the sidewalk. For a moment he chatted up Sarah who acted like a coquette. The old man appraised her pretty blatantly, then doffed his hat and walked on.

Marc sipped his tea and reflected back to his conversation with Minnie in Muir Woods. He'd left Minnie that afternoon certain that she was going to shut down whatever scheme Jeanette was up to. Minnie was too commanding, moral, and pragmatic to have done otherwise. But to see her on the street with them, all three dolled up in new clothes and hairdos, with shopping bags from Saks, Magnin, and Macy's, it was plain Minnie had buckled.

What had made his conservative, law-abiding aunt think this was a good idea? Was it a mid-life crisis, or insanity? Or worse, far worse: had he said something in Muir Woods to encourage her, even advise her? Marc scoured his memory but couldn't think of a thing he'd said that equated to a green light.

His stomach sank; he was about to be linked to the next Bonnie and Clyde gang. Obviously that was what was going on. His aunt and her crew were using credit cards like submachine guns.

No longer hungry, he pushed aside his plate and motioned for the waiter to bring his check.

For the last four months, someone had been using Edith Clarke's credit card. But Edith Clarke was dead. Died December 12th, 1975.

Sergio wasn't puzzled. He'd seen this sort of thing before. He was a bill collector in the City Security Bank Master Charge department, so it was his job to notice discrepancies.

This was clearly a case of fraud, though the card user was definitely not a professional. Pros move fast, maxing out stolen credit cards within hours. Certainly by Christmas, the damage should have been done and the card abandoned.

The sales drafts had started coming in slowly and systematically right before the holidays. This didn't set off any alarms because there had been no reason to suspect a problem. After all, the bank hadn't been notified of the cardholder's death. The balance remained below the established credit limit and there had been no delinquency. Someone was making the minimum payments in cash by the due date at a different branch every month.

Four months had passed before the account warranted serious attention. Now the balance had skyrocketed over the credit limit. Mrs. Edith Clarke's phone was disconnected and according to the manager, Lorna Klydesdale, she was deceased.

Sergio returned his attention to the coroner's report. A bus had hit Edith Clarke. There was no purse, no ID on the victim. Her cadaver lay in the county morgue until December 16th when it was matched with a missing person's report. Three women had identified and claimed the body. They had the same street address as the deceased, different apartment numbers.

Sergio reviewed the customer history file. The account opened in 1968, probably part of the first-year frenzy at the introduction of credit cards and the saturation marketing campaigns. Anyone who had a checking or savings account at City Security Bank was mailed a preapproved credit card. Every bank in the nation was doing it, providing Americans the shovel to dig their way into debt.

Unsolicited credit enticements were now illegal. But in the late sixties, at the beginnings of credit card accounts, there were no rules. Just sign here.

The computer summary report showed Sergio very little activity over the card's eight-year history. The small periodic balances had always been paid in full before the due dates in the subsequent month.

Thumbing through the most recent sales drafts, Sergio muttered, "Pandora's, Pandora's, Pandora's, everyday Pandora's." The signatures on the drafts didn't match Edith Clarke's signature on the original credit application. Still, the large flourish appeared to be made by a feminine hand. Other drafts revealed charges at expensive boutiques around Union Square, some meals at the Cliff House, and box seats at the symphony, plus one authorization refusal at Bass Ticket Outlet for a Barbra Streisand concert.

Sergio copied down the names of the three women who claimed Clarke's body. He dialed an internal extension. "George, it's Sergio. Listen, I've got one for you." Sergio filled him in. "Can you hit it this afternoon? Great. Let me know what you find out. We want to get whoever's doing this and we want the card back. Looks like one person, probably a woman. I'd be willing to bet it's one of the three, I have their addresses. Thanks, George. Yeah, I'm putting a seven on it right now."

Sergio hung up, then moved to the CRT monitor. He brought up the Clarke account and flagged it with a code seven, for lost or stolen. If anyone attempted to use the card again, the police would be alerted.

Minnie set down the big Saks bag first, then the one from Neiman Marcus. She hung the Nordstrom wardrobe bag on the doorknob then rifled through her purse for her apartment keys.

She did not hear the man's approach.

"Excuse me, ma'am. Are you Minnie Barlow?"

She whirled on him. He loomed well over six feet tall, intimidating as hell. He was some sort of rough-around-the-fringes businessman, in a gray suit. His crimson tie was loosened and the white shirt looked like it needed an iron. He looked uncomfortable, as though he preferred blue jeans.

"Who wants to know?"

The man fumbled in a pocket to retrieve a picture I.D. "I'm George Post, from City Security Bank."

Minnie's stomach tightened. This was exactly the person she had feared. She tried to maintain her composure as he studied her. Forcing a smile, she parroted a line she'd rehearsed many times.

"I'm not overdrawn, am I?"

"No, no, nothing like that. I thought maybe you could help me. I understand you were well acquainted with Edith Clarke?"

"She lived on this floor."

"She passed away in December."

Minnie retrieved her keys. "Yes, poor thing. It was terrible."

"I'm sorry." George indicated Minnie's packages in the hall. "Do you need some help with these?"

"I can manage." Minnie fiddled with the door lock, to give herself a moment to regain her calm.

George picked up the Saks and Neiman Marcus bags. "Let me give you a hand anyway." She pushed open the door and he followed into the apartment.

Remembering the condition of her living room, Minnie stopped abruptly in the foyer and turned. He came dangerously close to toppling her over.

She asked, "How exactly can I help you?"

George Post regained his footing, then looked over her head into the living room filled with bags from Macy's, Neiman Marcus, Emporium, and City of Paris. She felt guilty as sin.

Wishing she had remained in the corridor for this conversation, wishing she hadn't been too tired from shopping to put everything away last night, Minnie stood in the midst of incriminating evidence and tried to think of what to say.

"Okay if I hang these here?" He hung up the two wardrobe bags on wall hooks in the foyer. "Looks like you've been doing a lot of shopping."

"Yes, as a matter of fact. Mr. Post, is it?"

"Yes."

"I'm really very busy. I have an appointment in half an hour. And I must freshen up. How can I help you?"

"Okay. On December 13th, Sarah Gardner filed a missing person's report on Edith Clarke."

Minnie nodded. The straps of the Nordstrom bag were cutting into her hand.

Mr. Post continued: "I believe it was you, Sarah Gardner, and Jeanette Compton who identified and claimed her body."

"That's correct."

"I assume the other two women are friends of yours as well?" Minnie nodded. "Mrs. Barlow, it seems that Mrs. Clarke's Master Charge has been used quite a bit lately." Mr. Post peered again into the living room.

Minnie had practiced for this moment. "You know, of course, they never recovered her purse. And they never arrested the muggers, never found them."

"Muggers? I thought she was hit by a bus."

Minnie sensed she'd gotten the advantage, and pressed on. "A bus did hit her, while she was trying to escape. A witness said she was running from three teenage boys who'd grabbed her purse."

"I see." George scratched his head under his jet-black hair. "Your landlady told our man at the bank that you and the two other women cleaned out her apartment and tidied up her affairs. Did you find any credit cards?"

"No, we did not."

"Any credit card bills?"

"No. Edith wasn't much on paperwork."

"Well, Mrs. Barlow, I'll be honest with you. It seems strange, the MO on this. When credit cards are stolen, the charges come in fast, within a few days, a week at the most. Then the card is abandoned. But there's been a steady stream of charging on this account for months. It started out slow, then it's escalated in the past few weeks. Like someone's going a little crazy with it."

He paused for Minnie's reaction. She got the feeling he was enjoying himself.

He added, "And someone has been making payments."

Minnie's nerves were wearing thin. Suddenly inspired, she asked, "Do you suppose those teenagers are making payments so they can keep using the cards?"

"That's entirely possible. But the strange thing is the charges. They're from expensive restaurants, the symphony, beauty salons, and spas. Places like Edward's Luggage."

Mr. Post did not hide the fact that, in plain sight on the floor between Minnie's sofa and the coffee table, lay a carton from Edward's Luggage.

He shrugged. "It doesn't make sense. If teenage boys are using the cards, we'd expect to see electronic stores, you know, TVs and stereos, maybe a Three Dog Night concert, but not a symphony and spas. No. I don't think teenagers are using the cards."

Minnie pretended to ponder over the situation. "Yes, that is peculiar. Don't thieves usually sell the credit cards to gangsters or something?"

"Sometimes. But in my experience, gangsters move fast. Use the cards right away."

"Well, you certainly have a mystery on your hands."

"It's an unusual set of circumstances." George drummed fingers on a bicep, waiting for Minnie to say something, or admit something. When she remained silent, he continued, "You know, Mrs. Barlow, I have to ask about all this shopping you're doing."

Minnie drew out her response. "Yes?"

"How can you afford it?"

"Saks doesn't match with subsidized housing, you mean."

"Precisely. You see my dilemma. You have to admit, it does look like you found Mrs. Clarke's Master Charge and have been using it."

"I can see how it would look that way."

"So, is that what happened? Are you using Edith Clarke's credit card?" He crossed his arms over his chest.

Minnie answered truthfully. "No, I have not been using Edith Clarke's credit card."

Jeanette had signed for everything.

Then she lied. "Another dear friend of mine died a few months ago and left me a little money. Not enough to move from this dump, mind you. But enough to treat myself to some of the things I've always wanted."

"This isn't an accusation. But I'm required to tell you, that if you and your friends, or anyone else you know, found Edith's Master Charge card and have been using it, and you, or they, come forward immediately, the bank will not prefer fraud charges against you. Or them." He cleared his throat, then continued. "They don't want negative publicity. And I understand you've been a customer of our bank for a very long time. They would even be willing to set up an affordable repayment program."

He didn't believe her. Of course he didn't. Without knowing what she might say, Minnie was about to speak, when laughter and chatter filled the hallway.

Without knocking, Sarah and Jeanette came through Minnie's door, wearing brand new outfits, tags still hanging from the sleeves, both in wide-brimmed straw hats. They were so engrossed in conversation that, for the first moments, they were oblivious to the man in Minnie's apartment. George turned to face them. Both women froze, startled.

Minnie made a throat-slicing gesture behind his back.

Jeanette untwisted her worried look into a smile. She cooed, "Hello." Sarah moved behind her.

George returned his gaze to Minnie, questions in his eyes.

"There were a few things my friends always wanted too. Now if you'll excuse us." Minnie placed her hand on his elbow. Jeanette slid out of the way as Minnie walked George from the apartment.

In the hallway, George stopped abruptly, plainly peeved at being propelled out of the apartment. He called back through the open door.

"Are you Jeanette Compton and Sarah Gardener?"

Jeanette answered, "Yes. Yes we are."

"Perhaps you have some information."

Minnie interjected, "This is Mr. Post from City Security Bank. He's here about Edith. They haven't caught the muggers. But apparently those thugs are using her credit card. He was hoping we'd know something to help him. I explained that we know less than he does."

George asked Minnie, "Do you have anything to add?" Past her shoulder, he called to the girls, "Do either of you?"

Jeanette replied, "Sadly, no."

With a sigh, George dug into his pocket for a business card. "If you hear of anything, or just want to talk, give us a call. Mr. Sergio Fernandez is handling this account. His extension is listed there." George gave Minnie the card, then walked toward the elevator.

Minnie rushed back into her apartment and closed the door before George Post could steal a backward glance.

Jeanette stepped up first. "What did he mean, 'if we want to talk'?"

"I think he's onto us. And just look at this place! First time I don't clean up and look. Guilty, guilty, guilty! Jesus."

With the plastic Nordstrom bag under her arms, Minnie sunk onto the sofa. "Tell me you destroyed those cards."

"Marc said not to use them, right? I haven't used them since you told me."

"I suppose that explains the price tags on your dresses. And those hats."

"Alright, I'll stop. Now."

"They're onto something. I'm a nervous wreck. I don't want to have to talk to that man again. And I'm sure he'll be back. We better move up our departure date. I think we should get out of here."

Sarah asked, "Today?"

"Tomorrow morning."

Jeanette cried, as she dashed for the front door, Sarah in tow, "Let's pack. I'll call the car rental agency and the hotel in Palm Springs and move up the reservations."

"Don't answer your door or phone."

"A code," Sarah thrust her forefinger into the air. "If we want to contact each other, let the phone ring one time, then hang up. Then call back. At the door, one loud knock. Count to ten then knock again."

They left, and Minnie then made a pot of coffee. She packed for two hours in her new Edwards Luggage cases, then took a break to call Sarah, using the code.

Sarah answered, "Yes," in a deep, genderless voice.

"God, Sarah, did you pack your trench coat?"

"Oh, hi Minnie. I'm just about packed. Do you think we should leave tonight, at midnight?"

"Midnight." If she weren't so nervous, Minnie would have laughed. "You've seen too many crime movies. Call

Jeanette and see how she's doing. We'll get the car in the morning and take off."

A loud knock sounded at Minnie's door. It wasn't in code. Minnie whispered to Sarah, "Someone's at my door. I'm going in the bedroom now. Remember, if someone knocks, don't answer."

"I won't. Be careful."

Minnie hung up and waited. The pounding continued, more insistently. Minnie tiptoed across the living room, ducking unnecessarily as she crossed the foyer to the bedroom. She sat on the edge of the bed.

The knocking stopped. "Na Na! Na Na! C'mon, answer the door. I know you're in there."

Minnie rushed to remove the chain and opened the door.

"What a pleasant surprise!"

"What took you so long?" He stood with hands on hips.

"I was in the bathroom. What's wrong? You look upset. Come in."

Open suitcases overflowing with new clothes were scattered about the living room. "I thought you weren't leaving for another few weeks."

"Change in plans. We've decided to go tomorrow."

"Were you going to call me?"

"Of course, I was. I just put on a pot of coffee. You want a cup?"

"Sure," Marc said, sullen.

In the kitchen Minnie poured two cups. Returning to the living room, she found Marc going through her new clothes in one of the suitcases, muttering under his breath. Seeing her, he clutched an evening gown.

"Five hundred and ninety-nine dollars and ninety-nine cents. You know, I always wondered why they put ninety-nine cents on the end. Why the hell don't they round it up to six hundred? After all, when you're spending that kind of money." He slapped the gown into the suitcase. "I didn't think you went in for this kind of stuff. Isn't this a little fancy for a farm girl?"

Minnie rested the cups on the coffee table.

"Not at all. I want to start dressing up."

He sat on the sofa beside Minnie. From the inside pocket of his sport jacket, he pulled a sheaf of credit bureau reports. Marc tossed them into her lap.

Minnie moved them aside. "What's all this?"

"Why don't you tell me?" When Minnie gave no answer, Marc sighed.

"I knew you were up to something. I didn't want to believe it. I hoped the whole time it was Jeanette. I figured the thing would play itself out. You and Sarah would put a stop to her. Then I saw the three of you today on Grant

Street. I almost didn't recognize you. I knew something wasn't right. So I pulled up all the credit reports, Edith's too. Every credit card Edith owned has a big fat balance on it."

"I never used Edith's cards."

"So you're just the accomplice, is that it? The recipient of stolen goods. You should see Jeanette's credit report. I had no idea she was such a con artist. Do you have any idea what she ran up in New York? My God, I'm surprised they didn't send out a hit man."

"A hit man?"

"Hell, yes, a hit man."

"What happened in New York wasn't Jeanette's fault."

"Whatever. I personally don't give a damn what happened in New York. I'm concerned about what's happening here and now."

Minnie stood to pace. "I suppose you would have found out sooner or later."

"Christ. Of course, I would have found out. They'll be knocking on my door looking for you. I'm listed on all your credit apps as a reference, remember?"

Minnie halted. "Oh no. Marc. I didn't think about that. I'm sorry."

"Well, shit. Excuse me. But what the hell do you think you're doing?"

"Don't get mad at me. Everything just evolved. We didn't intend to get this carried away."

"But you did."

"We did."

"The day we talked in Muir Woods, Jeanette was already in trouble, wasn't she?"

"Yes. I didn't want to get you involved. I didn't want you to worry."

"Well, I am involved. Did you sign any of the sales drafts from Edith's accounts?"

"No, Jeanette did all of it. I already told you that."

"Okay. But you're going to need a lawyer. So will Sarah."

"No. We're leaving. We're using my cards, legitimately, from here on out, just like you told me to do."

"Like I told you?"

"You said we could probably make it to Spain without getting caught. You said I wouldn't go to jail, that it's not fraud if I use my own cards. No debtor's prisons, remember?"

"I can't believe we're having this conversation. At your age, you should have some morals. You always did. Jesus. You're little gray-haired grannies. Oh wait, I see the gray is gone now. You're supposed to be knitting booties, making bread, going to museums. Not acting like this."

Marc thrust out his arms. He drew a deep breath then brought the volume down a notch.

"Edith's accounts are maxed out. And I can see you've already started on yours. I'm going to ask you again. Did you destroy Edith's cards?"

"Yes, as soon as you told us to. Jeanette took care of it."

Marc eyed her skeptically. "I can help you get out of this. I'll help Jeanette, too, and Sarah."

"No. You have your career to think about. We'll leave. You can say that we've been estranged for years and you know nothing."

They went round and round a while longer; neither relenting nor softening their point of view. Marc brought up all the values she'd ever taught him but Minnie continued to justify her actions.

Marc gave up. "You're stubborn! Willfully, stupidly stubborn!"

"That's one of my better qualities."

Marc played nervously with the end of his tie. "So there's no stopping you?"

"We're leaving tomorrow. You'd be wise to stay out of it. By the way, do you know George Post?"

"Yeah, I know George. He's the field rep for Master Charge. Oh, damn. Was he here?"

"That's why we're leaving tomorrow." Minnie filled him in on the conversation with George Post, ending with the statement to call Mr. Fernandez if she 'wanted to talk.'

"It's a good thing you told me. I don't know Fernandez. Don't worry. I'll take care of things somehow. I'll find a way to protect you."

Minnie hung her head. "You really need to just stay out of this. I don't want you jeopardizing your career."

"I'll come by in the morning. Are you renting a car?"

"Yes. Jeanette's got the arrangements made. But I don't want you to come by. It's too risky. If that Post fellow comes back and you're throwing stuff in the trunk, it's going to look bad for you. Promise me you'll stay away."

"Okay. But promise me you'll call at least once a week to let me know what's going on. If you need anything, anytime at all, I'll take care of it."

"You're an angel."

"There's one more thing. Give me a paper and pen. I'm going to give you some inside baseball."

Minnie retrieved a notepad and pen. Marc squinted at the lined paper, hesitating.

"You definitely won't reconsider?"

Minnie shook her head, chin thrust out.

"I just know I'll regret this. But there are certain things you should know." Marc scribbled rapidly. "This is a list of floor limits. We talked about some of this in

Muir Woods that day, but I'm not sure you remembered everything I said. Now look, you better memorize these and have Jeanette, especially, and Sarah memorize them too. If you don't stay below the floor limits, you're going to be in huge trouble. If the clerk has to call for an authorization, just leave the card in his hand, and walk out the door. Otherwise, you'll be dealing with the cops and jail time. So get the hell out of there as quickly as possible. And I'm not just talking about getting out of the store, I'm talking about getting out of town.

"And don't stay in any one place for very long. Keep on the move. No more than three days, even fewer if possible. Don't use the same cards for more than one day. Spread them around. Use a Master Charge for one day, then switch to American Express the next, Diner's Club the next. At gas stations, use a gas credit card. Do you have any of those?"

"Yes, we've got Shell, Chevron and I think there's a Union 76."

"Good. Don't use the bank cards there."

"Why not?"

"Location. They'll be looking at every charge you make. So they'll see which direction you're headed. Or where you are staying. Gas station collection departments don't cooperate much with banks, so you'll be able to better keep your itinerary a secret.

"Once a week, call the 800 number on the back of the card to find out the status and the balance. And for God's sake, mail in payments, so the cards don't go delinquent. In fact, after I leave, call all those numbers. If any of them show as being reported Lost or Stolen, then cut it up and discard it. Don't use them again. George Post is not done with you. He's a free-lance rep who works for every bank. He will be on your tail from here on out. So be careful." Mark let out a burst of breath, detached the pages from the tablet and handed them to Minnie.

Chapter 8

His assistant's voice crackled over the intercom on Sergio's phone. "Mr. Fernandez, line two."

Sergio punched the intercom button. "You just love this new phone system, don't you, Frannie."

"Yes, I do, Mr. Fernandez. Over."

Frannie, stationed only two desks in front of him and one row over, the administrative assistant for the City Security Bank Master Charge Collections Department, was Sergio's good buddy.

She had her back to him. Sergio took the opportunity to lob a paperclip over Bob's unsuspecting head, dead center into Frannie's back.

She deadpanned into the intercom. "That was totally unnecessary, Mr. Fernandez. Over."

"Who's on line two?"

"Some asshole deadbeat with a good story for not paying. Over."

"Does he have a name?"

"You haven't been saying 'over.' No. He is a she and I didn't ask for a name. I just work here. Over."

Sergio picked up the phone. "This is Sergio Fernandez. May I help you?"

A woman's shrill voice shrieked over the clamor of a TV game show and a barking dog. "They're gone! They didn't even give notice. And they didn't pay their rent!"

"Whoa. Wait, wait. Who am I talking to?"

"Lorna Klydesale, the landlady. That man you sent, George Post? He gave me your card and said to call you if I had any new information."

"I appreciate the call. And who was Mr. Post inquiring about?" It never ceased to amaze Sergio that every contact seemed to think he spent his entire day poised over the phone waiting only for their call.

"Edith Clark. She's dead. But it's the other three, Minnie Barlow, Jeanette Compton, and Sarah Gardener. They just up and left, right after that George Post fellow came. I haven't seen hide nor hair of them since. That was two weeks ago."

"Can you hold for a moment while I look up the account?"

"Fine."

He pressed the hold button then dug through his overstuffed file drawer. A paperclip bounced off his scalp.

Working in collections at the bank was barely an okay job, tolerable because his co-workers were young and fun like him and the pay was decent. They were all fresh out of high school or college, all on their way up to better things. Of course, there were those who never made it and got stuck as career bill collectors. These bitter old-timers hated life and the bank but loved their jobs. After all, they were paid to vent their wrath legitimately on flakes who dared to get behind on their Master Charge payments.

Sometimes Sergio feared he'd turn into one of the career collectors. At twenty-five, the time had come to make his mark, move on to something better. Recently, he'd applied for an opening as a credit analyst but some new jerk who looked better in a suit was promoted by Mr. Jenkins, the boss who did not seem to like Sergio.

Sergio re-familiarized himself with his collection notes on the Clarke case. George had made contact and was suspicious of Mrs. Clarke's three neighbors, the women Mrs. Klydesdale was referring to.

When George returned the next day to get signature samples, the women weren't home. After numerous attempts, he'd been unable to make any further contact.

The account had been referred to Jenkins for a decision about preferring fraud charges; the case was no doubt beneath a stack of other accounts that required attention. It pissed off Sergio that the bank complained about delinquency and fraud ratios, holding the collectors responsible, when it was their own slow, debilitating system that caused or worsened the problems.

Sergio pulled the data card, then pressed the button on the blinking line. "Okay, Mrs. Klydesdale. Thanks for holding. You're the manager there?"

"I already told you that. Mr. Post went to talk to those women and the next morning they were gone. Jonesy in two-oh-three told me just now that he saw them packing luggage into the trunk of a Lincoln Continental. I don't know why he waited two weeks to tell me, except maybe he thought I already knew. I usually see everything, but damn it, they must have left while I was watching the game shows."

In the background a dog's yapping once again pierced the air. "Shut up, Mama's on the phone." To Sergio, she said, "Then Jonesy tells me that from what he overheard it sounded like they were moving out for good. They were saying 'Let Lorna get rid of all that crap.' So I got the master key and went into each apartment. Their clothes are gone. Mrs. Compton left dirty dishes in the sink. You should have seen the cockroaches."

"Mrs. Klydesdale."

"The rent is past due. The nerve, not even giving notice."

"Mrs. Klydesdale."

"I got to thinking about Mr. Post and what he said about somebody using that credit card. I put two and two together. They were the ones who cleaned out Mrs.

Clarke's apartment. Go in the other room and stop that barking. Go!"

"Mrs. Klydesdale."

"Sorry 'bout that, anyway."

"Stop! Do you know where they went?"

With raised eyebrows, Frannie wagged a finger at Sergio.

Mrs. Klydesdale said, "You don't have to yell at me. No, I don't know where they went. Those three always kept to themselves. But I always knew everything that went on. Now that Marc fellow was here the other day."

"Marc? Marc who?" Sergio readied to scribble a name.

"I don't know his last name. Mrs. Barlow 's nephew. Some hotshot at some bank. She bragged about him. My nephew this, my nephew that."

"Do you know which bank?"

"I don't recall. Get down. You get down from there right now. Oh Christ, can you hold on a second?" The phone clattered. Sergio heard a ruckus in the background. The yapping continued but seemed to come from behind a closed door.

"Okay, I'm back. Are you there? I told that Mr. Post they'd been doing a lot of shopping. I'm on the first floor, next to the elevators. When that front door opens, you can hear it. I always check through the peephole. I'm not being a busybody, it's a security thing. Every day, and

I'm not exaggerating, they got these bags and boxes from these fancy stores. They're laughing and having a good old time. How could they afford all this stuff? Last week I came right out and asked them. The tall one, Jeanette, she tells me it's none of my business and walks off with her nose in the air. But Sarah, now she's sweet. She told me that Edith had left her some life insurance money. I guess that's possible, as good of friends as they all were. I didn't think nothing of it until now."

"Mrs. Klydesdale, do they own a Lincoln Continental?" Sergio studied the sales draft from Hertz Rent-A-Car, dated the day after George's visit. The first part of the signature had been thoroughly crossed out but below the blotchy ink he thought he could make out the first letter, a J.

"None of them own a car. They must have rented it. Probably using that credit card."

"Do you have rental applications for them?"

"I sure do. Big long forms. This is government subsidized housing, you know."

"Could you bring those down here? We'd like to compare the signatures with those on the sales drafts."

"I don't know if I'm allowed to do that."

"You want your rent money, don't you? The sooner we find them, the sooner you get the rent."

"I'll bring them down this afternoon."

"I appreciate your cooperation." Sergio hung up. He went to the CRT to check the status of the account. New charges filled the screen. A restaurant and hotel in Monterey, a gas station in San Luis Obispo, another hotel in Beverly Hills, Universal Studios tour. Every charge stayed under the floor limit.

The account showed as Closed with a status Six. Sergio could have sworn when he'd closed the account two weeks ago it was with a status Seven, lost or stolen. He must have hit Six by accident, closing it as Derogatory Overlimit/Delinquent, but that sort of error wasn't like him at all. Sergio was meticulous, always. Nonetheless, there it was, a Six, and charges were still filtering in because the account wasn't listed on the warning bulletin. A new bulletin had just been distributed; if he changed the status to Seven right now, it would be another week before the alert hit the warning bulletin. By that time, at the rate the charges were ballooning, the balance on this account could be huge.

Sergio closed the account with a status Seven and then waited for the verification to flash on the screen. Looking at the familiar verification sequence, he pondered what else might have gone wrong to change the status; what if it hadn't been him? Sergio was positive it had gone through as a Seven two weeks ago, but he had no idea how else the change might have happened. So, it must have been him.

Mrs. Klydesdale arrived in the afternoon, in a froth of strawberry and gold taffeta that clashed with her short red hair. A big woman, she tugged a rhinestone-collared toy poodle along.

"Sorry it took me so long. By the time I went through all those files...sit." The dog ignored her while sniffing Sergio's pants.

"Let's go into the conference room."

"I would never have thought those three would do something like this. Mrs. Compton, maybe. She barely qualified to get the apartment." Mrs. Klydesdale followed Sergio to the conference room. She sat and put the dog on the table. "I wouldn't have let her in. But that was before my time. Old Mr. Gibbs was manager then." She opened one of her files. "Look at this."

Sergio reached for the file; the little dog lunged for his hand. Sergio jerked back.

"Stop it, stop it right now!" Mrs. Klydesdale tugged the dog's collar. She smacked it on the head, "Bad doggie."

She rattled on. "That's Mrs. Compton's credit report. I wouldn't have rented to her with a report like that. But poor Mr. Gibbs. She's something of a tramp, I hear. She probably turned his head. Or more than that, if you know what I mean."

Sergio studied the report and the rental applications. The dog pounced again but Mrs. Klydesdale yanked the leash.

"Excuse me. I'll go make copies."

When he returned he found the mutt tugging on the drapes. Mrs. Klydesdale was kneeling, detaching his teeth from the fabric.

Sergio sat. Mrs. Klydesdale and the dog rejoined him at the table. Sergio pulled up a notepad, eager to finish the interview. "You saw the three women returning from daily shopping trips. When did this start?"

"Before Christmas."

"Do you remember which stores the shopping bags came from?"

The woman looked to the ceiling as if the answers were written there. She reeled off store names; Sergio wrote them down.

"Do you know if they went to the symphony, or to a spa?"

Mrs. Klydesdale recounted a recent episode where the three returned from Saks Fifth Avenue lugging wardrobe bags. "They all had new hairstyles, lots of makeup. Mrs. Gardener said that was the first massage she'd ever had. And Mrs. Compton said, 'Get used to it, dear.' That's exactly what she said. I can't be sure about the symphony.

Sometimes I'd see them all dressed up to go out for the evening. I'll bet it was a symphony."

Sergio had talked enough with Lorna Klydesdale and her mutt for the day. He rose. "Mrs. Klydesdale, thanks for coming."

"I almost forgot. You asked about the nephew, the one who works at the bank." She kept her seat.

"I'll walk you to the elevator. You can tell me on the way."

"I found his business card. Mrs. Barlow gave it to me a year ago when she was bragging about his promotion. He's some sort of computer whiz."

Sergio slouched in the open doorway waiting for her to let him escort her out.

Mrs. Klydesdale said, "He must have a key to her apartment. I saw him a couple of weeks ago. I don't know if it was before or after they left. He was putting some boxes in the trunk of his little sports car. He's a suspicious looking character, if you ask me. Driving that fancy car. Here's the card."

She rose from the table. When she extended the card to Sergio, the dog snarled.

Sergio said, "Leave it on the table."

At the elevators, he said, "Thanks again." Sergio turned away.

Mrs. Klydesdale shouted after him, "If that Mr. Post needs any more information, ask him to drop by. I'm home all the time. He's more than welcome."

Sergio collected the nephew's business card from the conference room. The card read: 'Marc Corbett, City Security Bank, Computer Applications Team Manager.' That was on the twelfth floor in this same building. Sergio returned to the elevators.

The main reception area on the twelfth floor was much more plush than the warehouse of desks on Sergio's level. Private offices lined the corridors on both sides of the lobby.

Artwork decorated the walls, and ficus trees and palms adorned the hallways. They must have hired a decorator. Even the receptionist's desk was of oak, not the steel and Formica of Frannie's. The mood was a library, not the constant chatter and ringing phones downstairs.

Sergio approached the receptionist and asked to see Marc. She motioned for him to take a seat, then dialed. After briefly murmuring into the phone, she directed Sergio to Marc's office.

The glassed-in cubicle had his nameplate on the door. Open Venetian blinds revealed that Marc wasn't in. Outside his door was his secretary, Nancy Schroth, according to her nameplate.

Sergio stood by waiting for her to finish a phone conversation. His ears pricked up when she said, "He's in New York this week, Mrs. Barlow. He's working on a program for headquarters on Wall Street. He'll be back Tuesday morning. I'll tell him you called."

When she hung up, she asked Sergio, "May I help you?"

"I think you just did. Next Tuesday, huh?"

"That's right."

"Do you have a number for him in New York?"

"I can give him a message. He calls in every afternoon. I've seen you before. Do you work here?"

"I'm Sergio. Downstairs in Master Charge."

"I've seen you in the cafeteria at lunch. Oh Christ. We've had more trouble with the system in Master Charge. It hasn't gone kaplooey again, has it?"

"Not that I know of."

"Thank God. There was some loop, something that doubled and tripled everyone's balances. Mr. Southern was furious. He fixed it himself, I heard, fixed the whole thing."

"I remember that. Jenkins panicked."

"Jenkins is so weird anyway."

"You know Jenkins?"

"He's up here all the time."

Mr. Southern's office was next to Marc's, and twice the size, not glassed in. Phil Southern was executive vice president in charge of the Computer Applications Department. Young, MBA, recent Stanford graduate, considered a top-rank genius of the blossoming computer age.

The door opened. Sergio's boss Jenkins walked out gesturing and arguing quietly with Southern. Jenkins had a data binder under one arm.

Pointing at Jenkins, Sergio said to Nancy, "Maybe there's still a few bugs."

"That and SuperCredit have been one big mess."

Sergio perched on the edge of her desk. "I didn't think SuperCredit was up and running yet."

"It is and it isn't. They've already approved a mess of applications but they can't figure out the billing program. They'd better hurry too, or someone's going to have to type up the statements. And it isn't going to be me."

Sergio said, "A minute ago, you were talking to Mrs. Barlow. That's Marc's aunt, right?"

"Yeah. She's so cute."

"Do you know her?"

"I haven't met her, if that's what you mean. She calls a lot."

"Is she still on vacation?"

"I didn't know she was on vacation. The message pad in front of Nancy said: "Na Na called." The space for a return phone number was blank.

Sergio gave Nancy his business card. "When Marc calls, ask him to call me?"

"Sure. He's already checked in for today. I'll tell him to call you Monday."

Back at his busy desk, Sergio found George Post sitting behind it, feet propped up, reading a report.

"Hey, Post."

"What's up, Serge?"

"I'm reopening the Clarke case. Some new charges have come in."

"Clarke, Clarke," George pondered a moment.

"The old lady hit by a bus last Christmas. You checked out her neighbors, then we referred it to Fraud."

"Why doesn't Fraud just handle it?"

"They don't have enough bodies. Besides, it's a skip now and that puts it back on my desk. You're going to have to find them and bring them in."

George swung his feet down. "What have you got?"

Sergio spread out the three copies of the rental applications he'd made from Lorna Klysedale's files. He lay six recent signed sales drafts from Edith Clarke's account on the desk next to them. Sergio and George compared the signatures.

"Hard to say," George said. "You'd need an expert to tell if they're the same. But it does look like Jeanette Compton is signing those sales drafts."

"Check it out. Sarah Gardener has loopy and round handwriting, but it's too small. It's obviously not Minnie Barlow signing the drafts either. Jeez. Look at her penmanship."

"She should have been a doctor."

Sergio tapped a finger on one signature. "Jeanette Compton. Big, flourishing, loopy, round, feminine. I'm surprised she doesn't dot the 'i' in 'Edith' with a heart."

Chapter 9

Pandora's was empty except for a janitor vacuuming the floor in the dining room and a busboy carrying silverware. George approached the Maitre d' station and motioned for the busboy to come talk to him.

"We don't open until 11:30."

"I'm not here for lunch. I want to see the manager." George flashed his bank ID.

The busboy returned to the kitchen. George tapped his fingers on the dais and scanned the open reservation book below him. Looked like it would be a busy Saturday.

The manager arrived. "I'm Mr. Phelps. May I help you?"

George showed his ID again. "We have reason to believe thata stolen credit card was used on almost a daily basis in this restaurant for several months, until a couple weeks ago."

"Mr. Post, is it? I assure you, we are scrupulous in our transactions. We check the warning bulletin before processing any charges."

"I understand. But this account just hit the bulletin. The card hasn't been used here since. See, it belonged to a woman who died last December. Edith Clarke. Someone else has been using her card."

"Like I said, we always check."

"Listen, you guys didn't do anything wrong, okay? I'm trying to get a description of the person using the card, that's all. I'd appreciate some cooperation. Now, the waiter's initials on all of the drafts are R.A. I need to speak to whoever this R.A. is."

"Rafo Andretti. I believe he is the only one here with those initials."

"Is he here? Can I speak to him?"

"Wait here. I'll send him out."

After the manager left, George hummed softly and picked up a menu. His hum changed to a low whistle as he looked at the prices.

Rafo made a tentative approach. "May I help you, Signore?"

"Shit, I should have known."

Rafo stopped in his tracks, took a quick look around, then motioned George off to the side. The Italian accent was replaced with his native Brooklyn.

"What do you want? I haven't done nothin'. I been walking a straight line three years now."

"Rafo? That's your handle now?"

"You work in a classy place like this, you can't be Ralph. Now what do you want?"

"I want Edith Clarke."

"I don't know any Edith Clarke."

"Don't give me a bunch of shit, Ralph. Now who is she?"

"Jesus. She's a woman who came in here all the time. Had lunch, that's all."

"Knock it off. You're a low-life hustler who knows a few words in Italian."

The janitor had just turned off the vacuum cleaner and the last half of George's sentence echoed into the dining area. The busboys setting up tables turned. Rafo took George by the elbow to walk him into the bar area, out of earshot.

"You're going to make me lose my job."

"So tell me what I want to know. Edith Clarke, the real Edith Clarke, is dead. Who was the woman using her credit card?"

"Swear to God, I didn't know she was up to anything. Her lunch charges always went through."

"You were having an affair with her. She must have told you something."

"We had a few flings, so what? I'm telling you she didn't tell me nothin'. She was a rich broad. Her husband's some big CEO. He's somewhere in Europe setting up some operation for a real estate company. She gets bored, feels lonely sometimes."

"What's her real name?"

"I knew her as Edie, okay? That's it. I don't know nothin' else."

"Were you hustling her?"

"Oh, hell no. She bought me a watch and a couple of sweaters. So what! I already told you, I'm legit. I learned my lesson. Can't you guys leave me alone?"

"I'm not a cop anymore. I'm retired. I recover credit cards for a bank."

"Then I ain't gotta tell you shit." Rafo turned to leave.

"I still got friends on the force. If you don't wanna do it my way, fine."

Rafo stopped. "Look, man, I don't need no hassle. I'm straight now and I got a good thing going here."

"Give me a description."

"She's tall, five eight, maybe five nine. Great build. A real looker. Green eyes and auburn hair."

"How old?"

"Please. I don't ask women their age."

"Give me a ballpark."

"Fifty."

"Where does she live? What was her real name?"

"I'm telling you the truth, I don't know. I never went to her place. She wouldn't tell me where she lived."

"Smart broad. So where would you meet her?"

"She would just show up at my place. Stay a few hours, have a good time. I only saw her for a few months. Then she disappeared."

"Tall and auburn. She ever come in here with anyone else?"

"Twice. One time two other ladies came with her. Then another time they joined her."

"What did they look like?"

"Hell, I don't know. Old ladies. Short. One was dumpy, the other skinny. Gray, they looked gray. I wasn't checking them out."

"Rafo, you've been a big help. Stay clean."

George left Rafo where he was standing. Even before he stepped out of Pandora's into the sunshine, he was sure: Rafo had described Jeanette Compton and her two friends.

Chapter 10

Southern peered over steepled fingers at Marc.

Only twenty-six Southern was already a Senior Vice President. He had an air of superiority, an executive appearance even though he was just five-feet-six.

Maybe it was because he was from old money. Maybe it was Stanford. Either way, Southern seemed to be bred to have confidence and arrogance. And he dressed really well.

Marc cared not so much about Southern's wealth or bearing. Phil Southern was smart. A quick and creative thinker. The talk around the office was that he had an IQ of 183. And to the surprise of the staff around him, he liked to work. He wasn't another country club pretty boy who got the job because someone on the bank's board owed his parents a favor. Southern had proven himself in every project he undertook. He'd brought the bank into the cutting edge of modern technology with the computer systems he designed.

"So how was New York?"

"Fine. Looks like everything's running smoothly now. The billing cycles are ironed out, no more overlap. SuperCredit is up and running at that end. We'll know more by the end of the week after they burn in the new mainframe."

"Good. We still have a few major problems before we can interface. I'll need your help with programming the billing phase. Your boys ran into some bugs while you were in New York. How's your schedule this week?"

"Just have to finish up CRT monitor distribution and training at the Gough Street branch. I'm pretty clear after Wednesday." Marc was eager to become more involved with SuperCredit, Southern's most recent development. A new frontier in financing, it would consist of large revolving credit lines offered at prime plus two to select, wealthy businesses. Programming the variable interest rates into the system would be the challenge.

"Great. Set up a meeting with Carl Jenkins for Thursday morning."

"Will do." Marc stood to leave but Southern motioned for him to remain seated.

"Listen. Melanie Duvall, head of product development for National Credit Clearing Association, is coming in from Chicago this afternoon. We're having a dinner meeting at the Fairmont. It will be something of a brainstorming session. I'd like you to be there."

"NCCA? I'd be honored." This was the break Marc had been looking for, to be included in high level decision-making processes. It was another sign of their respect for his abilities and input. He'd proven himself in New York. The major problems here should have been solved while he was gone but apparently they weren't so they'd asked him to step in. Now this - an executive level meeting. Maybe he'd make vice president sooner than he'd believed.

"One other thing, Marc. I'm tied up so I need you to pick her up from the airport. I've already made the arrangements. The limo will be downstairs at three."

"Happy to do it."

Back in his office, Marc slung his briefcase on top of his desk and sank into his chair. He'd just come from the airport, having come straight to work after landing from New York. In forty-five minutes he'd head back to the airport, this time in a limo. His meeting with Southern had left him high with hope and promise, but physically he felt tired, rumpled, and jet lagged. Marc opened his briefcase for his Rubik's cube and idly toyed with it. He'd solved the puzzle on the flight from New York. The rows of colors were now perfectly aligned, order out of chaos. Marc twisted and turned the levels until it again became a challenge.

Then he leafed through the stack of messages resting on his telephone. Dorothea at the Gough Street branch wanted to know what time his team would arrive tomorrow. Na Na had called but left no number, smart girl.

Below that were four messages from a Lorna Klydesdale bearing a local phone number. They were marked personal. The name Lorna was vaguely familiar. Was that the girl he'd picked up at the Fern Bar on Van Ness two weeks ago? Marc drummed his fingers on his desk, hoping it wasn't her.

Na Na was scheduled to call tonight. Marc returned Dorothea's call. Lorna whoever could wait.

Just as he finished the call, Nancy poked her head into the doorway. "Sergio Fernandez from Master Charge is here to see you."

"Have him wait a second." Nancy disappeared. Marc peered through the open Venetian blinds; a tall Hispanic man stood by his secretary's desk. "Shit."

Marc cleared his desk. He wished he had had time to check Na Na's accounts before any encounter with Sergio from Master Charge.

Opening the door, he motioned Sergio in. The young man was muscular with unruly brown hair. The two of them crowded the small office.

"How can I help you? You aren't still having program problems are you?"

"Not my department. I'm in collections." Sergio took the chair next to Marc's desk, unbuttoning his blue blazer. "I'm here about your aunt, Minnie Barlow."

Marc sat, trying to stay nonchalant. "My aunt?"

"Do you know where we can find her? We need to talk to her."

Marc shrugged. "Last I knew she was on vacation. I just got back from a week in New York an hour ago, so I'm afraid we haven't been in touch. What's this about?"

Sergio filled him in on Edith Clark's stolen credit cards and the suspicions that Minnie's friend Jeanette Compton had been using them. Jeanette, her friends Sarah and Minnie had left town together, without paying their rent. Minnie's Master Charge account was also up to the credit limit.

"My understanding is that she's on vacation. That's when you use a credit card a lot. I don't know anything about the rest of it."

"The manager, Mrs. Klydesdale, said she saw you removing boxes from Mrs. Barlow 's apartment."

Klydesdale. That's why that name seemed familiar. "That's right. My aunt wanted me to store a few things for her. I finally got around to it."

"When will you be speaking with your aunt again?"

"Hard to say. Probably when she gets back."

"Are the two of you close?"

"Not really. I take her to dinner once in a while. See her on holidays."

"What about Compton?"

"I met her a few times. Listen, I think you've got a case of mistaken identity. I can't picture any of her friends doing this."

"We're almost positive the thief is female. You just never know what's going to motivate somebody. The way this thing is playing out, it's certainly not professionals."

"That's all well and good. But I grew up around my aunt. She's a straight arrow."

Sergio tapped a forefinger against his bottom lip. "You have any ideas?"

"Edith was mugged. They never recovered her purse. Somebody out there has her cards. But I can practically guarantee you that it's not my aunt or her friends."

"Where are your aunt and friends vacationing?"

"They're taking a road trip."

"Down the coast? Monterey, San Luis Obispo?"

Marc tried to not look alarmed. Charges must have come in on Edith's card on their way to Palm Springs. Damn it, they hadn't destroyed the card. "I was under the impression they were heading north. Gold country, Feather River, maybe Reno."

Sergio considered this, then stood to leave, buttoning his blazer. "I appreciate your time. Say, you worked in collections a few years ago, didn't you?"

"Yep. I was a night collector when I was in school."

"That's what George told me. He said you were at Berkeley, trying to get into medical school."

Marc thought back to those days. It seemed the entire night staff had applications in at medical and dental schools. They were a support group for each other and were all good friends. It didn't matter that he was Phi Beta Kappa, the best he got was an interview at Tulane, followed by rejection. Only one of the crew got in, on the waiting list. He'd been happy for the guy, but the memory of his own failure still stung.

"Yeah, well. Getting in isn't easy. That's just the breaks." Absentmindedly he took up the Rubik's cube and twisted it. "How is ol' George doing? I haven't seen him in ages."

"I've got him busy on this case. He's on the road right now."

Marc shifted the colors of the Rubik's cube while fighting the heat rising in his belly. "Will there be anything else? I just got in and I've got a lot to catch up on."

"If you hear from your aunt, ask her to call me." Sergio left Marc his card.

After the man was gone, Marc examined the card. He hoped he'd manifested the proper amount of evasiveness, misdirection, and disbelief in his aunt's treachery. Marc wished he had a number to reach her; they were still using Edith's credit card and they had to stop. Now. He slapped the card down and rubbed his face.

"Goddammit it, Na Na, you couldn't have picked a worse time to pull this shit."

Chapter 11

Entering the Stardust, Minnie halted just inside the door. Patronizing a place such as this was not her style.

Sarah rushed to the cashier's cage, pulling her wallet from her purse. Jeanette strolled elegantly, blithely behind in a black sequined jumpsuit, making eye contact with people she passed. Jeanette looked like she was twenty, maybe twenty-five, certainly not a day over thirty. Was it her undergarments rounding and slimming, or had Jeanette kept that nice fanny doing all those donkey kicks, or both?

Clanging bells and a delighted whoop pulled Minnie's attention to a nearby slot machine. A beer-bellied, red-faced, middle-aged man clapped. "See that, Sue? I hit it, girl, I hit it!" The twirling red light above the machine bounced off his bald pate. A hefty woman, probably his wife, moved down two stools and, grinning widely, peered in at the display. She hugged his neck and a small crowd began to gather.

It figured the winning machines would be by the door, to reel the doubters and chicken-hearted deeper into the casino. Minnie took in the confetti-patterned carpet, vibrant party colors, chaotic confusion of bells and whirling red lights that summoned cashiers carrying platters of bills, because no machine could hold the fortune owed to the lucky suckers. Long- legged girls in itty-bitty black velvet dresses bore drink trays through the crowds. Men and women plunked chips on the tray, tips for the waitress. A wooden five-dollar token felt like a nickel in here. The drinks and cigarettes were free to make sure the gamblers stayed a long time. Most would end up losing more than their inhibitions. They gathered at the thirty-nine cent breakfast buffet behind stacks of pancakes and bacon, trying to recoup something from their disappointment.

In search of Sarah, Minnie made her way through mazes of people and bright silver machines, past a raucous crowd of cigar-smoking men shooting craps, all flanked by lovely young women. Past security guards, past pasty obese women who had no business wearing shorts. She passed through a ring of blackjack tables overseen by pit bosses in three-piece suits, a uniform in itself. Arms crossed, pinkie diamonds glittering in the soft vibrant light, these overseers watched the action with gangster-like stoicism. Sometimes they'd glide beside a dealer to say something sidelong behind a hand. Nobody seemed to care how scary it really was.

When she reached Sarah and Jeanette, they'd already changed dollars to silver coins that filled big popcorn containers.

Minnie asked, "Did you get butter?"

Sarah didn't fathom the joke. "What?"

"Never mind. What do you want to play?"

"First get your quarters. Here, I have a coupon for a free roll."

"I'll just watch for a while."

"To the slots!" Sarah beamed, and off she went into the crowds and din.

"She's never gambled before,' Jeanette said. "Never been in a casino."

Minnie and Jeanette followed into the heart of the casino where Sarah took up residence at a slot machine. Jeanette joined in and for half an hour the two girls eagerly fed coins into the slots under Minnie's watchful eye. Their enjoyment was contagious; Shrewd Prude began to feel the temptation. Around them, more machines hit, bells rang, players rejoiced. Jeanette and Sarah won, too. It was a carnival; the silver and glass faces of the machines reflected like fun house mirrors. Shrewd Prude grinned at her distorted reflection, then scrounged around the bottom of her purse for spare change.

Sarah shrieked again as quarters flooded into the bin and spilled on the floor. Sirens wailed and the flashing lights revolved. Minnie and Jeanette rushed over. Three Sevens: one red, one white, one blue. Five hundred dollars!

Sarah grew flushed, and the kaleidoscope of colors reflecting off her glasses hid her eyes.

"Look at this! Help me pick it all up!"

A cashier pushed a cart to them. She handed Sarah some cardboard buckets and managed a dull "Congratulations" before moving down the line.

Sarah scooped up quarters and stuffed them back into the machine. Frenzied, she jerked the handle then tried another batch of quarters. Going for a third batch, Minnie stopped her.

"Don't give it all back, Sarah."

"I'm on a roll! I'm on a roll!" She yanked the handle again.

A cocktail waitress slid to a stop before them. "Would you like drinks here?"

"Of course!" Sarah replied. "We have to celebrate! I'll have, oh, where did that woman go? She was having some sort of coffee drink. Oh yes, that's right. A Karaoke coffee."

The waitress, whose name plate indicated she was from New Jersey, smiled knowingly. "Kioki. Okay." She asked Minnie and Jeanette, "What would you ladies like?" Both ordered strawberry daiquiris.

Sarah busied herself yanking the handle, and squealed when she hit a seven, an orange, and a cherry. Three more quarters clanged into the bin.

Minnie soon ran out of the coins she'd scrounged from the bottom of her purse. She retrieved the coupon for a free roll of quarters from Jeanette. What the heck, it was free money.

The ten dollar roll rose to fifty, shrank back to ten, climbed to one hundred, then disappeared into the smoke-filled air. They'd played the slots for three hours and three drinks. Thanks to Sarah's first-timer's luck, they were collectively up eight hundred bucks.

Sarah massaged her biceps while the dials spun on the machine before her. Minnie said to Jeanette, "We've got to get her out of here."

"Leave her alone. She's having a good time."

"I'm getting hungry. We haven't eaten since this morning." She looked at her watch. "Good grief!"

"What?"

"It's almost eight o'clock."

Jeanette looked at her own watch. "I thought it was around four."

Minnie searched the casino. "There's not a single clock on the walls."

Jeanette nodded, appreciating the cleverness of that.

Minnie said to Sarah, "Why don't we change this for paper and go have some dinner?"

"I'm not hungry. You go ahead. I'll see you later." Sarah yanked the handle again. Minnie tugged on her arm.

"No! I'm on a roll!"

"Sarah!"

"This is my lucky machine. It's going to pay. You'll see."

"For crying out loud. You're coming with us." Minnie tugged on her again. "Do you know it's already eight o'clock?"

"What?" Sarah let go of the handle. She stopped pouting when she cashed in her winnings. "Give me hundred dollar bills."

They took the elevator to their rooms to change for dinner.

Minnie said as she unlocked her door, "This cash will come in handy for incidentals."

"We'll double it. Triple it!" Sarah disappeared into her room.

In her room, Minnie laid out her blue evening dress then called Marc. He answered on the third ring.

"I was afraid you weren't home from work yet."

"I was just coming in the front door. Na Na, where are you?"

"Vegas."

"Is everything all right?"

"We're having a great time. I'm beginning to suspect that Sarah's a compulsive gambler. She won $750.00 off a quarter machine, then lost it all on a dollar machine. Imagine! Just now she won $500.00 on a slot and went berserk. I had to drag her off the floor."

Marc chuckled. "Who knew?" Then his voice took on a firm tone. "Listen, Sergio Fernandez, that collector from Master Charge, came to see me. Jeanette is still using Edith's cards."

"I know. Yesterday, Jeanette got a call in Palm Springs from her waiter friend from Pandora's. He tipped us off. George Post went to see him. What did the collector say?"

"He suspects you and Sarah are in on it, though he can't prove anything. Besides, you two never signed any sales drafts. You haven't signed any of the sales drafts from Edith's card, have you?"

"Of course not."

"Good. They're just guessing. I played dumb. Said all I knew was that you were on vacation. I don't think he believed me. Minnie, you need to know George is coming after you. Edith's card was used in Monterey and San Luis Obispo."

"What?"

"I thought you said Jeanette had destroyed that card."

"I thought she had, too. That's what she told me."

"You better get it away from her and destroy it yourself."

"Oh, Goodness, now what are we going to do?"

"Just remember everything I told you. Keep your eyes open. He's probably in Palm Springs right now. You're going to have to keep moving. They won't know where you've been until the sales drafts come in. By then, you need to be gone. Don't stay anywhere more than a couple of days. Keep below the floor limits. If somebody calls for an authorization, they'll know exactly where you are at that moment. Just remember everything I told you."

George Post was a new dynamic. Minnie had felt safe after they left San Francisco. They'd had a relaxing weekend in Palm Springs; now they'd have to live the fugitive life. She expected this to happen, but not so soon. Maybe they should hightail it out of the country right now.

Marc said, "I've been worried sick and didn't know how to get hold of you."

"Sorry. We're planning to head out tomorrow anyway."

"Where are you going?"

"We'll overnight at the Grand Canyon. Then go to visit Sarah's son David in Albuquerque. He's got a big house, so we'll hide there for a few days."

"That's good. Be sure you use cash in Albuquerque."

"We will. That is if I can keep Sarah from dumping it all back into one of those one-armed bandits."

"Excellent. By the way, I've got some good news. I might end up a V.P. before the year is out. Last night I went to a dinner meeting at the Fairmont. Mostly department heads not just from City Security but from other banks as well. Southern asked me to attend. They picked my brain about the projects I'm working on and about this new code I'm using. It kind of surprised me to be invited. It's looking really good for me, Na Na. Really good."

"I'm so proud of you. I know that whatever you undertake, you'll knock 'em dead."

"That's the idea."

"Now all I have to do is get you married off to a nice girl and I can quit worrying."

"Funny you should say that. I met someone."

"Naturally, as soon as I leave. Tell me about her."

"She's a hotshot from NCCA. She developed a new technology, a zero floor limit machine. They're going to test market it in L.A. early next year. It'll do away with floor limits altogether. It's hooked up to the mainframe at NCCA. The merchant swipes the credit card through it for every transaction, big or small. The mainframe can read it and automatically checks the account instantly authorizing or declining the charge. It'll eliminate losses by the likes of you." Marc laughed alone. "Anyway, she's a genius."

"So for that, you've fallen in love?"

"I didn't say love. But I'm certainly captivated. You know I've always had a soft spot for the smart ones. And she's gorgeous."

"Where did you meet?"

"I picked her up from the airport yesterday for Southern in the bank's limo. She was at dinner last night, too. I'll probably be working with her on the software end of the new machine. And."

"And?"

"I had dinner with her tonight, too. Alone."

It was a privilege that Marc would confide in her about his love life. The only other time he'd spoken about a girlfriend was when he was staying with her his senior year in high school. He was taken with a girl named Claudette. She had what Minnie suspected was a phony French accent. Marc wanted to marry her on graduation. Minnie panicked at the idea of Marc giving up college and marrying so young. She called her brother and he told her not to worry. Graduation was eight months away. Marc would change his mind by then and if he didn't, he'd come out there and give his son a good ass whipping.

Marc did change his mind. It wasn't just the accent that turned out to be phony. Marc caught Claudette having sex with his best friend. That ended the affair. In fact, he spoke no more of women at all after that, though he dated quite a bit. Minnie worried that his wounded high school heart might not recover and would stop him from getting serious about any woman.

This new girl must be very special.

"Call me when you get to Albuquerque? And get that damn card away from Jeanette."

"I will, sweetheart. Bye for now." Minnie hung up and thought it through. Jeanette would never give up the card. She would continue to lie about using it. A confrontation with her, a willful, stubborn woman, could spoil the trip. Besides, it wouldn't work.

Minnie might recruit Sarah to help. She dialed Sarah's room, then quickly hung up. She lay back on the bed and looked at the ceiling. Minnie had explained the "rules" to her friends; she could hear their retorts. Jeanette would say she'd stayed below the floor limits, which is why they weren't caught in Monterey or San Luis Obispo. She would get sarcastic and tell Minnie she worries too much. She might even blow off the threat to Marc's career, stating there's no proof whatsoever, short of a confession, that Marc is involved.

Sarah would side with Jeanette again, too fond of the drama of it all. Besides, it was obvious, though unspoken, that Sarah felt using Edith's cards in some way kept Edith alive. No, Sarah would be useless. Minnie would have to do this on her own.

She had to find the right opportunity to snatch that card.

◈

The girls dined sitting on the floor at a Japanese restaurant. Sarah produced a Master Charge to pay; Minnie made sure it wasn't one of Edith's. Rising after the meal, they felt creaky from sitting cross-legged too long, so they took a walk to stretch.

On the main drag, the bright lights of Vegas created a festive atmosphere. Barkers tried to lure them in for shows and gambling. Sarah stopped in front of a sandwich board outside a small casino. Her joy at being in a party town, having won so much money her first time out, and the love of life and adventure that had propelled her heart and soul of late fled her in a single instant. The board advertised a bridge game: 'Win $25,000.00 - Swiss Team Event, ten p.m." It didn't seem right for Sarah that everything she'd escaped should suddenly crash in on her, but she couldn't stop thinking of Edith, her favorite bridge partner and best friend.

Jeanette and Minnie called to Sarah, pointing at a white stretch limo across the street at Caesar's. The chauffeur opened the door and out stepped Sally Field and Burt Reynolds.

Sarah couldn't stop staring at the sandwich board, her mind on the past. If Edith were here, the four of them would enter the tournament for sure. But, if Edith were alive, they absolutely would not be here, or even thinking about being here. It was a confusing and emotional twist.

Jeanette said, "Maybe we can pick up a fourth. You want to try it?"

Minnie squinted at her watch. "It's only ten of ten. Sure, let's do it. Sarah?"

"No." Sarah walked away.

The next morning, after checking out of the hotel and loading the car, Sarah pleaded with Minnie and Jeanette for one more hour of gambling. Her profit was burning a hole in her pocketbook.

Minnie relented. "Okay, fine." Sarah headed for the slots.

Jeanette said, "You've been awfully hard on her lately. We're here to have fun and you seem to be uptight."

Minnie sighed. "I just hate seeing people suckered in like that. Besides, Marc told us we should keep moving."

"It's a form of entertainment for her. Just let it be. Shoot. That field agent is probably on his way to Puerto Vallarta right now. I'm going to hit the roulette table."

"We'll meet you back here in an hour. I'll go look after Sarah."

When the hour was up, Minnie and Sarah waited for Jeanette. They ventured back onto the casino floor, and found her at the roulette wheel seated beside a portly man. The man whispered in Jeanette's ear, then they put their chips together on number seventeen. "Give me a kiss for luck," the man said in a robust voice.

Jeanette planted red lip prints on his bald spot. He laughed heartily and the wheel spun. The ball lodged on number twelve, then lurched into another spin to clatter to more numbers before settling on seventeen.

The crowd cheered. The grinning croupier shoved two big stacks of chips toward Jeanette and her friend. The big man clutched Jeanette in a hug.

Sarah said, "Let's give her another half hour. We'll go back to the slots."

Minnie said, "How convenient for you."

Walking toward the slots, a familiar man strode past, eyes fixed on the roulette table, and on Jeanette.

Wheeling, they looked after him. Minnie said, "It's that man from the bank. George Post."

"Oh God! Oh look! He's heading straight for Jeanette!"

Sarah asked, "What are we going to do?"

George Post closed in on the crowded roulette wheel. "How did he find us so fast? We've got to get to Jeanette before he does." They hurried toward the roulette wheel but too late. George tapped her shoulder.

Minnie and Sarah stopped in their tracks.

Jeanette turned. Suddenly she was up and out of her chair, exclaiming, "Look, everyone, it's James Garner! Maverick! Can I get your autograph?"

Enthusiastic fans mobbed George Post, clutched at his arms and lapels. A drunk blonde in a red satin mini dress shoved Jeanette into his chest then yanked her out of the way. Lunging, she grabbed George and kissed him. Jeanette regained her balance and edged to the back of the gathering crowd. Sarah and Minnie took her hands and together fled to the car they'd already packed.

A pit boss and two security guards made their way through the mob. "Okay folks, settle down. Break it up. What's going on here?"

The drunk girl in red satin hung on George. He said, "Get off me."

The pit boss told them, "You wanna take it outside?"

The girl in red satin said, "You can't talk to James Garner like that!"

"That ain't James Garner."

The girl let George go. "You're not James Garner?"

"No."

"How dare you!" She slapped him.

George didn't try to find Jeanette Compton in the crowd. That woman and her friends were cagey enough to be long gone. The James Garner bit was brilliant. He found a pay phone in a quiet corner of the casino, and called Sergio.

George described how close he'd gotten, even laying a hand on Jeanette Compton's good-looking shoulder. Sergio howled when George told him how Compton had played him and the crowd.

"James Garner? Seriously?"

"Sergio, shut up. I need your help."

Sergio struggled to quit laughing.

"I've been told I look like him." Sergio didn't seem to hear, busy sharing the tale with his coworkers.

"Pay attention. I need your help here."

"Sure, Jim, sure. Sorry." Sergio sniffed back his mirth. "What do you need?"

"Someone lifted my wallet. Fix me up and get me out of here."

Another hyena laugh erupted, another exchange with the office group, more catcalls. Someone shouted loud enough for Sergio's phone to pick it up: "Hey, Maverick, use that hundred dollar bill you've got pinned inside your lapel."

"Just Western Union some money and a new card to me at the Stardust. I need some credentials too."

Hanging up, George went to the bar. He had just thirty bucks. He ordered a Johnny Walker Red neat. It had never been this way when he was on the force. He was never taken by surprise. Hostage situations, disarming felons, whatever, George exercised solid professionalism and had received commendations and promotions. His career as a cop had been moving up. He stopped thinking about it when the bartender set down the drink. George downed it in one swallow. "Give me a double."

"Losing streak?" The bartender poured George's double.

"My whole life is a losing streak."

Sarah exclaimed, "That was too close for comfort!"

Minnie wheeled onto the interstate. "You never cease to amaze me, Jeanette."

"He lost that smug look pretty fast." Jeanette mimicked George Post's deep voice: "No! No! I'm not James Garner! No! No!"

Once they stopped guffawing, Jeanette said, "Honestly? For a second I thought it was actually James Garner! Or else, I don't know what I would have done."

Sarah said, "Ingenious."

Jeanette grinned broadly, a Cheshire cat smile. "That's not all. Look what I got."

She held up a brown calfskin wallet.

Minnie strained to drive straight and put her eyes back on the road.

"You stole George Post's wallet?"

"Look! He has a gold key card! Who wants to pretend they're George next time we go shopping?"

Sarah leaned over the seat. "Let me see."

"Are you insane?" Minnie tried to slap down Jeanette's hand but couldn't while driving. Jeanette handed Sarah the card.

"Some woman pushed me right into him. With all those hands on him, it was a cinch." Jeanette dug through the other pockets of the wallet. "He only has one credit card. Oh, look at this." She held up a picture of a woman with two small children.

Sarah took the photo. "A married man. I wonder what his wife thinks about him being gone all the time chasing crooks."

"That's what we are," Minnie said. "We're crooks who steal wallets now."

Jeanette held up a memorial card that had been tucked behind the picture. "I don't think he's married anymore."

Minnie asked, "What does it say?"

"It's the Lord's prayer. Oh my God, his wife and children died on the same day. December 31, 1971. Wow. She was only thirty-one and the kids were seven and nine."

Sarah said, "New Year's Eve. Maybe it was a car accident."

Minnie said, "We'll mail his wallet back to the bank."

Jeanette held up cash, lots of it.

"Five hundred dollars." She fanned the bills then tucked them in her purse.

Minnie asked, "What are you doing? You can't take his money. Put it back."

"Like we aren't already thieves?"

Sarah came in on Minnie's side this time. "Jeanette, it's not the same thing and you know it."

"When we get to the Grand Canyon, I'll mail the wallet. But everyone knows you're not supposed to send cash through the mail."

Chapter 12

Minnie took the off ramp for the Grand Canyon.

Jeanette asked, "What are you doing?"

"What do you mean? We're going to the Grand Canyon."

"Why do we have to stop to look at a big hole in the ground?"

"Big hole in the ground?"

From the backseat, Sarah said, "It's a sightseeing thing. We're right here, why not do it?"

"Have you ever been there?" Minnie kept driving, she wasn't about to pull over to discuss this.

"I've seen postcards. That's enough for me." Jeanette rolled her eyes at Minnie. "I know, I know, it's beautiful. One of the Seven Wonders of the world." She put a hand to her forehead. "It's going to be hot and dusty there."

"There's nothing wrong with getting a little hot and dusty. That's why they invented bathrooms. It'll be fun. C'mon."

Jeanette studied the map. "If we keep driving, we can get to Albuquerque by nightfall."

"It's six hundred miles to Albuquerque. We won't get there until after midnight. I don't want to spend that much time in the car. Besides, I think we have a better chance of hiding out at the Grand Canyon."

"There are no nice hotels there."

"I'm thinking cheap motel, phony names, and pay cash. Make it more difficult for him to find us."

Sarah said, "I have some brochures. They've got cute little cabins."

"Cabins?" Jeanette turned to Sarah. "Cabins? Like Davy Crockett? Isn't cabin just another word for spiders, crappy water pressure, rusted sinks, raccoons under army cots, and rattlesnakes? No thank you." Jeanette slapped the map in her lap, crossed her arms and stared out the window. "Please turn the car around."

Minnie looked in the rearview mirror at Sarah, who shrugged and sat back. "Well, say something. Majority rules, right?"

Sarah said, "Whatever you two decide is fine by me."

"Look, see that sign? It's only fifty-two miles from here. We can see it, then come back to Highway 40 and find a motel."

Minnie's friends stared out the windows. Minnie made another attempt. "Sarah, you carried on about how you and Don had plans to go there in your Winnebago."

"Don't drag me into this."

"What do you mean, drag you into this? You are in this. Give us your verdict."

Sarah remained silent, disconcerted, and indecisive.

Minnie pulled into a turnout and screeched the brakes. Jeanette gave a little shriek of surprise.

"What are you doing?"

"Look." Minnie turned on Jeanette to blurt, 'Give me that damn card.' The animosity in Jeanette's green eyes would be fire on fire, so Minnie stared out the windshield and softened her tone. "Look. I spent years teaching about the Grand Canyon. I want to see it for myself."

"Suit yourself." Jeanette returned her eyes to the passenger window.

Minnie drummed her fingers on the steering wheel. In the backseat, Sarah also avoided her gaze.

"Fine. We're going to the Grand Canyon." Minnie pulled back onto the road, and within seconds was directly behind an old and very large Winnebago which made her cut her speed in half.

A yellow tarp sporting a Happy Face covered the RV's spare tire, the antithesis of the mood in the car. Stickers of travel destinations were plastered over the van's back: Fort Knox, Remember the Alamo, Petrified Forest. The vehicle was so huge it blocked any other view that Minnie could have appreciated.

She slowed to thirty miles per hour, sometimes fifteen or twenty on the curves. It was hard work to keep the car at that pace, as if the Lincoln wanted to pass the

RV on its own. The grade increased and the Winnebago downshifted, spewing a cloud of noxious exhaust from its corroded tailpipe. Even with the windows rolled up the girls could smell the fumes.

In the rearview mirror, Sarah seemed amused at the great yellow smiling Happy Face stuck in front of them. Minnie's glare caused Sarah to titter, then burst into full-blown laughter.

Jeanette whirled on Sarah, annoyed. The Winnebago farted another plume; Minnie hunched over the steering wheel in frustrated concentration. Sarah pointed at the RV; Jeanette, seeing how miserable the big mobile home was making Minnie, stinking and crawling up the mountains, its Happy Face bobbing before them nonstop, joined Sarah in laughter.

Minnie asked, "What's so damn funny?" The Winnebago backfired again. Minnie cracked a grin and that did it. She joined in the full hearted gales of Jeanette's and Sarah's laughter.

They followed the sluggish RV on the curving road for two and a half hours. Jeanette and Sarah engaged in a debate on travel: Sarah believed a Winnebago was efficient and much more comfortable for road trips; Jeanette likened it to a snail carrying his house on his back. "Besides, what about the gas? What do they get, three gallons to the mile?" Before Sarah could respond,

Jeanette waved a hand. "Whatever it is. You could fly first class, stay in the best hotels, and eat the best meals for whatever you'd have to pay to keep that thing gassed up and oiled up. Who wants to spend their vacation cooking and doing dishes? What kind of vacation is that for a woman?"

By five thirty, exhausted, they reached the first overlook. They'd left Vegas seven hours ago. Minnie was so tired from driving, she doubted she'd be able to stay awake for the sunset. They got out of the Lincoln, stretching and yawning, to a ferocious blast of dry heat.

"Good grief." Minnie had been fooled by the air conditioner in the car.

"I told you it would be hot."

A passing car raised dust that the breeze threw in their faces.

"And dusty?" Minnie swiped at her nostrils.

Jeanette and Sarah brushed themselves off. Sarah, indicating a lineup of blue Porta-potties, said, "Bathroom." She headed that way; unhappily, Jeanette joined her.

Minnie walked to a chain link fence. For the first time in her life she looked at a view she'd only seen in pictures. Though the Grand Canyon was breathtaking, the panorama was affected by the fence, by lines of cars in the parking lot and acres of people, by a fenced path leading the droves to a gift shop on a hill, trash cans everywhere, and by the Porta-potties.

Minnie shut her eyes to close out the irritating sights, sounds and smells. Somehow, she'd expected to be there alone with her friends in perfect solitude. She'd pictured a picnic lunch on a cliff, a train of pack mules in the distance. She saw herself breathing in the quiet air redolent of fresh, raw earth. Minnie would examine stones for bits of crystal, quartz, even gold. There would be a leisurely hike, stopping to take in the clouds, the changing colors against the rock faces while the sun set. Serenity, majestic nature, the raw quiet canyon with no human touch.

She hated to admit it, but Jeanette was right. It looked better in the postcards.

Sarah joined Minnie at the fence. "I doubt we can convince Jeanette to hike down a ways. I wonder if there's even a trail from here."

Numerous brown signs surrounded them, but none hinted of a trail name. The placards proclaimed only 'Gift Shop' with an arrow pointing as if someone might miss the only obvious structure and mistakenly go into the Porta-potty to buy a postcard, or 'Keep Back,' 'Keep Off,' 'Don't Litter.'

Minnie said, "Uh, oh, here she comes." Jeanette marched toward them, plainly vexed. "I don't want to hear it. I'm going to that telescope over there." She left Sarah to contend with Jeanette.

◈

"I knew it would be like this!"

Sarah tried to nip Jeanette's tantrum in the bud. "Take a look." She leaned against the handrail to give the canyon her full attention.

At her side, Jeanette lay a palm against the gunky metal rail and looked out. After a long moment, Sarah said, "Look at the way the sun's shining against that bluff. So red, so golden. It's like that painting at the De Young. Wagner, I think. Hudson River school. Tom Wagner. I'm glad we came."

Many years ago, she and Edith had begun planning a trip here. Their husbands drank beer out by the barbeque, talking about how they could take turns driving the Winnebago. They were all pumped up. It never happened.

The breeze lifted again. Sarah felt Don's presence in it, sailing through the peaks and valleys. She sent him a silent hello.

Their son David had never been here, either, though as a young boy he would excitedly participate in helping plan the adventure to the Grand Canyon. Now he seemed too involved with ambition, money, negotiating, and country club tennis to take the time to look at something he couldn't acquire. At least that was her take. She hadn't talked with him in ages.

Sarah equally feared and desired to see him again. She wanted to understand the reason for his coldness since he left home twelve years ago. Hopefully, he would bring up the subject himself. She needed to clear the air, desperately.

Jeanette's hand lay on hers. "What are you thinking?"

"Just how magnificent this natural architecture is. The whole bit about how small and insignificant we all are in the grand scheme of things. It is incredible, isn't it?"

"Yes. Yes, it is." Jeanette seemed to have forgotten her petty complaints. She was leaning forward over the railing, an expression of awe.

Jeanette straightened up. "I'm famished."

"All we had in the car were those potato chips and apples. I could eat."

Thirty yards away, Minnie was peering into a telescope, into the deep chasm. A pair of twins scurried by her with ice cream bars in their hands. One boy tripped and grabbed Minnie's pants leg as he tumbled. She helped him up, and the twin raced off after his sibling.

Then Minnie looked down at her slacks. Chocolate handprints streaked the pure white seersucker.

Minnie stamped and shouted after the child. This surprised Sarah, who'd seen Minnie deal with children many times. Minnie's patience with children was an amazing thing, with no trace of the intolerance and impatience she was capable of with adults. In fact, Minnie would become something of a child herself. On other days, she would have laughed, helped the boy up, and checked his little knees for scrapes before taking him back to his mother.

But those pants cost a hundred and fifty dollars. Sarah didn't like this thought at all. Perhaps that was what David was caught up in. She began to wonder if she was changing in some way, as well. And if so, how?

"There was nowhere to eat coming up the road." Sarah jolted back to Jeanette's voice. "You'd think a tourist trap like this would have plenty of restaurants."

"I guess it's mostly campers who come. They bring their own groceries."

As they walked towards Minnie, Jeanette took Sarah's arm. "Listen, I wouldn't mind indulging Minnie in this. She's had a rougher day than we have. Maybe we could drive up a little further and find a nice hotel. Have a little dinner somewhere then lie down for an hour or so. Maybe we could find a place that has a nice balcony off the room. Get a wakeup call in time to watch the sunset. Instead of going out, we could get room service. I'd love to dive into a bubble bath, come out to a nice Caesar salad, chardonnay and an Arizona Highway's view of the sunset. What do you think?"

"Sounds wonderful."

When they caught up to Minnie, she was still in hissy mode. She spread the stained pants leg for them to see. "Look at this. It's never going to come out." Minnie flung her hand over her breast with a gasp. "I don't know why parents can't keep better track of their children. None of my students were this rude. Hippie families! Communes! That's what it is. These kids probably don't even know which ones are their parents."

"I was thinking," Jeanette said, "let's just find a place to eat and get a room. We'll get some soda water too. Maybe there's hope for that stain yet."

Minnie was already striding to the car, still incensed. Jeanette whispered to Sarah, "Better let her have the first shot at the bubble bath."

After inquiries at the gift shop, a couple of phone calls, and a bit of driving around, they discovered the only motel; it had one room left, with two double beds and a rollaway they could rent for an extra three dollars a night.

Jeanette maneuvered the big Lincoln through a cloud of dust down a potholed dirt drive. "Number six, right?" The shabby dark brown cabin stood at the end of the line under a tall spreading tree. The covered wooden porch tilted at a dangerous angle. "Is that safe to walk on?"

They managed their way, luggage in tow, over the uneven rocky path, then onto the creaking porch.

Jeanette unlocked and opened the squeaky door. "Look at my shoes." Her little white sling-backs were scuffed and covered with a layer of brown powder, as was the hemline of her pink and white jersey shift.

Sarah said, "They should clean up okay,"

It took a while for their eyes to adjust. The light switch clicked on a ceramic cactus lamp with a yellowed shade on the nightstand between the beds. It barely lit the darkened room. Drapes covered the dusty windows and greenery around the cabin blocked any further light.

Sarah tugged open the curtains. The filtered light that spilled in illuminated a spider web. With a tissue from her purse, Sarah swiped it out of existence, then turned to see if Jeanette had noticed. She hadn't. Jeanette was peering into the open bathroom door, balled fists on her hips.

"Well, there's no bathtub. It's so tight we're going to have to shimmy in sideways to get to the toilet."

"Don't start." Minnie flung herself onto one of the lumpy sagging beds. It groaned and a spring jabbed into her back. "All I want to do is take a nap."

From Minnie's suitcase, Sarah took a knee-length Palm Springs t-shirt. She laid it beside Minnie. "Change into this and give me those dirty slacks."

Sarah took a little bottle of club soda from the cabin's small refrigerator onto the porch with Minnie's pants. The stain was stubborn; Sarah struggled with it for a while before giving up. When she went back in, Minnie was sound asleep. The thundering pipes and squeaky faucet fixtures revealed that Jeanette was showering. Sarah lay on the other bed, and was soon out like a light.

They overslept, missing the sunset, almost missing dinner. The dining hall, a large tin-roofed building a quarter-mile away, was old cafeteria-style, reminding Minnie of her teaching days. The cracked linoleum floor probably had its last update in the forties. Tankards of bitter coffee were on a table against the wall. A three-bar rail for sliding dinner trays was attached to the large stainless steel buffet table. An elderly hair-netted woman in a faded turquoise uniform looked up from behind the buffet. "You just made it. I was about to close up." She served up the girls' meals of chicken tacos, Spanish rice, and refried beans advertised on the handwritten sign outside.

Jeanette asked, "Do you have any salad greens?"

"Over there." The server pointed her long-handled spoon to a weathered pine buffet. Plates of shredded iceberg, chopped tomatoes, diced jalapenos, and grated yellow cheese slopped over into each other.

Jeanette smiled at the server then made a yuck-face for Sarah and Minnie. "Don't worry. At this point, I'll eat almost anything."

She did.

After dinner, at bedtime, the rollaway was the worst of the worst of the beds in the cabin. Jeanette fidgeted and tossed but could not get to sleep, and this kept Sarah awake. Finally, Jeanette rose with her pillow and blanket and tiptoed for the door. It creaked open. Sarah asked, "Where are you going?"

"Shh. Don't wake Minnie. I'm going to sleep in the backseat of the car."

"Do you want my bed? Take my bed. I'll sleep over there. I can sleep anywhere."

Jeanette moved to Sarah's side. "You're already tucked in." She touched Sarah's cheek. "Besides, I think there're spiders in your bed. Go back to sleep now."

Sarah got up to peer through the drapes as Jeanette got in the car. Minnie slept on. Lying in bed, Sarah stared up at the ceiling. Maybe the overlong nap was the culprit, but she stayed wide awake. She closed her eyes but shutting out the visual world didn't close down her mind.

Tomorrow night at this time, she'd be in David's guest room. Minnie and Jeanette, too. It had been such a long time. How would it go?

David had distanced himself soon after Don's death. At first she thought it was the way he handled grief. David cried and cried when his older brother was killed in a hunting accident. He was only nine then. After Don died, he didn't cry, not that she knew of. Instead he went into a stony silence.

At first, Sarah blamed it on the physical distance between them. He left soon after the funeral for college at MIT. He was far away, focusing on studies, a new social circle, the fresh excitement and curiosity of independence. Her calls to him were short, he was impatient always. Sarah felt like she was intruding and gave up phoning him, in fear of the inevitable rejection.

After college, David went to work for a lab in New Mexico. In the twelve years he'd been gone, he never returned home, rarely called, and remembered her birthday occasionally. She couldn't put her finger on why and couldn't get him to talk about it. This time she would.

A noise made her eyes fly open. Minnie had slipped out of bed. Sarah quietly picked up her glasses from the nightstand and put them on.

In a white t-shirt, Minnie huddled over Jeanette's suitcases.

"What are you doing?"

"Go make sure Jeanette's not on her way in here."

"Why are you going through her things?"

Minnie took up Jeanette's purse. She parted the drapes, peered out, and satisfied, sat on Sarah's bed. She rifled through the purse.

"We've got to get Edith's cards away from her. She's still using them and she's going to lead that man right to us. That's how he found us in Vegas."

"Why didn't you say anything before?"

Minnie looked at Sarah over her glasses. "Please."

"You're not going to find them in there."

"Where does she keep them?"

"In her travel belt. You didn't know that?"

"She wears a travel belt? Right now? She's wearing it while she sleeps?"

"I'm not sure she even takes it off when she showers."

"What are we going to do?" Minnie tapped a fingernail against her chin. "You have to help me get them away from her."

"You want me to hold her down for you?"

"No. Just talk some sense into her. She won't listen to me."

"What makes you think she'll listen to me?"

"Why are you suddenly so argumentative? Won't you just help me with this?"

Sarah was the peacekeeper, not the warrior. Was that how she had changed? She said, "There's no talking sense into that woman, for one thing. And for another, that's all she has. She doesn't have any credit cards of her own. No cash either."

"But we'll use ours!"

"Don't you see? Jeanette has her pride. She doesn't want to have to ask you or me to buy her anything." Sarah tried to reassure Minnie. "In that restaurant in Monterey, nobody called the cops on us.

"So you knew she used the card there? I was in the restroom. I thought you said you were going to pay."

"I was going to put it on my card but Jeanette said the total was under the floor limit. She knows what she's doing. She's real savvy about all this stuff. I don't see the problem."

"The sales drafts are coming in and the bank knows where we've been."

"The operative word there is 'been.' By the time they show up, we're gone. Look how long we stayed in Palm Springs. That George Post didn't come around then."

Minnie put the wallet and purse where she found them, then tidied and closed Jeanette's suitcase. "Now you know why I was trying to find them on my own. I knew you wouldn't help me." Minnie got back into bed and snapped off the light.

Sarah fell asleep puzzling over what tomorrow would bring. Minnie was surely coming up with an alternate plan, and she'd be caught in the middle. Again.

Jeanette said, "I thought New Mexico was one big desert. But look at all the evergreens."

Sarah said, "The desert starts after Albuquerque. Here it's all mountains and cattle country." She quoted the Atlas in her lap: "And rich in Native American culture."

At twilight, when they dropped into the valley surrounding Albuquerque, the mesa and butte landscape of the Colorado plateau looked like something out of a western. Behind them the sun waved goodbye with long red arms. The only sound was the humming of the motor. Jeanette pulled to the side of the road.

Sarah asked, "What are you doing?"

"Let's stop for a minute and look."

They got out to stretch. In the west, silhouetted against an artist's sunset, stood a distant pueblo beside an abandoned stone church. Sarah felt she'd been dropped back a century in time. Beyond, the valley extended forever. Long shadows painted abstract designs on the desert floor. A faraway rumble of thunder reached them on the warm evening breeze. The three friends leaned on the trunk of the car to witness the still life before them.

"So beautiful," whispered Sarah. "I've never seen anything like it."

Minnie said, "This is so much sweeter than any tourist trap."

Thunder roared again, and the sun sank lower.

Suddenly a clunking, chugging clatter came up the slope of the highway. Dust and fumes swirled around them as the big Winnebago passed. As if on cue, it backfired. Minnie groaned as the RV disappeared over the summit. The yellow face, crimson in the sunset's afterglow, grinned at them happily.

Chapter 13

At David's house in Albuquerque, they sat in the car in the street.

David had done well for himself. The house was large, modern, beautifully landscaped, in an expensive neighborhood.

In her thick bifocals, Sarah reread the address, then matched it to the number on the stone pillar at the entrance to a circular driveway. She was proud of her son's accomplishments in the world, tempered by shame that Minnie and Jeanette were witness to the fact that he'd had the means to help yet for years had done nothing to assist in her struggles for money. She'd never once been invited to this house.

Minnie said, "The gate is open. Shall we?"

Sarah said, "I wonder if this is such a good idea. Maybe I should call first."

"Nonsense." Jeanette wheeled into the long driveway, then stopped in front of the house.

Sarah said, "Okay, we're here."

Jeanette asked, "Do you want us to come in with you?"

"Come with me, of course."

At the front door, standing on imported Italian tiles, they admired the potted desert blooms while waiting for David to answer the doorbell. Sarah fought her shock, held her ground against the urge to retreat a step, when a blond woman answered, an infant in her arms.

"May I help you?"

Tears began to well in Sarah's eyes. David was married? Had a baby, and didn't tell his mother? Sarah had not known she had a grandchild.

Jeanette came to the rescue. "We'd like to see my friend's son."

Sarah barely squeaked out the words, "My son."

The woman's eyes widened, then narrowed. "That's impossible."

"Impossible?"

"Yes. Impossible."

"Why? Did he tell you I was dead or something?"

"No. It's impossible because his mother lives here with us. In the guest house in the back."

Jeanette put an arm around Sarah. "We must have the wrong house, Sarah."

The woman blinked. "Sarah?"

Feeling a bit of hope Sarah said, "Yes."

"You sent that huge Saguaro cactus?"

"Yes." Minnie answered for her. "From Palm Springs."

"Oh gosh, no wonder. At first we had no idea what that was about. The previous owner of this house was named David."

The woman' smoothed her baby's tiny wisps of hair. "We've been here for two months. Your son was transferred to Baltimore. We have his address. We send him monthly payments on the second mortgage. Would you like to come in? My name's Emma. Would you like something to drink? I just made a pitcher of lemonade. I'll put Brandon down and be right back."

She swung the door wide and moved through the foyer to the stairs. She whispered, "The bathroom's over there. Make yourselves at home."

Emma disappeared up the stairs. The girls stayed on the imported Italian tiles, this time inside the front door in the wide foyer. A lavishly framed mirror showed Sarah what she was, small, alienated, and sad. A nothing.

The living room spilled from the foyer down a single wide step. Sarah tried to imagine her son in that room. What had his furnishings been like? She had no idea where David's tastes ran, could not picture his living style. Sarah didn't know him.

The living room was immaculate, decorated in Southwestern style with palm trees rising nearly to the top of the two-story ceiling. A beautifully landscaped yard was visible through tall, elegant windows. Fifty yards away was a darling cottage; blooming succulents filled planter boxes below shuttered windows. That was where the mother lived. That should have been hers. The cactus she'd sent David as a gift poked out of the shipping crate in front of a garden shed.

"My goodness," Minnie said, "this place is gorgeous."

Jeanette sat. "Right out of Sunset Magazine,"

Emma returned with a tray of glasses and a pitcher of lemonade. Sarah's attention was yanked away from her gloom, from what should have been.

At Emma's bidding, Sarah took a corner of the couch. With a tremble, she took the proffered lemonade. Emma was sweet and amiable. She seemed to understand Sarah's sorrow and embarrassment; she made small talk about her own family and how they loved the house. She inquired about the three friends' road trip. Jeanette and Minnie took up the slack, chatting to let Sarah remain wordless.

When the glasses were drained, Emma retrieved a slip of paper with David's Baltimore address.

At the front door, Emma asked Sarah, "The cactus. What should I do with it?"

"Well, dear, a plant like that has no business in Baltimore. I noticed a spot next to the cottage. I think it would be lovely there. You should get it into the ground soon. I believe it's ready to bloom."

Emma blinked, openly sympathetic. Before her was a woman whose son didn't want to be found. Emma stepped onto the porch and surprised Sarah with a hug.

"Thank you." She said this simply, then disappeared into the house.

Chapter 14

Jeanette drove through New Mexico, then over the border into Texas. She, Sarah, and Minnie stayed somber and quiet, making only small talk between long swaths of silence. It was best to leave Sarah to her thoughts, at least for a little while.

They drove through San Antonio; on the edge of town, before leaving the city limits, Jeanette suddenly pulled over.

"My God! I just remembered. Madame Viola lives here now."

Minnie asked, "Who?"

"Madam Viola Vallé. A psychic. She had a little studio on 47th Street in New York. There's a lot of fake clairvoyants, but Madame Viola was the real deal. She knew everything. She even predicted Alex's arrest. She retired then came to live with her daughter in San Antonio. We kept in touch until she went into a rest home. She would write the most insightful letters."

Sarah perked up. "There can't be that many old folks homes in San Antonio. It's not like we're on a schedule or anything. You want to look her up?"

Minnie said, "I've never met a psychic before. I'm sure it's hogwash. But it could actually be interesting,"

Jeanette pulled next to a gas station phone booth. She tore out the yellow page with all the rest home listings.

In the car, Jeanette held the page in her palm. Closing her eyes, she circled her forefinger in the air and landed it on the page.

"Country Hills Retirement Estates. The spirit guides tell me that this is the one."

Jeanette got directions from the gas station attendant. She drove to the opposite side of town. A few blocks from the rest home, Jeanette pulled into a parking space in front of a curio shop that displayed hunks of amethyst and scrimshaw pieces in its murky windows.

"I want to bring her a gift. Maybe they have prisms. She can hang them from her window to give her a room full of rainbows. It'll remind her of the old days."

This new adventure made Sarah smile. She said, "Perfect idea."

They all got out of the car. "My regular appointment was four o'clock. Perfect timing for a rainbow show." Minnie and Sarah followed Jeanette to the door. "She must have had dozens and dozens of crystals on strings."

In the doorway, Jeanette whispered, "Viola said crystals attract spirits." She put one foot inside the store and came face-to-face with a life-sized sculpture of the grim reaper, scythe raised above his hood. Jeanette shrieked and leaped back, gouging the top of Minnie's sandal with her heel.

Minnie yowled in pain; Jeanette turned to apologize. A hand on her shoulder made her jump and whirl back again. Not the grim reaper but a tall eccentric-looking gent with a halo of frizzy silver hair stood in front of the statue, looking every bit its tall, gaunt, pale twin. Jeanette let out another shriek.

He didn't flinch; perhaps he was accustomed to this reaction. In fact, he grinned as if he anticipated it.

"Ah, yes, the crystals," he said in a soft hypnotic voice. "Right this way." He shuffled towards the back of the shop, his suede moccasins making no sound.

Sarah said, "He couldn't have heard you talking about crystals."

They followed through cluttered aisles. Shelves held pieces of semi-precious stone dimly lit; hanging on cracked plaster walls were paintings of the famous burnings of Salem witches and Joan of Arc.

The clerk removed a string of dusty prisms from a display in a window. He rubbed them on the sleeve of his gray flannel shirt; he held them up but no sun invaded the shabby shop.

"These are beauties. From the apartment of Harry Houdini's mother, they are. I was a very good friend of hers. After Harry's death he would visit her daily through the crystals."

"Really?" Jeanette had moved closer to better hear his breathy voice.

"I was her medium. I became well-acquainted with Harry, too."

Sarah said, "Oh my. You knew Harry Houdini?"

"Not in life, unfortunately. Only in the spirit realm. She sought me out after his physical death." His lined face creased as though he were remembering some distant memory. Abruptly, he brightened. "Excellent choice. Are they for you?"

Jeanette said, "For a friend." Alluding to the arcane atmosphere of the shop, she asked, "Perhaps you know her, Madame Viola Vallé?"

"Madam Viola." The clerk mused skyward and tapped his chin. "Lived down on the boulevard. Used to come in with her daughter. Haven't seen her in years. Figured she had crossed over. She's still with us, you say?"

"Hopefully. I knew her in New York and last I heard she was in a rest home here. We're passing through on our way to Mexico, so I thought I'd look her up."

"Very kind of you. I imagine she would be grateful to see you again." They followed the round-shouldered clerk as he drifted towards the counter where he wrote up the sale. "That will be eighty-two dollars and six cents."

Jeanette pulled out a Master Charge card and handed it to him. The clerk moved to a desk in an alcove. He fumbled for an old black rotary phone buried in a mound of papers.

"I just have to get an authorization."

Minnie asked, "Which card did you give him?"

"I don't know. I wasn't really paying attention."

After hanging up, he scratched his head and looked the card over. Turning his back to them, he dialed again. They couldn't hear his conversation.

He returned to the counter, frowning. "I'm sorry, Mrs. Post, but it seems you can't use this card."

Minnie pulled Jeanette aside to whisper, "You gave him that investigator's card. Let's get out of here."

Jeanette waved her off and turned back to the counter. "I'm sorry. That was my husband's card. I gave you the wrong one. He would have a hissy if he knew I had it. Here." She handed him an American Express.

"Sorry, we don't accept American Express."

Minnie spoke up. "You made a second phone call. What was that for?"

"I thought there might have been a mistake, so I called back to try again."

"Here." Sarah threw four twenties on the counter. "This should take care of it, let's go."

Jeanette held her ground. "No, I want to charge it."

Sarah tugged Jeanette toward the front door. She hissed, "He called the police."

"Don't be ridiculous Sarah."

Minnie added her hands to towing Jeanette from the store. "Don't you be ridiculous. There's got to be a stolen alert on that card now. He's supposed to call the cops. Don't you remember a damn thing I told you? Let's go."

Jeanette turned walking quickly back to the counter. The clerk said, "I'll just wrap this for you."

"No, that's okay." Jeanette reached for the crystals, but he held them away from her.

"It will only take a moment." He ducked under the counter. George's card still lay on the countertop, Jeanette tucked it into her jacket pocket.

When the clerk reappeared with tissue paper and bag, Jeanette reached across the counter and deftly slipped the crystals from his hand. "Thanks just the same." She left the clerk in mid-sentence she couldn't hear not because of his gentle voice but because of the police sirens. Jeanette ran the length of the shop.

Screeching brakes and flashing red lights flowed through the front windows. Two uniformed officers bounded from the squad car. Minnie and Sarah had already left the shop, Jeanette was there alone. She took a deep breath, formulating a plan. If it didn't work, she hoped she could make bail on American Express.

She stepped through the doorway with a worried look, coming face-to-face with two young San Antonio policemen.

She looked back over her shoulder, feigning fright. "Officers, the clerk, the clerk in there, he's got someone cornered. You better hurry."

"Thanks, ma'am." The cops rushed past, pistols in hand.

Jeanette rushed toward the Lincoln, dismayed to see it empty. Suddenly, two familiar heads popped up. Behind the wheel, Minnie started the car. Jeanette jumped into the backseat, barely closing the door before Minnie squealed out and rounded a corner. After two blocks, she sped down a side street. In the distance they heard sirens.

"There, there! Turn right!" Jeanette pointed at a sign for Country Retirement Estates. Minnie turned sharply and sped through the parking lot, Minnie drove behind the building and halted so fast Jeanette and Sarah were slammed forward and back in their seats.

"Get down." Minnie ducked; Jeanette and Sarah obliged. They waited while sirens passed on the street.

After a full minute, the sirens faded into the distance. Minnie peeked, then ducked again. "Let's go."

Sarah said, "Let's get out of town."

Jeanette said, "No. We don't want to be on the streets. We got to lay low."

Minnie said, "Lay low. For heaven's sake, you sound like a gangster. We can't get any lower than this. Let's just hope this is the place. We're not going to cruise around town trying to find her."

Minnie gave Jeanette a hard look. "I want every single credit card you've got stashed in that travel belt."

Jeanette flung open the passenger door. "We'll talk about that later. This is not the time."

Before Minnie could say another word, Jeanette was out of the car and striding toward the back entrance of the rest home.

At the front desk a burly woman pointed them in the direction of room eighty. "She's probably in the day room, though."

Jeanette winked at Minnie and Sarah. "The spirit guides are with us."

Down a fluorescent-lit hallway the odor of urine hit them. In her calfskin bag, Jeanette found a linen hankie to hold over nose.

Patrons lined the corridor, asleep in wheelchairs, others gazing at them expectantly. A few muttered.

Sarah said, "How very strange."

"What's that?" Minnie asked.

"Room eighty. That's the exact amount of money I threw on the counter at the curio shop."

Room eighty was a four-bed ward. One elderly woman in a gray hospital gown slept fitfully. The room was clean, the floor a shiny black-and-white speckled linoleum. The beds were metal-framed, walls barren, and a small window overlooked a busy intersection.

A tiny woman in a wheelchair was at the window. Jeanette approached tentatively. "Viola?" The woman didn't seem to hear.

A nurse's aide entered. "Are you looking for Viola?"

"Yes."

"Follow me. She's in the day room."

The aide led them back down the corridor. An elderly gentleman with a brightly-colored afghan around his shoulders reached out, mumbling incoherently to the aide. She strode past him without a glance.

Sarah paused to take his hand. "Hello."

He answered in a slow, slurred voice.

Not understanding, Sarah gave him a smile. "I hope you're having a wonderful day." When she let go his hand dropped.

The day room was furnished in modern functional furniture. The focal point was a fireplace with a colorful floral print on the wall above it. Heavily draped windows with tie-backs let in afternoon sun through a center panel of sheers.

Two elderly gentlemen in plaid bathrobes played cards quietly in a corner. When the ladies passed, one pinched Minnie on the bottom.

The aide wagged her finger. "Mr. Patterson, you know better than that." Chuckling, he tried to pinch her, but being used to the attempts she swished away from him still wagging her finger.

She led the way to a small, frail woman asleep in a wheelchair by the window. She wore a gray hospital nightgown and a tattered black shawl across her shoulders. Her bifocals rested on the tip of her nose. Her tiny legs were tucked under a blanket.

The aide stopped them six feet away. Softly, she said, "I'm so glad you're here to see her. Three months ago, her daughter was killed in a car accident in Fairfield. She's always asking for her. No one visits now. She has Alzheimer's, you know. So it might be a little difficult."

The aide approached the wheel chair and gently nudged the slumbering woman. "You have visitors, dear."

The chin came up, the eyes opened and flitted dazedly at the group around her. The aide repositioned her to a more upright posture and pushed her glasses up to the bridge of her nose. With a burst of energy the little woman came fully awake and smacked the aide's hand.

"It's okay, Vi. You have friends who've come to visit."

"Jessie?"

The aide said to Jeanette, "Jessie was her daughter."

As she walked away, Viola called, "Jessie, Jessie! Bring me my toast!"

Jeanette pulled up a chair. "It's me, Madame Viola. Jeanette Scapelli. From New York. Remember?"

"You're not my daughter. Where's Jessie? They promised me Jessie would come today."

"Yes, dear. She's sure to be along later. It's me, Jeanette. From New York. Remember?"

The tiny woman squinted fiercely. "I'm closed today. Come back tomorrow."

Minnie and Sarah sat in a semicircle around Madame Viola. Emphatically, the woman told them, "You're not Jessie either!"

Jeanette brought out the prisms from her purse. The old woman's eyes widened in recognition. The crystals swayed and sparkled in the afternoon sun casting the hoped-for rainbows on the cream walls. Madame Viola gasped. Then her eyes closed and her head rotated into a downward nod.

Jeanette whispered, "Goodness, I think she's going into a trance."

Suddenly Madame Viola sat straight up. Her eyes were heavily glazed, focused on nothing. She swayed gently then extended a thin wrinkled arm to Sarah.

"Sarah," she whispered. "Sarah."

In amazement, Sarah looked from the woman to Jeanette. "How does she know...?"

Jeanette shushed her, not taking her eyes off Madame Viola.

"You are full of words and more strength than you know. Your love will blossom again."

Still unfocused, Viola moved her gnarled hand to Minnie, who took it. The medium told her, "The clock of life is wound but once."

Minnie nodded and understood. You only get one chance. Take advantage of it.

The old woman sneezed. Her eyes returned to normal; Jeanette handed her a handkerchief. Viola removed her glasses to wipe her rheumy eyes, then blew her nose. She lay the glasses on the end table next to her water glass.

"Why Jeanette Scapelli. Of all people. It's so very nice to see you."

Jeanette sat up straighter, happy at the recognition. "It's wonderful to see you too, Madame Viola."

The old woman turned to Sarah and Minnie. "Lovely. You've brought friends."

Jeanette made the introductions. Madame Viola nodded to both women. She lifted the gift of the crystals from her lap. "Did you bring me these?" She smiled and dangled them. Rainbows fluttered again on the walls. "Look at that sparkle."

Her face fell. She dropped the crystals to her lap and focused on Jeanette. "Oh dear, Jeanette. Child, you haven't lost your sparkle yet, but you will. In order to get what you want, you must give it away."

"What does that mean, Madame Viola?" Jeanette leaned in.

"I don't know, dear. Only you can interpret. I feel the spirits. I can give you a reading, if you like."

"Yes, please do."

Viola fixed again on the crystals. Her voice lowered and became querulous. "You'll have to come back tomorrow. Jessie. Jessie. You quit that, quit it." She flailed; Jeanette pulled back to avoid a slap.

Refocusing, Viola said, "Oh, hello, Jeanette. You've come for your reading. Let me touch something of yours. Something of metal. Perhaps your emerald ring. Let me hold your hand."

The old woman stroked Jeanette's hand. "Ah, the sparkle, the sparkle." Lowering her face, she nodded, then lifted her eyes, again fogged and unfocused.

"You'll soar through the skies on a bird in flight. You'll get the credit you deserve, if you play your cards right."

Sarah said, "My goodness."

Madame Viola continued: "The man from Panama is not your friend. If you have courage, you'll win in the end.

Escape is easy, if you are aware. The voice of destiny is clear. The solution is illusion."

Viola fell silent, head bowed and veering. "I see a man traveling with you. You left him in a dark place, but not far behind. Don't postpone your departure."

Minnie said, "Post. George Post is chasing us. I'm convinced. Let's get out of here."

Minnie's voice seemed to pull Viola out of her trance. The old woman called for her daughter. "Jessie. Where's my toast? I want my toast and jam."

Her urgings brought the nurse's aide who bent over Viola consolingly. "We'll get that toast now, dear. Just calm yourself." Then to Jeanette, she said, "I think she's had enough for today."

George asked the embarrassed young cop to talk out on the sidewalk. It was too dark inside the curio shop.

The cop said, "She looked like a nice lady. An older woman, five nine, auburn hair, dressed real good. She said the clerk had the perp cornered in the shop. So we rushed in. By the time we got back out here, she was gone."

"Did you get a plate?"

"No. It was a silver 1976 Lincoln Town Car, I can tell you that much. I lost them."

"Don't worry about it. You're not the first one she's tricked. Got an APB out?"

"Yeah."

"If you pick 'em up, do me a favor. Call Sergio Fernandez at City Security Master Charge, okay?"

George handed him the business card. "The bank doesn't want any publicity on this. I'll come back to bring 'em in."

George went inside the curio shop; a life-sized grim reaper greeted him. The statue was supposed to be fearsome but it didn't scare George. He was too familiar with the reaper.

George found the shopkeeper hanging prisms in a window.

"Excuse me. Are you the owner?"

In placid tones the man said, "Yes. May I help you? I have some beautiful crystals from the home of Houdini's mother. Just came in. I'm putting them up now. Care to take a look?"

"My name is George Post. A woman attempted to make a credit card purchase here a little while ago. I'm here to pick up the card."

"Are you the husband?"

George flashed his ID. "I'm with City Security Bank in San Francisco. Have you got the card?"

"I'm afraid I don't. They scurried out of here before I had a chance to stop them."

"You had the card in your hand when you made the call. You were supposed to cut it in half and return it to us. So what did you do, give it back to them?"

"The woman just grabbed it and ran."

"Ran to where?"

"How should I know?"

Quickly, George studied the alignment of the cash register, the counter, the phone on the desk beyond. "I see your phone is well behind the counter on the desk over there. Was anyone behind the counter with you?"

"No."

"Then how could she grab the card from you?"

"I had the card in my hand when I gave the woman her purchase. That's when she grabbed it."

"By returning the credit card to her you're in violation of your merchant agreement. You understand that you can be stripped of your rights to accept credit cards because of this?"

"I am aware. But she was very quick, Mr. Post. Very quick. And quite distracting looking."

"If you can tell me where they were headed, we might let it go this time. We depend on the cooperation of our merchants. You realize you lost out on a fifty dollar reward?"

The old man heaved a weary sigh. "The tall one, she has a friend. A medium, Madame Viola Vallé. Apparently she lives in a local rest home. She said she wanted to visit her before they left for Mexico."

George took out his notepad. "Mexico?"

"That's what she said."

"Which rest home?"

"Honestly, I don't know which one."

"You got a phone book?"

The old man trudged to his desk to rifle through stacks of papers. He returned with a thick volume that seemed an effort to carry.

George flipped to the yellow pages. "I'll need your phone."

The clerk hesitated then motioned George to come around the counter.

On the third call, George located Madame Vallé. He got directions and headed to the door. The clerk stopped him with a touch on his shoulder. George turned to find the man expecting a handshake.

"I'm sorry I didn't recover the card for you. This is a hard business. But they paid for their purchase, you know. With cash. They didn't steal."

The man had an honest face. "I appreciate your cooperation. Don't worry about it, okay?" He shook the clerk's proffered hand.

The clerk said, "The pursuit of innocence can be unrewarding. See instead the intent of the heart."

"Yeah, yeah." At George's exit, the string of bells on the door clanged loudly.

◈

Inside Country Retirement Estates, an aide showed George to the day room, another visitor for Mrs. Viola Vallé.

The aide led him down a long corridor. "This is so nice. Mrs. Vallé hasn't had a visitor in months. You'll be her fourth caller today."

"So my aunt and her friends have already been here?"

"You just missed them, honey."

George pretended to check his watch. "I would have thought they'd wait for me. Did they say where they were going?"

"I'm sorry. I don't know. You may want to check at the front desk. It couldn't have been more than an hour ago."

They entered the day room. An old woman by the window was shouting. "Jessie! Clean up your room, right now."

The nurse shrugged and pointed to the little ranting creature in the wheelchair.

"Is she coherent?"

"She goes in and out. Good luck."

George pulled up a chair. Oblivious, the old woman continued disciplining an imaginary child. "Don't give me any of your back talk, young lady."

George lit up a Marlboro. He tossed the match into an ashtray.

The old woman viewed him through rheumy eyes. "You're not Jessie."

"I'm George, Mrs. Vallé. I understand you've had some other visitors today. Was it Jeanette Compton?" He tried to spur her memory. "Minnie Barlow? Sarah Gardner? Just a little while ago."

"You're not Jessie."

George dragged on the cigarette. He noticed the string of prisms lay on the little end table beside the ashtray. He held them out to her. "They brought you this present, remember?"

Viola Vallé examined the prisms in the sunlight. "You're in the dark, traveling stranger. A black heart will bring you danger. The pursuit of innocence is unrewarding. Look to the intent of the heart."

George dropped the prisms onto the tabletop. He'd puzzle later about the oddity of hearing those same words in the curio shop and in a rest home.

"Where did they go?"

But the spell was broken. The woman resumed raving at unseen Jessie. George stood to leave. Behind him,

Viola shouted, "Let my people go!" Then she muttered something unintelligible. George returned to her side and squatted beside her wheelchair.

"What did you say?"

"There is no party, no Mardi Gras." She clenched her jaw and stared out the window. George waited but nothing more was forthcoming. He left the building.

In the parking lot, George spread a United States map on the hood of the car. Where would they go next? Mexico wasn't their destination; that was just to throw him off the scent. He traced his finger the route from San Francisco to Palm Springs to San Antonio, then east until it stopped on New Orleans. The old medium had said something about Mardi Gras.

"Good a place as any." At a gas station pay phone, he checked in with Sergio.

Chapter 15

Sergio hung up with a hearty laugh.

He'd been teasing George, despite the fact that George was royally pissed. "It's personal now," George said. "They're trying to use my card."

Even funnier were the leads George was following: one from an eccentric mystic shop clerk with prophetic observations; another tip from an Alzheimer's patient, to head to Mardi Gras which had been over for four months. Sergio also took a jab at George's supposition that this job would be 'a piece of cake.'

Tom the collection manager approached. He plopped a data binder on Sergio's desk. "Here's the new EAJ. There's more activity on the Clarke account. The balance is over twenty grand now. Doesn't look like anybody's bothering to check the Warning Bulletin. They're all small purchases, under the floor limit. Weren't you investigating a Minnie Barlow in that case?"

"Yep."

"Well, check this out." Tom ran his finger down the EAJ. "Looks like we've got another card to pick up. Barlow's fifteen grand over her limit. Put George on it."

Sergio couldn't believe it. Only last week the balance was hovering at the credit limit. In a short span she'd gone way over. Minnie Barlow must've been having one hell of a vacation.

Compton had stolen Clarke's card, then George's card, and now this. The time had come to take some serious action. At the CRT, Sergio placed a closed status on Minnie Barlow 's account. Then he ordered up the sales drafts. She was working it like a pro. Someone must have taught her the ropes. Perhaps that 'someone' was her nephew, Marc Corbett.

Sergio took the elevator to the twelfth floor. Nancy intercepted him in the hallway.

"Hi, Sergio."

"Hey. Is Marc around?"

"He went to lunch with Ms. Duvall."

"Did he say what time he's coming back?"

"Probably by two unless." With sarcasm, she added, "Unless they decide to have another nooner."

"Jealous?"

"Hah! Of her? I've got no respect for a woman who sleeps her way to the top. She makes a bad name for all of us." Phil Southern rounded a corner. Nancy sweetened. "Hello, Mr. Southern."

Sergio decided to seize the opportunity. "Mr. Southern, I wonder if I could have a word with you."

Southern handed Nancy a sheaf of papers. She retreated without a word.

"What's on your mind?"

"Can we go into your office?"

Southern led the way. Inside, Sergio explained the circumstances around the Clarke and Barlow cases. He was cautious when bringing up Marc Corbett. Sergio only alluded to it, and let Southern draw the conclusion.

When Sergio finished, Southern leaned back and looked skyward. "Sounds like you believe Marc Corbett has given them inside information."

"I don't want to make a direct accusation, but it appears so."

"What do you want me to do about this?"

"I thought I should inform you, that's all. Perhaps you have an insight. Perhaps there's something I've overlooked..." His voice trailed off as he realized this move might have been inappropriate.

"Marc is a valuable employee, dedicated, loyal, hardworking. Hard to believe he'd be part of a conspiracy like this."

"A conspiracy isn't what I'm implying."

"I think you're barking up the wrong tree. It's not as if all this information they're using for personal gain isn't readily available."

Did Southern always talk this way, like he was writing a business letter? Sergio thanked him for his time and left worried that he'd made a mistake, a drastic political mistake, by talking to Southern. But if he had spoken to Marc, he would just have gotten another Gee-whiz-I-don't-really-know-what's-going-on response.

The next morning, the sales drafts arrived in a brown envelope via interoffice mail. Sergio arranged them on his desk chronologically, trying to read Minnie Barlow's mind through her transactions.

Among the dinner, spa, concerts, gift shops, clothing stores, and luxury hotel tags was a sales draft for a helicopter ride over the Grand Canyon. Sergio admired their bravado; his own grandmother rarely left her knitting.

All the signatures on the sales drafts matched the one on Mrs. Barlow's credit application. It appeared she was responsible for the charges.

Sergio went to the CRT monitor to punch in Barlow's account number. The screen filled with the account history. Sergio paged down until he saw it.

The balance was zero.

A bank-originated entry made this morning had reversed the balance. It wasn't a payment. Someone inside the bank had created the entry. The closed status was removed, allowing Mrs. Barlow to continue her spending rampage.

When Sergio tried to return the status to closed, the computer issued a warning: "Unauthorized, Access Refused."

He called Frannie over.

"Look at this shit. The Minnie Barlow account. Fifteen grand on a skip and someone reversed the balance. What the fuck?"

 Who would do that?"

"Barlow has a nephew working upstairs. And he's a computer programmer. How much you want to bet it's him?"

Before Frannie could reply, Sergio was out of his chair and headed to Carl Jenkins' office. He called to Frannie, "Get a hard copy of that reversing entry for me."

Wearily, Jenkins said, "Thanks for the information. Bring me everything you have on the Barlow and Clark cases. We'll handle it from here."

"I don't understand. Why..."

"And you shouldn't have bothered Mr. Southern yesterday with your crazy theories."

"I'm just trying to get to the bottom of this. But Jeanette Comptom. She's the one..."

Again Jenkins cut him off. "You don't have proof." He leaned forward and smiled, a surprise to Sergio. "You've been working too hard. Why don't you take the rest of the week off?"

"Please, sir, you have to listen."

"I told you we'll handle it from here. You've ruffled some feathers. You've got a stack of sick time coming. Just bring me the files and take off." Jenkins waved him toward the door, then picked up his phone and swiveled to face the windows.

Sergio returned to his desk, astounded that he hadn't heard Jenkins say, "Good work." He needed to find a way to prove his suspicions about Jeanette Comptom, or face reassignment to the basement file room.

Slump-shouldered, Sergio filed the other accounts he'd been working and closed his follow-up book. He reflected how, finally, he'd gotten an interesting case, and they snatched it away. He put on his sheepskin jacket.

Frannie poked her head around the corner. "Data Processing just called. They won't have that bank-originated on Barlow until six o'clock. They'll messenger it over."

"Call them back and--" Sergio stopped. Carl Jenkins wanted proof? Fine. This could be proof. The bank-originated entry would bear an authorized signature.

"Scratch that. I'll be back at six. Thanks, Frannie. If it comes before I'm back, put it in my top drawer."

"What's going on?"

Sergio rested his palms on her desk. "I don't know yet. But don't talk about this to anybody okay? Promise me."

"Tell me."

"I can't right now. I'll call you tonight."

"Okay. But you're going to owe me a drink for this."

"I pay for your drinks half the time anyway."

"Top drawer. You got it."

Sergio headed out.

Melanie lay beside Marc on the king-sized hotel bed. The afternoon sun glistened on her sweat.

Marc caught his breath then found he had to catch it again. Never had he met anyone so aggressive, so exciting, and so beautifully formed. She lay with eyes closed and one arm thrown across her forehead.

He propped his chin on one hand, and with the other reached for the glass of ice water on the nightstand. The clock there told him the time.

"Shit!"

"What's wrong?"

"It's three thirty. I've got to get back to the office."

"Don't worry. I told Southern you were taking me sightseeing." She dipped fingertips in his water then walked them up his chest. Marc resisted the allure and cool of it.

"I've got to finish up something on the SuperCredit project."

"Southern put Brad on that."

Marc fell back on the pillow. "Great. That means I'll have to redo the whole thing tomorrow."

"No you won't. I've got a surprise for you. We're leaving tomorrow for Hawaii."

"What?" He sat up again.

"Yep. A week in the islands. NCCA is paying for me and a guest. I got a bonus. I told Southern I'm taking you and he agreed to it. You won't even lose any pay."

"No shit?"

"No shit, big boy."

He kissed her lightly, not to start another fire but to thank her. This was what he'd been waiting for, working for, the ladder up.

Melanie whispered, "I'm famished." She swung her legs over the side of the bed.

He took up the room service menu. She pushed it down. "Let's go to the restaurant. I'll take a quick shower."

After Melanie finished in the bathroom, Marc took his own shower. When he emerged in a towel, Melanie had slipped into a tight white dress. Her tanned legs curved in delicious lines below the short hemline.

Marc said, "You won't make it out of this room looking like that."

"Get dressed."

Marc dropped the towel, spread his arms wide to make her one last offer then threw on his clothes.

In the Fairmont's restaurant, they were seated in a sunny booth surrounded by flowering plants. Melanie ordered oysters on the half shell, green salads, and a bottle of Chablis.

"Like we need oysters," Marc took her hand. "I've never met anyone like you, Mel. You're incredible."

"You're not so bad yourself."

He wanted to tell her he was in love. Intuition told him to keep it to himself; he'd only scare her off. Besides, even though they'd spent every day and night together since they met, it had been only ten days. A whirlwind.

She was worldly in ways he was not. Not only was she three years older and obviously more experienced but Melanie was in the big leagues of the banking world, on a par with executives and board directors.

And the news had gotten even better. NCCA had transferred her to San Francisco. Melanie's two-week stint had turned into a permanent assignment. Marc was joyful, and hopeful their fling could become something loving and lasting.

She interrupted his daydream. "How's the SuperCredit project coming along?"

Her input could be valuable. Marc told her his concerns with the programming elements. Finishing, he said, "From the way Southern told me to set it up, it looks like those balances will just disappear into outer space a month after they're posted."

She set down her wine glass. "I don't see how you come to that conclusion. You don't know much about accounting, do you?"

"I took one-oh-one at Berkeley. But I don't see how it's an accounting problem."

"Believe me, it is. Okay. A customer gets an advance for a hundred thousand on his SuperCredit line, right? The receivable is debited, funds are credited. Interest is computed. That's the variable you programmed in, correct?"

"Right."

"Okay, that's debited to the receivable, credited to interest income. So what's the problem?"

"There's one program string Southern gave me. It appears to be a reversing entry."

"Impossible. It's probably a payment accommodation string."

"That's in there already. This is something extra."

Melanie lit up. "Oh, I know what you're talking about. It's the same thing we have at NCCA. It looks really weird doesn't it? Is this the first time you've programmed variable interest?"

"Yeah, it is." Marc was starting to feel stupid.

"No wonder. Freaked me out the first time I saw it, too. But when I traced it out, it made sense. Don't worry about it. Listen, you really should take some more accounting classes. Most computer applications are for accounting programs anyway. I majored in computer science and minored in accounting. It really helped me understand debits and credits."

She took a sip of white wine then scooted closer. Taking his hand, she placed it high on her thigh, moving his fingers, encouraging him to roam behind the private long folds of the linen tablecloth.

And roam he did.

Sergio didn't get back to the bank until six-thirty. He signed in with the security guard then took the elevator. The crew of night collectors was busy calling the sixty-day delinquents.

Frannie had put the envelope from Data Processing in his desk drawer as promised, with a note: "Come to the Sails and buy me that drink." He ripped open the envelope to find a copy of a microfiche copy, barely discernible due to lack of contrast. In the half-page explanation box where one would normally see "merchant return authorization," or "customer service dispute resolution," was a single word: "Credit." At the bottom above the line marked 'authorized signature' he could barely make out the scrawl. With a magnifying glass, Sergio read: 'Marc Corbett.'

Sergio headed briskly to Jenkins' office. Everyone had gone home at five, but In Jenkins' corner office behind the closed Venetian blinds, a lamp burned.

Jenkins wanted proof. Sergio had proof. He tapped the envelope against his palm. It was hard to believe Marc would do something so stupid. But family always had family's back, so maybe it wasn't so tough to believe. This would justify Sergio's talking to Southern. He'd exonerate himself, save his job, and his career.

Jenkins' office door was ajar. As he approached, he heard Jenkins on the phone. Jenkins said two familiar names: Corbett, and SuperCredit.

Sergio crept closer.

Jenkins laughed. "Hawaii. Good idea. Mel's all over him, he won't be able to see straight. No, no, don't worry about Brad either, that dumbass has no shot at figuring this out."

Jenkins' voice rose. "What was I supposed to do? You jumped the gun so I took the case from him. Yes, the sonofabitch knows. But he's only here for a paycheck, he won't give it another thought. Jesus, I thought *I* worried too much. Stop acting like a goddamn child. The timing isn't that fucked up. I'm telling you, we'll be in the clear."

Jenkins lowered his voice again. "Get a grip, we're close. Remember, we're talking about forty million bucks."

A long silence was followed by more laughter. "We'll keep Post on it. He'll bring them in. Barlow will be the clincher."

Noiselessly, Sergio backed away and hurried for the elevator. He punched the call button over and over again. "Hurry up, hurry up."

Forty-million bucks? Brad, Mel, who were they? Sergio didn't know either of those guys. Jenkins was part of the development team for SuperCredit, but how did that tie in to the Barlow Master Charge account, and to Sergio? And what was Jenkins saying about Corbett?

The elevator doors couldn't open fast enough to get Sergio away with all his questions, all those secrets.

Jenkins set down the phone and noticed for the first time that his office door was ajar. He went to it and peered out, but no one was lurking, the large room and halls were empty and dim.

He finished his work, and when he was done a half hour later, the plan was in motion. On his way out, he stopped at Frannie's desk to see if the envelope from DP with the Barlow credit had arrived. He didn't see anything from DP in her in-basket. He checked her desk drawers. Maybe DP hadn't gotten around to it yet.

Downstairs, he signed out at the guard desk. Every night, he chatted baseball with the security guard Frank, an Oakland A's fan. Carl was a devoted fan of the Giants.

"Somebody ought to shoot Billy Martin."

Frank said, "Hell, Billy's the star of the show. I like watching him more than the team."

Carl signed in the Out column. "Of course you do. The A's can't play for shit."

Sergio's signature was right above where Carl's pen paused. He'd signed in at six thirty-five and out at six forty-seven. Twelve minutes. What was Sergio doing here? Carl's watch said it was seven ten.

Frank made some sarcastic remark about the Giant's pitching; Jenkins didn't hear.

"I left something upstairs. I'll be right back."

Carl went directly to Sergio's desk and searched it. He found nothing, but every instinct told him Sergio had the copy of the credit.

Sergio would see Marc Corbett's signature. He'd come straight to see his boss, try to be a hero, try to save his fucking job. He'd see the lamp shining in Carl's office, the door cracked open, wait outside to avoid interrupting Carl's phone conversation, and listen.

"Goddammit." Mentally, Carl kicked himself. Something would have to be done about this. Right away

Chapter 16

"I'm glad you called, Na Na. I'm leaving in a couple of hours for Hawaii.

"That's wonderful. But I didn't know you had a vacation planned."

"It just came up. It's a bonus from the bank. Melanie and I will be on Kauai. Let me give you the phone number at the hotel there."

Minnie scribbled the number in pencil in her address book.

Marc said, "I want you to check in with me every couple of days."

"I will. So, this thing with Melanie, is it getting serious?"

"I've only known her for a week and a half. But she's something. I'm liking her more every day. So, enough about me. Where are you?"

"New Orleans."

"What's the latest?"

"You tell me."

"No one's been nosing around me for a while. And I don't want to do any nosing of my own, it would look suspicious. I figure if I run into Sergio in the elevator or something, I'll just casually ask him what's going on. So, are you and the girls having fun?"

Minnie didn't want to worry Marc. "We're having a wonderful time. I finally got to see the Grand Canyon." That wasn't a lie. It was simply half the truth.

She wished Marc a fun-filled vacation and lots of good luck with Melanie, then hung up.

Minnie examined her dogeared address book. An entire page had been devoted to Marc over the years. At the top was the farm's number in Missouri, followed by the hallway pay phone in his UC Berkeley dorm; next was the phone for his Berkeley apartment where he roomed with two chums, then his studio on Green Street in San Francisco; near the bottom of the page was the info for his one-bedroom on Parnassus where he'd been so proud of the view of Golden Gate Park and the top the Golden Gate Bridge. Finally came the address and numbers for his beautiful house in the Marina district overlooking the Bay. The page was a history of Marc's ascent in the world. She hoped that she hadn't screwed it up for him.

She regretted she couldn't be present to celebrate his upcoming promotion and to meet this woman who seemed to have captured his heart. He refused to admit he was in love, but Minnie knew by the lilt in his voice and how he downplayed his enthusiasm.

Her phone rang.

"Hello?"

No one answered, only the faint sibilance of breathing, then a click and dead air. Minnie hung up.

Sarah, waiting in the doorway of Minnie's hotel room, asked, "Who was that?"

"They hung up. Probably a wrong number." Minnie rose from the bed. "We better get going before we lose our dinner reservation. Is Jeanette ready?"

Sarah looked down the corridor. "She's coming now." Sarah beamed, "My, she looks like a movie star."

Minnie and Sarah met her in the hall. Long folds of green-black satin swished over the carpet at Jeanette's feet. A chinchilla stole draped her shoulders in soft folds. Her hair was done up in a French twist, secured with an alabaster fan-shaped barrette. Emerald earrings and necklace completed the glamor.

Jeanette said, "Minnie, look at you. Absolutely gorgeous."

Minnie never thought of herself as gorgeous even in her youth. Her eyes had always been a deep blue that changed to purple gray in some light, but they were small, efficient eyes like a bird's, spaced too close together. Her high cheekbones could have been dramatic if they were not on such a long face. Her thin lips were nicely defined and shaped, her teeth even and straight, but nothing about her mouth was sensuous. Still, she had a perfect nose, nicely upturned, and she never had to worry about weight. Minnie was athletic, small-breasted and upright.

Tonight, as she had for the months since they'd begun this adventure with credit, Minnie felt young. Beautiful. The colors of her eyes and the shape of her body could assert themselves again. The gray was gone from her hair and her life.

"Thank you. But you. You are definitely the glamor queen."

Jeanette curtsied. "And Sarah. Fantastic!"

The simple black dress Sarah wore with a chevron shaped golden belt elongated her body, minimizing her plumpness to make her appear taller and slimmer. Sarah glowed. "Thank you."

Walking down the stairs, Sarah said, "I wonder about that call. I hate it when people just hang up. It's so rude and unnerving."

Minnie said, "You don't suppose that was George Post? Is he in New Orleans? Let's check with the manager."

Jeanette made a show of consulting her diamond-encrusted watch, and complained they were going to be late.

At the front desk Minnie spoke to the clerk. "I'm Minnie Barlow, room twenty-two. Did someone call my room a few moments ago?"

"A gentleman tried to reach you. It was an outside call. Didn't he get through?"

A man. A man who heard her say hello. It wouldn't have been Marc, unless somehow the connection was lost. But he surely would have called back. "He hung up just as I answered. Did he happen to identify himself?"

"He didn't. As a matter of fact he seemed more interested in acquiring your room number than in talking to you."

"You didn't give him my room number, did you?" Minnie asked.

"We never give out that information." The clerk sounded offended.

"Sorry." Minnie bit her lip.

The clerk leaned across the front desk. "Is something wrong?"

From her purse, Minnie pulled a twenty-dollar bill. "Please, if he calls back or comes by looking for us, would you tell him we checked out?"

The clerk took the bill. He whispered, "Of course. I can't help but observe that you are perhaps in some trouble?"

"I hope not. Thank you."

Minnie and her friends left the hotel, looking about as they walked down Canal Street.

George Post parked his rental car in front of the hotel. He lit a Marlboro, then stepped out to lean against a wall where he could watch the entrance and see up and down the street. Frannie had rented him a Ford Maverick. For James Garner. Smart aleck Sergio was probably behind that. George flicked his cigarette in a line drive to the curb. He entered the hotel and approached the front desk.

"I'm here to see Minnie Barlow."

The desk clerk, whose name tag read Lavon, said, "Mrs. Barlow has checked out." Lavon returned his attention to some paperwork.

George didn't buy it. It was eight p.m. and Minnie had answered the phone only fifteen minutes ago. Credentials and straight talk didn't always work in New Orleans; he dangled a hundred dollar bill before Lavon. It got his attention. George said matter-of-factly, "I don't think so."

Checking to see that no one was looking, Lavon reached for the bill. George pulled it back.

"Are they in right now?"

"Money first."

George laid the bill on the countertop, one hand covering half of it. Lavon laid his hand on the other half and spoke softly. "They went out. I don't know where. They were all dressed up. Probably for dinner. If you'd like to wait in the bar, I'll let you know the moment they return." Lavon tugged at the bill but George held fast.

"How long do they plan to stay here?"

"They're checking out tomorrow."

George snatched the bill away from the counter and Lavon's hand. "I'll be in the lounge. You let me know the minute they get back. Here." He dug into his pocket again for a twenty, which he flung onto the counter. "You'll get the rest when I see Barlow."

George stalked off to the bar.

Minnie whispered, "Jeanette, stop that."

"I can't help it. Look at him, he's gorgeous. And that smile." The lone diner at the next table had noticed Jeanette and was eating up the attention.

Minnie asked quietly, curiously, "Have you ever had a one night stand?"

Jeanette did not take her eyes off of her object d' arte. "What do you think?"

Minnie chose instead to chew on a shrimp. Sarah paused, a spoonful of turtle soup at her lips, to ask, "I've only been with my husband. Never thought about it before. What's it like, you wild woman?"

Jeanette's admirer smiled and winked as he worked on his salad. Jeanette said to Sarah, "Imagine what it's like. And it's like that."

When the bill arrived, Minnie was ready with her Master Charge card. The waiter said, "I'm sorry, cash only." He put the tray on the corner of the table and left.

Minnie said, "Give me some money. I've only got twenty dollars on me."

Jeanette had no cash, Sarah only ten dollars.

Minnie groused. "I can't believe they don't take credit cards. The bill is eighty bucks."

Jeanette's man came to stand beside their table. Well dressed in a tailored dark suit with white tie, he must have been at least six-foot five.

"Good evening, ladies. I overheard your predicament. Please, allow me." He lay a hundred dollar bill on the tab.

Minnie said, "No, we wouldn't think of it."

Jeanette smiled up into his chocolate eyes. "You're a lifesaver."

Minnie told him, "We'll pay you back. We have the money, just not here."

"You can repay me by being my guests tonight. I'm playing at the Famous Door. It's on Bourbon Street. We start in an hour."

"We'd be delighted," Jeanette said. "I thought you were a musician. Isn't that what I told you, Minnie?"

Minnie said sullenly, "Yes. We'll bring the money."

"No need for that. It's my pleasure. See you in an hour."

Jeanette watched him walk out. "He's so sexy, don't you think? Tall, dark, stunning. Such fine clothes. It's so hard to tell an older man's age. What do you think? Sixty? I'd guess sixty."

Sarah said, "Kind of old for you, isn't he Jeanette?"

Minnie said, "I don't think this is a good idea. Let's just go back to the hotel and get some money."

"You should never decline a gift from a man. What's wrong with you?"

"What's wrong with you? You're creating an obligation."

"An obligation to honor him with my presence, that's all. Let's walk to his club."

Arriving at the Famous Door, the maître d ushered them to a table marked 'Reserved' in front of the bandstand. A waiter approached; before they placed their drink orders, Minnie asked, "Do you take credit cards?" The baffled server said, "We do."

"I'll have a glass of house white."

Sarah ordered the same; Jeanette, a champagne cocktail.

The lights went down. A five-piece jazz combo opened with a bouncy number. Center stage was Jeanette's tall friend on trumpet. At the end of the song, he winked at Jeanette.

"I'm dedicating this next little ditty to Sweet Thing here." He gestured to Jeanette, then raised his trumpet.

"He's good." Jeanette said. "I love jazz."

At the end of the first set, he joined them and bought rounds. His name was Tone Palmer.

After a few white wines, Minnie seemed to forget her reservations and tapped her fingers to Tone's melodies. Sarah bummed a cigarette from a man at a neighboring table then ended up with him on the tiny parquet dance floor.

Minnie and Jeanette were repeatedly asked to dance. Jeanette declined, staying at the table to stare at Tone.

The combo broke into a fast tune, a favorite of the locals. The crowd sang along to the words about a Creole and an alligator.

When the final set ended, Cajun music from a jukebox took over. Minnie and Sarah stayed on the dance floor. Tone joined Jeanette at the table.

"How'd you like to take a stroll along the river?"

"That would be wonderful. I'll tell my friends when they quit dancing."

"I'll pack up and be back in ten minutes."

"I'll be right here."

Minnie fretted throughout their walk back to the hotel.

Minnie said, "A total stranger. And a musician."

Sarah waved Minnie's concerns off into the scented evening. "She's having fun. The manager told us he's been playing there for fifteen years. He sounds okay."

"I don't like it."

"The clock of life is wound but once."

"So you think that's what it means, huh?"

"I do."

Reaching the hotel, Sarah put a restraining hand on Minnie's arm. "What if Post is in there waiting?"

"Let's use the side entrance."

Minnie and Sarah followed the cracked sidewalk around the side gate of the ancient hotel to the central courtyard. They paused behind the gate's wrought iron curlicues to peer into the lush courtyard. Tables and chairs surrounded a bubbling fountain on a brick patio. The French doors were open, the desk clerk was at his station beneath a humming ceiling fan.

The rooms were stacked in three stories overlooking the courtyard. Minnie opened the gate for Sarah and her to slide inside. Quietly they ascended the stairwell to Minnie's room.

"We made it." Sarah shut the door. Minnie reached for the switch on the bed lamp.

Sarah whispered, "Leave them off."

"You're being overly dramatic."

Just as Minnie was about to click on the lamp, a tapping came at the door.

The two women froze. Sarah put fingers to her lips, then moved to the window to peek out from behind the heavy drapes.

"It's the desk clerk."

She opened the door to motion him in.

He stepped inside. "Mrs. Barlow. The man who called has been waiting in the bar for several hours."

Sarah threw her hand to her mouth to stifle a gasp.

Minnie asked. "Didn't you tell him we checked out?"

"Of course. But he didn't believe me. Not only that, but he was willing to pay me a hundred dollars to alert him to your return."

"Did you take the money?"

"He's been waiting quite a while. He'll be mad if I don't tell him you're here now."

Sarah pleaded. "But, you can't tell him."

Minnie said, "You took the money, didn't you?"

"If you make it worth my while, I can think of something better to throw him off track. A hundred fifty would do it."

"That's blackmail."

"I'm trying to help you out. Would you rather talk to him?"

"No."

"Well?"

"Just give him the money," Sarah said.

"I don't have a hundred-fifty," Minnie lied. "I can pay you a hundred."

"Okay, a hundred."

"What are you going to tell him?"

"That you never came back."

Minnie pulled open the nightstand drawer. Turning her back to the clerk she removed a hundred dollar bill from a stack hidden inside the Gideon Bible.

"Pleasure doing business with you." The clerk left.

Minnie and Sarah still felt unsettled. The possibility of being double crossed again was disconcertingly high.

Minnie said, "Even if Jeanette was here, we can't leave with Post downstairs."

"This is like the movies." Sarah's face was rosy, luminous from the drinks, dancing, the walk, and something else. Excitement.

"Are you okay?"

George rubbed his face. "Yeah, fine. You got a Bromo?"

The waitress said, "I'll be right back."

His watch said it was two forty-five in the morning. How long had he been passed out? Drinking on an empty stomach was never a good idea.

George downed the Bromo and tried to suppress the accompanying belch. He threw some twenties on the bar and went to the lobby. Walking was difficult, his back was killing him.

"Goddammit," he said to the clerk. "Where are those women? Did they come back yet?"

"Ssh, please, sir." The lobby was completely empty. "No, they haven't."

George continued in the same loud tone. "I've been sitting in that bar for six hours."

"This is New Orleans, friend. People party all night long in this town."

George scratched his head. Had this little weasel double-crossed him? He looked like the type.

At the point of exhaustion, George found it difficult to think clearly. "I'd like a look at their room."

"I can't…"

"Why don't we just have a look at that room? I'd hate to think you're jerking me around."

George balled both fists on the check-in counter where the clerk could see them, and his intent for them.

"I don't want any trouble." The clerk retrieved a room key from a brass hook.

The room was empty, the beds unmade. Towels littered the bathroom floor.

"What the fuck?"

"Well, I'll be. They must have come in another way and cleared out. The boss is gonna be pissed. They didn't pay their bill and that's going to come out of my pay." The clerk extended his hand expectantly toward George.

"Fuck you." George lowered himself wearily onto the edge of the bed, wishing for sleep. He'd had it for the day. "Why don't you just check me into this room right here."

"But it's not made up."

"I don't give a shit. Get rid of those dirty towels and have housekeeping bring me some clean ones and some soap tomorrow morning."

The clerk gathered up the soiled towels. He left the key on the nightstand and went quietly out the door.

George undressed down to his skivvies and fell back onto the unmade bed, disappointed.

They strolled arm in arm along the riverbank. Though it was three in the morning, other walkers were about on the warm full moon night. They passed couples embracing on the edge of the wall overlooking the Mississippi.

"Do you know? I was here for Mardi Gras thirty years ago, and I saw you play."

"You remember me from back then?"

"In the restaurant, I didn't. But, Tone, as soon as you lifted that trumpet, it came back."

"Tell me."

"God, those were wild times. The night I saw you, we were at a party on St. Charles Street. Big mansion. Everyone was drunk and carrying on. There were couples making love in the yard, in the fountains. Tabletop dancing. Your band was in the ballroom at the De Bonneville's."

She put fingertips to his face.

"I remember a younger version. Very handsome, with that birthmark on your cheek. It had to be you."

They strolled to the short wall overlooking the Mississippi.

"I remember the lights lowered and a single spotlight on you. You played a solo, soft and sweet, it had a plaintive quality. Joel and I danced to you. That's a special memory in my book."

"I wished I would've seen you. Don't know how I could have missed you. I would have snapped you up and we could have made a lot of good memories of our own. So, where's Joel now?"

"He died. He died that night. That's why my memory is so clear. I don't think I could ever forget that night as long as I live. It was the sweetest time with him. But it was the last."

"I'm so sorry. What happened?"

"He was called back to New York on business. He was scheduled for a charter flight at 2:00 a.m. so he left right after that dance. I was staying on in New Orleans for the rest of the week with friends. His plane crashed over Alabama, in the mountains." Jeanette shuddered and rubbed her arms.

Tone pulled her to his chest and kissed her forehead. "Ah, little Sweet Thing. Sometimes life shows us the back of her hand."

"Then life goes on." Jeanette took his hand and began walking again.

"You married now?" he asked.

"I've had my fill of marriages. I've been on my own for the last seven years and it's been kind of rough. But I'm at that point where rough or not, I enjoy my independence. It's kind of nice not having to answer to anybody. How about you?"

"I'm a New Orleans fixture. Never been married. Come close a couple of times, but they all came to their senses and left me. Pretty sure I got a few kids scattered about. What about you, you got children?"

"One daughter in New York. Natalie. Joel was her father. I'll be seeing her and my little granddaughter in a few weeks."

"Grandkids. Now that's something special, Sweet Thing."

"No one ever called me that before. It's cute."

Tone put his arm around her shoulder and turned her. They kissed gently.

"My place is just around the corner, Sweet Thing. How about a night cap?"

"That sounds wonderful." The full moon caught the sparkle in his chocolate eyes.

◆

"God, it's four in the afternoon." Minnie pulled Jeanette into their room. "Where have you been? We've been worried sick."

"You have no idea what's been happening." Furtively, Sarah checked the hallway before slamming the door. "We haven't dared to leave the room all day. That George Post was waiting for us last night when we came back."

Minnie asked Jeanette, "Did he see you?" She peeked through the drapes.

"I didn't see anyone. I doubt he saw me."

"We're all packed."

Sarah said, "And claustrophobic." Sarah pointed outside. "George Post spent the night here. Right here, in this hotel. We paid the night clerk to keep him off our trail, so he showed Post an empty room and said it was ours, and that we'd just left."

Minnie picked up the thread: "Post had breakfast in the courtyard. Stayed there sipping coffee watching the entrance and the lobby. Then he started knocking on doors room to room. I called the desk and told the day manager. The manager said he didn't like the look of the guy so he told Post we'd already left."

Sarah said, "He could be just sitting in his car waiting for us. Did you see anything?"

Jeanette grabbed her face in both hands to escape the hangover and the ping-ponging between her two friends.

"I came in through the back, so no." Jeanette bit her lip thoughtfully. "I'm supposed to meet Tone for dinner at seven."

"Oh, for heaven's sake!" Minnie came off the bed. "You can forget about that. We've got to come up with a plan. Now think, girls, think."

Jeanette and Sarah, together, rattled their heads. They had nothing.

Minnie put hands on her hips, standing between them.

"I hate to have to do this. But I'm going to call Marc."

The phone rang in the tiny bungalow. In a silver bucket, ice settled with a scuttling sound. A gecko skittered along the top of the big picture window that looked out over swaying palms, white sand, and an azure ocean. Marc chased Melanie, both nude, across their private beach. He caught her, and together they dove into the clear, warm Pacific.

"He doesn't answer."

"Let's just make a break for it." Sarah paced. "I've been in this room too damn long."

Minnie said, "He sees our car. That's why he's still here."

Jeanette said, "Girl, stay calm. I have an idea. I was just in the back of the hotel. If Post is out front, he can't watch every exit. We'll get a cab to pick us up in the back. We can sneak out through the delivery entrance where I came in. We'll go to the airport and fly to Miami."

George stubbed his Marlboro in the overflowing ashtray. He sipped a coffee gone cold on the dashboard. It was starting to get dark; the Lincoln Town Car hadn't moved. He'd circled the hotel ten times, then parked in different spots, always with a view of the Lincoln.

That weasel clerk Lavon came up the street. The shifty little bastard had steered George wrong and taken his cash. He must be headed in for the night shift. George got out of the car.

Time for a little exercise.

Chapter 17

Sergio opened one eye. The clock on the bedside stand said it was already eleven-thirty.

He hadn't slept in like that for ages. And never on a Wednesday. As he sat up, a throb started above his right eye then swept across his skull into his shoulders. He groaned; he and Frannie had shut down The Sails, drank way too much. He sat for a while gently rocking his neck back and forth, trying to release the tension. No one was on the other side of the bed. Good.

He stumbled to the kitchen to start the coffee and suck down four aspirins.

Sergio rubbed his eyes and drank the brew staring out the window. It was a painfully blue-skied day in Noe Valley.

After a hot shower, three cups of coffee and a few shoulder rolls, he could focus. Time for a fishing expedition. He lay back down in bed and called the main number for the bank.

After a transfer, Nancy answered on the first ring, "Marc Corbett's office, Nancy speaking."

"This is Sergio Fernandez from Master Charge. Is Marc in?"

"I'm sorry he's out of town."

"That's right. He's in Hawaii, but I can't remember where he said he was staying."

"Would you like me to take a message?"

"Can you tell me where he's staying? It's really important."

"No, Sergio, I can't do that."

"Well, at least tell me what island he's on."

"Kauai. I can tell him you called if he checks in. But he hasn't checked in so far."

"When's he coming back?"

"Sunday afternoon. Due back in the office on Monday."

"Thanks Nancy." Sergio hung up. So it was Marc they sent to Hawaii. Piecing that together with what Jenkins had said, it sounded like they'd gotten rid of Marc for a week, too. Maybe Frannie was right. Maybe Marc wasn't a conspirator, just a pawn.

It looked like a set up. They probably forged his name on the credit reversing his aunt's card balance, making it look like he was helping her. But why? Sergio puzzled over this only for a moment, then kicked himself. He should have asked Nancy about Mel, the guy who was keeping Marc distracted. Nancy had been guarded, but not altogether closed-mouthed. He toyed with the idea of calling her back. No. Best not to press his luck. Later.

Sergio dialed Frannie.

"Hey, it's me. You find out anything yet?"

Frannie whispered so low that he had to strain to hear. "Jenkins keeps all the SuperCredit applications locked up in his credenza. And he's been in his office all morning."

"No shit."

"He was at my desk first thing. Wanted to know if anything came in on the Barlow account from DP."

"What'd you tell him?"

"I said that nothing came in. He told me to call down there to find out what the holdup was. Then he asked what time I left last night. I said 5:00. He asked if I saw you last night. I said no."

"Do you think he knows I met you at The Sails?"

"I don't know. It made me nervous. What if he knows I lied to him? Lots of people from the bank hang out there."

"That's the least of our worries. Guess what? Marc's in Hawaii. I just talked to Nancy."

"I knew it."

"Can you meet for lunch?"

"Where?"

"Clown Alley. One o'clock."

"Okay."

"Can you do me another favor? Can you get the sales drafts for the Barlow account?"

"Jenkins has the file."

"But DP is supposed to deliver new drafts this morning, the charges from last weekend. Can you intercept them?"

"For you, Sergio, of course."

"Oh, and if George calls in, ask him to call me at home."

"He already called in. They ditched him in New Orleans. He fell asleep staking out their car and woke up to it being towed away."

Sergio laughed with her.

"Then I told him Barlow was on the authorization approval list this morning. She bought three airline tickets from New Orleans to Miami. George freaked out. Wanted to know how the hell that could happen. I didn't tell him any of the stuff you told me last night. I did tell him you're off the case. He freaked again."

"Thanks. I want to talk to him myself next time he calls."

"I'll give him your home number. I got him on a flight to Miami. He asked me to transfer him to Jenkins."

"No, no, Frannie, next time he calls, keep him away from Jenkins."

"Shit. I got to go. Speak of the devil, here he comes. See you at one."

"Bring those drafts with you."

How could they get to those applications? The way he figured it, those apps were phonies. Once approved and processed, the credit lines would be funded, obviously to the tune of forty million dollars. To get the funds out of the country, they'd have to be untraceable.

How?

Sergio pulled out the San Francisco phone book. He opened to the listings for City Security Bank, the Wire Transfer department, in the main branch on California Street around the corner from headquarters. He dialed.

"Wire transfer, Rachel speaking.

"Is Mel there?"

"Mel? Sorry, there's no one here by that name."

"Is there another Wire Transfer department besides this one?"

"No, this is it. Maybe if you tell me what this is regarding?"

"I got a message to call Mel in Wire Transfer. This was the only listing in the phone book."

"It could be someone from one of the branches where the wire originated. What branch were you dealing with?"

"Maybe you're right. I'll check with the branch. Thanks."

That was a dead end.

Sergio was on time to meet Frannie. He ordered two burgers, a plate of fries, a Diet Coke for Frannie and a lemonade for himself.

When Frannie arrived, she pulled an interoffice envelope from her handbag.

George arrived at the Miami airport still hungover. He was more than exhausted; he was distraught over the twists and turns this case was taking and his inability to stay on track. Was he losing his edge? At a bank of pay phones, he called Frannie.

"I just arrived in Miami. What have you got?"

"I got a credit card charge for a Cadillac and an oceanfront hotel."

"Now we're talking. Where?"

"St. Augustine. Stay at the airport. You're on the next flight out."

"What?"

Chapter 18

Minnie drove the whole way, six hours north from Miami up the A1A. The power and style of the convertible Cadillac was like nothing she'd ever driven. The wind in her hair, behind the wheel, glimpses of turquoise waters and white beaches, even the motorcycle gang who surrounded them on the road, a shouting, revving escort for fifty miles, thrilled her. She would not share the wheel with Jeanette or Sarah, even though it was Sarah who'd picked the Caddy convertible to rent in Miami.

They arrived in St. Augustine in early afternoon. Their beachfront, three-bedroom bungalow was quaint and spacious, with a generous living room with a stone fireplace. After settling in, they met in the living room.

"This is just like home." Jeanette said. "The home we deserve."

Minnie said, "I want to get to the bottom of something that's been bugging me."

Jeanette said, "The airline tickets in New Orleans. We know, you've mentioned it a hundred times already."

"The girl called for an authorization. Isn't that bugging you, too? How could that charge have cleared?"

"I don't know. I don't care."

Sarah asked, "What difference does it make?"

"I can't stand it anymore. I'm going to call the 800 number on the back of the card."

Jeanette said, "Make sure you tell them where we are."

Minnie pulled the credit card from her wallet and dialed. A customer service rep answered; Minnie gave her the account number and asked for her balance. After the clicking noises of a computer keyboard, the rep said, "Your balance is $1150.00. There is a payment pending for that amount."

"A payment?" The outstanding balance was the exact amount of the security deposit on the Cadillac rental.

"I'm sorry, Mrs. Barlow, it's not a payment, it's a credit. Also, I see your credit line has been increased to ten thousand dollars."

Minnie was stunned into silence for moments, then asked, "What about the airline tickets to Miami?"

"That's been taken care of. The credit posted yesterday so the charge has been reversed."

"Thank you." She hung up so slowly, Sarah said, "Uh oh," and Jeanette asked, "What's wrong?"

"Wow. There's some huge mistake going on."

Minnie explained the reversals of their charges, and the ten thousand credit limit.

Jeanette, never easily shocked, slurred when she asked, "Did you say ten thousand?"

"I should call Marc and ask him about this."

Jeanette said, "No way. Leave well enough alone."

"I wonder if they've pulled George Post off the account, too. Could be he's not even following us anymore."

"One way to find out." Jeanette popped to her feet. "Let's go shopping."

From the beach it was a short walk into town. Over their heads, palm trees swayed and seagulls swirled. They strolled at a leisurely pace through the old shady streets and down narrow ancient walkways where Spanish settlers had trod centuries ago. Stone houses and shops with clay-tiled roofs and bright awnings lined the avenues.

They toured the town in a horse-drawn surrey. The atmosphere was so heavy with history they expected Ponce de Leon to burst forth brandishing a sword. Newer buildings blended with the ancient Spanish architecture.

In the main shopping area, they went crazy with the credit cards again. They made frivolous purchases, and shipped gifts to friends and family.

Outside what looked like a charming little restaurant, Minnie and Sarah examined the menu on the wall outside while Jeanette peered through a window.

With a gasp, she drew back and tugged Sarah's sleeve. "My God!"

"What's wrong?"

"It's that man. Post. He's here, in the restaurant. He's sitting at the table next to the window I just looked into."

Jeanette grabbed Minnie and Sarah and rushed them around the corner.

Sarah asked, "Did he see you?"

"I don't think so. He was looking into his soup bowl."

"Are you sure it was him?"

"Of course it was!"

"Settle down, Jeanette."

"Settle down? It was a shock. He could have seen me."

Minnie asked, "What are we going to do?"

"Let's follow him." Sarah said with a mischievous grin.

"Have you gone completely out of your mind?" Jeanette pointed back to the restaurant. "He'd spot us right away. You're just asking for trouble."

"But if we could learn what he's up to, we'd have an edge."

"Minnie's right," Sarah said. "We have the advantage. I've got it. I'm the most common looking of the three of us."

Jeanette and Minnie both tried to undo this opinion of Sarah about herself.

"Stop, really, both of you. It's true. Let's all pop into a shop and get a wig and sunglasses. He won't spot me.

I'll follow Post and find out what I can. You two go on to dinner. I'll eat here. Wait for me back at the hotel, and don't worry if I'm late."

Minnie asked, "You sure you're up to this?"

"Absolutely."

Minnie stroked Sarah's cheek. "Just like the movies."

Sarah took a seat four tables behind George Post. She kept her sunglasses and wide-brim straw hat perched on her long blond wig. George was just tucking into his main course, crab cakes and rice. As he ate, he read a local newspaper.

Sarah, too, ordered crab cakes and rice.

Midway through her meal, the waiter brought George his check. He paid with a credit card. She motioned for her waiter, sad she wouldn't have time for dessert.

She paid with her Visa card which had been maxed out on their Miami shopping binge. No worry; dining alone, she was sure to be under the floor limit. The waiter processed her sales draft and checked the warning bulletin. Without any fuss he returned for her signature. The first time Jeanette had used Edith's card at Pandora's, Sarah had been so nervous. Now, she felt only calm and confidence.

Before Sarah could sign her check and leave, George disappeared from the restaurant. She signed her check and hurried outside, almost plowing into him.

He stood on the curb, back toward her, lighting a cigarette. Sarah eased her hurried pace and blithely walked past George Post. She paused at a window display in a candle shop and studied his reflection. He flicked his cigarette into the gutter, removed his jacket, and strode down the street.

She followed twenty feet behind. Post's quick pace made her worry about keeping up. Almost in a trot, Sarah cantered in his wake around a corner. He'd stopped to contemplate a Greyhound bus station across the street; again, Sarah almost bumped into him. She turned her back, smoothed the lapels of her apricot silk pantsuit, and did not lose her confidence that Post would not recognize her in wig and sunglasses, that she was not notable or memorable. Sarah dug through her Gucci handbag as though looking for something.

When she turned to check on him, Post was headed into the terminal. She entered behind him.

George approached a bank of payphones. Sarah took the telephone in the alcove next to his.

George Post tapped her shoulder.

"Excuse me, do you have change for a dollar?"

Still confident, Sarah said, "Well, let me see, young man." In her wallet she found four quarters. "Oh dear, I'll need this quarter for my phone call."

"Fine, fine. Here's a buck, keep the change." Post turned his back and dialed.

Sarah dropped the remaining quarter into the telephone and called the bungalow.

When Minnie answered, she said in a cheery voice, "I'm here at the bus station. I've come to meet the young man. He's arrived already. He's in the bathroom."

George kept his back to her, and Sarah eavesdropped.

"Hi Carl. I'm in St. Augustine. Just got here... No, I had dinner first." An announcement from the bus station intercom announced the arrival of a bus from Miami, covering George's words. He put his hand over his free ear.

When Sarah picked up the conversation again, George was writing in a pocket-sized notebook. He repeated, "Cadillac convertible, powder blue. License plate?"

The intercom blasted again. George shouted into the phone, "What hotel? On the beach. Got it." He put the notebook in his pocket. "Okay. I'll call back after I check it out."

George hung up and hurried away.

When he was well out of earshot, she said to Minnie on the phone, "Get packed. Get out of there now. Leave the car and get a cab to the Greyhound station. He's on his way there right now. I'll buy the tickets. We're taking the bus."

Chapter 19

From the black leather of the convertible Caddy's passenger seat, George lifted a straw hat that sported a pink band and a trail of long blond hair.

The bus station. The woman beside him at the payphone. Big round sunglasses, blonde hair, this same hat but with an apricot band. 'Yeah, keep the change.' She used the extra quarter to call her friends and warn them.

George tossed the hat back into the Caddy. He didn't bother to look around, he knew by now there'd be nothing to see. They were gone. Just like New Orleans.

George entered the hotel lobby. They sure knew how to pick places to stay. The lobby was furnished in plantation style. A waterfall slid over a rock wall into a pool of Koi fish, potted palms reached to the open mezzanine level above. The front desk was polished mahogany.

Behind it was a woman he thought he knew. George wracked his brain but could not place her.

She was exquisite. Long brown hair framed an angular, shining face. She appeared to be in her early to mid-thirties. Looking up from some paperwork, she flashed a beguiling smile at the couple she was waiting on. George drew closer, and as he did his surroundings disappeared as if she were the light at the end of a tunnel.

He didn't know her. She didn't look like anyone he knew, or had even known.

The couple took their key and departed.

"Good afternoon, sir. May I help you?"

The attraction to her was instant; heat flooded George's cheeks, so much that he became aware that he was blushing.

Five years had gone by since he'd been drawn to any woman at all. Five years since he'd been with a woman, or felt anything but the desire to run when they made passes at him.

"Sir? Are you all right?"

George found his voice and slid into his professional demeanor. "I'm George Post, from City Security Bank." He presented his credentials.

He went through the motions inquiring about the three women. She listened carefully, then dialed their suite. No one answered. As she hung up, he turned his gaze to the Koi pond; he didn't want her to know he'd been staring.

"They must be on the beach or in Old Town." She consulted a log. "They haven't checked out yet. I'm afraid I can't disclose any further information." She leaned on her elbows. "Something else seems wrong. Are you okay?"

She caught him by surprise. "I've been on the go all day. I think I'm a bit road worn."

He rubbed the stubble on his chin. How must he look to this young woman? Old and bedraggled. George groaned inwardly.

She smiled, and her brown eyes sparkled with curious regard. "I'll bet you are. I think you need to check in and rest up. And since you represent the bank, I'd like to offer you a complimentary room." She straightened up and reached for a form.

"That's very nice of you. You can do that? I wouldn't want to get you into any trouble. And I can pay. I mean the bank can pay."

"No need, George Post from the bank."

She ran a finger down the log. "Here we go. Bungalow seven."

George peeked at her hands as she wrote up the form. Long delicate fingers, French-manicured nails, smooth tan skin, a small amethyst in delicate curlicue silver on her right hand, no wedding ring on the left. She was left-handed.

"I'm Valerie." She handed him a key. "If you need anything, just give me a call."

There was something in her tone, an inflection. Wasn't there? An indication. Was she hitting on him? George couldn't tell. He used to be able to fathom these things, but he'd lost the ability to spot the signs. She liked him. She liked him? George cleared his throat.

"Thanks. I'm George. Wait, you already know that. You wrote up the room thing and I already told you that anyway." His voice trailed off.

"Are you in the front parking area?"

"Yes."

"Follow the lane marked 'Bungalows one through seven.' Go to the end. You're in number seven."

George repeatedly thumped the key against his palm as he backed away from the counter. Pointing the same direction she'd just pointed, he said, "Follow the sign for the Bungalows."

"Yes."

"At the end."

"Go, George."

He continued walking backward, enjoying her amusement and feeling idiotic at the same time.

"If you get lost, come back. I'll draw you a map."

He gave his best smile and turned away. Still thumping the key in his hand, he turned as he left the lobby. Valerie gave him a little wave.

George had no problem finding his bungalow. Driving down the lane, the ocean view was beautiful, the beach was brown sand. When he pulled into the space for number seven, he realized she'd given him the most private and luxurious accommodations on the grounds. The sound of the waves was soothing, the bungalow was private. Yes, the ladies did know how to pick their hotels.

Inside the bungalow, he dropped his luggage and went straight to the bathroom. To the mirror. "Ah, Jeez. Look at you." George rubbed his bleary eyes and five o'clock shadow. "She's probably just making fun of you." He splashed cold water on his face.

In the living room, he opened the double doors to the veranda. On the beach, a couple of kids ran up and down the sand with a dog.

George rifled through his canvas bag for a pint bottle of Jack Daniels. In the kitchen he stood a glass on the counter, then stared down at it for a long time.

"Fuck this. You're not your old man." George filled the glass with water.

He had gotten royally tanked in New Orleans but hadn't had a drink since. His father wasn't a mean or a stupid drunk, he just looked bad all the time. Lines broke his face, his skin bloated, and liquor reeked from his pores. It seemed like every time George wanted to have a talk, he'd find his dad passed out in a chair. George became a teetotaler. That changed when his life changed. He drank at first in moderation, although there had been binges. Like recently. George gulped down a second glass of water.

On the couch, looking through the French doors to the ocean, he picked up the phone.

"Master Charge, Frannie speaking."

"Hey, Frannie, it's George. Is Carl still there?"

"No. He and Southern went out to catch nine holes."

"How you doing?"

"I'm okay. I miss Sergio."

"Give it up, girl. He's never going straight for you."

"You never know. You just never know."

"Yeah, you do. So when's he back?"

"I think Monday. Did you make it to St. Augustine?"

"Yep. What have you got for me?"

"Hang on." George listened to rustling files and papers until Frannie said, "Mess of charges in Miami. Hotel. Clothes. Restaurants. Oh, they went sailing."

"They're living it up alright. That's all ancient history. What have you got that's new?"

After more paper rustling, Frannie said, "Here we go. A shopping binge in St. Augustine. A candle shop, this boutique, that boutique, lots of freight charges. I wish they'd send me a present. They're like a little band of Robin Hoods, stealing from the rich and giving to the poor. You think their mission is to help the economy?

"It occurred to me."

"Carl wanted me to ask if you'd checked the hotel yet."

"I'm here right now. You oughta see this place."

"What about the women?"

"The Cadillac is out front. The clerk said they're out shopping."

"What a life. Sometimes I wish I was with them."

"Nah. You don't want to go to jail."

"Jail? The bank's going to press charges?"

"That's what Carl told me yesterday."

"That's stupid. Ridiculous."

"Why? Because they're women they should get away with it?"

"No. That would be terrible PR. Because they're old. Because they're poor. I read your field report with Klydesdale, the manager."

George realized he hadn't removed his shoes and wondered why. He cradled the phone between his ear and shoulder and bent to unlace his wingtips.

Frannie continued making her case. "You've got Sob Story one, Sob Story two, and Sob Story three here. They were all pretty well off, then got screwed over one way or another and ended up damn near homeless."

"Yep." George slid off his shoes and socks. He loosened his tie. "These women got a lot of guts. They're clever. They might just get away with it. Now, what does Jenkins want me to do?"

"Catch them."

George sank deeper into the cushions. He yawned. "Man, this is nice."

"What is?"

"This couch. Listen, I'm gonna sack out for a while."

"Jenkins said to call him first thing Monday morning."

"Okay. You have a good weekend. What are you doing this weekend?"

Frannie made no answer for moments, then whispered, "George."

"Frannie, you okay?"

"There's a lot going on."

"I take it you can't talk right now, right?"

"Right."

"They're still having that computer glitch?"

"Something like that. Everything is still zero." Her voice dropped lower. George sat upright on the sofa, straining to hear Frannie.

"Every charge they make gets reversed. Sergio wants you to call him tonight. Seven, at my place."

"Got it. Be careful, girl."

"You, too."

George hung up, then stretched out on the couch. An ocean breeze riffled the curtains beside the French doors, the smells of salt and warm sand wafted over him. He was close to collapsing into sleep, but not just yet.

So, the balances were still being reversed. According to what Sergio had told him two days ago, Marc Corbett had signed the credits that zeroed out the account balances. George recalled Marc from Master Charge before he got bumped upstairs into computer programming. George didn't know any of the night collectors, the college crew, but the few times he'd seen Marc, the kid seemed to be a straight shooter. It made sense that Sergio thought there was something, or someone, else behind all of this.

And there was Valerie. The hotel clerk.

George awoke groggy. He'd napped on the sofa for an hour. He stumbled into the bathroom for a hot shower and shave. This time, the mirror revealed a different man, refreshed, clean, damn near handsome. He put on a pair of shorts and a tee shirt for a walk on the beach.

Tying his shoes, ready to head out, a knock came at his door.

He opened to find Valerie smiling. Her blue hotel uniform had been replaced with pink shorts and matching golf shirt.

"You left this at the front desk." Valerie held out his billfold with his bank credentials.

His fingers brushed against her hand when he took them. "Thanks. You didn't have to go out of your way."

"I just got off work and the employee parking lot is nearby. I thought I'd drop this off. Say, you clean up nice."

"Thanks. So, you're off work now?"

George was flummoxed; he couldn't figure anything to say more interesting than that flat question. You're off work?

"I am."

Valerie waited moments, and when nothing was forthcoming from George, she said, "Well, I hope you enjoy your stay. Bye." She turned to leave.

"Wait. I was just."

"Just what?"

George ran a hand through his still-damp hair to buy himself a second, to compose himself and speak in complete, coherent sentences. He'd get one shot at this.

"I was just going to take a walk on the beach."

"That will be nice. You'll like it."

"I mean, would you like to join me?"

She seemed to hesitate. Had he made a mistake inviting her?

She smiled. "Okay."

The ocean ran mild this afternoon. The waves did not crash so they could speak to each other quietly. They strolled on the wet sand beside a white lace of froth, and as they walked, George grew more confident. Or Valerie made him more confident.

He asked questions about her. She was from Los Angeles, had moved east for college. She liked Florida better than L.A, despite the hurricanes and humidity. "Humidity's a great moisturizer." Valerie turned the talk soon to George. She was curious about him, and this touched him.

"Do you like your job?"

"Yeah. I do. There aren't that many options for ex-cops. I didn't want to go into security work. That's boring. The bank's been good to me. I work alone, travel a lot. It's cool."

"You seem like a loner. Are you?"

"I wouldn't say loner. Really? You think of me as a loner?"

"Maybe it's just the cop vibe." Valerie shifted gears. "Tell me about these women you're chasing. I checked them in myself. They seemed like sweet, innocent gals on vacation."

"They're not pros, that's for sure. I've never had a case like this one. Usually I'm out tracking real crooks, you know, bad guy types. Or I get assigned to pick up credit cards that families have been living on after Dad got laid off. That's always embarrassing for those folks, so I try to be nice with them. But, you know, I have to do the job. These gals are a different story. They're using the cards of one of their dead friends, plus they're running up their own balances. They've been jumping around the whole country doing it."

"Are they really criminals, though? A couple of old gals having a fling together? I mean, what's their story?"

"I know their story. It's sad enough, sure." George snorted. "But everyone has the capacity for crime. You just need the right set of circumstances, mix in a little ill-conceived justification, some indignation, and voila, you've got a criminal."

"Do you ever feel sorry for any of them?"

"Sometimes, yeah. But these three old gals? No. Not at all. They're sharp. Actually, I find them pretty entertaining."

The sun sank behind them. George took Valerie's hand when she skipped away from the lace of a wave sliding towards her feet. He didn't let go as they walked on, and she didn't disengage. His heart began to flip.

He asked. "Do you like your job?"

"It's fun. But I'm back in school again. I want to go into interior design."

"Really? An artist."

"My parents can't believe it. I spent all those years in college, went on for my MBA. Got this nice managerial position at the hotel with a chance at promotion. My dad asked, 'And now you want to do what?' I guess it takes some people a long time to decide. Mom reminded me how gung ho I was about the hotel industry. She's afraid I'll get a few years into interior design and decide I want to be a brain surgeon."

With the sun resting on the horizon, they headed back to the hotel. Along the way they talked of common interests, hobbies, places they always wanted to visit. Valerie was easy to talk to, she gave honest answers. And her questions about him were polite, gentle.

Back in his room, George offered a drink from the Jack Daniels bottle. Instead, she took a Coke from the mini-bar. He poured it into two glasses with ice and sat with Valerie on the big couch.

More conversation flowed with ease. She made George laugh often, deeply, and honestly. It had been a long time since he'd laughed so freely with a woman. After a bit, the conversation lulled, and he went into his thoughts. George ached for what he'd missed, the years spent in grief and isolation. Now here he was with this sweet, beautiful woman. And she lived on the wrong coast.

Her voice brought him back. "What is it that's making you so sad?"

"What do you mean?"

"Maybe I'm wrong, but you seem to be weighed down with something."

He tried to look confused; she sighed patiently and continued. "You hide it with work." Valerie nodded toward the still-unopened Jack Daniels bottle. "Maybe with drinking? I see you as a people person, but you've got some sort of self-imposed alienation going on."

How did she know? George felt like he'd been caught in a lie and had some explaining to do. Pride and self-pity had kept him from talking about it to anyone. And things had been really going downhill lately. He'd lacked focus, and that put him in a downward spiral.

But something about Valerie felt open, accepting, healing; something made him feel safe in confiding. As if he could take the burden in his heart and give it to her, tell it to her, and maybe rid himself of it. Or at least share it and make it lighter.

"I don't talk about this much. Actually, not at all."

George cleared his throat. She didn't recoil but appeared expectant, like she was being flattered that he would speak to her with this kind of candor and vulnerability.

"Except to the SFPD shrink. With him I just played the game. But something horrible happened in 1971."

The story came out in a gush of words. "New Year's Eve. I was a cop. I'd brought down this guy, a big time drug dealer. He had this big time attorney and instead of getting life for murder, transporting, and on and on, he got two years. Two lousy years. Okay, that was 1969.

When he left the courtroom after sentencing, he made a throat-slicing gesture to me."

Valerie said, "He sounds awful."

"You don't want to know. Anyway, two years go by and I'd forgotten all about this guy. Until New Year's Eve. My partner tells me this clown's been sprung a few days ago. I was a little worried, but figured this shit happens all the time, these threats, you know. They always say they're gonna get you, but they cool down in the can. I get off work and go home. It's just before nine o'clock at night. My wife, the kids, and I were going to watch the big apple drop in Times Square on T.V. I thought I made it home just in the nick of time. I had these two kids; they were great kids. Brian was six, Debbie, nine. When I got into the house, I found them."

She asked softly, "He'd killed them?"

"Shot them all. Jesus."

His hand went to his mouth. George felt like he might vomit.

"Well, I..."

His voice trailed off. Before his tears could boil over, George swiped angrily at his face. He'd be damned if he was going to cry in front of this young woman, this new person in his life who he wanted to stay, not run from a weeping fool.

Valerie's arms encircled him.

Chapter 20

Jeanette, Minnie and Sarah took their seats on the bus out of St. Augustine. Sarah and Minnie sat together, Jeanette took the open aisle seat beside a handsome young man in a cream linen suit with a pale straw Panama in his lap. After polite nods, she peered out the window to scan the boarding area for George Post.

"Good afternoon, ma'am," the passenger beside her said cordially. "Looks like we're riding together. My name is Jasper C. Cornell."

Jeanette smiled at her seatmate. "I'm Jeanette." She leaned forward looking past him out the window again. George was nowhere in sight. With a roar and an undecipherable message over the intercom, the bus pulled out. They'd made a clean getaway, once again by the skin of their teeth.

"Where you headed, ma'am?"

"New York. What about you?"

"Savannah first. That's my hometown. Then on to New York. I start an internship next week."

Sarah and Minnie were silent, relieved to have escaped. Jeanette was wired from another close call and she wanted to talk. He seemed a courteous young man.

"Internship?"

"I just graduated law school. Went to Cornell because it matched my name." He grinned broadly. "I'll be interning at McGee, Phillips, Brockman, and Hastings in Manhattan."

"That sounds wonderful. Good for you."

"My father's an attorney in St. Augustine. I was just visiting him. So what about you?"

"Traveling with my friends." Jeanette indicated Minnie and Sarah two rows ahead. "We're heading to New York for the Bicentennial celebration in Central Park and to see my daughter and granddaughter. We're taking our time, seeing the sights. Then from there we're off to Spain."

"Ah, so you're married."

"Yes, I am. Very happily."

Jasper C. Cornell looked her up and down.

"Where's this husband? Is he in Spain? Why'd he let a beautiful woman travel with the girls like this?"

"Yes, he is. He's setting up a big real estate deal. I'm meeting him in Paris next week. Jeff's a wonderful man. I was supposed to go to Spain with him, but my friend Sarah recently lost her best friend – she passed - and needed a diversion. Minnie and I decided a little road trip would help distract her. He understands."

"That's a very kind thing you're doing. I hope you've been enjoying it so far."

"Oh yes. A wonderful time." Minnie and Sarah looked back at her and Jasper C. Cornell. Both were wide-eyed and twittering to each other, probably scandalized anew at Jeanette's continued brazenness. Quietly, Jeanette was delighted to see them whispering, aghast and tickled by her behavior, all of them together on this adventure.

"And Spain. Now that's one place I've always wanted to go. I'd like to run with the bulls. Saw that on TV once and since I ran track in high school, I think I'd do okay. Maybe, the first time I get a break in the action, I'll come to Spain and you can cheer me on while I outrun all them bulls."

Jeanette grinned. "I'd like to see that." She peered out the window at the urban landscape receding to soft country. Suddenly, Madame Viola's words returned to her – 'take the bull by the horns.' She looked at Jasper full on as he absent-mindedly rubbed a spot on the band of his panama hat. Hmmm. Take the bull by the horns. Maybe she shouldn't dismiss this young man so quickly. Maybe he would prove to be a fun diversion while in Savannah.

Jasper looked up at her and smiled. She returned his smile adding a smidgen of seduction. Jasper grinned wider, looked away shyly, cleared his throat, then said, "Tell me about your daughter."

Jeanette settled back in her seat. "Natalie. My little angel. She went to art school in New York then went into interior decorating and has made a name for herself in New York, not an easy thing. She married a wonderful man, an architect she met at a fundraiser for the homeless. She has her own little girl now, three years old."

Jeanette and Jasper talked about Savannah. He filled her in on points of interest, a little of its history, and how Jasper hoped he could find time in his upcoming internship to travel a little more.

"I wonder what the weather will be like in Savannah," Jeanette said.

"That doesn't change much. Hot and humid. It is late June, after all."

For the next hour of highway, Jeanette enjoyed the conversation with Jasper C. Cornell. He was smooth, no question, and probably a liar. But people on a bus had to entertain themselves, so why not adopt a persona? Jeanette did the same, told pleasant stories of a life she did not lead, and did not begrudge Jasper if he did the same. He was good company and had a lively sense of humor.

Jeanette dozed off. She had a dream, a brief but vivid scene. She was with Madame Viola Valle, both younger, the way they knew each other in New York. They rode in a limousine, traveling toward a mountain peak with a lion and a peacock. The lion had immense paws. Madame Valle said something Jeanette couldn't hear.

Jeanette awoke, unable to remember more of the dream. Night had fallen, and Jasper slept beside her. A hush like a reverence filled the bus, only the humming of the engine. Minnie and Sarah nodded in their seats. Jeanette shut her eyes trying to recapture the dream. Madame Viola had been speaking with urgency, Jeanette fell back asleep wondering what it was about. She didn't awaken until the static from the intercom jolted her.

Jasper awoke, as well. "Dang, I'm hungry."

"I was just thinking the same."

The big coach rolled into the downtown Savannah terminal. The driver announced, "We've arrived in Savannah. We're going to stop here for forty-five minutes."

As the bus came to a stop, Jeanette looked out the window for signs of George Post.

Off the bus, Jeanette introduced Jasper C. Cornell to Minnie and Sarah. "His family lives here in Savannah."

He tipped the brim of his Panama hat and smiled broadly. "A pleasure, ladies."

"He's offered to show us a good fried chicken place around the corner."

Minnie grunted, skeptical as always. "Do we have enough time?"

Sarah was overjoyed. "I'm starving."

"I was thinking maybe we could stay here a few days. Jasper says it's a very elegant city."

Minnie said. "Maybe. I've had it with this bus anyway."

Sarah rose to her toes. "Oh, I don't want to get back on this bus either. I could use a good bed right now."

Jeanette beamed. "First, let's get some of that famous fried chicken. Then we'll come back for our luggage."

They made their way through the noisy terminal, away from the smell of buses and tired people. Jasper paused to straighten his tie and smooth the lines of his white linen suit.

"Right this way, ladies."

Jasper led them outside the bus terminal. They strolled together for several blocks; the neighborhood adjacent to the Savannah terminal began to tatter and grow rough-looking. Jasper led the girls down littered streets, past neon-lit small stores, men on corners idly watching them pass, and women who hip-checked each other when tall, good-looking Jasper paraded by in his white suit and straw hat, Jeanette on his arm, followed by Minnie and Sarah. All three girls still dressed for a casual evening.

On a dim side street, Minnie asked, "How much further is it?"

Jasper pointed to a wide boulevard ahead. "It's at the end of this block."

At the corner, an orange sign on a decaying brick building read: "Fanny's Fried Chicken." On the sidewalk, an old woman with a shopping cart rifled through a city trash can. She examined a broken umbrella, then added it to her collection in the cart of clothing, bottles, and odd boxes. She wore layers of sweaters, all too big for her tiny frame. A red felt hat topped tendrils of fine gray hair. It looked like someone had taken a bite out of the brim.

The woman turned sharp, parrot eyes to them. "Do you have any spare change?"

Jasper said, "Ignore her."

He led Jeanette past her, but Sarah said, "Wait." She gave the woman a dollar bill. The woman snatched it and gave them all a broken-toothed scowl. "Tightwads."

An alley approached. Jasper tugged Jeanette's elbow to lead her and the girls into it.

"I know the owner of Fanny's. We'll come in the back way."

Jeanette followed. Sarah, too. But Minnie pulled up short, staying in the street.

"I don't think so."

Jasper let go of Jeanette. He took long strides to Minnie. He peered first to see if the coast was clear, then took Minnie firmly by the arm.

"Think so."

Jasper dragged Minnie to Jeanette and Sarah. His demeanor did not change, he remained the stylish and graceful Jasper C. Cornell. But his eyes and his voice carried threats.

From his waistband at the small of his back, he pulled a small black pistol. He waved it first at Jeanette, motioning the barrel down her royal blue linen suit.

"That a Paco Rabanne?"

"Yes. Yes it is."

"I've seen the shoes in Bloomingdales. Italian, very nice. That bag is Hermes. Seen that, too."

"What do you want, Jasper?"

"Your purses. All of them."

Madame Viola. In the dream she'd tried to warn Jeanette, that's what Jeanette hadn't heard clearly. The same words she'd said in her trance in San Antonio: 'The man from Panama is not your friend.' Jasper's straw hat.

Minnie was speechless, Sarah burbled, "But...but..."

Jasper grabbed all their handbags. "Give me your jewelry." He waved the gun at Jeanette's right hand. Jeanette struggled to get the ring off her finger.

"Hurry up. And the watches, too."

He snatched them off their wrists and stuffed all his lucre into Jeanette's bag. He waved the snub nose of the pistol at Jeanette, waggling it upward.

"Pull up that blouse, darling."

"No. Absolutely not."

"Either you do it or I will."

Jeanette marshaled all the indignation she could but Jasper C. Cornell was unmoved. He stepped to her. She barked, "Alright."

She exposed her bare midriff, and the travel belt. Jasper did not ask her for it, but enjoyed taking it off her.

When he had everything, he surveyed the three women from whom he'd taken everything, almost.

"That ring, Jeanette. Emerald, isn't it? Haven't gotten a good look."

"It's just glass."

"It's not. I'll take it."

Jeanette froze, unable to respond. Jasper grabbed her hand to yank at the ring. It did not budge.

"Oh please, please, you're hurting me."

He tugged harder but the ring wouldn't slide off.

The shriek of sirens on the boulevard ahead made him more desperate and hurried. Jasper spit on Jeanette's finger, twisted and turned the ring but it wouldn't slide over Jeanette's knuckle.

"You're going to rip my finger off!"

The sirens seemed to be closing in; they weren't for Jasper, not yet, but if they came close enough Jeanette would scream and see if she couldn't change that.

The three purse straps slid down Jasper's arm as Jeanette struggled. To use both hands, he tucked the small pistol under his arm. Jeanette saw her chance to save her ring, maybe more. She swung at the handle of the gun stuck in Jasper's armpit. She knocked it loose.

The gun landed at Sarah's feet. Thinking fast, Sarah kicked it away.

Jasper quit wrestling with Jeanette, to swivel his head in search of his gun. Minnie moved in fast.

She kicked Jasper C. Cornell fiercely in the groin. Jasper shoved her away before stumbling backwards against a dumpster.

He said, "Bitches."

Jeanette said, "What did you just say?"

Together, all three rushed Jasper. Sarah swung her nails at his face while Jeanette and Minnie pulled at the purses to free them from his grasp. Jasper couldn't protect his face, his groin and the purses for long. He flung out one beefy arm and big hand, sending Minnie flying onto her backside.

Jeanette pulled Sarah off him. She grabbed Minnie off the ground and they fled the dim alley to the street, leaving Jasper C. Cornell doubled over and groaning.

The sirens and flashing lights were speeding their way on the main street, only blocks off. Sarah stepped into the road to flag down a cop car. Minnie hauled her back to the curb.

"We can't talk to the police. Let's get back to the bus."

"But our purses."

Jeanette said, "My travel belt!"

In the alley, Jasper scrambled over a wall and disappeared.

"He's got everything." Sarah's voice climbed at the extent of their predicament. "Oh, God, what are we going to do?"

Minnie herded them along the street. "We're going to catch that bus. Let's go."

Before they could hurry off, a half dozen police vehicles skidded to a halt haphazardly, lights flashing, in front of the liquor store across the street. A young uniformed police officer climbed out of his car to hustle toward the girls. Behind him, more policemen flooded into the liquor store.

The officer asked "Ladies, have you seen anybody run by here? There's been a holdup."

"Yes there has," Sarah blurted. "He stole our purses."

Minnie leaped in. "We haven't seen anyone. We're fine. Everything is fine."

The officer looked beyond them to the alley. He asked Sarah, "What direction did he come from?"

"He was on the bus with us."

Minnie stepped in front of Sarah. "Nothing happened, officer."

"Who stole your purses, ma'am?"

"No one."

The officer put his hands on his hips. "Then where are your purses?"

Jeanette strode between the young officer and Minnie.

"Young man. Take a good look at us. Honestly. Do you see criminals?"

The cop considered the question. He said, "No, ma'am."

"Then you go be safe out there. Come on, girls."

Minnie wouldn't let them go the direction that Jasper took. They went the other way, the long way around the block, she figured, past Fanny's Fried Chicken. As they scurried past, the wonderful aromas of fried chicken made them lick their lips.

Sarah stopped walking. "Chicken."

Minnie propelled her onward. "No money and no time."

After two blocks of speed walking, Jeanette said, "We turn here."

"No, that's not right. It's one more block then we turn."

Jeanette insisted, "I remember this sign."

"I do, too. But it's one more block then we turn."

"You're going to get us lost. I know we're supposed to turn there."

"You've already gotten us lost enough times." Minnie stopped to glare at Jeanette. "If you weren't so gullible. Madam What's-her-name in San Antonio. Tone in New Orleans. Jasper in Savannah."

Minnie marched on, increasing her speed to distance herself from Jeanette.

"Whatever!" Jeanette crossed the street by herself.

"Oh, shut up."

Sarah caught up to Minnie. "I think she's right."

"What?" Minnie wheeled on Sarah with a hard look. Halfway down the block, Jeanette's defiant strut carried her around a corner and out of sight.

"About the direction. Come on. Let's catch her." Sarah crossed first and called for Jeanette to wait up.

Minnie muttered, "Idiots."

She caught up to Sarah and Jeanette after a block of running. Closing in on Jeanette's back, Minnie said, "You better be right about this. I don't want to miss the bus."

Jeanette wheeled on her. "Oh for Christ sakes, we already missed the damn bus."

Sarah stamped her foot. "That's enough out of both of you. We have got to get back to the bus station. Then we'll get this whole thing sorted out. In the meantime I'd like a little silence so I can think how we're going to get out of this jam."

Jeanette turned away and burst into tears. Minnie wanted to say she was sorry for yelling; she closed the distance to Jeanette to say it with a hand on her friend's shoulder. But before she could reach for Jeanette, the bag lady in the sweaters and hat pushed her cart between them.

She looked at them full on. "If you'd given me a dime, I would have warned you about Jasper. It serves you right. Now you're in a jam without a spoon."

Sarah said, "Excuse me. I gave you a dollar."

"I didn't need no damn dollar. I asked you for change. I needed a dime." The old woman plucked a newspaper off the heap in her cart. "This is why I needed a dime. Johnny Mercer died today. One of Savannah's own."

Sarah asked, "Who?"

"Who?" The old lady dug for the umbrella she'd rescued from the trash so she could wave it at Sarah like a sword. "Johnny Mercer, fool. You know the song. It was your joke."

"Jeepers Creepers. Where'd you get those peepers?" She lunged at Sarah as though she might stick her with the umbrella; Sarah drew back in alarm while the old woman cackled crazily.

Minnie took Jeanette and Sarah by the wrists and dragged them away at a fast pace. Once they were a safe distance from the madwoman, Minnie slowed to ask Sarah, "What was she going on about? Why would you know that song? What joke?"

"Oh my goodness. Johnny Mercer wrote Jeepers Creepers."

"So?"

"That was a joke between me and Edith, whenever she wanted to make fun of my big glasses."

"Now what? You think that old lady's psychic?"

Jeanette said, "Like Viola. Yes."

"All she had to do is take a look at Sarah's glasses to figure that one out."

Sarah tapped the face of her watch. "Our bus left ten minutes ago."

Minnie puffed her cheeks, looking about for a way forward. Sarah and Jeanette were useless right now, both still agog at the soothsaying bag lady.

On the next corner, outside a restaurant, stood a phone booth. "I'm going to call Marc. I'll ask him to wire us money."

The booth was shattered but the phone worked. Out of habit, Minnie reached for her purse. She dialed the operator to place a collect call. After waiting with dead air, the operator returned to inform her there was no answer.

Minnie snapped her fingers. "That's right. He's still in Hawaii. He won't be back for two days. Who else can we call?"

Sarah said, "Without my address book, I'm at a loss. Where's he staying in Hawaii?"

"I don't remember! Some resort with a lot of K's and vowels in the name."

Jeanette asked, "What are we going to do?"

"Let's get back to the bus station and tell them what happened. Maybe we can catch up to our luggage. Maybe they'll let us take the next bus out."

"No bus tickets, no baggage claim ticket and no ID. I'm afraid I can't help y'all. If you like, I can call ahead to the Charleston station, give them your names, and ask them to pull your luggage off the bus and store it for y'all."

Minnie asked the clerk, "Can't you get us on a bus to Charleston?"

"Ladies, I'd like to help. But we get a lot of crazies in here trying to swindle free bus fare out of us." She shrugged indifferently.

Jeanette stepped up to the counter. "Do we look like a bunch of crazies?"

The clerk slid the glass booth door shut.

Minnie shouted, "Please make that call for us!"

Jeanette said, "Well, I never."

Minnie ran her hands over her ruined clothes, then flicked her finger over Sarah and Jeanette, the runs in their nylons, smudges on their dresses and faces, tatters and rips here and there.

"Well, we're a sight. We look like we just got in a fistfight with a mugger in an alley."

They slumped onto a nearby bench, too weary to laugh at the obvious joke.

Sarah said, "I'm just going to sit here until we hear from that bus clerk that our luggage is safe."

Minnie added, "We can keep trying to call someone until we can get the money wired."

A big clock on the wall told them it was ten p.m. Jeanette groused. "Just how I want to pass the time."

At midnight, a security guard came through the terminal. He'd been eyeing them since they first sat down.

"Sarah, wake up." Minnie prodded a thin finger into Sarah's hip. "Wake up."

Sarah came awake abruptly but woozy; she looked to be trying to figure out where she was.

The guard approached. With his nightstick he pointed to a 'No Loitering' sign. "Ladies, I'm afraid I'm going to have to ask you to leave."

Jeanette stepped forward. "We're waiting to hear about our luggage." She tossed him a coquettish smile.

"You'll have to check back in the morning."

"But you don't understand. We've been mugged, our purses stolen. Now we've missed the bus. We don't know what to do." Jeanette's eyelashes fluttered.

"I suggest you take that up with the police."

"If we could just wait here a bit longer."

"I don't want to have to ask you again." He pointed his truncheon toward the exit.

Jeanette crimsoned, then turned on her heel. Minnie and Sarah followed.

Outside, Jeanette broke into tears. Sarah tried to console her. "Now, now, sweetheart, it's going to be alright."

"No man." Jeanette rattled a finger in front of her own face, as if to make the point clear to herself, "no man has ever been that rude to me before."

Minnie added her voice to Sarah's, to try and soothe Jeanette. "Honey..."

"When my ring wouldn't come off, I knew it." She looked at them bleary eyed. "I'm gaining weight. I'm fat! And now this...this insult. I knew it."

"Knew what, honey?"

Jeanette pinched her lips tight to quell her crying. Then, as if making an admission, the reveal of some bold secret, she said, "I'm getting old. Old and fat."

Minnie and Sarah together touched Jeanette's still lovely face. At the same time, they said, "We all are."

Jeanette walked on ahead of them into the hard neighborhood beside the bus station. Minnie had nothing more to say; Jeanette would have to find her own consolation and come to her own peace with aging, as Minnie must, and everyone else if they were lucky enough to live so long. Add to that, Minnie was too exhausted, and had too many more important things to think about than Jeanette's flirtation failure.

They wandered the opposite direction of Jasper's crime, the alley, and the liquor store. No matter how bad their situation, a chat with the police would make matters worse. The bus terminal's neighborhood didn't improve after midnight. Sketchy characters roamed the streets, and from the shadowy alleys and crevices where the streetlights did not reach, whispers and quiet laughter followed the three girls who walked nowhere in particular.

Sarah said, "This is a horrible neighborhood to be stuck in."

Jeanette said with conviction, "What you have to do in a scary situation is walk with purpose. Walk with confidence. No one is going to mess with The Three Musketeers. Now watch and copy."

She strode off at a brisk pace, carriage erect and head held high. As she stomped along the pavement, the heel broke off one shoe.

"Damn." When she bent to pick up the heel, the rear seam of her skirt tore. The comb fell from her hair and her auburn locks tumbled unkempt onto her shoulders. Again, tears shined in Jeanette's eyes.

"This is just too awful."

Minnie and Sarah came to her side, again murmuring reassurances to keep Jeanette's emotions from overwhelming them all.

A clattering racket interrupted their ministering to Jeanette. A singsong voice sang out from the depths of an alleyway: "Round and round she goes, where she stops nobody knows." The noises stopped suddenly, replaced by a rocking clamor and curses. "Rutting rut! Rutting, rotting rut!" The clatter struck up again and the old bag woman emerged from the alley pushing her overflowing shopping cart.

She stopped at the sight of the trio poised indelicately on the sidewalk. Jeanette still had one unshod leg upraised and her hand on Minnie's shoulder for balance. Sarah was holding parts of the shoe in each hand.

The bag lady whooped, "Allie's one-time special! New arrivals right here, yep."

"Jeanette said, "It's cold. Why not?"

One shoe on and one shoe off, she clomped unevenly toward the woman and her full shopping cart. Minnie and Sarah followed.

On top of the cart's heap lay a maroon velvet jacket. Minnie checked the tag.

Allie said, "It's from Saks Thrift Avenue."

Jeanette asked the old woman, "You're Allie?"

"Right here. Living color." She slapped Jeanette's hand away from the jacket. "You're the gal wouldn't give me a dime. If you're gonna pick through my stuff, you got to trade me something."

"We had everything stolen from us. We don't even have our purses."

Allie pointed to Jeanette's blue and white sun hat in Minnie's hands. "That hat looks like a good start."

Seeing the jacket made Jeanette realize how cold the night had already become. Not only did she need to replace her torn skirt; an extra layer would help her make it through the night.

Her hat had cost sixty dollars in St. Augustine. Jeanette told Minnie, "Give it to her."

Minnie handed it to Allie who examined it and cooed extravagantly.

The old woman put it on and danced a little jig, both hands on the brim to keep it secure from a nonexistent wind. She ventured over to a shop window to see her reflection through the bars.

Minnie lifted the maroon jacket from the cart and fitted it across Jeanette's bent back as she was foraging further through Allie's merchandise.

On the other side of the cart, Sarah tried on a heavy taupe cardigan sweater with the matching belt still in the waistline loops.

Jeanette discovered a pair of black slacks. She held them to her waist; the size was close enough. She nudged Minnie, indicating the dumpster in the alley.

"Come with me."

"Why?"

"I need to change clothes and I don't want to go behind a dumpster to do it by myself. So come on."

Hidden by the dumpster, Jeanette said, "That guard kicked us out before I could pee. I've got to go something fierce."

"This is as good a place as any. I'll stand guard."

"We don't have any tissue."

"I guess you'll get one last use out of that old skirt."

Holding onto the dumpster for balance, Jeanette removed her underwear. She couldn't avoid the splatter on her unshod feet. She danced her feet wider apart.

From above, a deep voice bellowed. "Showtime." Jeanette froze in midstream, feeling like a cornered animal. Minnie had hands on her hips, head tilted upward and a fierce tone in her voice to a large bald man sitting in the window of a second floor apartment.

"Give us some privacy, you pervert."

The man puffed on a cigar. "Take your time, ladies."

Jeanette finished her business, pulled up her underwear and slipped into the slacks to find them two sizes too big. The only way she could keep them up was to bunch the waistline in her hands. Jeanette tramped from behind the dumpster to glare up at the bald man with Minnie. He gave her a thumbs-up and a last puff of smoke.

Minnie handed her the maroon coat, also a few sizes too big; the sleeves reached Jeanette's knuckles. Disgusted, she walked barefoot back to Sarah and Allie. "For heaven's sake. How did we come to this?"

Behind her, Minnie jeered. "You know how. Jasper C. Cornell."

At Allie's cart, Sarah continued to dig into the tiers of clothes and street jetsam. Noting Jeanette clutching her waistband to keep her trousers up, Allie said, "How are you girls doing? Would you like me to check for another size?"

"Back off," Jeanette said.

"I found these." Sarah offered a pair of smudged white tennis shoes.

Jeanette cleaned her feet on her discarded skirt and tried them on. They fit, but she cringed at the warm moist lining. "I'll probably end up with foot fungus."

"And this." Sarah produced a short length of rope, perfect to hold up Jeanette's pants.

Jeanette said, "Let's get out of here." In the window, the leering bald man was gone with his cigar. "Jesus, I hope he's not on his way down here. Hurry up!"

Sarah asked, with alarm, "Who?"

Minnie said, "Your next husband, if you play your cards right."

Allie pointed to the cardigan Sarah had selected. "Must have something for that." She indicated Sarah's glasses.

"Oh, no. You can't have my eyes for this old thing. I gave you a dollar earlier on the street. Don't you remember?"

"I didn't ask you for a dollar. I asked for change."

From the pocket of the sweater, Sarah produced the key ring she'd found there. "Take this."

Allie's eyes lit up. "Ah, I have a collection of these. Keyless rings to homeless houses." She accepted Sarah's offering, then turned on Minnie. "Not shopping today, dear?"

Allie handed Minnie a pink and white baby afghan. "You'll need this where you're going." Allie gave her cart a push and headed down the street. When the women didn't follow, she called. "Well, c'mon. You'll need shelter."

The three women shrugged at each other. "We don't have anything better to do."

They followed Allie at a short distance, following her singsong voice and occasional titters as Allie conversed and exchanged inside jokes with herself.

After several blocks behind Allie, exhaustion blotted out the girls' fears of what lay ahead. Allie may have been a demented guardian angel, but she seemed harmless - even well-intentioned.

Allie rolled around a white "Caution" sawhorse with a flashing yellow light, and moved down a darkened alley. With a finger to her lips, she indicated they should keep quiet.

She stopped the cart by a door that began two feet above street level; it appeared that a short flight of stairs had been removed.

With the handle of the umbrella, she pushed the heavy door creaking inward. "Ssshh," Allie whispered to the door, then wagged a finger at it.

"Go on in," she rasped.

Jeanette asked, "In there?"

Allie said no more. She gave the cart a shove and started her song again: "Round and round she goes, where she stops nobody knows." Allie disappeared out onto the boulevard.

Jeanette, Minnie and Sarah hesitated at the missing threshold to the shambles that would be their shelter for the night.

Jeanette pressed a hand to her forehead and leaned against the wall. "There could be anything in here. Rapists. Murderers. Rats. Spiders."

Minnie gestured like an usher to Jeanette, whose escapade had led them to this place.

"You first."

At noon, George awoke to a ringing phone. Valerie hadn't moved in the bed. He put the receiver to his ear and whispered "What."

"George, it's Carl."

George hung up. Let Valerie get some more sleep; they hadn't closed their eyes in this bed until 5 a.m. He stroked her hair gently, then slipped quietly from the bedroom. In the living room, he called back.

"Hey, Carl. Sorry. I was dripping wet from the shower. What's up?"

"We got an authorization request last night from a massage parlor in Savannah, Georgia. And a charge came in this morning from a gun shop on the same street."

"A massage parlor? A gun shop?" George rubbed sleep from his eyes.

"I want you to get your butt up there immediately, get those goddamn women and bring them back. You've got until Tuesday. If you're not back, with them, by then, start looking for another fucking job. You understand me?"

The call ended with a dial tone.

George leaned against the cushions of the couch. A massage parlor and a gun shop? What were these women up to?

The phone rang again. He scooped up the receiver.

"What is it now?"

"Whoa, settle down, big guy."

"Serge, that you?"

"Yeah, man. You were supposed to call me last night at Frannie's."

"Ah, shit. Sorry about that. I got involved in something. Tell me what's going on."

"I wish I knew. Sergio told George what he'd discovered about the 'computer glitch,' which was really a series of bank-originated entries reversing the credit card balances of the three women George was pursuing. Each had been signed by Marc Corbett.

"So you think Corbett's helping his aunt and risking his career in the process?"

"I don't think so, but I have to admit it looks like it. You knew him when he was in collections, right?"

"Not very well. He was one of the night collectors. He wasn't in charge of assigning cases to the field so we never had direct contact. But yeah, I knew who he was."

"He's upstairs in computer programming now. What do you know about SuperCredit?"

"SuperCredit? The new department? Not much. Unsecured credit lines for business clients."

"Well, there's some bullshit going down about that as well. I swear to God, there's some kind of fraud in process. Someone is going to scam a shitload of money off the SuperCredit program. Like forty million dollars. And guess who's in charge of the computer programming for it."

"Corbett." George picked a cigarette from the pack on the coffee table. Lighting up, he settled back into the cushions. "Marc always seemed like an honest guy, Serge. Where'd you get this about scamming forty million off SuperCredit? Somehow I'm not buying it. You think he'd fuck around like that?"

"I don't. I did at first, believe me. It just looked obvious, or so I thought. But it's Jenkins. Him and someone else, I don't know who."

"Carl Jenkins? Our Carl Jenkins?"

"I overheard a phone conversation Jenkins had with someone. That's the number he said, forty million. He specifically said that someone named Mel was keeping Marc distracted. I think Marc's being set up. I think someone's forging his name on those credits to make it look like he's reversing his aunt's credit balances. And since he's in charge of the computer programming for SuperCredit, everyone is going to suspect he's the one who stole the forty million when it goes down."

"If Corbett looks guilty for the smaller crime of helping his aunt, he's a shoo-in to go down for the bigger fraud. Sweet. Makes sense."

"Exactly."

"Jenkins just told me that if I don't get these women back by Tuesday, I'm fired."

"Tuesday. That means they're going to transfer the funds pretty soon. Jesus. They want the women busted by Tuesday to finish the setup."

"Sounds like it. Shit, poor Marc. He's fucked, isn't he?"

"Yep."

"Sounds like you might be fucked yourself, Sergio."

"What do you mean?"

"It's no news flash that Jenkins hates your guts. He'll probably implicate you too. After all, you were working the Barlow account. And now they've dumped you. Better watch your back. They might be setting it up to make it look like you and Marc are in on it together."

"Ah, damn it. I didn't think about that. Should I go to the cops?"

"Cops don't know crap about white collar crime. This is the FBI's jurisdiction. But you know if they're called in, they're going to want to see some evidence. Otherwise they're just going to think that you're some disgruntled employee making trouble. You said you know where those SuperCredit applications are?"

Sergio brightened. "Yeah, I do. Locked up in a credenza in Jenkin's office."

"Have you talked to Marc about any of this?"

"He's been in Hawaii all week. He's flying back tomorrow afternoon. I guess I better look him up."

"I guess you better. Keep me posted. I'll call you back tomorrow night." George hung up.

His head was reeling. Forty million dollars. He could barely think about that much money, there wasn't enough room in his head right now, not after his night with Valerie.

With a sigh and a heavy heart, George started packing.

Chapter 21

Minnie awoke first, coming out of a dream about sleeping on concrete. Then she remembered where she was and flipped open her eyes. Sunlight angled in through a slit in one boarded window to catch dust motes drifting inside the beam. A cobweb glistened inches from her nose.

She stifled a squeal and rolled off the wooden palette that had been her unforgiving mattress through an interminable night.

"Wake up."

Jeanette and Sarah stirred. Each, upon seeing their surroundings in the light of morning, muffled their mouths in shock.

Minnie saw her own state of mind reflected on the faces of Jeanette and Sarah, confused but comforted by the fact that they were all still intact. They sat upright on a plywood floor in a dusty, musty living room, with a small kitchen adjoining. Years ago this had been a modest family home. In the kitchen the metal cabinets were chipped and barely clung to the walls. The sink was a nightmare, the faucet turned green. Smudged outlines showed where pictures had once hung on the peeling yellow walls. One greasy square of linoleum marked where a refrigerator had been.

Jeanette said, "I have to pee."

Minnie shook her head. "If you're thinking about finding the bathroom in this place, you go alone."

As Jeanette considered her options, the wail of an infant came from an adjacent room.

Minnie said, "Oh my goodness. We're not alone."

This put them on their feet fast, stiff and achy. Jeanette said, "Let's get out of here."

Before they could head for the door, the floor and walls shuddered to the roar of an immense machine. Outside, an engine cranked up and revved, sounding like an angry Goliath beyond the dirty windows.

A voice outside boomed, "Okay. You're all clear!"

The house tilted, swayed, and shook. Off balance on the trembling floor, the three women stumbled sideways and grasped a door frame.

Terrified, the women hunched together, arms around each other. Loose plaster fell, smashing and scattering around them. Minnie managed a few steps on the quaking floor towards the kitchen, to see what was happening. From the bedroom, the child's cries grew louder.

Out of the room flew a frantic toddler, barefoot in denim overalls, running straight at Minnie. Seeing her there, the child reached up. Reflexively, Minnie swept the little fugitive into her arms.

Her little hands wrapped around Minnie's neck. In the room, the infant wailed again. From inside, a woman's panicked voice called, "Jamie, Jamie!"

Minnie answered. "She's okay. She's here with me." She stroked the child's head to calm her, caressing a rainbow of barrettes that adorned tiny braids sticking out at many angles. Jamie clung tight, and Minnie did, as well.

Another jolt quivered through the building. The great engine's rumbling swelled and strained.

"It's moving," Jeanette announced the obvious. "We slept in a house that's moving."

Out of the bedroom limped a tall, lanky black man in his early thirties. His bare arms were corded with muscle and his eyes, though kind, took in the situation with apprehension: the three women huddled in the living room, one woman holding the child, the shaking floor, and the sense that his world was on wheels.

Minnie asked, "Is she yours?"

The little girl twisted and stretched her arms to him. Mildly, he took her from Minnie.

"Yes. C'mon now, child." His voice was deep and resonant. He winced as he took on her weight. "Thank you." He called into the bedroom, "Jolene, I got Jamie. C'mon out now. It's okay."

Jolene emerged with her wailing infant. She wagged her finger at Jamie in her man's arms.

Jolene was short and plump, a pretty redhead. A sprinkling of freckles speckled her nose and cheeks. Her high cheekbones were accentuated by hair pulled back in a bun. She carried an infant only a few months old who was sucking on her mother's forefinger.

An oversized drawstring bag hung from her shoulder. The string slid down her arm and the packed bag knocked against her legs. She halted, juggling the baby and struggling to pull the bag back into place. Jeanette stepped forward.

"Let me help you, dear."

Sarah hurried to the kitchen window, and narrated what she saw through a break in one of the boards. "We're behind a really big truck. On a road."

With the floor still quaking, Sarah said, "We should leave."

Jeanette said, "You think?"

The man seemed to be in some pain; Minnie offered to hold Jamie. At first he seemed reluctant to let her go, but Jamie reached out shyly for Minnie. She brought the little girl close and warm against her throat.

"Your name's Jamie? My name's Minnie. How old are you?"

The tyke held up all five fingers. "Free."

Minnie said to the child's father, "These are my friends, Jeanette and Sarah."

With a friendly nod, he said, "Jerry. And the baby there," he pointed to the infant in Jolene's arms, "that's Janice."

Jolene slumped into a sitting position against the living room wall and unbuttoned her blouse. She revealed one breast and cuddled Janice to it. Jeanette sat beside her. She ran a finger through the baby's soft fine curls. "Look at how much hair she has."

The suckling infant made Jolene's voice soft. "My lil' tulip's two months old today."

The house lurched as the driver slowed to negotiate a corner. Jerry moved hand-over-hand to the door. He opened it. With care, Minnie moved beside him to gauge their situation.

Jerry hollered to a man in a hardhat walking alongside the rolling house.

"Hey, Hey! There's people in here!"

The hardhat man waved at the driver, who braked instantly; the house teetered badly. The driver climbed down from the cab and tromped alongside his long trailer, to the door, and with hands on his wide hips, yelled up at Jerry and Minnie.

"What in the hell are you all doin' in there? Didn't you see the signs? Y'all get down. Right now!"

Minnie was the first out the door. The driver made no move to help her clamber down the side of the trailer. Jerry did his best to lend her a hand from above but his bad leg made him little use. Minnie wound up helping him down to the street. The driver belted, "Move it!" Minnie whirled on him with a glare that clamped his lips long enough to get Jerry on the ground, gritting his teeth in pain. Bravely, he reached up to help Jeanette. Jolene handed down her infant before lowering herself. Sarah brought little Jamie to the door and coaxed her into Minnie's waiting arms. The driver's impatience renewed, he shouted for Sarah to get down and this time it was Jerry who turned on him with a stare that shut him up while Sarah left the house.

The driver asked Minnie, "Any more of you up in there?"

"No. And you could be more understanding."

The driver lacked either the time or the heart to be bothered with that. He returned to his truck cab, gunned the engine and with a lurch slowly rolled the house away.

Minnie swept up little Jamie and led the way for everyone out of the road, across the street to a church.

Once they reached the safety of the sidewalk, Jerry lowered himself to the ground in a shady spot against a stone wall of the church. With a blue bandana he wiped his forehead. As he coughed into it, blood stained the kerchief.

Minnie and Sarah went to him, and sat on either side. Sarah asked, "What can we do? Water? Do you want some water?" Jerry nodded, then coughed again. Jolene brought a baby bottle from her bag. Sarah unscrewed the top and handed it to Jerry; he sipped gratefully, fighting the spasmodic cough that soon halted. He let his head drop to his pulled-up knees.

Sarah said, "We'll get you to a doctor."

Minnie tried the doors to the church, to find them locked. A cardboard sign read "Food and worship. Everyone welcome. Sunday 7:00 a.m."

Today was Saturday. She groaned, and her stomach groaned with her. They hadn't eaten in almost twenty-four hours.

She walked past the church, up the block to a vacant lot beside it. A volleyball net had been rigged up between metal posts grounded by cement-filled tires. Beyond a stand of eucalyptus trees stretched a field of flimsy, thrown-together shelters made from wooden crates, corrugated tin sheets, cardboard boxes, canvas tarps. They used bushes and trees for support and tiedowns.

Some metal barrels burned, pulsing heatwaves and smoke into the already steaming air. Haggard-looking people surrounded them, stirring their meals on aluminum pans. One man circulated, pouring steaming coffee into metal cups. Even from a distance, Minnie smelled the coffee and food, and longed to make friends.

Minnie returned to her little group in the shade of the church. "It's not the Hilton, but come over here and I'll give you a tour."

Jeanette's eyes were fixed on the street. She breathed. "No, don't look."

"What? What is it?"

"It's him. It's Post."

George Post, of all people, sat in a white Ford sedan, three cars deep at a red light, directly in front of them.

He smoked and stared out his windshield waiting for the light to change. Then as if on cue, he turned and looked straight at Minnie. She dropped her chin, turned slowly and moved to block the view of Jeanette still seated against the wall.

They remained that way, terrified, until the light changed and the idling engines accelerated. Together, they watched his taillights vanish in the traffic.

Sarah said, "These are our best disguises yet."

Minnie said, "Yep. He found us and he didn't. I suppose he'll be checking every hotel in town. Maybe he'll find Jasper."

"Wow!" Jeanette exclaimed. "Wouldn't that be something if Jasper took the fall for the whole thing?"

Sarah laughed in an uncharacteristically wicked way. "That's right. He's got those cards."

Jeanette said, "Uh oh."

"What?"

"He's coming back."

The white Ford had turned around and was making its way back towards the church. Minnie herded Sarah and Jeanette around the side of the church, out of sight. The Ford didn't slow and continued on its way.

The familiar clatter of a shopping cart brought Allie to them up the sidewalk.

"Enjoy your taxi ride? Welcome to the neighborhood. Better get busy and join the group."

In the daylight Allie seemed scarier. What appeared to be knife wounds scarred her face. Needle-sharp tiny eyes scanned the sky. "Looks like rain."

Sarah asked, "How can you tell?"

Allie ignored the question. "Someone's chasing you. Don't worry, you're safe here."

Gathering sticks, rocks, unclaimed cardboard, and a plastic tarpaulin abandoned in the bushes, Jerry and Sarah constructed a shelter in an open spot between two eucalyptus trees.

Minnie surveyed the clear sky. "It doesn't look like rain."

Jerry said "It gonna rain all right. Take a whiff. And look. See those clouds? Before sunset. Maybe sooner."

Minnie crawled under the hasty shelter, lay the pink baby blanket on the raw ground and lay back to rest. Jeanette sat beside her, rocking slumbering Janice in her arms. Little Jamie crawled next to Minnie. Sleepily she nuzzled into her side.

Jolene sidled beside Sarah. "Oh good. The children are sleeping. Clinic's not so far from here and I gotta get Jerry there. We'll be back. Do you mind watching them?"

"Of course not."

Sarah took a seat on a rock outside the shelter. She wondered about the stories of the other inhabitants, and whenever one of them returned her attention, she glanced away bashfully. She dared not linger over any one face too long. Sarah felt vulnerable with Jerry and Jolene gone and the others asleep, knowing so little about the people surrounding her. Were they dangerous, like trapped animals? On every face throughout this community, she sensed the pain of homelessness, their hopes and hopelessness.

She rose from the stone, massaged her lower back and peeked into the shelter. The girls and children were sound asleep. She took a walk to the deepest part of the property. The tall fence ended there. Someone had cut a hole into the open lot next door. Sarah went through to a graveyard dotted with tall trees drooping Spanish moss. Under one, a wooden bench faced a family crypt with six headstones.

With the sleeve of her cardigan, Sarah brushed away spider webs and took a seat on the dirty but sturdy bench.

Headstones overgrown with moss jutted at odd angles, weeds grew up their sides. The graves made Sarah wonder what would happen if they were to die in this place - who would know? Just three more vagrants with no I.D. Three bums, not worth the taxpayer's money to investigate, laid in unmarked paupers' graves. David would never know what became of her. Perhaps he wouldn't care.

How quickly things had changed for them, starting last night with the mugging by Jasper. Did Edith feel the same terror in the last moments of her life? What a cruel fate, and the same had almost befallen Sarah.

Beyond the still branches above, thunder rolled and the first drops of rain fell. Sarah stayed on the bench, studying the tombstones. A flash of lightning made the forgotten graveyard even more eerie and frightening.

Sarah couldn't accept Edith's death, the suddenness of it. Living without her best friend of forty-two years was surreal and sad. In the rain and the cemetery, Sarah cried and screamed her friend's name to the cracks of thunder. Though she was afraid of her own death, Sarah feared, just as much, forgetting Edith, her face, all the times good and bad they'd shared. She feared her fading memory. Alone and unabashed, Sarah cried harder with the rain.

When she'd had a good cry and did not know her tears from the rain on her cheeks, Sarah swiped her eyes and tried, as she always did, to find some bright side to her situation, any silver lining. She could find nothing good or pleasant right now, but a lesson: she reprimanded herself for taking so much for granted. She pictured her shabby San Francisco apartment; at least there was paint to peel, plumbing to go wrong, a radiator to break down. Sarah took in her soaked third-hand clothes. She wished she were in her apartment right now, in the shower instead of on a bench in a scary cemetery. She had a hearty laugh and imagined herself griping about the water pressure. She was still alive. What more could she ask for?

Sarah sent a silent prayer for Edith's soul into the enormous gray and white clouds. Was Edith looking down at her right now? Sarah smiled to the heavens, sent greetings and love, and could almost hear Edith's chuckling at what her dear friend had gotten herself into. The rain stopped, and in the breeze that took it away, Sarah felt Edith's presence.

Two hours passed with the rain; the tarp kept them dry inside the shelter. Jeanette awoke when the baby cried. She emerged with Janice to the dripping field, a warm afternoon sun, and Sarah sitting on a rock.

When Jerry and Jolene returned, Jerry stood a bit taller. They bore gifts of fruit: two bananas and a bruised apple. For the first time a smile edged Jerry's lips. Jolene seemed more relaxed, the furrows gone from her forehead.

They lay the tarp on the damp ground, arranged some of their bulky clothes as cushions and huddled together. They shared the fruit, and despite their hunger, the three women took only small bites of the apple, letting Jamie devour most of it.

Jolene described their journey to the clinic. The medicine they got for Jerry would only temporarily help the pain and symptoms. He had enough for seven days of relief. The doctor confirmed what they suspected: Jerry had an acute ulcer. The cure required continuing medication, a proper diet, rest, and relief from stress.

"There's the catch," he murmured. "I don't know how we're gonna get out of this mess. I can't help but worry what with a wife and two young'uns."

Jolene looked at him lovingly. She lay Jerry's head back in her lap and stroked his brow.

"Shhh. Now don't you fret now. You need your rest. You lay back."

Jerry seemed to doze off, or he might have been awake behind his eyelids, but he did not interrupt when Jolene began to tell Jeanette and her friends the story of her family.

"Sweet baby. He's worked so hard, he tries so hard. And what does it come to? I can't see God's blessing in this. This man is always so strong, even in sickness. But I just can't see why God lets it happen like this."

Jolene described the time when Jerry had a good warehouse job. At night he went to school so he could advance. He'd study half the night, sleep four hours most of the time. Then go to work and perform heavy labor all day.

"I cooked for him, fed him well, encouraged him to take time off but he'd say they couldn't afford to let things slip away. He's a worry wart. And I think that's what made him sick."

Then Jolene became pregnant. "That didn't help. Jerry was an hourly worker and didn't have health insurance.

The bills piled up, and Jerry worried even more. Then he got ill and lost his job because of it. The landlords made us move. I had little Janice in a motel room we paid for by collecting cans to recycle."

Janice, apparently aware of her role in the story, made herself known in Jeanette's arms. She cried in hunger; Jeanette handed her to Jolene to be suckled.

"Shh, li'l tulip, don't wake your daddy." Jolene smiled at Jeanette, Minnie and Sarah. "Now, don't y'all look so stricken. Things will be better. You wait and see. Jerry will get back on his feet and we'll be fine. I didn't mean to carry on like that."

"Take it from me," Sarah said, "it's good to let things out."

Sleepy Jamie snuggled deeper in Minnie's lap.

Jolene said, "I suppose you all are here because the government doesn't treat retired folks right. We've seen so much of that, too. Old folks getting sick with no place to go and nobody cares. Some of them even have family who don't do anything to help. They just let them stay sick on the street and fade away to nothing. At least Jerry and I have a chance, being still young and mostly healthy."

Jeanette exchanged sympathetic glances with Minnie and Sarah. Silently they agreed not to add their own stories to Jolene's sad, brave tale. They let her think they were here, in a homeless camp wearing rags, because it was someone else's fault.

Minnie slept long and well, and did not dream. The morning dawned sure and clear, with dew on the field. The sun rose in a cloudless sky, promising a dry, hot day.

The noise that awakened Minnie and the girls had a familiar sound.

Someone whacked against the cardboard wall of their shelter. Then a shrill, madcap voice belted, "Get in line! Get up. Time to get in line." More whacking on the tarp was followed by: "Get up you, hobos. Get in line!" Whack, whack, whack.

Allie's face peeked in under the tarp. Her old umbrella was her alarm clock.

Jeanette muttered, "Room service," and freed her arm from between Minnie's head and the cardboard floor. A sour taste fouled her mouth, and still groggy, she wondered where her toothbrush was. Rising, she said to no one, "I need a cigarette and some French roast. And a little mouthwash."

Jeanette's remark made Allie cackle and Minnie sit up.

Allie said, "French roast, wrong coast. Looks like y'all stayed dry overnight. Told you it would rain. Better get in line before the food's all gone."

She moved on to the next flimsy shelter, smacking it to wake the inhabitants to some semblance of breakfast.

Jeanette wound her matted hair into a loose bun. Beside her, Jolene cradled the baby to her breast. "Sometimes I can't figure if that woman is a guardian angel or the devil herself."

Jerry rolled over; he kicked Minnie in the shin and grumbled an apology. It took a few minutes for them to unpeel themselves from each other and make their way out to the marshy ground. Sarah laid out her still-damp cardigan to dry in the sun.

Jerry stood more easily than he had the day before. He stretched and Jolene beamed when he grabbed her for a morning kiss.

"Ain't this just the most beautiful day ever?"

Little Jamie rubbed the sleep out of her eyes. "I'm hungry." Jerry swept up his daughter for a bear hug, making her squeal with delight. "Hey little blue jay, you sleep alright? Ready for some groceries?"

"Can I have cake?"

"Maybe so, little girl, maybe so. Let's go see what they got. Hey, see those pink flowers? God put them there just for you. Go get one for your mama." Jerry put his little girl on the ground so she could run to pick some.

They stood in line for half an hour, for hard-boiled eggs, oatmeal and oranges provided by a local church.

Jeanette was ravenous; they all were. This may have been the best breakfast of her life.

They stayed with Jerry and Jolene for the worship service in the field that followed. Jolene's faith and spirits seemed buoyed by the sermon as much as by her husband's recovery. Every time she said Amen the word rang out; she went up front to thank the young pastor at the conclusion.

Walking back through the field, she said to Jerry, "Baby, God is going to take care of us."

Jeanette stepped forward. "I'm so glad you're feeling better, Jerry. We're going now. We've got to figure out a way to get to Charleston."

Jolene's freckled face filled with gratitude. "Glad to have met you. Thank you so much for caring for my li'l tulip." She embraced Jeanette.

To Minnie and Sarah, Jolene said, "And my li'l blue jay. I'm grateful to you all."

Sarah squeezed Jerry's arm. "You take care of yourself."

Minnie wrapped up Jamie in an embrace. Jerry offered handshakes all around. "Thank you all for everything. You're the only folks we've ever trusted our young'uns' with. Ever."

Jeanette was happy to see that his grip was strong. As his grasp receded, Jerry accidently pulled Jeanette's emerald ring off her finger. The ring fell to the trampled grass and weeds.

Jerry picked up the ring. Handing it to her, he said, "This is a pretty ring. But it doesn't sparkle like you do."

Jeanette flushed. "Are you saying I sparkle?"

"Oh, yes, ma'am. Don't you know it? You've got to know it. Come on. Did you see the way little Janice took to you? The way your friends look at you? Yes, ma'am. Indeed you do."

"Oh my." Jeanette covered her mouth to quash a cry. "I suppose I may have forgotten." Jeanette was tall enough to kiss Jerry's cheek without going on tiptoes.

She gazed into her palm at her precious ring. The ring symbolized her old life, the one that was gone forever. Madame Viola's words came back in a rush: You haven't lost your sparkle yet, but you will. In order to get what you want, you must give it away.

Jeanette took a last admiring look at the beautifully set emerald circled by diamonds. She held out the ring. "Here."

He took a step back, surprised and refusing. She moved to him and pressed the ring into his palm. "It's worth a lot of money. And I mean a lot. Ten thousand dollars. Don't be swindled when you hock it."

He started to say something, but she cut him off. "Don't even think about not accepting this. You have a family." With that, Jeanette walked away into the field.

Minnie and Sarah caught up with her. Jeanette glanced back over her shoulder. Jerry held the ring up to the sunlight. It sparkled as she turned away.

Chapter 22

Marc unlocked his front door and set down the suitcase in the foyer. He reset his watch from Hawaii time where it was only noon. Yesterday at this time they were still in bed. He smiled at the memory and all the others they'd made: snorkeling, a cruise of the Na Pali coastline, the falls, hiking through Waimea Canyon. Though so much of the scenery was extraordinarily beautiful, Melanie lived at the heart of his thoughts.

He headed toward his refrigerator. He was apart from Mel for the first time in a week, and even a few hours away from her was hateful. A foul odor swept out of the fridge.

"Christ, I should have thrown that salmon away before I left."

He tossed the plastic-wrapped fillet in the garbage. He took a beer into the living room and sat on the couch with a week's worth of mail.

Among the junk mail and bills was a New Orleans postcard from Na Na and a letter on the stationary of a hotel in Miami. There were also two postal attempted-delivery cards for packages from New Orleans and Miami. It appeared Na Na was trying to make him an accomplice one way or another.

The New Orleans postcard bore a Miami postmark. It read, "You're not going to believe this, but I danced 'til 2:00 a.m. last night. They play great music in New Orleans. Real fanny swingers. Love, Na Na. P.S. Pralines and Carnival masks to follow."

The letter from Miami read: "Dear Marc, I tried to reach you in Hawaii, but you were never in. Figured you were in the surf all day. Something strange is going on that I thought you should know about. I thought we were under the floor limit, but they called for an authorization on the flight tickets we bought from New Orleans to Miami. And the charge was approved. I don't see how that could be possible. In fact, I charged a few other things in Miami (you'll be getting a package any day now) just to try it out and those charges cleared as well. By the way, we've managed to keep George Post postponed. I'll call in a couple days. We're on our way to St. Augustine. Here's something you can appreciate: we're driving a Cadillac convertible. How's Melanie? Love Na Na.

Marc puzzled over the situation with her credit, despite the fact that she was defrauding the very bank he worked for. That fact still surprised him and made him nervous as hell. He made a mental note to check her accounts at the office tomorrow.

The doorbell rang. Did Melanie miss him already? Marc switched on the intercom.

He crooned, "Who's there?"

"Sergio Fernandez. We've got to talk."

"What the hell do you want? You've got a lot of nerve coming to my home. Especially on a Sunday."

"Just give me five minutes. I swear, it's important."

"Two minutes." Marc buzzed the gate and then covered Na Na's postcard and letter with an issue of Forbes. When he opened the door, Sergio rushed in.

"Sorry to bother you at home. I couldn't do this at the bank. There's something going on."

"What are you talking about?"

"SuperCredit. It's a fraud."

"What do you mean, fraud?"

"Your boss and my boss, they've got a scam going."

"What makes you think that?"

"I overheard a phone conversation. They're framing you. They did it while you were in Hawaii for a week."

"Bullshit. Get out."

"You don't believe me?" Sergio handed over a brown envelope.

From the interoffice envelope Marc pulled a sheet of paper. He read the bank-originated entry reversing the balance of Na Na's account. No wonder she could continue charging.

Sergio asked, "Is that your signature?"

Marc studied the signature line. Fighting shock, he said. "It's fucking close. But no."

"They're reversing every charge that comes through on her account. I'll bet they faked your signature on those, too. Now your aunt has a ten thousand dollar credit line. Want to bet you approved that too?"

Sergio had sniffed something out, something big and nasty. Marc hadn't signed anything on Minnie's behalf. Sergio seemed to know this, otherwise he would have accused Marc.

"Want a beer?"

"I'll take a dozen."

Marc went to the kitchen examining the signature on the dark, hardly legible microfiche copy. When he returned with two cold beers, Sergio was pacing the living room. He took the beer and lowered himself onto the leather couch beside Marc.

"What's this about SuperCredit?"

"They're going to embezzle forty million dollars."

Marc whistled. Somehow this didn't surprise him. Phil Southern came from money, but was ambitious and ruthless. Marc had pegged him with a short man's complex, the way he barked orders like an arrogant snob. The dismissive way he dealt with women. Melanie had complained about him in Kauai, she could barely tolerate the guy.

"How'd you find out about this?"

"I overheard Jenkins and Southern talking about it on the phone the other night. As soon as Jenkins knew that I knew about the credit reversal," he gestured toward the paper on Marc's lap, "he took the account from me and told me to take a week off. That gave me a few days to think about it while you were in Hawaii, and do some snooping on my own. I think they're working the computer system, loading it with phony credit line accounts. SuperCredit accounts. They were talking about the timing getting fucked up, though Jenkins said the timing was fine. He said Southern jumped the gun, I noticed it, and that's why they took your aunt's account from me. I figure they're going to fund all the credit lines on one day, then somehow get the money into a safe place."

"Where do I come into all this?"

"They said they'd gotten you out of the way, in Hawaii. They said Barlow was the clincher. And they would get away clean."

"Slow down. Why are they forging my signature all over the place? Why are they making it look like I'm helping my aunt?"

"Come on, man. You've got a background in collections. They're going to make you the fall guy not just for your aunt, but for the bigger scam they've got going. Marc, you're a shoo-in for that role."

"Have they already done it? Taken the money?"

"I doubt it. But it's going to happen real soon. You're back now and you know how quiet it is down there on the weekends. Tonight, tomorrow. I'd bet you anything."

Marc had suspected something was wrong with the SuperCredit program from day one. Even Melanie's explanation of the debit and credit situation hadn't satisfied him. The credit going to outer space was probably, in reality, going to an offshore bank account.

Suddenly, it all fit together. They waited until he was out of the way in Hawaii so they could complete the string. As project manager, he'd be the responsible party, thus the embezzler.

Marc was shaken. "We've got to take this upstairs, to someone we can trust. But we've got to have solid proof. More than just this." He slapped the paper.

"I know. Listen, we've got to get hold of the SuperCredit apps and get evidence from the programming to prove Southern's role. That's got to be where he comes in on this thing. We do that, we prove you're innocent. But we've got to get to someone before they make the transfer."

"Why do you care? You don't even know me."

Sergio walked to the window and the view of boats docked on the Marina. He took a swig of beer. "I'm not here to save your ass. I've got to save mine. My career's in the shitter, too. I was in charge of the Barlow account, and

I figure they'll frame me along with you. Jenkins already suspects I'm on to them so they might try to shut me up. Maybe permanently. I've been hiding out and looking over my shoulder all week."

Sergio finished off the beer, then turned from the window.

"They've got somebody named Brad finishing up your project. And they sent you to Hawaii with another guy named Mel who was supposed to keep you distracted."

Marc dropped his beer bottle, it foamed onto the carpet.

Mel? Melanie?

They sent him to Hawaii? No, no. She invited him. He was in love.

Marc couldn't, wouldn't, believe that she was in league with Southern and Jenkins.

Sergio read something in Marc's reaction. Gently, he said, "Marc, it's true. They said that."

If Sergio was right – and he seemed to be right about everything else, the papers, his forged signature – then Melanie had been playing him, keeping him distracted, as Jenkins put it.

Melanie had blown off the programming problem, she'd attributed it to Marc's lack of accounting knowledge. Oh, Jesus. He swiped a hand across his forehead.

Marc went to the window and stood beside Sergio gazing out, thinking. A barge made way toward the port of Oakland. The bay was calm. Sunshine glinted on the masts of the sailboats at harbor.

Sergio said, "With your pass we can get into the bank tonight. I know where Jenkins keeps the SuperCredit apps. We'll break into his office, get them, and take them to the authorities. If those apps are fraudulent, it'll be easy to prove."

Sergio put his back to the bay and leaned against the glass.

"You in?"

Mel. Melanie. He'd chased her into the surf and caught the top of her bikini. It came off. She laughed and said, 'God, I love you,' then dove into a blue wave before he could say anything. He'd wondered then if she meant it. Meant it the way he did.

What was her part in this? Jenkins was needed to process and approve the phony credit applications. Southern's part would be to set up the computer program in order to divert the funds to an offshore bank account. They needed someone inside NCCA to process the approvals, authorize the fund's destination. Melanie. Of course.

Sergio said, "You've got a nice place, man. I love the view. You know, San Quentin has the same view, only from the other side of the bay."

Marc's hurt faded faster than he'd wished it to. He tried to hang onto it a moment more, because if he hurt he still loved. But it curdled into anger.

"Yeah. I'm in."

Marc snapped open his briefcase and brought out the crowbar.

Though it was the middle of the night and the floor was deserted, Marc was on edge. It was unlikely Carl Jenkins would stumble in on them, but he listened for any sound.

Marc inserted the edge of the crowbar between the door and the jamb. Sergio threw a hand over his arm to stop him.

"Man, what the hell are you doing?"

"I'm breaking in. You said we'd break in."

"I didn't mean to tear up his door. Jesus Christ, anyone who sees this will know someone was in here."

"That's what break means."

"Move aside."

From his wallet, Sergio extracted his Master Charge card. He slid it into the opening.

Marc said, "Like that's going to work."

"How's your tennis game?" Sergio kept working the plastic card between the door and jamb.

"What's that got to do with anything?"

"I'm saying…" and with that the lock clicked - Sergio turned the knob and pushed the door open for Marc to enter first – "…that we grew up differently."

Marc put away the crowbar and stepped into Jenkins' office.

Behind the desk stood a trio of two-drawer oak filing cabinets. Sergio said, "That's where they are."

All the drawers were locked.

Marc asked, "What do we do now?"

"Well, we tried to be neat." Sergio put out his hand. "I've been dreaming about this. Give me the bar."

Inside a minute, Sergio pried open three of the drawers, leaving splintered wood on Carl Jenkins' carpet. He peered into the third, finger-flipped through a few files, then said, "Got him."

Sergio heaped fistfuls of SuperCredit applications into Marc's briefcase.

"Okay, let's get up to twelve, back up the program and get out of here."

They avoided the elevators and climbed the stairs to the twelfth floor. It too was empty. From behind the closed door of the clean room came the whir of the mainframe computer. Sergio stepped forward with the bar upraised, nudging Marc out of the way.

Marc grabbed his arm. "Whoa, whoa." He dangled his key ring in front of Sergio's face.

Marc unlocked the door. The mainframe took up most of the room. Reels of tape spun on the floor-to-ceiling behemoth. Three illuminated screens flashed ever-changing rows of numbers. Marc opened a drawer and pulled out a blank tape.

"This might take a little time." He inserted the tape into a drive, and typed instructions into the computer. The light on the drive came on and the electronic whirring grew louder.

"Now we wait while it backs up."

Sergio opened the briefcase and pulled out a handful of documents. Among them was a blank white envelope. He opened it and handed it to Marc. "Look at this. A note to Carl Jenkins."

The note said nothing, just a phone number with a 212 area code. New York.

Marc dialed but got no answer. "Hold on to this. Maybe we can find out who it's listed to."

Sergio folded the note small and tucked it into his shoe. He examined another handful of credit apps.

"All we have to do is make a few calls to verify these businesses don't exist. Look at these signatures. The apps are typewritten, same font and size, but the signatures are the same handwriting."

Marc recognized his own script spelling out dozens of different phony names. "Shit."

The computer beeped and the light went out on the backup drive. Marc stowed the ejected tape. Sergio was busily going through another stack of papers. "Let's go through this stuff later. While I restart this program, you pack up. We got to get out of here."

"Check this out." Sergio pushed forward one of the credit apps. "Did you know your aunt owns a furniture store in New Jersey?"

"What!" Marc grabbed the paper. 'Approved' had been rubber-stamped across the top, and written beside it was 'seven hundred thousand dollars.'

"And her dead friend, Edith Clark, owns a string of gyms. Pretty good for someone not feeling too hot."

Marc said, "While you're at it, look for Compton and Gardener." He turned back to the computer and focused on typing.

"You said Compton? Oh, this is good. You approved a million for her. Seems she owns a string of modeling schools on the east coast." Sergio scooted his chair toward Marc. Together they studied the application. "Ice cream parlors too." Sergio pointed to an item on the paper.

From behind them, Phil Southern said, "Don't forget about the Andalusia horse farms."

Swinging around they came face-to-face with Southern and two burly men. Southern had a small caliber pistol.

"I'll take that." He snatched the paperwork from Sergio's hand. He perused it, chuckling softly. "Your aunt's friend is a naughty girl."

Marc tensed. He was an athlete, he might be able to take one of the big guys.

Southern seemed to read Marc's intention. "We can do it the hard way, if you like. Go ahead. But don't think I won't use this gun. And Roscoe, here," Southern indicated the goon on his left, "did two tours in Vietnam. Vinnie did two, but he was Navy."

"Hey," Vinnie protested.

Roscoe told Vinnie it was okay, he served.

Southern kept talking. "Jenkins had a feeling you might be here tonight. Actually this works out just fine. You broke into Jenkins' office to get your hands on all the evidence he had on you."

Southern shoved the gun in his waistband. "Watch them."

He stuffed the remainder of the SuperCredit apps into Marc's briefcase. "This is sweet. Not only are they going to see your signature," he patted the case, "but your little programming reconfigurations you did tonight. It is definitely looking like you two boys did it."

Southern patted Sergio's cheek, almost tenderly. "Sergio, you're a stupid fag, just like Jenkins said. You should have done yourself a favor and kept your ass out of this."

Before Marc could blink, Sergio roared out of his chair to take Southern by the throat, almost lifting him off the floor. Southern's eyes bulged with surprise and fear, then smoked in anger. He flailed and fumbled at his waistband, trying to get the gun, but Sergio, bigger and stronger, took a hand from Southern's throat to go for it, too. Vinnie jumped on Sergio to pry him away.

In the confusion of the melee, Marc grabbed the crowbar. He leaped at Vinnie, hitting him square in the back; when he reared back for another blow, Roscoe caught his wrist and grabbed Marc by the hair. With a powerful grunt, Roscoe drove him face-first into the computer console. Marc's forehead and nose broke the screen, and when Roscoe hauled him upright, blood obscured Marc's vision.

Roscoe punched him in the stomach, then caught his chin with an uppercut. Woozy, Marc was shoved back into the chair.

Through a screen of blood Marc watched Roscoe turn on Sergio. Sergio took several merciless punches, but when Marc tried to rise to help, the decisive click of a handgun's hammer made him stop.

"If you want to live, stay where you are." Marc stared into the black snub barrel of the pistol while Southern rubbed a purple streak around his neck. Roscoe relented his beating of Sergio when Southern told them, "That's enough. Tie them up and hood them."

Roscoe bound Marc's sore hands behind his back. Then a cloth bag was yanked over his head.

"Get them up. Let's get out of here."

Chapter 23

After a summer storm, Savannah was a soggy metropolis of muggy air, muddy puddles, and a dampness like sweat on every bit of concrete and greenery.

Jeanette slumped on a curb, feeling limp. She hugged her legs between ragged velveteen arms. She brushed away a tear and kissed the pale band of skin on her ring finger.

Minnie and Sarah sat on either side. Minnie said, "That was the most beautiful gesture I've ever seen anyone make." Sarah put an arm around her.

"The only thing I want right now is a good stiff drink."

Minnie stroked Jeanette's matted hair. "Once we get to Charleston and get our luggage, we'll be fine. Once we get a shower."

A roll of thunder made them all look up. Sarah said, "The sky's clear. How can it rain again?"

Jeanette said, "I swear, if it does, I'm going to strip naked right here."

A pair of motorcycles rounded the corner; this was the source of the thunder. They sped through a puddle and splashed mud and water on the three women.

Minnie wailed, "Look at this mess!"

Sarah removed her glasses to clean the lenses. "What difference does it make?"

At that moment, a five-dollar bill swirled down the street before them. Jeanette leaped up from the curb to grab it with grimy hands. As she did, the rope holding up her pants loosened and the waistline slid down. Minnie grabbed the back to pull them up. "You're losing your pants."

Jeanette snatched the five dollar bill off the street. Madame Viola's intoning voice returned: In order to get what you want, you must give it away. "Five bucks for an emerald ring. Okay, I see Viola still has a sense of humor. Let's find some food."

Minnie said, "Better than a stiff drink. I'm starving."

They walked south toward a retail area. Passersby gave their tattered, muddy figures a wide berth. Quickly they found what looked like a neighborhood bar, called Hog Heaven. In the parking lot, a truck boasted a flag that read: "Charity Ride for Muscular Dystrophy, D.C. or Bust. Happy 200th!" A hundred motorcycles stood in rows of chrome, rubber and steel.

Inside, in the dim light of sconces, purls of cigarette smoke mingled with the pungent odor of unwashed bodies. The jukebox played Janis Joplin. The chairs and booths were all upholstered in red Naugahyde, and every pool table was occupied by hard-looking men, grizzled and muscled, pot-bellied and ponytailed, guzzling, laughing men holding onto shapely, tattooed women.

Minnie found the only table not filled with motorcycle riders. The three girls sat; before they could settle, a great-sized man in a sleeveless leather vest at the next table leaned toward Sarah.

In a southern drawl, he said, "Why, ma'am, you look just like my Aunt Sophie." He called over his shoulder to a pool player: "Bart, don't she look like Sophie?" He pointed to Sarah with a plastic fork.

Bart's leathery hand plucked a cigarette from his weathered face. He hollered "What?"

"This gal here. Ain't she the spittin' image of Sophie?"

Bart squinted in the poor light. "Yeah, Pit Bull. Is it Sophie?"

"No, numb nuts, but don't she look like her? Ah, hell, never mind." Pit Bull turned back to his food, shaking his head.

"Oh, oh yeah." Bart swaggered from the pool game, cue still in hand. He came close to scrutinize Sarah with wizened blue eyes. Then he lit up and shouted, "Hey, damn. It's Sophie! Girl, you look like you fell into a pool of magic and came out a fairy princess."

Sarah dipped her head genteelly. "Why, thank you, sir." Bart made a short, princely bow, and returned to the pool table.

Pit Bull rolled his eyes, still leaning towards Sarah. "That's my cousin. He ain't all there." He tapped the fork against the side of his head. "Took one over the high side and ended up with a plate in his head. Told him to wear a helmet."

A big fellow sidled up beside Jeanette. She greeted him with a muddy but coy smile. He asked, "Ma'am, may I buy you a drink?"

"Yes." He pulled out Jeanette's chair for her to stand. "A stiff one." She went with him to the bar.

While Pit Bull engaged Sarah in conversation, the man next to him grabbed his beer bottle by the neck and sat in Jeanette's abandoned chair. He was handsomely rugged, without a beard but attractively unshaven, and beefy shoulders under his leather jacket.

"I'm Rudy." He reached a massive paw to Minnie; her hand disappeared into his strong mitt.

"Are you a Hell's Angel?"

When Rudy smiled, wings appeared beside his eyes.

"No, ma'am. I'm an accountant."

"A what?"

"I ride on weekends. Our club does a lot of charity work. It's good for our image. But we can party down like anybody else. Then on Monday, back to the suit and tie."

Sarah excused herself from Pit Bull's charms, and said to Minnie, "There's the bathroom. I hope they've got lots of soap and paper towels."

Rudy kept Minnie's attention with stories of his weekend rides. Jeanette sipped a whiskey at the bar with her new friend, and the pool tables resounded with laughter and the clack of the game. When Sarah returned from the bathroom, her face and hands were fresh and white, her hair less in disarray, and she looked closer to herself than she had in days.

Bart stopped in mid shot and looked at her from the pool table, squinting again.

"Sophie, you like you been dyed, fried, and swooped to the side." Bart grinned again and looked at Pit Bull. Bart added, "And that's comin' from a lewd, crude, tattooed dude."

Pit Bull walked to his cousin, plainly fond of him. "That ain't her, dipshit. Sophie's been dead ten years." Pit Bull slapped Bart on the back of the head. "Here, let me reset your plate."

Pit Bull leaned in to Sarah, grinning with mischief. "But you do look like you been clubbed, mugged, and scrubbed in the tub."

Bart wouldn't quit. "Like you fell off the porch and got dragged through a brambleberry patch."

Sarah said, "Alright. Point taken."

Pit Bull asked, "So. Who are you?"

"I'm Sarah. And these are my friends Minnie and Jeanette."

Bart took another turn: "They look like they been waylaid, not paid, and left in the shade."

Pit Bull called to a blonde woman at the bar. "Irene." When Irene turned, she revealed a snake tattoo rising from between her bosoms, which were propped up by a black leather bodice. Pit Bull said, "Get over here and lip lock this boy."

"Dang it, Pit Bull! I lost a handful of hair the last time."

"C'mon, girl. I need him to calm down. You know how he gets."

She bounced off the barstool, and jounced over to Bart at the pool table. As she closed in, Bart said, "You look like you been tossed, turned..." Irene silenced Bart with her ruby lips. His cue stick clattered to the floor as he threw his arms around her and backed up to a barstool. Irene attached to his face.

Pit Bull said to Sarah, "You don't mind my saying so, lady, you look like you fallen on hard times."

"Just lately."

"What the hell happened?"

"It's a long story."

Pit Bull pivoted on his black boots, and in short order returned to the table with cold bottles for Minnie, Sarah and himself.

"You can talk 'til they run out of beer."

Sarah and Minnie explained their mishaps in Savannah, leaving out the credit cards and George Post. They spoke of Jasper, Jolene, Jerry, Jamie, and lil' tulip Janice.

Pit Bull listened keenly, with sympathy. He seemed to understand bad luck and hard times.

When they'd caught up to the present moment, Minnie said, "Pit Bull, we could sure use your help. We're stranded and we've got to get to Charleston. Do you think you could give us a lift?"

The old biker cracked his knuckles like he was getting ready for action.

"Hell, girl, you all don't have to ask twice."

The pair of very flattering black leather pants Rudy chose for Jeanette fit her perfectly. So did the ebony knee-high boots. She turned in the mirror to make the fringe on her jacket sleeves and pant seam flare together.

Jeanette couldn't suppress a giggle. In the dressing room alongside hers, Minnie giggled too.

Exiting at the same time, they measured each other in their new outfits. Minnie looked like an adventurer in leather chaps over black denim jeans. Sarah admired herself in blue denim coveralls.

Jeanette asked Sarah, "Did you bother to look at the back of those overalls?"

"No. Why?"

"Look in the mirror."

Emblazoned on Sarah's back was a red oval patch reading: 'Harley Hog.' Below the patch, a pink pig on a motorcycle gave onlookers the finger.

"Here, throw this on." Minnie handed Sarah a black leather jacket fringed at the chest and sleeves. Sarah slid it on and smiled at herself from every angle.

Rudy passed the time conversing with the clerk, Marty, a wiry man in his fifties. When the ladies were properly outfitted to his approval, Rudy produced a credit card.

Marty laughed when Rudy laid the plastic on the counter. "Where'd a shit-heel like you get a credit card?"

"Oh, sorry." Rudy reeled the card back from Marty the clerk. "That's my corporate card. Here's my personal one. Ring it up, asshole. All of it. I'm treating these ladies, and it's my pleasure."

Minnie and Sarah picked out boots to match their ensembles. After they were fitted for helmets, Sarah said to Rudy, "Thanks. You're a sweetheart."

"Not as sweet as you, Auntie. Alright, girls. You're looking sharp. Let's roll."

They walked a block back to the bar where the entourage was lounging outside. Minnie donned her new leather gloves and took a deep breath. "Well, we saw Savannah, girls."

Jeanette said, "I can't wait to tell Susan where we stayed. She'll be green with envy."

Minnie rode an enormous Harley with a tall biker named Spider, likely because his bald head was tattooed with a web. Jeanette joined forces with Rudy. In the din of the engines jumping to life, Sarah struggled to sling her leg over the sissy seat of Pit Bull's BMW. Pit Bull plucked her up, light as a dishcloth, and planted her on the back. Straddling his bike, he kick-started it and a fiery blast spit from the chrome tailpipes. He and Sarah shot like a bullet from the curb; Sarah clutched him tight about the chest. Excited and thrilled, she shrieked so loudly that Minnie heard her clear as a bell over the growl of a hundred thundering beasts.

Chapter 24

Marc walked on a dock with his hands tied behind his back. He was blinded by a hood over his head but a foghorn's distant moan, the salt smell of brine, planks under his shoes, and the tumbling tide against the pilings betrayed where he was. Several gashes in his forehead stung; they'd bled into his eye sockets to make a crust that kept his eyes shut. His shirt was damp from the fog; he shivered, feverish and cold.

One of Southern's thugs gripped his arm, propelling him forward. Disoriented beneath the hood, Marc stumbled; the henchman smacked the side of his head. "Keep moving."

After a nerve-racking walk on the pier, the thug jerked his arm to turn him left. "Keep going." The surface under Marc slanted upward. "Keep going," the voice repeated. Then a push in the back made him fall headlong. Marc, unable to use his hands, landed on his shoulder. The hood was snatched off. He lay on the deck of a large wooden sailboat. Beside him, unconscious, lay Sergio.

Phil Southern said, "Take them below. Then get the cooler out of the van."

Marc was yanked to his feet. The other thug slapped Sergio awake.

They were taken below, through a galley and wide settee area. The sailboat was well appointed in polished teak accents and plush cushions; on a captain's desk lay charts and navigation tools. Marc and Sergio were hustled through the common area and stuffed into a small stateroom in the bow. The room was poorly ventilated and smelled of damp wood and musty bed sheets. With stiff corded ropes, Roscoe tied Marc into a chair, leaving his hands tied behind his back, while Vinnie lashed Sergio onto the stateroom mattress. Sergio's hands were left tied, too.

When Roscoe finished his knots, he leaned close to Marc's face, studying his brow. With pinching fingers the kidnapper plucked a shard of computer screen glass out of Marc's forehead.

He showed the blood-tipped sliver to Marc, then tossed it away. A warm dribble ran between Marc's eyes and dripped crimson off his nose.

Roscoe asked, "You boys got everything you need? Sorry, there's no room service."

"Hot tub on the third deck. Jacuzzi on the second."

As they left, Vinnie said, "No funny business. No one onshore can hear you if you start yelling. But if we hear you, we'll be back to quiet you down."

The door closed. Sergio rolled over on his side because he could not lie on his arms and hands. His face was swollen and purpled around one eye. Blood caked around his lips.

Marc asked, "You okay?"

"Been better."

"They beat you up pretty bad."

"A little dizzy. A Jacuzzi will be good. Second floor, right? Get the towels, will you?"

Sergio's face was so bruised Marc couldn't read his expression.

"You terrified or do you just joke a lot?"

"I'm way past terrified. Coming back around to I-don't-give-a-fuck. Where are we?"

"On some sailboat. We did a lot of driving. I think we crossed the Golden Gate. Fort Barlow's my guess. We didn't go very far after the rainbow tunnel."

"That's a relief."

"What do you mean?"

"All this rocking, I thought I was really fucked up. So I guess tonight is it. Tonight they get the money."

"Could be."

"I guess all they gotta do now is finish framing us. Then they'll let us loose so we can get caught."

"Yeah. Right."

"What do you mean, 'Yeah right'? Did I miss something while I was out?"

"They're gonna fuckin' kill us, Serge."

"You've seen too many movies. These guys are thieves, not murderers."

"Think about it. We're talking about forty million bucks. They can't afford loose ends."

Sergio's head bobbed, slowly, painfully, calculating along with Marc.

"I suppose you're right. They don't want us talking, no matter how guilty we look."

"They'll deep six us off this boat somewhere. The cops will think we pulled a disappearing act, like we're in Mexico somewhere sipping Margaritas. But we won't be."

"Great."

"Serge?"

"What."

"How are we going to get out of here?"

Sergio shifted positions; he groaned and rolled back to where he was on his side.

"You okay?"

"I think it's a broken rib."

Marc tested the ropes that bound him. They held tight, and every attempt cut his wrists and ankles deeper.

"They got all the evidence. They got the credit apps."

Serge said, "Yep."

"And the backup tape."

"Did they? Are you sure?"

"Shouldn't I be?"

"I mean, how could they figure out which one tape it was with all that mess in the clean room? There was a whole library of shit on the floor and desk. They cleared it off when they took us, remember?"

"But I gave you the tape and you put it in the briefcase with the apps. Southern took the case."

"I didn't put it in the case. I was busy looking at all those credit apps, so I put the backup on the desk."

Hope surged in Marc's chest. "Oh my God. They probably don't even know we made a backup."

Serge agreed. "If we can get out of here somehow and get hold of that tape, we can blow this whole thing out of the water. What time do you think it is?"

"Two or three in the morning."

"Which morning?"

"You weren't out that long. It's Monday morning."

"I'm wasted, man. You're not going to believe this, but you know what hurts the worst?"

"Your dignity?"

Sergio's laugh turned into a coughing jag. "No, aside from the damn rib, it's this fucking paper cut on my thumb."

"Paper cut?"

"Cardboard cut, actually. Got it after I busted open Jenkins' file cabinet. Off those files I shoved in the carry case."

"Hurts that bad?"

"It's searing, man. I ripped it open real good grabbing Southern by the neck. Maybe I can get Workers Comp."

Marc's thoughts spun fast to find a way to escape. Each plan fell apart. He worked at his bonds again, to no avail. He asked Serge for his ideas but got no answer. Marc worried that Sergio had passed out again, but his concerns disappeared momentarily when Sergio began to snore.

Chapter 25

George sat on the bed and lit a smoke. It was Sunday night and he was exhausted. He used to love being on the road, chasing crooks city to city, new places, new adventures. But this trip left a bad taste in his mouth, especially after his conversation with Sergio yesterday about bank fraud.

The silver lining was Valerie.

But even she, the first woman who'd touched his heart in five years, the reason why he'd finally considered letting his heart come back to life, couldn't keep his head from tumbling back to Sergio, Marc Corbett, and the three women he was chasing.

He had to admit, they'd given him a run for his money. But then, he hadn't been on his A game, hadn't from the beginning, not for those five years. Suddenly the statement made by the curio shop owner in San Antonio, repeated by the psychic Madame Viola, sprang to mind: The pursuit of innocence is unrewarding. Look to the intent of the heart.

Way too weird. George dialed Sergio's number. He counted fifteen rings, then hung up. He'd try later.

With a smile, he dialed again. Valerie answered at the front desk; he'd hoped she was on duty. When he'd left this afternoon, she was still sleeping. He'd stood watching her, taking in all that she was. If he'd woken her up, he'd never have been able to leave. So he had slipped out. But he hadn't gotten any information about her, her last name, home phone number, nothing.

"Hi, Angel."

"George?" She sounded relieved and happy to hear from him.

"Honey, I'm sorry I had to leave like that. Did you get my note?"

"I did. I understand. Are you in Savannah?"

"Yes." George swiped his hand over his mouth; he felt his words begin to scatter again. "I just had to tell you...I mean...you know...ah hell, Valerie, what I'm trying to say..." His eyes rose to the ceiling in frustration, his stomach twisted.

"I feel the same way, George."

"You...you do?"

"There was an immediate connection between us, wasn't there? When you walked up to the counter, I felt like I already knew you."

"That's what I felt too. Man, I was afraid I'd gone over the edge or something." His tongue came untied; this was what Valerie did to him, tied him in knots, and the next moment freed him. "At first I thought you were someone I already knew but couldn't think of who it was."

"I know what it was."

"What?"

"James Garner."

"Ah, Jeez. This again?"

"What do you mean?"

"Never mind. It's an office joke. No, I don't think I look like James Garner. Not the way I came into the hotel. I was beat."

"Okay. James Garner having a bad day."

George laughed, not at the Garner bit but how this woman had changed him so quickly, almost overnight. A void had been filled. Even if the two of them never made it, heaven forbid, his life was better and would stay that way.

"Val, I've got to see you again. We've got to figure something out. I mean it. I know we've only known each other about sixteen hours, but I swear to God, I think it's worth going after it. Do you want to try?"

"Yes."

"Good. Good. Man, okay."

"What are we going to do?"

"I was thinking. There's an excellent design school in San Francisco." She made no quick reply, and perhaps too soon, George prodded. "Val?"

"This is all pretty sudden. I don't know about just up and relocating. Think about it, George. Like you said, we've only known each other for sixteen hours. And we were asleep for three of those."

"I thought it was only two." George paced the room. "You're right, you're right. It's too soon. We need time to get to know each other."

"That would be the wise thing to do. Yes. That would be the wise thing."

George tapped his forehead, chastising himself for moving too fast. But he could barely contemplate being without her.

"Listen, I've got some vacation time coming after all this is over. Maybe I could come back down, spend a week or two with you. Can you get time off?"

"I could manage that."

"Excellent." George stopped pacing and knocking himself in the head.

Valerie shifted gears. "Have you caught your little bandits yet?"

"No. Some charges came from here yesterday and a few today. I've checked all the hotels and they aren't registered anywhere. I figure they're under phony names and paying cash."

"More than likely. George, I'm so glad you called. You know what?"

"What's that, Angel?"

"I slept until three this afternoon. I'm glad you put the Do Not Disturb sign on the door. I could just picture Evangelina coming in to clean up and finding me there nude under the covers."

"You'd have some explaining to do."

"You should have seen me checking out all the windows and doors before I headed out to my car. I was like one of your criminals. Ran the whole way. So what fine hotel are you staying in now? Is it our sister hotel?"

George's surroundings were bleak. He was back on the bank's per diem, and that meant discount accommodations. "Not exactly. Not unless your sister hotel's a dive above a biker bar."

"Oh my God. Really?"

"Really."

In the street below, the rows of motorcycles parked there roared to life.

George had to shout into the phone. "You hear that?" With the floor vibrating under him, he carried the phone to the open window. "There's got to be a hundred of 'em. And a red, white and blue truck with, I swear to God, no muffler. It looks like some sort of charity drive. You hear that noise? And there they go."

They looked dangerous as they strode into the Charleston bus terminal. Jeanette, Minnie and Sarah, in black leather and rawhide and denim, covered with road dust, appeared every bit as intent and disdainful as every member of the motorcycle gang who'd dropped them off. They looked like no one was going to mess with them again.

Jeanette said to Minnie, "Let me handle this."

Minnie patted Jeanette on the back to send her onward. A young man gaped openmouthed from a bench in the waiting area. Minnie winked.

Sarah trotted along behind holding her black, flame-covered helmet like a trophy. She could not manage a scornful leer; she grinned from ear to ear.

Jeanette arrived at the counter where a clerk was busy writing in a log. She pushed her road-grimed face into the open window. Minnie waited behind her, hands on hips, leather fringe dripping off her arms. Sarah plopped on a bench, flaming helmet in her lap.

When the bus clerk didn't bother to look up right away, Jeanette slapped the window. "Hey."

The clerk looked up startled. Jeanette said, "We're here for our luggage. Names are Compton, Barlow, and Gardener."

"Okay," the clerk said indifferently, "Let me check." He walked away to the far end of the enclosure. He opened a door and flipped on the light. He called back to Jeanette, "Do you have any ID?"

"I have an ID of what my bags look like."

"Okay, tell me."

"Ten Louis Vuitton pieces altogether. In black with taupe piping."

The clerk pointed, counting with his forefinger. "I don't know what the hell taupe is. But I got ten black bags right here. Come around to the side door and see if they're yours."

Minnie and Jeanette looked to each other, disappointed in no prospect of an altercation.

Chapter 26

Monday morning, Frannie got off the train at Third and Townsend. Instead of taking the number forty-three bus up Sansome Street to City Security headquarters, she chose to walk.

Today there was no fog to frizz her hair, and she needed the exercise. Sitting at a desk nine-to-five was taking its toll. Even at twenty-one, she noted the first signs of secretarial spread and love handles.

At Market Street she waited for a green light. Though business people swept by, crossing against the red, dodging buses and cars, hurrying to their jobs, she was not about to jaywalk, not in her brand new black strappy heels. Sergio would say they were too slutty for the office. But the red piping matched her black and red mini dress, so she had no choice but to wear them.

Sergio was due back today. She hoped Jenkins hadn't transferred him to another department, but she feared that was exactly what had happened. It seemed they never fired anyone who'd been around for more than a couple of years, especially if their performance was good. Management just dumped them somewhere else, somewhere they would hate, then hoped they would quit. Sergio was probably in the basement sorting file boxes.

She'd miss going to lunch with him, exchanging friendly barbs. But they got together quite a bit after hours, so at least they wouldn't lose touch. Getting through the workday without Sergio would be a little tougher.

The light turned green. Frannie practiced her sexy strut crossing the street; the shoes were surprisingly comfortable. If only Sergio wasn't gay. She'd thought this for the three years since she joined the bank and was stationed near him in Collections. He was so tall and strongly built. She flirted with him in those first days. Later, when they became pals, they laughed about that. She began to view him as a brother.

But scared of staying at his own place, Sergio had spent most of last week at Frannie's place, and her romantic feelings returned. They stayed up late Friday talking about the situation at the bank and their dating problems over her spaghetti and a bottle of wine.

By midnight she was soused and made a pass at him. Sergio had been sweet about it but she still felt foolish. And now she hadn't heard from him since he'd left Saturday morning.

In the alley next to the twenty-story City Security Bank headquarters, Sergio's navy blue VW bug was parked in the loading zone. Three tickets had been crammed under a wiper blade. The fender under the driver-side tail light was dented.

Frannie peered inside. Sergio's briefcase lay in the back seat, a 49ers' mug beside it. Why all the tickets?

She plucked the tickets from the windshield. Sunday night, 11:00 p.m.; another at 2:15 a.m., and the last this morning at 7:45.

Strange. The last thing he told her was that he was going to Marc's house, to wait for him to come home from Hawaii.

"Hey, is this your car, lady?"

A construction worker approached in a hardhat and concrete-spattered clothes.

"It belongs to a friend of mine."

"Can you move it? We need the space. We got some work to do upstairs."

"What's going on? More remodeling?" Frannie tucked the tickets back under the wiper blade.

"Someone tore up one of the executive offices and the computer room. Like a break-in or a fight or something. We got to replace some cabinets, computers, there's blood on the carpet. That sort of thing."

The computer room? Was this Sergio and Marc? Sergio had told her he was planning to go in after hours with Marc to find the credit apps and clear their names. Did they get caught? Was there a fight? Was Sergio safe?

"So can you get this car moved?"

"Yeah, sorry. I'll try."

"Thanks. Sooner the better, lady." The construction worker walked away.

In the headquarters, Frannie stopped at the security station.

"Hi Ralph. Were you on duty over the weekend?"

"Nope. I haven't worked weekends in seven years. Won't do it, either."

"Do you have the sign-in sheets from the weekend?"

"Right here. They haven't been picked up yet." He patted the clipboard.

"Can I look at them?"

"Don't see why not. Help yourself."

Frannie thumbed through the pages. Sergio hadn't signed in on Saturday. "Where's the page for Sunday?"

"Huh? Let's see."

Ralph thumbed through the pages. "That's odd." He looked around him on the floor, checked under the newspaper spread on the desk. "Don't know what to tell you. Nobody comes in on Sunday anyway."

"Even if nobody does, wouldn't there be a Sunday page?"

"Yep." Unconcerned, Ralph returned to reading his Sports section.

Frannie headed for the elevators. At her desk, Sergio still wasn't in. He could have been reassigned, but her gut told her no, something was wrong. She dialed his apartment and got no answer. The time was 8:15. If he were coming in, he'd have been here by 8.

Sergio's desk was always well organized and clean. His In and Out boxes, pencil holder, stapler, and scotch tape dispenser were lined up in orderly fashion. Frannie frequently marveled at how he managed such tidiness with the amount of paperwork he generated each day.

Frannie went to the other side of the floor, to Carl Jenkins' office. The door was closed and the Venetian blinds were closed tight. She tapped on the door. No one answered, which was unusual because Jenkins was usually in by 7 a.m. At the desks cluttering the big room, everyone performed their duties as though it were a normal Monday, as if nothing were amiss.

Walking back to her desk, Frannie passed the coat rack next to Jenkins' office. On a shelf above the rack, Sergio's sheepskin jacket lay folded neatly, the way he always did it. So he had really come in after hours. Sergio was after the SuperCredit apps in Jenkins' office. A fight, a break-in? He must have gotten caught and put up a struggle. Where was he?

She checked to see no one was watching her before searching the pockets of the jacket. She found Sergio's keys and a brown envelope.

She took the keys and envelope back to her desk. In the envelope she found the credit reversal, over Marc's signature.

One of the keys bore the VW emblem. Sergio's car.

Downstairs in the alley, Frannie started the VW. At the sound of the engine, the contractor shouted to another worker, "Hey, I'm gonna move the truck. Head up to twelve and I'll meet you there."

Frannie circled the block to repark Sergio's VW. Walking back to the front entry, it hit her. Twelve. The twelfth floor. Marc Corbett's office was there. And the computer room, where there'd been a fight, and blood.

Frannie took the elevator. On the twelfth floor, she found the computer room. The door was open and she glanced in. A toolbox lay on the vinyl floor and a wide, splintered slab of wood, like a desktop, was propped against the wall. Frannie approached Marc's assistant Nancy at her desk.

"I'm Frannie, from downstairs in Master Charge."

"I've seen you around. Good morning. Can I help you?"

"Is Marc Corbett in?"

"No. Mr. Southern says he's out on an assignment. I don't know where. Nobody tells me anything."

"It's like that on my floor. Trust me. Do you know what's going on in the computer room? What happened?"

"The workers told me there'd been some sort of accident, something electrical that blew up the monitor. They told me to order a new one."

"Did anyone get hurt?"

"No. It happened over the weekend. Mr. Southern said no one was around when it happened."

"Nobody runs the computer on the weekend?"

"It's on automatic. Someone usually checks it Saturday afternoon and again on Sunday. Guess it blew Sunday night. You should have seen the mess. Tapes and paper everywhere. Lucky there wasn't a fire."

"I heard there was blood on the floor."

"No one said anything about that. Where did you hear that?"

"It's probably just someone making up tales. Trying to make something exciting out of a blown fuse. Don't worry about it."

"Okay. Let me know if you hear anything else?"

"I will. You do the same. Thanks, Nancy. See you around."

"You want me to give Marc a message?"

"I'll catch him later."

Passing the computer room, the door was still open and the contractor from the alley was busily measuring a cracked desktop. His assistant, on his hands and knees, used a screwdriver to loosen the desk where it was secured to the wall.

Frannie looked in. "Hi." Indeed, the computer room was a wreck, as if a ferocious fight had taken place inside. Tables were knocked akimbo, one was cracked, and computer monitors had been knocked askew. Several red dots marred the linoleum floor. Someone had bled in here. Frannie caught her breath, prayed it was not Sergio, and feared instantly that it was.

The contractor smiled. "You work on this floor?"

Before she could answer, make up some lie to learn more about what happened in the computer room, the contractor's assistant plucked a cardboard box out of the debris on the floor. He opened it. "Hey, look at this."

He closed the box to toss it to the contractor, who opened it.

Frannie asked, "What is it?"

"A computer tape."

"Is it labeled?"

"Nope. You said you work on this floor?"

Frannie arranged one knee in front of the other to draw the contractor's attention to her miniskirt and matching shoes.

"I do, in fact, work on this floor."

"Then, I reckon I can give this to you."

"I reckon you can."

Frannie took the tape.

Behind her, Phil Southern said, "Actually, I'll take it."

She handed it over as meekly and innocently as she could.

"What are you doing up here?"

"Oh, sorry. I was just on my way to ask Nancy if she wanted to make lunch plans. This nice man and I," she gestured to the grinning contractor, "we met out in the street. I was only saying hello."

One more time, Frannie worked the new shoes and the long legs they were on.

"You better get back to work, Frannie."

He knew her name. A chill went through her. It was a big bank, and she was a nobody.

"Of course." She conjured up a smile before heading to the elevator.

Returning to her office, Frannie broke out in goosebumps. No doubt, Southern had something to do with Sergio's disappearance. A scribbled phone message lay on her desk. George Post had called. He'd call back after lunch.

As the morning wore on, Frannie stayed on edge, hardly able to concentrate on her work. She couldn't go back to the twelfth floor to investigate more, Southern would be onto her, if he wasn't already. Southern's mean eyes seemed to follow her everywhere.

At noon, she grabbed Sergio's brown envelope and keys. There was a new ticket on his VW, the meter had expired. Frannie headed toward Guerrero Street.

She used Sergio's keys to enter his building. When she reached his apartment door, the key wouldn't slide in, the lock was jammed. Something, someone, had broken it. Frannie tried the door knob and pushed. The lock was busted open, and stayed open. She entered.

A stack of unopened mail was scattered on the carpet. An acrid smell hung in the air. Frannie went to a window to let in some light and fresh air. Sergio's many small potted plants on the ledge of the bay window had been knocked to the floor.

When Frannie pushed back the drapes and opened a window, it became instantly clear that Sergio's apartment had been trashed. He never left the place in disarray. The mess and the broken lock told her the obvious: someone had forced their way in here. Frannie rubbed her sweaty palms on her miniskirt.

In the dining room, several decorative china pieces lay broken on the hutch. A ceramic souvenir bell from Washington D.C. was in pieces on the floor.

In the kitchen, the trash bin had been overturned, garbage strewn across the linoleum. More plates had been smashed.

She opened the door to Sergio's bedroom. The mattress had been tossed and the contents of his closet and all the dresser drawers had been thrown on the floor. She moved down the hall to the second bedroom, Sergio's home office. It, too, had been ransacked. A worktable was toppled over, electronics and computer gear, gadgets and wires, all were reduced to jumbled litter on the floor. Books and manuals had been swept off a bookcase.

Frannie fought down a panic attack. Her friendship with Sergio had immersed her in some dreadful conspiracy. Someone had forced their way into Sergio's home, to look for what? The credit reversal slip? It couldn't be that. Anyone with authorization could get a copy of that from DP.

Sergio had been caught in the computer room at the bank Sunday night. By whom, Southern? And what about Marc Corbett? Where was he? And Carl Jenkins?

Back in the living room, she collapsed on Sergio's sofa in the light and fresh air pouring through the bay window. Though the room had been turned upside-down like the rest of the apartment, Frannie took comfort that Sergio's stereo system, an amplifier, turntable and two small speakers, had been left untouched on a bookcase. Below them, several records from his expansive album collection had been cast on the floor, but most of the LPs were safe and standing upright on their shelf.

Her worry over Sergio made Frannie miss him terribly. It might make her feel better, even think more clearly, if she had some evidence of him to cling to. She turned on his stereo amplifier and turntable, then fingered through his albums, looking for one of her favorites to play.

She started on the left, in the *A*'s of Sergio's alphabetized collection. She flipped through the *B*'s, then found several *F*'s in the *C*'s. *J*'s, *K*'s, *L*'s and other letters were jumbled in the middle of the collection, haphazard and out of alphabetic order, something Sergio would never have allowed.

Someone had taken them down and put them back in a hurry.

Frannie pulled a dozen LPs from the shelf, then another dozen, and looked behind them. The white edge of an envelope showed against the bookcase, behind the albums. Frannie fished it out and peered inside. On many sheets of paper, the City Security Bank logo appeared above the words: *SuperCredit Application*.

So Sergio had gotten his hands on them, after all! He'd gotten away from the bank with them. But his car. It was still at the bank. Maybe he had to ditch it to escape whatever happened in the computer room. Maybe Marc was with him at the bank and they left in Marc's car.

But it still didn't make sense. Sergio's apartment was trashed, the albums were out of order. If Sergio had hidden these apps, he'd have moved just a few records out of the way, stuffed the envelope behind them, then put them back in order.

Whoever searched Sergio's apartment had been pretty damn thorough. If they were looking for this envelope, they would have found it.

This was planted.

In sudden tears, Frannie plopped onto the couch. Jenkins was setting up Sergio, making him the fall guy. Sergio had disappeared with Marc; the presumption would be that they'd skipped town together, with the money.

What to do?

George Post. George was the only person Frannie could trust. But he was on the opposite coast. How could he help?

Frannie couldn't go to the police, not right now, while Sergio looked so guilty. Frannie needed more information. What to do? She sat pondering, but knew one thing for sure. She was not going to let Sergio down.

Frannie shoved the envelope of SuperCredit applications into her handbag. Sergio had to be alive. She wouldn't let herself believe otherwise. It wasn't too late. She was going to save him.

Chapter 27

Frannie sat outside the bank, drumming her fingers on the steering wheel of Sergio's VW. She was still scared but not as much as earlier. She grew angrier by the hour at anyone who would endanger Sergio, a good man.

She watched the exit to the parking garage. A stretch limo pulled out; she couldn't see past the tinted windows. More cars carrying strangers made Frannie impatient. She considered going upstairs to see if there was any gossip, if Jenkins had come in. But she'd already called in sick for the afternoon.

On another day, for a different friend, Frannie might have quit after an hour of waiting, and definitely after two. But three hours later, near the end of the workday, she was still watching when Jenkins' gold Mercedes emerged into the alleyway. She ducked down in the VW; the Mercedes drove into the alley and away. Frannie fired up the VW to follow. At the intersection, Jenkins turned onto Montgomery, headed in the direction of North Beach.

Frannie kept him in sight, and her excitement mounted. She knew, just knew, that Jenkins would lead her to Sergio.

Chapter 28

Marc awoke to gray morning creeping in through a porthole, and Sergio's grunts.

Sergio struggled to swing his legs off the bed. Even with his hands behind his back, he sat up to face Marc. Sergio gritted his teeth to breathe down a terrific pain.

"Fucking busted rib."

"Man, you look pretty bad."

Sergio managed a small smile. The caked blood on his swollen lip and his purpled cheeks made him look like a macabre clown. "I'll live. If I don't, it might be a relief."

"You know we're going to have to figure out how to make a break for it."

"Maybe they'll let us have some Wheaties first. I'm starving."

"We've got to figure something out. And quick. We're probably in Sausalito, maybe Fort Baker. I doubt we're as far north as San Rafael. So I'm thinking, if we can make it off the boat, we can grab another boat and make it back to the City."

Marc had strained at his ropes several times, and did it again. Nothing gave way, but the bonds on his wrists seared.

"Damn, that hurts."

Sergio said, "Show me your hands."

Marc held them up into the foggy light. Sergio did his best to lean his slatted eyes closer.

His right wrist was swollen and discolored. Small red streaks trickled up his forearm.

"It's infected, man. We've got to do something about this quick." Sergio faced the stateroom door, and yelled: "Hey! We need some help down here! Hey! Get down here!"

"Sergio, don't do that!"

Sergio ignored him. "C'mon! We need help! Now!"

Vinnie's voice boomed down through the wall. "Shut up."

Sergio muttered, "Sons of bitches," before bellowing again. "Get down here!"

Heavy footsteps tramped down the companionway, then the stateroom door flew open. Roscoe and Vinnie sneered in at them.

Vinnie said, "I told you to keep your trap shut."

"Look at this, man. A judge is going to wonder how he lost his hand. Southern said we had to look pretty for court, right? Your ass will be grass if you don't get him a doctor."

Vinnie bent over Marc to examine his wrist. "Nice job, Roscoe."

"Thanks, Vin." Roscoe puffed up proudly.

Vinnie stabbed a finger at Sergio's disfigured features. "Look at that face. Now, that's art right there. You did a good job, Roscoe."

Southern's voice rang from up on deck. "Bring them up."

Vinnie untied the ropes from Marc's and Sergio's feet and tossed them aside. Unsteady on cramped legs, with no help from either thug, Marc and Sergio made their way topside.

Hunched and groaning, they were led into the wide cockpit where Southern sat on a green-cushioned deckchair. The early fog dissipated enough to spot the large pylons supporting the Golden Gate Bridge.

Sergio said to Marc, "You were right. This is Fort Baker."

Marc wasn't listening. On the foredeck fifty feet away, reclining in a beam of summer light the mist could not hold back, lay Melanie. She didn't sit up and look back, though Marc glared so hard she might have felt a shove from his eyes.

Southern said, "Don't worry, you guys are going to live. If all goes well, you'll go home today. And wait for the cops."

Every part of Marc pained him from the beating the thugs had put on him. His wrist was in danger of rotting off, his face ached with every flinch from the many cuts.

But none of it ached like his heart at the sight of Melanie on Southern's boat.

He muttered, "Bitch."

Southern rose from his deck chair. "What was that?"

"And fuck you, Phil."

Southern stepped back to regard Marc. He was the sort who would hit a man whose hands were tied. He was a little shit, an entitled bore, and a criminal, and the worst Marc could wish on Melanie was that she would end up with an asshole like this. Southern balled a fist.

Melanie arrived just in time to grab his arm.

"Don't."

Southern's jaw worked, his anger with Marc plain and unfazed. Melanie changed her tone to cajole him.

"Phil, we need to get them cleaned up, not more messed up."

Sergio said, "Take a look at his wrist."

She examined Marc's wrist. He looked for any sign of concern from her, and believed he might have seen a glimmer, but brushed it off as hope and imagination. Melanie had betrayed him, used him. No need to search for a sign of love. Marc sighed in resignation to the obvious.

"His hand's infected. Let me at least wrap it."

Southern's icy eyes slid from Marc to Sergio. "Take them inside."

Sergio met Southern's gaze. "I'm going to fucking kill you when this over. You know that, right?"

"You don't got the balls."

"Oh, trust me." Sergio grinned as far as his bloodied lips allowed. "The one thing I got is balls."

Phil said to Vinnie and Roscoe, "Get them out of my sight."

The pair of henchmen led Marc and Sergio out of the growing sunlight, into the pilothouse. Melanie had them seated at the galley table. Vinnie cut the ropes off both their wrists.

Melanie busied herself with a first aid kit. She kept her voice low to Sergio: "Please don't say anything more to him. He really would just as soon kill you." She poured peroxide onto a cotton ball, then swabbed the purpling cuts on Marc's wrist. "He's capable of it. Believe me."

Marc had nothing to say. She didn't look at him, refused to meet his eyes. Sergio asked, "What the hell do you care?"

She worked to clean their cuts and gashes, applied antibiotic cream and bandages, and wrapped Marc's wrist in gauze. She dabbed his forehead with a damp cloth. "You've got a fever." He snatched the cloth from her. "Don't touch me."

Expressionless, Melanie rose from the table. She filled two glasses with water and set them on the galley table with aspirin tablets. "Drink. You're both dehydrated." Before they drank, Melanie set another pill in front of Marc. She said only, "Penicillin."

Again, she did not let her eyes catch on his. She asked Vinnie, who stood with arms folded across his big chest, "You got the fresh clothes?"

"In the state room."

"Get them changed."

Melanie must be placed highly enough to give these goons orders.

"C'mon boys." Vinnie yanked Sergio to his feet. "Let's get dressed." Marc rose on his own, still staring at Melanie. He wanted to say so many things, all hateful. Instead, he let his eyes burn into her, but she only looked away, out to the marina and the windy bay beyond.

Sergio and Marc were walked back to the stateroom. Roscoe entered long enough to toss a jumbled pile of clothes on the bed. Sergio picked up a shirt.

"This is mine. Did you bring this from my apartment?"

"That's right."

"So you're saying I have to get dressed in an ensemble you picked out for me?"

"Shut up."

"Will the horrors ever cease?"

Vinnie shut the door. Gingerly, Marc and Sergio helped each other dress in fresh duds.

Chapter 29

Groggily, Marc awoke. He lay on the mattress beside a snoring Sergio.

What had happened? Had they passed out? The last thing Marc remembered was Melanie applying first aid, then he and Serge changing clothes. That might not have been aspirin she gave them.

Marc's wrists and feet were not bound, nor were Sergio's. His injured hand felt better, the swelling had gone down and the red marks leading up his arm had receded. At least the penicillin pill had been for real. Marc's head felt dull but the fever was gone. He elbowed Sergio.

Sergio snorted himself awake. He bolted upright, and seeing Marc awake, said, "What the hell?"

"I think we were drugged."

"Well, we're still alive." Sergio rubbed his head furiously. "I've had better drugs."

Marc took a peek out the porthole. They were still in the marina at Fort Baker. He put his ear to the door.

On the other side, Marc heard nothing. He tried the latch, already knowing it was locked. They might get through the door with a few good kicks, but that would just bring Vinnie and Roscoe down on them with a vengeance. The porthole was too small, it might help an infant escape.

Through the porthole, Marc could see activity on the dock: a slightly drunk couple staggered onto a small sailboat, two pot-bellied men in galoshes drank beer on a fishing vessel in the spring evening. From another big sailboat at the end of the pier came music and laughter; the ship's mast had been decorated with lights, someone was having a party.

Phil Southern walked past.

"Southern's leaving."

Sergio said, "Good. Now all we have to deal with is Roscoe, Vinnie, and Melanie. It's time to make our move."

Sergio rifled through several drawers in the stateroom until he found an old brass compass. He hefted it. "I'm going to smash this into Roscoe's face. Maybe Vinnie. Definitely Phil when I see him."

Marc said, "Whoa."

"Whoa? Seriously?"

"What if they have guns?"

"Marc, they do have guns. But there are plenty of people on the dock. I doubt they'll shoot us with people everywhere. Marc, they're not going to let us go. You know that."

"I don't know that."

"Either way, I'm not going to wait to find out."

"You think they're going to kill us?" Marc licked his lips. "Really? Kill us? Then why haven't they done it already?"

"Think about it, man. They must still need us alive for something. Who knows? Probably they're planning to take the boat out a few miles tonight and dump us over the side with bullets in our brains. That way, it looks like we grabbed the money, erased the paper trail, and disappeared never to be heard from again. Marc, buddy. My signature is all over a bunch of credit apps. Then there's you. You've been helping your criminal-ass aunt steal from the bank. All those bank originated entries reversing her balances. SuperCredit, the computer room. Need I say more? You're fucked, man. And I'm the guy next to you. So I'm fucked."

Sergio hefted the large compass, feeling the weight. "Ready?"

Marc displayed his purpled wrist. "I'm kind of helpless here."

"You got legs don't you? You ever do any kickboxing?"

"Nope."

"Nothing to it. Just kick the shit out of them."

Movement outside the porthole caught Marc's attention. Roscoe walked off, counting dollar bills. Through the door came Vinnie's shout after him: "Don't forget anchovies. I want fucking anchovies this time."

Roscoe had been sent for pizza.

Sergio said, "Two left. And one is Melanie. You okay with this, man?"

Marc took down the brass curtain rod from above the porthole, to use as a cudgel. It wasn't much, but it was better than his bad right hand.

"Do it."

Sergio kicked the door.

"Hey, gotta use the head. Open the door!"

Footsteps came up the companionway. Sergio continued kicking until the latch released from the outside. Sergio nodded to Marc, who was crouched low gripping the brass rod hard. The door opened; Sergio raised a hand to Vinnie in greeting. The thug in the doorway cocked his head, distracted by Sergio only for the one moment Marc needed to surge at him. He swung the brass curtain rod one-handed, but with all his strength, into Vinnie's knee. Vinnie didn't see it coming and the knee buckled.

Vinnie doubled over, grabbing at his leg. Sergio, holding the compass like a softball, swung an uppercut into the bottom of Vinnie's jaw. Vinnie's head snapped up then he keeled over, knocked out cold. Sergio folded in two, wrapping both arms around his torso. His busted rib must be on fire after the might of that blow.

Marc checked on Sergio, then tied Vinnie hand and foot with the ropes the thugs had used to bind Sergio's and Marc's feet. When Vinnie was secure on the floor, Marc stuffed a corner of the bedsheet into his mouth, then covered his big head with a pillowcase. Sergio stared down at helpless, unconscious Vinnie like he wanted to work him over a little more with the compass.

Marc checked the porthole. The dock was empty. "Let's go, now."

Sergio grunted as he rose to his feet. The pain in his side registering with a searing heat. He carried the compass in case he needed it as a weapon again; Marc held fast to the curtain rod. They made their way out of the stateroom, through the galley and up the companionway steps.

At the top of the stairs, Marc stopped short; Sergio bumped into him from behind. Sergio urged, "Go, man. What are you waiting for?"

Melanie sat on a green cushion in the cockpit, calm and wicked. She looked particularly gorgeous in pleated white pants, white button-down shirt, barefoot, her hair in a ponytail beneath a 49ers' ball cap. She rose, planting her legs apart and pointed a capable-looking handgun at Marc's chest.

Chapter 30

Marc stepped forward. Behind him, Sergio urged, "Whoa, whoa, whoa."

He put a hand on Marc's shoulder to stop him. "Man, look at her. She means it. She'll kill you."

"I will," Melanie said.

The gun she leveled at his chest did not quaver, but her eyes revealed fear. Marc tapped his heart.

"You already have, Mel. May as well finish the job." He took another stride.

"Stop, Marc."

"Is this what you were the whole time? A crook, a liar, a thief? What an asshole I am."

"You're not, Marc. Where's Vinnie?"

"We beat the shit out of him and tied him up down below."

"Impressive. I didn't think you had it in you. Either of you."

Sergio said, "Fuck what you think, lady."

"I can't let you leave this boat. There's too much at stake."

Marc asked, "Too much at stake with Phil Southern?"

"It's not about Phil. It's about my cut of forty million dollars."

Marc took one more step. "So that makes you a murderer, too?"

Melanie matched his advance with a step in retreat. Marc had to make a move now, before Roscoe came back with the pizza. He swallowed hard and made a guess: she wouldn't pull the trigger. If she did, he'd at least go down on his feet, trying to live, to understand, to do better, all the things a man promises himself when he stares down the wrong end of a gun.

Melanie backed up one more time, the pistol still at the end of her extended arm. Marc stepped around the ship's binnacle and wheel, he covered the distance to her until he pressed his chest against the snub nose of the revolver. Melanie's eyes were nothing like they had been in Hawaii, loving and naughty, as though she were honestly falling in love. She'd played him, and played him hard.

Marc gripped her wrist to push the pistol away from his chest, pointed down. Then he squeezed and twisted until she yelped in pain, until it was Melanie on her knees, the gun in his hand, and Marc standing over her.

He shoved the pistol into the waistband of his jeans, looking down on the top of Melanie's head. Sergio came to the bow.

"We need to go, man. Now."

"Where?"

"I got an idea."

Sergio stepped over the stainless railing at the bow, onto the transom. He reeled in the inflated dinghy tied behind the sailboat. When the small rubber boat was close enough, he climbed in. Sergio primed the outboard motor, then with two powerful yanks that cost him two grunts from his busted rib, he got the engine started.

"Marc, come on, man. We gotta split. Say goodbye."

Marc laid a gentle hand on the top of Melanie's blonde head. Like a benediction, with finality, he said, "Goodbye."

He climbed over the rail, and kicked the dinghy off from the sailboat as he climbed in. Sergio throttled up the outboard motor and the nose of the little craft lifted as it surged into the harbor's smooth water.

Sergio pointed back to the pier, at Roscoe who'd dropped the pizza and was running after them.

Chapter 31

Frannie followed Carl across the Golden Gate Bridge. When he turned down a dirt road leading to the docks at Fort Baker, she grew afraid of being caught by following him too closely. Instead, she took the upper parallel road with a view of the unpaved track. When Carl pulled into an isolated dirt parking lot, Frannie pulled over in a grove of trees. Below, Jenkins got out and leaned against his car.

Above, Frannie quietly closed her car door, then bent low in a cluster of bushes. From here, well hidden, she could keep an eye on Jenkins.

He lit a cigarette and waited, smoking, until he took a few steps, shading his eyes with his hand to look down the dirt road. Jenkins waved to someone.

Phil Southern arrived on foot, up from the dock. Southern slapped Jenkins on the back.

Frannie could not move closer to listen in, not without being seen.

The physicality of the two men changed suddenly, they appeared to argue. Carl shook his fist in Southern's face before Southern swatted it down.

Carl stepped back, suddenly frightened of Southern. Then, in a moment, Frannie could see it wasn't Phil he was afraid of, but something else. Carl rubbed his left arm, then took a heaving step forward as if he wanted to run from this place. He clutched at his chest, managed one more halting step, crumpled first to his knees, then keeled over onto his back. Southern stood over him, hands on hips, plainly puzzled. Carl, face up, fumbled in his suit pocket. With a shaking hand he withdrew a vial of pills. Frannie knew the same moment Southern did; Carl was having a heart attack.

Carl's hands quivered so much he couldn't get the pill bottle open. Southern kneeled beside him and took the pills from him. Carl extended a trembling hand for a pill to save his life but Southern backed away, holding the vial.

Frannie could do nothing but watch from the bushes as Carl, lying on the ground, begged for a pill, both arms up beseeching while Southern gazed down like a buzzard on a branch. One of Carl's arms came down, then the other, and he lay still. Frannie bit her tongue, stunned, and pressed both hands over her mouth to hide her shocked breathing and her desire to scream.

Phil squatted and peered closely. He put fingers to Carl's neck, then tossed the pill bottle into the dirt beside him. Surveying the hillside, Southern even looked straight at Frannie's hiding place. Then, satisfied, he walked back the way he'd come.

Frannie, freeing her hands from her mouth, wiped away tears. She'd never liked Carl Jenkins but didn't wish this on him. She stayed hidden, unsure what to do, while Southern strode to the docks, to the end of the pier where he stepped aboard a large sailing yacht.

Frannie kicked off her heels to run down the hill. She hurried to where Carl lay and kneeled beside him. He didn't respond to his name or a shake of his shoulder.

Frannie ought to go find a payphone and call the police and an ambulance. Or she could keep an eye on Southern.

Chapter 32

Roscoe tore along the dock. Marc said, "Go, go."

Sergio twisted the throttle wide open; the inflatable dinghy sped up. Both Sergio and Marc looked back at the pier where big Roscoe galloped after them.

Marc said, "We made it."

Sergio at the helm didn't turn away as fast as Marc, and did not see the fishing boat putter into their path. He swung the motor to dodge the craft and barely missed it. The older man in the boat, a fellow in fishing gear readying for a day casting his lines in the bay, flung curses at Sergio and Marc as they flashed past, rocking his boat in their wake. He was still shaking his fist when Roscoe leaped and landed in the water beside him. Roscoe, a large man but nimble and athletic, hauled himself over the gunwale before the fisherman could raise a hand in his own defense. In seconds, he was tossed overboard and his fishing boat commandeered.

Marc's elation crashed. "Shit, Sergio. He's got a boat. Hit it!"

Sergio ran the dinghy's outboard flat-out, around sailboats at anchor and on mooring balls, past the breakwater and into the bay. Roscoe flew after them, gaining on them, with a heavier hull and a bigger motor.

Marc said, "He's gonna catch us. Head for Fisherman's Wharf."

"I'm trying, I'm trying."

They carved around slower boats on the bay. The water rattled the plastic hull under their feet through the floorboards. Roscoe bounded over the small chop on the water, bearing down on them.

Marc shouted. "He's gaining!"

"This is all she's got." Sergio pushed the lightweight dinghy as fast as it would go toward the San Francisco skyline and Fishermen's Wharf, three miles off. "Fuck!"

Roscoe's boat poured on a speed that Sergio couldn't wring from the dinghy. Sergio hunkered behind the wheel; Roscoe's craft pulled even, twenty yards off to the right and stayed there, wake for wake, matching speeds.

The thug made a show of drawing a pistol. He held it up, showed it to Marc as if to say there was nothing Marc or Sergio could do about it.

But there was.

Marc produced the gun he'd taken from Melanie, and showed this to Roscoe.

The thug fired first. Marc screamed at Sergio, "Get down!" and leaped at him; Sergio lost his balance, spinning the speeding dinghy hard to the left, away from Roscoe just as the report of another shot coursed by. Marc had to hold on to keep from being thrown out. Roscoe missed with both bullets, but his faster craft was going to get him more, and better, shots.

Sergio drove scrunched over, and his bad rib was clearly killing him. Roscoe corrected course and came back in hot pursuit. Every second, he closed the gap.

Sergio said, "You want to shoot back maybe?"

Marc had never fired a pistol before and had no reason to believe he'd be any good at it. But the life and death circumstances, the rush of adrenaline, the angry gray water flying past, flashes and bangs from Roscoe's gun, the hurt from Melanie and the fear of Southern, all combined in Marc's breast to make him dizzy. The thing that cleared his head, while Sergio fishtailed and zigzagged to dodge Roscoe's weapon, was firing back.

He pulled the trigger, the pistol recoiled; the round sailed high over Roscoe's fishing boat. Roscoe shook his head, sure that he was in no danger from an armed Marc.

Roscoe fired again to make his point. The bullet whizzed past Marc's ear like a hornet. Sergio bellowed for him to get down. But Marc didn't.

He was done being beaten and fooled, used and threatened. Marc put both hands on the revolver to get a bead on Roscoe. Even bumping over the bay, Marc was able to bring the gunsight over the thug's big frame.

Before he could squeeze the trigger, he was knocked off his feet by a pain like a mule's kick in his left shoulder.

Marc fell to the floorboards, still clinging to the handgun. Every bit of his anger, all his will to live through this dangerous day, curdled into fear. He'd been shot.

Roscoe's bullet had dug a trench through the meat of the upper arm. Crimson swelled into the fleshy groove and soaked into his torn shirtsleeve. Despite the searing pain and the copper stench of his own blood, Marc could still move his arm. His instant fright subsided. He was still in the fight.

Sergio hollered down, "You all right, man?"

"I got hit. Fucking stings. But I think I'm okay."

Marc sat up, gun in hand. Where was the son of a bitch? San Francisco was a mile and a half off, plenty of opportunity for Roscoe to finish what he'd started. Sergio couldn't make a beeline straight for land, but had to continue to slalom the dinghy in wild serpentines to throw off Roscoe's aim.

Sergio said, "Here he comes."

Marc sat up to his knees. Staying low, he tested his left shoulder; he could hold the revolver well enough to have a chance.

"Let him come even, then let him pass us."

"What?"

"Do it."

"Alright, man. Glad someone has a plan."

Sergio straightened the dinghy's course, which let Roscoe gain on them faster. Roscoe raced up on the left, keeping his distance, knowing he was the better shot. He raised his pistol.

Marc said, "Now."

Sergio cut the speed, only for a moment, but enough to let Roscoe scoot past. Then Sergio shoved the throttle to the stops and swerved directly behind Roscoe. Moving into the fishing boat's wake leveled out the dinghy's ride; Marc had a clear shot before Roscoe could react and bank away.

Marc emptied the revolver, five more rounds. The last bullet found the target; Roscoe's outboard motor spewed a puff of gray diesel smoke. The engine coughed, then made a dying, grinding sound. Sergio swung the dinghy away sharply, rolling Marc onto his wounded shoulder, and barely missed hitting the slowing fishing boat in the butt.

Sergio screamed, "Get down!"

Marc hugged the bottom of the dinghy; Sergio ducked so low only his hand and arm were visible. They flashed by Roscoe who bellowed curses and emptied his own gun after them.

Chapter 33

When Southern emerged from the big sailboat moored at the end of the pier, Frannie ducked down in Sergio's blue VW bug.

A motorboat eased into the marina, towing a fishing boat; a large man stood in the stern of the disabled craft. When they reached the pier, the big man tied the fishing boat up to the pilings, cast away the towline, and shouted thanks to the skipper who'd tugged him in from the bay. The big man stepped out onto the pier; Southern walked his way.

Instantly, an old fellow stamped up to shake his finger in the big man's face, visibly furious. Southern stepped between them to peel off a bunch of bills from a wad he pulled from his pocket. The old fisherman, still beet-red, took the money and stormed back to his broken boat.

Southern and the big man held their own heated conversation. Southern's hands flew up and down, stabbing the big man in the chest with a pointed finger. He flung an arm in the direction of the parking lot where Carl's body lay. The big man pointed out to the bay, seeming to explain himself, but Southern wouldn't have it.

The two men headed towards the parking area.

Frannie couldn't decide if she should fire up the VW and drive off or not. She feared calling attention to herself and being recognized. She stifled another sob and told herself to get a grip. And what about Carl's body, left lying there in the parking lot?

No one had yet discovered Carl. The big guy dragged the corpse to Carl's Mercedes and stuffed it into the passenger seat. It made sense; a dead body would draw police to the marina, and that was the last thing Southern wanted. The big man rifled through Jenkins' pockets, found his car keys, then got behind the wheel. Southern bent to the driver's window where the two had another brief talk. Southern collected the vial off the ground and handed it to the burly man who drove off in Carl's car with Carl's body. Southern took off in his BMW.

Frannie was parked on the exit road to the parking lot. It was the only road out; they were going to drive right by her. Would they recognize Serigo's blue VW? In terror, Frannie slid down in the seat as the BMW sped past followed by the Mercedes.

Both cars disappeared up Sommersville Street. Frannie waited, afraid to get out of the car in case Southern should double back. She tasted vomit, and dug through her purse for a piece of gum.

Carl was dead. Southern took away Carl's pills, and that killed him. Frannie had witnessed a murder. The thought chilled her, she tried to shake it off. "C'mon, Frannie, don't panic."

She took a few deep breaths, willing herself to think logically. She figured they were going to leave the body somewhere in the Mercedes. It would look like an innocent, timely death. Then they'd return.

All Frannie wanted to do was run. But Sergio might be down there on that sailboat, and that helped her find her courage. She drove down the hill and parked at the edge of the dock. If Sergio was on that boat, was he guarded? Or was he left tied up without a guard when Southern and his man-ape drove off with Carl's corpse? Frannie would have to move carefully and fast.

She hurried up the dock, then slowed to creep up on the yacht. She peeked into several portholes but saw no one, and no sign of Sergio. Frannie took off her new slutty shoes, and gripped one stiletto heel like a weapon. She climbed up the short gangplank and stepped quietly onto the deck. Her heart beat hard and fast in her ears; she had to listen keenly for any other sounds. Frannie inched through the cockpit, past green cushions and the big wooden wheel at the helm, to stand at the top of the companionway steps leading below. Still she saw no signs of life onboard.

She willed her heartbeat to slow. Frannie listened very carefully, trying to leach out any sound of danger, any hint that Sergio was still alive and on this ship. She heard nothing and sensed only the gentle water of the harbor beneath the ship.

Frannie held her breath as she stepped down the companionway stairs, into the settee and galley areas. She tiptoed towards the bow and a series of stateroom doors. She held the stiletto by the toe, cocked at her ear. Frannie was as ready to strike as she was ready to turn and run. But Sergio could be inside one of these doors.

She pressed one ear to the first door, then gingerly opened it. The empty room was a mess, as if a violent altercation had occurred. Bloodstains marred the bed, even the walls. A heavy brass compass with a broken face, a bent curtain rod, and lengths of rope lay on the floor.

Had Sergio been in this fight? Was this his blood?

Where was he?

Behind Frannie, an unfamiliar voice made her start.

"What are you doing here, Frannie?"

Turing with dread, Frannie marveled how so many bad people knew her name.

Chapter 34

On a crisp sunny afternoon, Minnie, Jeanette, and Sarah arrived at David's home in Baltimore.

They did not replay the scene in Albuquerque. Sarah wasn't nervous or paralyzed in the car seat, or suggesting they call first. She'd been thinking about her son quite a bit since New Mexico, had rehearsed her words, and built her courage and confidence one solid brick at a time.

His Baltimore house was as grand as the one in Albuquerque, situated on a tree-lined street of brick homes with peaked roofs above garden walls, all estates in this hilly part of town.

Jeanette drove through the gates. "I see he still likes circular driveways."

After parking, they approached a columned front porch. Sarah stopped them. "How do I look?"

Minnie said, "Beautiful." Her face had a rosy, healthy glow, her hair shined a glossy strawberry blond from a color treatment that morning. She wore a lavender raw silk wrap that made her look as lovely as an orchid. Most importantly, her adventures and travails with her friends, from San Francisco to Savannah, had made Sarah not only look stronger, but act it, too.

David answered the door. Before she said a word, Sarah took him into her arms. "David. I'm so glad to see you. It's been years."

"Mom?" The son extricated himself from her embrace. "Did I miss a letter saying you were coming to visit?"

"I didn't have a chance to write."

"Well. Here you are. Let me look at you." With hands on her shoulders as though to keep her back, he said, "You look good. Different, you know, but good."

"You've changed too, dear. Twelve years is a long time."

David was tall, bespectacled, and big-boned like Sarah. His sandy brown hair was thinning, his midsection had thickened. Wrinkles framed his eyes and lips, something she'd never imagined. She'd always pictured him the way she'd seen him last, an athletic young man, full of energy with a tanned, smooth face.

"Who are your friends?"

David had not yet moved out of the doorway, had not invited them in.

"You should remember Minnie and Jeanette. Although you haven't seen them for a long time."

"Of course. How are you?"

This was the boy Minnie had built forts with in the backyard when he was ten. The one she took to see "Cool Hand Luke" when he was fourteen; he'd bragged about how she was so cool. She'd bought him a drafting board when he was seventeen and first showed an interest in architecture.

She shook his outstretched hand. "Come on, David. It's Auntie Minnie. You can't have forgotten me, all the fun we used to have."

His coolness remained. Jeanette tried next. She beamed her best smile, but David's face stayed as bland and flat as an ironing board. "I haven't seen you since you were six. I doubt you remember me. Your mom and I have been friends forever."

David shook her hand, and said, "Yes, yes," absent-mindedly.

Sarah asked pointedly, "Would it be okay if we come in? We've been driving for an awfully long time."

He finally stepped back from the doorway. "Of course. Please, come in." Clearing the way, he glanced at his watch.

Minnie followed Sarah and Jeanette through the marble foyer, then down a step into a sunken, circular living room.

Minnie eased onto a long couch upholstered in white silk. The entire room was decorated in modern furniture with chrome accents. A jungle of large potted plants, some flowering red, provided the only colors in the tastefully-decorated but sterile-feeling room. Even the plush carpet was spotless white. Black and white abstract paintings and photographs hung in silver frames. Floor to ceiling French-paned windows and doors overlooked a redwood deck lined with pots and planters of more flowering plants. Beyond an immaculately landscaped and precise English garden was a tennis court and a waterfall that spilled over boulders into a black-bottomed swimming pool.

It was a dream house out of Architectural Digest. Again, as she had in Albuquerque, Minnie wondered how he would let his own mother live in the Tenderloin of San Francisco, why he wouldn't at least send for her on holidays. He could afford it.

Jeanette said, "This is a beautiful home. And enormous."

"I entertain a lot. Mostly business." David sat in one of the matching black leather armchairs opposite the couch. He tamped a pipe into a heavy crystal ashtray. From a humidor he packed the bowl with sweet-smelling tobacco, and lit up.

Jeanette wore a frozen smile. Sarah's cheeks were flushed with pride; or was it embarrassment and anger at how she and her friends had been greeted?

David was a non-stop talker. He spoke a lot about his house, then under Sarah's questioning lapsed into bragging about a recent promotion, and how his company couldn't exist without him.

Sarah patted Jeanette's hand. "I told you my David was brilliant."

David leaned back, crossed his legs, and sucked the end of his pipe. He squinted back and forth between his mother and her two friends unexpectedly in his house.

Sarah used the pause to tell her son about the plan to live in Spain. "An old friend of Jeanette's has left her a villa on the Spanish Riviera. When we finish our tour of the United States, we'll leave from New York."

Sarah seemed to have taken on a pretentious air, waving her hand about to be debonair and impress her son, as if to say, 'I'm doing well, too, you know.'

"Imagine, Spain. Oh, and we've been to New Orleans. I wish we could have planned it around Mardi Gras. And Jeanette wants to stop in New York to visit her daughter and grandchild. That is a priority." She rested a hand lightly on Minnie's knee, to include her friends in her sudden role of braggart. "We've traveled the southern states, Miami and..."

Minnie said, "Tell David about that incredible place we stayed at in Savannah."

Her son cleared his throat, stood, and put down the pipe. "How about that? It sounds fabulous, Mom. I mean it. Listen, I have to get over to the lab for a meeting at

4:00. It's 3:00 now. Why don't you girls go check into your hotel? Then we'll meet at the Monte Carlo for dinner. Say at 7:00. How's that?"

Sarah kept her disappointment out of her voice, but Minnie knew her well. Sarah was wounded.

"We haven't gone to a hotel yet."

"There's a Motel 6 on the highway. You probably passed it coming in. I'd let you stay here, but the head engineer from our Cincinnati lab's coming in tonight. We've got a working weekend planned, so he'll be staying here."

Jeanette rose. "Would you mind terribly if Minnie and I took a quick walk around the grounds? We'll just be a moment. I know you have to leave."

David checked his watch again. "Of course. Help yourself."

They let themselves out the French door onto the deck. Minnie whispered, "So much for Sarah's weekend with her son."

"Really. And Motel 6? That's insulting. He didn't offer us a glass of water or a place to freshen up. And I would have loved a tour of this house. You'd think there'd be enough room for us and a fleet of engineers. At least for his own mother. He acts like he hates her."

"Sarah's too sweet for anyone to hate her. He treated you and me the same way. I don't understand. He must only have a few months to live."

"Do you know something I don't?"

"He looks at his watch so much, I figure there's some sort of countdown."

"Seriously. Couldn't you just slap him every time he does that?"

"Or every time he says, 'Of course.'"

Jeanette said, "Sarah's got to be crushed. But I have to say she's handling it well. I'm proud of her."

"It's painful to watch. Let's go get her out of here."

Minnie opened the sliding door off the deck to go back inside. Sarah's and David's voices rose from the foyer, arguing. Minnie shut the door. "We should wait out here a bit."

Even in her anger and hurt, Sarah stayed collected. If she didn't, she would break down in front of her son, and she refused to do that "You can't even tell your own mother that you moved?"

"I was going to tell you. Look, I'm sorry. We'll have a nice dinner."

"I thought that man was coming in tonight."

"Not until nine o'clock. I can fit you in for dinner."

"You will fit me in for dinner. How lovely. You have all but ignored me for the past twelve years. I want to know why."

David looked at his watch. "I don't know what you're talking about."

"Stop that right now, young man." She slapped his hand, apparently surprising him as much as she surprised herself.

"What's gotten into you?"

"You know exactly what I'm talking about. You've been this way toward me, cold, even mean, ever since... ever since..." The tears welled behind her eyes; Sarah fought to dam them in. "Ever since Papa died. "Damn it, this is probably going to be the last time you ever see me. So tell me. What's eating at you?"

Slack-jawed, her son said, "I've never seen you like this."

"Why should that surprise you? It's been building forever. Now, what is it? I'm not leaving until we sort this out."

"Fine. You want to know? You should already know. You're the one who killed him."

Sarah was flabbergasted. "What are you talking about?"

"I was right there when you told them to pull the plug. All you could think about was the insurance money."

Sarah shrieked, "What? You were seventeen. I talked to you about the decision. In fact, your father himself made that decision. He wanted to pass at home. There was no hope by then. I thought you understood."

"I understood one thing. Two-hundred-and-fifty-thousand dollars. I saw the policy on the desk. You were sick and tired of taking care of him. Waiting for him to finally die. You just wanted to be free of him and have all that money."

"How can you say that? I loved your father. He was terminal, there was nothing that could be done. And all that money? You're supposed to be so damned brilliant, then where's the money? If there was money to be had, why did we lose the house and have to move to that crappy little apartment? But you wouldn't know about any of that would you? You went straight off to college. You had no problem calling me when you needed money. Did you think the money I sent came from the insurance? Did you?"

His mouth opened, but before he could reply, Sarah rushed on: "I worked two jobs. Two jobs. And I lived in squalor while I did it. You don't think that wears out a damn near fifty-year-old woman? And what do I get from you in return? Nothing but this distance, this hatred."

David's face began to flush; Sarah couldn't discern if it was more anger or confusion. He started to speak but stopped himself.

She realized she'd been shouting. Sarah drew one calming breath before continuing in a more soothing tone. "We borrowed on that insurance policy to pay the medical bills long before he passed away. There wasn't any money left. None whatsoever."

Sarah shuffled her feet, buying herself moments to process what she'd just been told, and decide what next to say to her son.

"So, that's it, huh? That's why I've had to suffer your coldness all these years? Why didn't you bring this up before?"

David looked like he was twelve again, when she'd grounded him for sneaking out at midnight on Halloween to toilet-paper houses. He reached for his car keys off the étagère near the door. He turned away and she couldn't gauge his expression. He said only, "Mom."

Sarah held her breath for his next words. Did he believe her now? Was he crying? She longed to know her David again.

Instead, his voice stayed cold. "I don't have time for this right now. We can talk more at dinner."

"What? At dinner? With Jeanette and Minnie sitting there? I won't burden my friends with our dirty laundry."

"I've got to go."

"Fine. Go." Sarah found the girls peering through the French doors from the deck. She motioned them to come inside.

"Let's go." Sarah marched away from David, out of the foyer, into the circular driveway. At her back, her son made his excuse to Minnie and Jeanette, "Sorry I have to rush off like this. Business."

Sarah turned back to watch Jeanette turn the faucet off her fake charm. "Of course. Thank you, David, for your warm hospitality. I'm just so...overwhelmed. One thing. I can't imagine staying at a Motel 6. What's the finest hotel in this little hick town?"

"There's a Hyatt, a Hilton. They're both pretty nice."

"Oh, and don't worry about your mother. We'll take good care of her. After all, we're the only family she has left."

Sarah went to lean on the car. By the time her friends reached her, she was sobbing. Minnie held her tightly while Jeanette glared at the closed front door to David's big house.

Through sniffles, Sarah asked, "How could he think that?"

Minnie said, "Now, now. He was young and full of grief himself. Just angry and looking for a place to put it. He'll come around. You'll see."

Jeanette opened the driver's door, to climb in and get them away from here. Before she ducked behind the wheel, she said across the car's roof, "That whole thing happened twelve years ago. You'd think the boy would've grown up and figured something out by now. It looks like he knows how to get around in the world." Jeanette waved a hand toward the house and grounds then leaning down to angle into the driver's seat. "It's not like he's stupid."

"I can be pretty stupid sometimes." David had crept up behind them. Minnie and Jeanette looked at him surprised at his admission but still angry in the same way they were when Jasper had called them all 'bitches.' They were ready to leap at him.

"Mom."

Sarah stood erect, away from the car. She was no longer crying but firm on her feet and ready to accept whatever her son said or did next. Nothing could be worse, so anything had to be an improvement.

He stepped close to Sarah, Minnie backed away to make room but stay close at hand.

David raised both arms, looking very young. Sarah held her ground, she made her son step up to take her in his arms.

Chapter 35

Marc didn't have his bank ID card with him. Earl wouldn't let him past.

"Go on down to the security office on California Street. They'll give you a temporary pass."

That would take Marc a half hour. Time was short. Of the essence.

"Look, Earl. I've been mugged. Look at my fucking arm. I've been shot."

"You need to see a doctor, Mr. Corbett. You look rough. You want me to get someone to take you to the hospital?"

"No, thanks. I'll go. But I've got to get upstairs first. I have spare house keys in my desk. I need to get to them or I can't get into my apartment or my car. Earl, you know me. Just let me sign in."

The old security guard looked Marc up and down. Marc grabbed up the pen and bent to sign. Earl put a restraining hand on his arm.

"Rules are rules. I can't let you sign in without your badge."

Marc shook his hand off and continued to sign the register.

"I already told you, I don't have time for this bullshit. Do what you have to do, Earl. Call the cops, whatever. But

I'm going to my office." Marc signed and headed for the elevator.

His clothes were still damp, rumpled and bloodied. His forehead stung from scabs, his wrist was still bruised purple and swollen. His shoulder throbbed from a gunshot wound. He could barely press the elevator button; how had he been able to shoot a pistol like this? Marc marveled at himself, at what he'd proven himself capable of.

He rode to the twelfth floor. He and Sergio had split up: Serge went to tell the cops what had happened at the sailboat, Marc to the bank for his last chance to find any evidence to clear his name. The bell rang for his floor, the doors slid apart, and Marc stepped out.

Southern's office was the last one down a short hall off the central lobby. His voice called cheerfully to his secretary, "Good night, Vicky. See you in the morning."

Marc hustled away from the elevators before Phil could enter the lobby, turn the corner and head for the elevator bank. Marc had nowhere to hide but behind a lush ficus tree at the end of the hall. He crouched behind the pot and the skinny tree trunk, certain that Southern would see him and there'd be another fistfight or some ugly new scene to further make this the worst day of Marc's life. Phil entered the lobby, then the foyer to the elevators. Marc willed him not to turn his head; Southern pressed the call button then stepped into the elevator without glancing around once. He rubbed his hands together gleefully, even greedily, and Marc could sense the little man's bubbling joy. The heist had been accomplished. Southern was on his way, scot free.

After the elevator closed, Marc emerged. He avoided the reception area where Vicky was putting on her jacket to leave for the day, as well. Marc headed for the computer room.

Inside, he sat at the new monitor. The wrecked room had been completely restored from the fight with Roscoe and Vinnie the night before. Marc worked the keyboard to bring up the history module in order to review the day's transactions. The screen read: "Transaction completed," followed by: "Log off." This confirmed what Marc suspected: Southern had made the funds transfer and erased the significant history that would ordinarily have been displayed.

Marc brought up the SuperCredit program. He glanced over his shoulder as he typed in code, nervous at first, but within moments he was propelled by the same adrenaline rush that had helped him escape Vinnie and shoot at Roscoe. Marc figured he had about ten minutes if Earl reported his security breach downstairs. He hoped Earl had let it go, but in case the old guard hadn't, Marc worked as fast as he and the computer could.

The computer beeped, alerting him to the completion of his requested task. There they were: row after row of names with amounts listed beside them. Cash advances supposedly taken that very day by all these 'customers.' Among them he spotted the names of Minnie and her friends. Some of his own friends were listed, too. How did Southern know about his tennis buddy, or his old girlfriend from college? Phil had done his homework in order to frame Marc; he'd told Melanie to get Marc to talk about his past, and Marc did. He tamped down a fresh surge of temper at her, and focused on the job at hand, of nailing all their asses to the wall.

At the bottom of the list he read the total: forty million two hundred and fifty-eight thousand dollars. Un-fucking-believable.

Marc pressed escape and went to another menu. This took him deeper into the program. As he'd guessed, the debits appeared to have gone into outer space. Outsource revealed nothing but gibberish; the destination of the funds was untraceable even to an expert like him. But Southern and Carl had left just enough history to incriminate Marc.

He cursed himself for his stupidity, for his belief in Melanie. He'd been so quick to please her, so in awe of her job title and smarts that he didn't question any further about the workings of the program. Of course, she didn't leave him much of a chance to reflect on it, either. He was whisked off by her to Kauai for just the right amount of time needed to pull off this fraud. The program had been the farthest thing from his mind.

The backup tape of Southern's fraudulent program was lost forever. How could Marc prove his innocence? There was no way to recover the money without knowing where it had gone. Marc thought hard, but it all seemed futile.

He typed in another string of commands. The computer screen returned him nothing he could use. Marc rolled his chair back from the keyboard. He stared at the screen, fucked.

Melanie was probably on a plane right now with Phil, on their way to someplace like Switzerland. Forty million bucks was a lot of money. He should have tied her up on the sailboat when he had her on her knees. Instead, he'd despise her for the rest of his life. And miss her.

The computer room door opened. A tall gray-haired man in a gray suit stood in the doorway. Behind him were three others, similarly dressed with identical scowls.

The tall man looked Marc up and down, then produced a badge.

"Marc Corbett?"

Marc sighed in defeat and nodded. "Yes."

"I'm Agent Paul Fellows with the FBI. You'll have to come with us."

Chapter 36

Sergio drove onto Sommersville Road in Marc's car. He crept toward the yacht club, scanning the area. The sun wouldn't go down for another hour.

He'd told Marc he'd go straight to the cops. But he hadn't, not yet. If he did, there'd be lots of questions and the delay might let Southern, Melanie, Vinnie, and Roscoe get away. Sergio told himself he was heading back to the marina to find a way to keep the bad guys from skipping town. Now that he was here, he admitted to himself he'd come back to Fort Baker to get even.

Instead of rolling straight into the yacht club's parking lot, Sergio thought it best to creep in by the exit road; the dirt lane ran along a hillcrest and afforded the best view of the marina. He'd park up there and stay out of sight while he formed his plan.

As soon as he turned up the one-way road, Sergio could see the whole marina. Southern's sailboat rested quietly at the end of the pier. Good, the sonsofbitches hadn't left yet. Sergio hadn't seen the boat from this vantage point; he'd been hooded when Vinnie and Roscoe tossed him on deck. That was just last night, but it felt like a week had passed.

In the waning daylight, a dim glow emanated from the ship's galley. She was a beautiful boat, tall-masted, well-kept and stately. All Sergio could think about was watching her burn.

He looked for a good spot to park Marc's car, to stay unseen from the harbor. As he rounded a line of bushes, Sergio's breath snagged in his chest.

His blue VW was parked haphazardly on the shoulder of the exit road beside a tall anise bush. Why was his car here?

There could only be one explanation. Frannie.

She must have come to help him, save him. Did those bastards have her? That glow from the sailboat's galley windows; did they have Frannie?

Sergio's heart thumped as he got out of Marc's car. Both doors of his VW bug were locked. He peered inside and saw no clue, but it had to be Frannie who drove it here.

He scampered down the hill, then made his way stealthily up the dock toward Southern's vessel.

Was she onboard with those two psychos Roscoe and Vinnie? Was she even alive? Sergio would never forgive himself if anything bad happened to Frannie. He crept near the boat, intending to peer into each porthole. Every quiet step closer made Sergio regret more that he'd dragged Frannie into this dangerous mess.

Sergio put Melanie's gun in his hand. If he was seen, if he encountered Mel, Vinnie, Roscoe, Southern, Carl, anyone onboard, he'd have to bluff his way through because the pistol had no bullets. Either bluff or be captured again, maybe gunned down on sight. Sergio was a great joker, a big enough physical specimen, smart and coolheaded, but this was a different game, played by real villains with loaded guns. Sergio had passed a payphone on the yacht club dock. Maybe it was time to admit he wasn't the right guy to play hero and call in reinforcements.

Hunkered low, Sergio moved away from the sailboat, headed back to the public phone. Then, trills of laughter issued from inside the hull, from the galley. Sergio stopped his retreat and inched closer to the boat. The laughter, unmistakably, was Frannie's. A man's merry voice joined her. It sounded like Vinnie.

What the hell? Sergio crept close enough to peer into one of the galley windows. There, at the table, sat Frannie, enjoying the company and witty banter of Vinnie the thug.

Was she in on the plot? Impossible. But Sergio, armed with a pistol, even an empty one, was damned well going to find out.

He stepped quickly across the plank to the deck, staying on his toes, and alert for anyone else he might bump into. From below came more conversation and giggles, like Frannie and Vinnie were on a date.

Sergio stood at the top of the companionway stairs. He steeled himself for what he was about to discover, held the gun menacingly, and descended.

Vinnie and Frannie were seated close together in the dining alcove, smiling and talking. Frannie drank a beer. A gauze bandage circled Vinnie's head. Vinnie placed one hand on Frannie's. She seemed not to mind and took a sip of beer.

Sergio trained the empty gun on Vinnie. Frannie rose from the table.

"Thank God you're alright!"

"What's going on here?"

Vinnie made no sudden moves. He held up both palms in surrender. "It's all right, Sergio. Put down the gun."

"What do you mean 'put down the gun'?" Sergio thrust the revolver at Vinnie to threaten him.

Vinnie raised both hands higher, above his shoulders. "Whoa, settle down, big boy. I'm Vincent Armada, FBI."

Chapter 37

Sergio asked, "Carl's dead?"

Frannie nodded solemnly. "I saw the whole thing. It was horrible."

Sergio listened to her story. When she got to the part where Southern took the pills from Carl who was lying on his back, choking and pleading, Frannie's throat caught and tears welled up. Vinnie patted her hand, then held on.

This was a hard sell for Sergio, the idea that Vinnie was FBI. He still looked like a henchman, but maybe you had to be some sort of thug to be in law enforcement.

He had to admit, Frannie and Vinnie looked good together. Both had Italian blood, dark hair and eyes. She could do worse, and had. At least this one had a job.

Vinnie said, "Roscoe got you pretty good."

"Looks like I got you pretty good too." Sergio gestured to the bandage wrapping Vinnie's skull.

"Yeah, you did. Had me out cold there for a few."

Frannie's eyes widened on Sergio. "You did that?"

"I did. Sorry about that, man."

"Part of the job. Don't worry about it."

Frannie squeezed Vinnie's hand. It looked like the FBI man might be around for a while. Sergio nodded at Frannie; Vinnie seemed okay.

Sergio asked him, "What about the bank plot? Is Southern getting away with it? He and Melanie? Did the transfer go through? Forty million?"

Vinnie let go of Frannie's hand. He sat up straighter, becoming his official self, the upright law enforcer.

"We've had our eye on Phil Southern for a long time. When he was fresh out of college, he went to work at First Bank of Marin. Some money came up missing then, but he's a natural at this crime thing. We couldn't prove shit."

"How about now?"

"Oh, he's gonna get away with it this time, too."

Sergio's mouth fell open. "What?"

"I told you, the guy's good. And he has pros around him. Melanie, Jenkins. I tell you, you don't see criminals this smart very often. Hell, I even infiltrated his little gang and I still didn't get enough to bust him."

Vinnie lifted an envelope off the cushion beside him and laid it on the galley table.

"Frannie found this packet of credit applications hidden in your apartment. It's incriminating as hell."

"Then use it against them."

"Incriminating for you, Sergio. Then there's all those apps with Marc Corbett's signature. The forgeries are good, they honestly look like Marc's. He's got no way to prove they aren't his. Especially the apps signed under his name for his credit-crazed aunt and her two friends." Vinnie chuckled, shaking his head. "No. Southern, Melanie, even old dead Carl, they would've gotten away with it."

Frannie, showing every bit of shock on her face that Sergio felt, asked, "What do you mean 'would've'?"

The FBI man laid a big paw on Sergio's shoulder. Sergio winced under the pressure on his bad rib.

"He kidnapped our buddy Sergio, here, and Corbett. He imprisoned them against their will. He instructed me and Roscoe to beat the snot out of them. Melanie aided and abetted the kidnapping, plus she aimed a lethal weapon at Marc Corbett with intent to kill. Let me see, what else? Oh, yeah. Miss Frannie here witnessed Phil Southern taking the pills from Carl Jenkins who died of heart failure as a direct result. Since these are all felonies, my guess is Phil Southern will be glad to bargain for a little leniency in return for clearing your name and Marc's. And if he won't, Melanie will, since she's already in custody."

"You got her?"

Vinnie checked his watch. "Fifteen minutes ago. She was arrested at the bank. Along with your boy Corbett. It's kinda funny, really."

"What is?"

"You and Corbett. You've been trying so hard to catch them in this bank scam. In the end, you came up just as empty as we did. But you wound up helping us put them away just by getting your asses kicked. Come on, Serge. Sorry, man, but you gotta see that's funny. I do."

"I don't. Speaking of getting my ass kicked, where's Roscoe?"

"In custody. Fucker dropped my pizza. No one drops my pizza."

"And Phil?"

"Southern's on his way here right now. He's expecting to meet Melanie onboard. I've got two men tailing him from the bank. The transfer's scheduled to go through at five o'clock. Once it's done, he and the girl figure they're gonna disappear on his sailboat to parts unknown, with forty million in a private account. You and Corbett take the fall. Aunt Minnie and her pals go to jail for credit card fraud. Happy ending."

Vinnie slapped his palms on the tabletop. "I have to call in again. See what's going on and get a car out here to take you guys to HQ. Wait here, okay? I'm going to the pay phone. I'll be back in a few minutes." Vinnie softened as he rose from the table, and asked Frannie, "You okay? You need anything?"

"I'm just scared."

Vinnie put his large hands over her small ones. "They'll be in jail soon enough. Don't you worry. I'll be your personal witness protection program."

After he left, Sergio grinned at Frannie, and mimicked her tone. "I'm so scared."

Frannie reddened then slapped at Sergio's hand. "Stop it. He's really sweet. I think it's love at first sight."

"So. Kinda looks like it's mutual?"

"Yeah, well, I dunno. God, he's such a fox. Isn't he gorgeous? And he's so nice under that big bear exterior. Do you think he likes me? I'm worried he's just being nice because I'm so upset after seeing Jenkins get killed and all."

"I think there's more to it."

"Do me a favor? Go walk with him. Kind of feel him out for me."

"Sure."

Sergio caught up with Vinnie on the dock. The big FBI man stopped walking.

"Sergio, I know what you're doing."

"What am I doing?"

"Pal, you need to understand what I do for a living. I figure people out. She sent you."

"Okay. She sent me."

Vinnie folded his meaty arms across his chest.

"You can tell a lot about people by the company they keep. I know Frannie's a good person, because I can tell you are. I like her, man. Right off the bat, I like her. Maybe a lot. How 'bout you give us some room to see where it can go? Not too much, but give me a chance with her. I'll appreciate it. And I won't plan to pay you back for splitting my skull. Okay?"

Vinnie put out one of his bear paws to shake. Sergio took it, and they walked together to the far end of the pier, to the payphone.

The big man put a coin into the slot and dialed. He said, "Hello," then listened, saying little more than "Uh huh," and "Yeah," before hanging up.

"He's on his way."

"What are you going to do?"

"I'll arrest him as soon as he gets out of his car."

Sergio turned to hurry back along the pier. "I'll get Frannie."

"Stay with her on the boat 'til this is over. It'll be safer."

"Got it."

Sergio made it to Southern's yacht just as a BMW pulled into the parking lot. He hustled onboard and down the companionway stairs. Frannie sat where he'd left her at the galley table.

"Vinnie says for us to stay here until they arrest Phil. He just showed up."

Sergio sat. Frannie took both his hands in hers.

"What did he say about me?"

"That's what you want to know right now?"

"Yep."

"He likes you. Jesus, Frannie."

Before she could ask more, the sharp cracks of gunfire erupted outside, then the thuds of feet running along the pier.

Sergio said, "Stay here."

He climbed the companionway enough to poke out his head. Southern sprinted the last distance along the pier, then up the plank to the ship's deck. He held a big gun, a hand cannon he fired at Vinnie and two other men, probably FBI agents on his team. All three threw themselves flat on the pier while Southern ran to the bow. There, he shot again as he slipped the docking line.

Sergio muttered, "Holy shit."

Something had gone wrong. Determined as well as greedy, Southern had somehow sensed the danger and started shooting before Vinnie and his team could grab him.

Southern ran about the deck, dropping lines, shooting at Vinnie, all the while shouting for Melanie. Sergio ducked back down below.

"Get up, Frannie. Now."

As he said this, the sailboat's diesel engine came to life. Phil was going to make a run for it on a sailboat. That didn't make much sense, but along with being evil and greedy, he was desperate.

Frannie scrambled from behind the galley table. Sergio scuttled into the bow, to find a place for the two of them to hide.

The boat surged away from the pier, its diesel engine at full throttle. Sergio threw open a door to a stateroom; he turned to push Frannie inside.

She was not behind him.

"Frannie!" Phil Southern said over the barrel of a very large handgun, "get up here. Now!"

Frannie willed herself not to look over her shoulder at Sergio. Southern hadn't seen him and she needed to keep it that way. With legs like jelly, she climbed up the companionway steps to the cockpit. With one hand he trained the gun at Frannie's chest, manned the big helm wheel with the other, and the yacht coursed at top speed through the last of the marina. Southern turned from Frannie to yell back to Vinnie and the other two armed men.

"Hey, Vinnie, you backstabbing piece of shit! You got Melanie?"

"We got her, Phil."

"Too bad. Tell her I was gonna use her for a hostage. That would've broken my heart. So this is much better. See you, asshole."

Vinnie's voice faded as the sailboat gained pace and distance from the pier, headed to the open San Francisco Bay.

"Phil!"

"What?"

"Don't fucking hurt her!"

Phil didn't answer Vinnie's last shout, but grinned knowingly at Frannie.

"Well, well."

Sergio hunkered in the passageway between the forward staterooms. He stayed low, out of sight from the cockpit above, where Phil kept his gun on Frannie.

The boat rocked on the chop of the open bay. Sergio had to do something, play hero for real, or else he'd wind up joining Frannie as Southern's hostage. Vinnie was no help right now, and though the FBI might apprehend Southern before the boat made it out to the open ocean, there was no guarantee Frannie and Sergio would still be alive when that happened.

Carefully he pushed open the door to one of the staterooms, the main one used by Southern and Melanie.

Sergio rummaged about but found nothing but clothes, cigarettes, and a travel magazine for tropical Pacific islands. Nothing he could use against Southern. Quickly he searched the stateroom where he and Marc had been tied up; again, he came up empty.

In the third stateroom, the smallest of the three, Sergio found in the bottom of a closet something he might make use of: one big can of spar varnish and two cans of paint thinner. A warning on all three cans read in big scarlet letters, CAUTION: FLAMMABLE. Sergio grabbed the varnish and slipped back into Southern's room. He dug through the drawers beside the bed until he laid his hands on what he prayed he would find: a cigarette lighter.

Southern stopped pointing the gun at Frannie and focused on getting all the speed he could out of his sailboat. He pointed the bow west for the Farrallones, still miles off, and then what, she wondered? The open Pacific? Tahiti? Did he have a plan? There was plenty of food onboard. Was he really going to keep Frannie hostage until he managed to disappear? And even if he managed it, then what? Send her home? Unlikely.

Where was Sergio?

At the wheel, Southern was facing forward; Frannie, frozen in the companionway, looked towards the stern.

Southern couldn't see the speedboat chasing after them, or hear it because of the whine of his own straining diesel. The small craft was still too far away for her to see who was coming after her. But she knew it was Vinnie.

Sergio poured the varnish over the mattress where he'd been tied up by Vinnie and Roscoe. He spilled a little pool onto the floorboards outside the stateroom door.

Sergio lit the mattress first, then laid the cigarette lighter's little fire to the floor. The varnish didn't flash at first but drank up the flame, held it, and spread it. He stepped into the stateroom across the hall, leaving the door cracked, to watch the fire grow.

"Mr. Southern."

"Shut up." He pointed the big handgun at Frannie for a moment to underscore his command, then lowered it.

Frannie raised her hand like a schoolgirl.

"Mr. Southern."

He raised the gun again, this time direly annoyed. He yelled, "What?"

"I smell smoke."

Southern left the wheel. "Get out of the way."

Frannie stepped out of the companionway. Southern moved into her place at the head of the stairs, to peer below.

He never looked back at Vinnie racing closer. Southern said, "Shit," and leaped down the stairs, leaving Frannie unguarded.

The fire in the mattress was building fast, billowing more black smoke by the second.

The flames on the floor grew to knee height. Southern skidded in the passageway, stunned to see his boat on fire.

Sergio burst out of the stateroom, ready with the same compass he'd used to knock out Vinnie. But Southern was a smaller man, more nimble than the big FBI thug. Sergio's swing with the compass missed Phil's head and glanced off his shoulder. The blow wasn't enough to drop Southern or make him lose his grip on the pistol, only push him sideways into the passageway wall.

Sergio didn't pause to take another shot, not while Southern held a gun. Instead, Sergio swept past him, out of the passageway through the smoke and fumes.

"Frannie!"

Sergio bounded up the companionway steps. Frannie stood in the cockpit, one arm raised, not at him but behind the sailboat, out over the water at a speedboat closing in.

She said, "It's Vinnie."

Sergio wrapped Frannie in his arms. With his rib stabbing him hard, he snatched her up and leaped with her overboard.

Strong arms lifted Frannie out of the bay. Then Vinnie reached down for Sergio, who collapsed beside her in the bow of the small motorboat. Shoulder to shoulder, both shivered from the cold waters.

"You're okay," Vinnie said, "you're both okay."

Frannie waved off the FBI man's ministrations.

"Don't worry about us. Go get that sonofabitch."

Vinnie gave her a thumbs-up. "Yeah, we're gonna get along just fine."

The sailboat smoldered in the middle of the bay, coursing smoke and fire even as it surged over the whitecaps. Vinnie brought the powerboat even with the dying yacht but kept a safe distance in case Phil Southern decided to shoot at them.

He eased the throttle to match the sailboat's pace. Vinnie cupped his hands over his mouth.

"Phil! Phil! It's over, man. Toss your gun in the water. I'll come get you."

Southern didn't appear to hear; he stood behind the wheel, the big gun hanging in his hand, and made no effort to answer. Smoke pulsed from the open companionway, blowing past him, leaving a gray trail on the water. Phil stood motionless, stoic, stunned.

Overhead, a helicopter zoomed out from the city. A San Francisco police boat powered away from the city docks with lights flashing and siren whooping. Vinnie shouted again.

"Drop the gun. Jump in the water. I'll pick you up."

Southern did nothing to show he'd understood. Vinnie nudged the motorboat closer. The tips of flames peeked out of the companionway to lick the salt air. Vinnie eased just close enough to speak to Southern in a normal voice. He kept his own pistol in hand.

"Phil. Please."

Southern seemed to register.

He said to Vinnie, "I went to Stanford."

"I know, Phil. You're a smart cookie."

"Where's Mel?"

"Under arrest."

The flames rippled higher, everything below decks had ignited. Sergio told Vinnie, "Back off the sailboat."

Vinnie said, "I got this."

"Listen to me. I started that fire. There's cans of flammable shit on that boat. They're gonna go up any second."

The FBI man tried one more time. "Phil. You're gonna die."

Southern exhaled a long breath, like a man who figured it was among his last.

"Yeah," he said. "That's what I told Carl."

Southern let go of the ship's wheel, to let the sailboat go its last moments wherever it wanted. Vinnie turned the motorboat away moments before a black and orange fireball tore the sailboat apart.

At the dock, Marc was waiting with two dozen FBI agents and city cops.

Sergio and Frannie sat together on the pier. Someone threw blankets over their shoulders. Vinnie came to slump beside her. A tall man in a blue suit, crewcut and steely-eyed, followed Vinnie to stand over him and continue talking in a clearly pissed-off tone.

"Goddamit, we wanted to take him alive."

"Well," Vinnie said, not looking up, "We didn't."

"No, we fucking well didn't."

"What about Roscoe?"

Vinnie said, "That idiot counts on his fingers. He wouldn't know anything about where the money went. You pick him up yet?"

"Half an hour ago."

"How about Melanie?"

"We got her. She's not talking yet but Fellows says they're working on a deal, leniency for information. But

I doubt she'll budge. After all, with Carl and Phil both dead, the score would be all hers. She'll do her time then when she's out, head to that Swiss bank to collect all forty million. And the Swiss show no inclination to help. They claim the privacy of their banking business is more important than solving our little crime. So, fuck them."

"You find Carl's body?"

"Mall security found him in his Mercedes in the Sears parking lot at Tanforan. And now that you cowboys decided to blow up Phil Southern, we got no trail."

The tall FBI agent stuffed hands in his pockets and surveyed the water, the marina, the world that would give him no break.

"Forty million dollars. And we can't find it."

The agent stalked off, probably looking for someone else to growl at. Sergio asked Vinnie, "Who's that asshole?"

"That asshole is my boss. Fellows. He's the agent in charge of the case."

Marc sat beside Sergio. He whispered, "He did it. The fucker did it. Moved forty million, and they couldn't stop him."

Marc looked as weary as Sergio felt. "Well, at least he's not alive to enjoy it."

"We saw that blast. You're lucky you're alive."

Vinnie leaned across Frannie to put out a hand to Sergio.

"That was brave shit, man. Thanks for saving Frannie."

She bussed Sergio's cheek. Marc drew back, surprised.

"He did what? He saved you?"

"Like a hero."

Agents and police swarmed around the dock, coordinating as best they could, dancing to Agent Fellows' aggravated tune. Frannie had long since lost her new shoes, the sharp stilettos she'd been so proud of were left behind on Phil's boat. Sergio untied his own sopping wingtips and socks to let his freezing feet dry out.

From his left shoe he peeled out his twenty dollar bill. Out of the right he plucked his ten dollars.

And a piece of paper.

Marc asked, "What's that?"

"Hey. That New York phone number. I forgot all about it."

Vinnie pointed. "What's that?"

Sergio explained. "When Marc and I were in Jenkins' office."

Vinnie raised a finger. "When you broke into Jenkin's office."

"Okay, technically yes. That we broke into." Sergio liked Vinnie, but told himself never to forget this was an FBI agent.

We loaded up a briefcase of paperwork out of a cabinet."

"That you stole from a cabinet you also broke into."

Frannie gave Vinnie's arm a squeeze, to tell him to stop being a dick.

Sergio handed him the slip of paper with the 212 phone number on it.

"We called this number but got a recording that it wasn't good anymore."

"What makes you think this is a phone number?"

"Ten digits. 212. That's New York."

"Serge. Marc. You know what this might be?"

"No."

Vinnie got to his feet, too excited to sit.

"Ten is also the number of digits for a Swiss Bank account. It could be a phone number but I have a feeling it's an account number at a Swiss Bank."

Vinnie took several hurried steps away, then stopped himself and returned. He laid a quick kiss on Frannie's cheek, then said to the three of them: By the way, if this is really a Swiss account number, and the forty million is there, the bank's offered a ten percent finder's reward."

Vinnie hustled off to find Agent Fellows.

Frannie beamed at Marc and Sergio.

"You guys are going to be millionaires."

"No," Sergio said. "All three of us are going to be millionaires!"

Marc agreed. Sergio asked him, "What'll you do with your share?"

"I'll probably have to use half of it to square my Aunt Minnie with the bank."

Sergio laughed, his first good laugh in a long, scary day. "Jenkins did one nice thing for you before he croaked. He reversed all your aunt's balances. She and her friends. They don't owe a cent."

"Well then, I'll probably have to spend half of it on lawyers for them. What they did is still credit card fraud."

Frannie nodded. "George Post isn't going to stop until he nails them. Sorry, Marc."

"It's okay. They're my family. How about you, Serge?"

"New car. I'm gonna run that VW bug off a cliff. Frannie?"

"The first thing?"

"Yeah. The first thing you're gonna buy."

Frannie gazed at her bare feet. "I really did love those shoes."

Chapter 38

George massaged the stubble at his jawline. He yawned, got up and tossed the half empty paper cup into the trash can. He took one last bite from the nasty concoction that was trying to pass itself off as a churro and dumped that too. Checking his watch, it was 7:47 p.m. He looked deep into the corridor. No sign of his three criminals. He turned his back on the crowds in the busy international terminal and stared out the floor-to-ceiling windows at the tarmac. Everything looked gray. With the exception of a few slices of red, blue, orange on the large jet liners pulling in or queuing up for their turns on the runway.

For two days he'd been slumped in the molded plastic chair near the check-in desk half hidden by a bushy fichus. Shifting and angling, he was unable to find any comfort. And definitely no sleep. But he had to wait it out. The last charges coming through were for three flights from Kennedy Airport in New York to Malaga-Costa del Sol Airport in Spain. Info that American Express had shared with the bank. Naturally, no date and time indicated. Even credit authorizers such as his all-powerful bank could not get detailed information from the airlines. Privacy acts and all.

◈

Minnie was slack-jawed as she hung up the phone. "You're not going to believe this."

"What?" Jeanette checked her watch, then started moving. "We better hurry to find our gate."

Minnie said. "Okay, I just called Marc. Jeanette! You with the long legs. Can you just slow it down a bit? I can't keep up. Anyway, Marc. He's going to be a millionaire."

Sarah and Jeanette stopped, mouths agape. Minnie said, "Yes. He busted open this forty million dollar fraud at the bank and discovered they were funneling money into a Swiss bank account. He even found the account number. The bank is giving him and two of his co-workers a ten percent reward. And the news gets even better."

Sarah asked, "How could it get better than that?"

"Our card balances are all zero. We don't owe any money."

Sarah beamed. "So we're in the clear?"

"No."

"No?"

Jeanette laid a hand on Sarah's shoulder. "It's still fraud. We're still crooks. So come on, we need to keep walking."

Minnie said, "We've got plenty of time before they start boarding. Look. A bar. I say we get a drink under our belts. And we can stay a bit hidden until take off. Just in case."

"Fine." Said Jeanette. The three found a tall cocktail table halfway in and settled in with screwdrivers.

Sarah exhaled in a rush. "I can't believe we made it."

Minnie said, "We haven't made it yet. I'm so antsy. I won't be able to exhale until that plane is in the air."

Jeanette said, "Did you see that Louis Vuitton store just outside the bar?"

Sarah grinned. "That red scarf in the window. And that bag!"

Minnie interrupted, "That was a gorgeous scarf. If you can wear red that is, which you two can. Maybe they have it in blue?"

Jeanette said, "I wonder if we can get some Spanish credit cards?"

Sarah said, "Shopping in Europe. Oh my goodness. Spain is close to Paris and Rome and even London. And the couture."

"Good grief," Minnie said. "This is going to be a long life."

Feeling a tap on her shoulder, Jeanette turned. A bedraggled version of George Post stood before her, his City Security Bank badge in hand. "The three of you need to come with me right now."

Jeanette said, "Oh no! Really? We're twenty feet away from boarding a flight to freedom and you have to show up?"

"Look, lady, I've been after you for a long, long time. I've been kicked around, bum rushed, embarrassed, outrun, tricked, and I'm plum burnt out. I've had it. And to tell the truth I'd just as soon shoot the three of you. So don't tempt me. Now, come on."

Once outside the bar, Jeanette started to walk toward their gate but George put a restraining hand on her arm. "I wouldn't do that if I were you. If you make a scene, you'll bring on airport security and they aren't as nice as me. Now come with me."

Sarah said, "I guess we always knew it was too good to be true."

With downcast eyes, they walked away from their happily-ever-after in stride with their pursuer. Minnie whispered, "What if we just took off running? You think we might make it?"

Sarah said, "You've seen too many movies. Besides, see that bulge in his jacket? Shoulder holster."

Jeanette put a hand on Sarah's arm. "Oh for God's sake. What the hell is he doing here?"

Above the thick crowd a white panama hat bounced along, moving in their direction. When Jasper passed them, a grin spread across his face. He had a carry-on bag in one hand, coke in the other but still managed to tip his hat, wink at Jeanette and say, "Well, well."

"I'll be damned." Jeanette hissed to Minnie. "That smug jerk! The nerve. You and Sarah enjoy Spain."

"What are you going to do? Jeanette, no. No."

Jeanette whispered. "Goodbye. I love you both. When I go that way, you and Sarah head to the gate. As fast as you can."

With a sudden roar, Jeanette burst from the group and rushed Jasper, fingernails and fists flying. The suitcase flew from his hand, the soda poured down the front of his white suit then bounced across the linoleum.

George ran after, leaving Minnie and Sarah unguarded. Neither said a word or looked behind them at the international gate. They took off after Jeanette and jumped on Jasper too.

Minnie and Sarah got in some thumps to the head and kicks to the shins while Jeanette clawed at his eyes and punched at his face.

Jasper screamed, blood trickling from his nose. "Get them off of me. Get them off!"

George hauled them off Jasper, shouting, "What the hell? What's going on here?"

"He's the one!" Jeanette said. "He's the one who robbed us."

George grabbed Minnie's hand and pulled her up from the floor. "Now settle down all of you. And stay put."

Jeanette said, "What the hell are you doing here? Are you following us?"

Jasper sat up from the floor. "Damn! It was your idea, lady."

"The name is Jeanette. I'd think you'd remember."

George said, "What idea?"

"Well, she's the one planted the idea in my head. I'm going to Spain."

Aghast, Jeanette echoed Jasper. "Spain?"

"Yeah, you said you had a villa in Spain. So I got to thinking how I wanted to travel and decided to go to Spain. I'm going to stay until they do that running with the bulls thing. Then I'm gonna outrun the damn bulls." Jasper stood with a little help from George, picked up his suitcase and hat which he planted atop his head.

Minnie took a step toward Jasper and said, "Well, I say, we grab this bull by the horns."

Jeanette gasped. Those were the very words Madame Viola had used. The old medium had predicted everything, including this moment.

George said, "Just relax. Everyone just take a breath, okay?"

Sarah said, "Mr. Post, he's the one who stole the credit cards. Don't you see?"

"These women are crazy. I don't know what they're talking about." Jasper made as if to leave.

George said, "Just a moment sir."

"Beg pardon?"

"I said you're not leaving. Not yet."

"Oh yeah? And who the hell are you that you're gonna stop me?"

George displayed his credentials to Jasper. "These ladies say you robbed them in Savannah. It's apparent you know each other. So is this true? Did you rob them?"

"It's bullshit, man. All I did was help them get to the bus station. That's all I did."

Sarah said, "He took our wallets. He took everything we had. We had to sleep in an old abandoned house with spiders. And we had to sleep in a tent with the driving rain soaking in on us." She stopped herself, then her face lit up. "Though we did meet some very nice people."

George asked Jasper, "You took their wallets?"

"Hell no."

"And you don't have their credit cards?"

"I got a flight to catch."

"Let me see your wallet."

"You're just some bank security guard. I don't have to show you shit."

George, a much bigger and more substantial man, brought his face close to Jasper's. "Either show me your wallet right here and now and maybe make that plane to Spain. Or show me at the police station and miss it." Suddenly quite mean, he added, "Or I can take it from you." He pulled back the buttons on his rumpled suit jacket to show Jasper his shoulder harness and black handled pistol.

Reluctant and sour-faced, Jasper handed over his fat wallet. An accordion sheaf loaded with dozens of credit cards tumbled down.

The three women edged backwards toward their gate, toward freedom. Sarah said it again, "He's the one. He's the one who stole the cards. Please. We have to catch our flight. Please let us go."

George kept a grip on Jasper's skinny arm as he peered at the credit cards. Most of them had Edith Clarke's name emblazoned across the front. Several belonged to Minnie Barlow and Sarah Gardener. George laughed.

He said to the women, "I wondered why you three started ringing up charges for men's clothes and massage parlors."

"Let me go." This time from Jasper, wriggling and indignant.

George shook Jasper's arm. "You, sir, are under arrest. You're gonna come with me."

George tucked the wallet in his coat. The lock he had on Jasper's arm looked unbreakable. Jasper glared at Jeanette, Minnie and Sarah, but George yanked his attention back to him.

"What kind of piece of shit mugs three old ladies?"

Sarah said, "Hey."

George apologized. "I mean three ladies."

"Thank you."

Minnie asked, "George?"

"Yes, ma'am?"

"Um, what about us?"

George Post considered Jasper's face up close. There was plenty of crime there. George had spent enough time as a cop to know it when he saw it.

"I'm sure there's a reward for this asshole. I suppose I can give it to you up front."

"Meaning?"

"Meaning, I need to arrest someone for credit card fraud, and that's exactly what I'm doing."

Minnie edged backwards a few steps. "So we can go?"

"Yeah you can go. And you better hurry. That flight is already boarding. And don't come back for a while, you hear?"

Sarah stood motionless. "Thank you, Mr. Post. Thank you. And I'm sorry for all the trouble we put you through. That must have been a really hard..."

Jeanette grabbed her arm. "Oh for God's sake, Sarah, move it. You can send him a thank you note from Malaga."

George pulled cuffs from the inside pocket of his suit jacket and snapped them on Jasper's wrists behind his back.

At a bank of pay phones, he stopped and placed a call. Valerie answered on the first ring. "George! I'm so glad to hear from you. I was afraid, well, you know, that it was just going to be one of those things. Where are you?"

"I'm in New York. I caught my crook. Going to turn him over to the authorities. Then I'm on vacation."

"Him? I thought you were chasing down those three women."

"Yeah, well, I'll tell you all about that when I see you. Uh, that is, if you'd like to see me again. I mean, I loved the time we spent together and I'd like to come back. You know, to see you. But if, you know, I mean, I don't know how you feel, but I do know how I feel..." his voice trailed off.

Beside him, Jasper snorted. "Smooth."

"George, it makes me so happy to hear that. I would love to see you again. When can you come?"

"After I dump this loser with the authorities, I'm taking the first flight out."

Jeanette, Minnie and Sarah boarded in their summer outfits from Bloomingdale's. Their fine linens and silks were wrinkled and spattered with blood and Coke. They settled into the comfort of their first class seats and laughed all at once.

A bottle of champagne in an ice bucket stood on a small cocktail table near Jeanette. Beside it, plump shrimp cocktails, lemon wedges and a tray of French bread waited to be served.

A steward arrived. "Would you like champagne?"

Jeanette said, "Yes. Yes. More than I can tell you."

The cork let loose with a loud pop, and the women applauded. The steward filled each glass. "If you need anything, press the red button on the console."

Jeanette fluttered her eyelashes.

The plane lifted through the darkening 4th of July skies. Over New York, the Bicentennial fireworks show erupted as if just for them and their departure together. They plastered themselves to the plane's windows until the explosions of color and light faded too far behind on the shores of America.

Jeanette, Minnie and Sarah raised their bubbling champagne flutes and clinked them together.

"To an enjoyable flight," said Minnie.

"To our flight from justice," said Sarah.

"To just us," said Jeanette, "in Spain."

421

The End

Acknowledgments

No creative work can be completed without input, advice, inspiration, and experience. For all of this I owe a great deal of thanks to many people and to many circumstances.

In my early 20s I worked in the credit card department at a large bank in San Francisco. During my four- year stint as a bill collector and skip tracer, I learned all the ins and outs of dodging the system and committing fraud. My mind started spinning this tale. What criminals could get away with back then would never be possible now. The 1970s were the wild west compared to current times with our advanced technology. Every clever ruse, every planned step our gangster heroines performed in this book was completely possible. Then. Not now.

Over the decades between other adventures, I put pen to paper to develop the story line. During that time, my sister Jessie listened and offered hilarious anecdotes and advice that I incorporated into these pages. We had a lot of laughs together over the predicaments and close calls encountered by the characters. Thank you, Jessie!

My Granny B was a great inspiration to the development of the three main characters who are patterned after three aspects of Granny's personality. She could be a vivacious and generous Jeanette; she could be a shrewd and conservative Minnie; or she could be a complacent and indecisive Sarah. I wish she were alive today to read this book. She'd enjoy a great laugh. And probably get a little ticked off at me, too.

Once the characters got going, they pretty much took over the manuscript. And for that I extend thanks to my imaginary friends who live within these pages. They rushed headlong into their various adventures and dragged my pen along with them. I remember running out of my writing den one day exclaiming to Jessie, "Oh my God, you're not gonna believe what Jeanette just did!"

Thank you to my writing group: Carole Kellerer, Tami Casias, and Patricia Henley for their encouragement over the years and for their sound advice.

David L. Robbins is a *New York Times* bestselling author who read my manuscript, loved it, and worked with me for several months editing it. I learned so much about writing during this time. The knowledge and experience he imparted, improved my way with words. He became my mentor and I'm proud to say, my friend. He also introduced me to Joni Albrecht, Little Star Publishing, who decided to take a chance on me.

Thanks to Cathy Plageman for her editing skills and Wendy Daniel for her creative talents with cover design.

Biggest thanks of all go to my husband, David Petri, who was a good audience and a patient man while I labored over the final document.

Then there's God and Country. Can't forget that!

About the Author

Bonnie Lee is an EA, Enrolled Agent representing taxpayers in all fifty states and is the author of fiction and nonfiction about life, love, and the IRS. *The Card Game* (Little Star Books, $19.99) is her fourth book and first full-length novel, following *Taxpertise, The Complete Book of Dirty Little Secrets* and *Tax Deductions for Small Business that the IRS Doesn't Want You to Know* (Entrepreneur Press 2009). Her tax novella for writers and other creatives is *Taxpertise for the Creative Mind*, because she "can't think of a single artist who wants to read a straight up tax book." Its sequel, *Taxpertise: The Heist, 50 Shades of Green*, is a fictional comedy adventure that provides factual tips and resolutions for the tax troubled. She is working on the third novella in the series on the topic of taxes and divorce. Bonnie Lee lives and writes in Sonoma, CA.

www.ingramcontent.com/pod-product-compliance
Lightning Source LLC
Chambersburg PA
CBHW021333150726
47989CB00005B/1969